THE BELGAE TORC

By
Kevin Marsh

For Lydia and Jonathan

Published by Paragon Publishing
© 2012 Kevin Marsh

ISBN 978-1-908341-82-2

Book design, layout and production management by Into Print
www.intoprint.net
+44 (0)1604 832149

Printed and bound in UK and USA by Lightning Source

Part One
The Dawning

*Take from thy neighbour that which is not yours and
thou shalt reap the consequences for all eternity*

I

Ban Mac Faelan held his hand above his head and bellowed out a call. Men fell back surrounding their leader to form a protective shield which was re-enforced as others arrived to join the circle. Thrusting their spears outwards they made a formidable barrier and like a giant porcupine began their slow withdrawal back towards the beach. Ban had lost more than half of his men and those left were either wounded or exhausted, the bodies of the dead lay strewn along the path leading from the village.

The Hibernians, seizing the opportunity, mounted a charge and the air sounded with screams and battle cries as they surged forward. Warriors cried out in agony and shock as they clashed, the attackers driven onto spears by the momentum of those following up behind. Deadly weapons found their mark and blood flowed as swords sang their songs of death. Men and women stood together fighting as equals and those who survived the initial onslaught came face to face with Ban and his elite guard. These were hardened veterans of the battle field, each one having earned the highest award for bravery and together they made a formidable killing machine.

Prisoners taken earlier were shackled together and herded into a miserable group behind Ban and his men. Of those captured one stood out above the rest, a red haired woman of noble birth who remained alert clutching a leather bag to her chest. Her eyes darting between the mêlée, she watched for an opportunity to aid her people, but she was chained to a woman who did nothing but hamper her movements. Her warriors were being systematically slaughtered and there was nothing she could do about it.

The struggle within the circle became desperate as the opportunity for escape receded, then Ban roared encouragement to his men and fearful for their lives the captives drew back into a tighter group.

Those left guarding the ships were led by Alma, son of Ban Mac Faelan and when he heard his father's cry he began to organise his men. One group was ordered to pull on the ropes, run the ships off the beach into the surf while the remaining men were formed into lines which Alma set at intervals along the beach, the pursuing army would have to negotiate this fresh fighting force in order to get at the ships.

The battle reached its climax and Alma re-enforced the dwindling circle of guards around his father securing the fate of the captives. He screamed a blood curdling cry as he faced down the charging army and hacking with his sword, the razor edge sliced into a warrior's arm before removing the man's head then he turned his attention to the next in line. Momentarily he glimpsed a woman who was fighting furiously, spittle spraying from lips that were drawn back over barred teeth and with a flash of blue, a swirling design etched onto her skin, she was gone.

The first of Ban's men were now in the water, the movement of the waves disturbed their balance, hampering their ability to defend themselves, and as if sensing victory the pursuing army followed resolutely, fighting even more ferociously.

The ships were close now, riding high in the water and men began to call out encouragement as they held the crafts steady against the rising tide. Warriors began heaving themselves aboard, aided by those on the decks, and as soon as they gained their footing they turned back to fight off attackers who were following up close behind.

Ban, standing waist deep in the water was set upon by two warriors, he made short work of them both before bellowing out another war cry. The water around him boiled red with blood and turning towards the shore he watched as more Hibernians poured onto the beach.

"Alma," he called out to his son. "Make sure that bag gets aboard a ship." Ban indicated towards the captives who were being dragged into the water.

Hampered by chains, they were terrified and half drowned, then Alma spotted the tall red haired woman who was struggling in the waist deep surf, he made his way towards her.

One of the opposing warriors broke away from the fight on the beach and charged into the water, he had also seen the women and was desperate to get to them before Alma. Lunging out with his spear he caught Alma a glancing blow and shocked by the sudden attack Alma stumbled forward unbalanced by the force. He managed to hold onto his sword as he struggled against the swirling water, but the spear tip gouged a groove along Alma's arm and he grimaced. Barring his teeth he recovered his balance, then driving his blade up sliced into the belly of his attacker. The warrior doubled over and roared with fury as he dropped his spear, then, Alma, sensing his opportunity, leapt onto the man's back and forced him under the water. Struggling and twisting they fought and all the time the water around them turned red as the warrior's strength faded.

5

Once the struggle was over, Alma reached out towards the woman who lashed out, with nails extended she began to scream obscenities in a language that he scarcely understood and recovering his sword he prodded at her. The sharpened tip cut through the fabric of her tunic biting into her flesh and she recoiled, hissing like a wounded cat screaming her indignation. Wound up with fury she launched herself at him, dragging the tethered woman along with her. Their combined weight was sufficient to knock Alma off his feet, but before she could hold him under he recovered his footing. Swinging his arm up in an arc his blade smashed down slicing through flesh and bone killing the half drowned woman instantly. The red head was pulled down by the dead weight of her companion and gasping for breath she found the strength to come back at him. This time her attack was ineffectual and Alma dodged her lunge, pushing her to one side he snatched the bag from her shoulder and swung it up over the rail of the nearest ship, then leaping up after it he grabbed hold of the rail and one of the men on the deck helped him up out of the waves. Gasping for breath he lay on the wooden planks, his chest rising and falling like bellows, then once he'd recovered he glanced back over the side.

The woman, struggling with the heavy chains and the weight of her dead companion disappeared from view as another wave rolled over her head. Reaching for his sword Alma leaned out and cleaved down hard severing an arm from the corpse, then the red head popped up gasping for breath, water streaming from her hair. Holding out his hand he almost recoiled when he saw the hatred burning in her huge green eyes. Recovering instantly he called out insisting that she took hold, but ignoring his pleas and spitting in anger, another wave washed over her head. A heavy wooden oar caught the side of her head as the men began to row and slowly the ship moved forward, all Alma could do was look on helplessly.

The sail was hoisted up the mast, it caught the breeze then the bow lifted and the ship began cutting freely through the water. Alma stared at the empty spot where the woman had been then suddenly she re-surfaced. Lifting her head she stared directly at him, her eyes blazing, he could almost feel her hatred. Her lips began to move as she recited an ancient curse, he couldn't make out her words but he knew instinctively what she was saying and the hairs on the back of his neck stood up. Watching as she disappeared for the last time, he called upon Bel, begging him to give her a free passage into the otherworld.

Ban made it to another ship with a handful of men and standing on the rail so his warriors could see him, he shielded his eyes from the glare and searched for his son. Alma lifted his hand in salute to his father and hoisted the leather bag high above his head. Ban smiled, he was satisfied the raid on Hibernia had been a success.

II

The feast of Imbolic had just come to an end, the celebrations a welcoming gesture for the arrival of new spring lambs. Many of the ewes, heavy with unborn, were brought into the village and the Goddess Bridget called upon to hasten their swift and safe arrival. This would ensure that the village was blessed with good luck for the coming year. The feast lasted for three days and had proven to be a boisterous affair, the cost was yet to be realised.

Luain Mac Lanis made his way through the village past the house that had been destroyed by fire, it had been devoured by flames when a careless occupant left a hearth unattended. He was not surprised, during most of the annual festivals there was trouble, a mixture of strong brew and bravado was a deadly catalyst. At least no-one had been killed this time, a drunken brawl could easily turn nasty, and once knives were drawn blood was sure to follow.

Luain was on his way to his forge which he had built some years earlier. It was situated on the outskirts of the village beside common land bordered by forest.

Villagers made use of this unrestricted area bringing their beasts in from the fields during the worst of the weather, the village was dependant on the survival of their animals.

Now that the festival was over it was time to resume work, Luain had jobs which required his immediate attention. Farming equipment had to be mended, plough blades straightened and sharpened, there was always something needing his skills. At this time of the season there was also a great demand for spear heads and knives, warriors relied on him for the manufacture of arms. The weather was beginning to improve and with the promise of summer came the threat of attack.

Rolling the stiffness from his shoulders, Luain smiled. He looked up at the clearing sky, his bones ached less each morning as the length of daylight increased and there was a little more warmth in the air. He was still wearing his winter cloak, a thick woollen garment lined with sheep's wool, this kept out the worst of the weather and pulling it tighter around his neck he quickened his step. Soon his forge would be glowing and his workplace filled with warmth.

Madb set out along the path that her uncle had taken earlier, she was carrying food wrapped in a cloth. This was her daily routine, just one of her jobs to ensure his welfare she also helped out at the forge.

"Hello Madb," a voice carried across the open space separating the houses.

Luigsech was not one of Madb's favourite companions, standing a head taller than Madb this morning she looked particularly attractive. Luigsech was wearing a blue woollen dress which complimented her emerging figure and her hair was perfectly plaited, tied with a strip of cloth which matched the colour of her dress.

"Where are you going?" she asked, dancing excitedly along the track.

"I have work to do at my uncle's forge," Madb attempted a smile.

"Oh," Luigsech wrinkled her nose.

She had no interest in the forge it was a noisy, smelly place which was much too hot during the summer.

Madb, glancing sideways at the girl, studied her thoughtfully and brushed a strand of red hair from her eyes with the back of her hand. Luigsech had rubbed ruan into her cheeks, the red dye applied too thickly gave her a constant blush, she had also darkened her eyebrows using black juice from last year's berries.

"So why are you dressed up?" Madb asked curiously.

"Well, as the cold weather has almost gone, I thought it time to wear something bright I've been too long in drab winter clothes. Don't you think I look good in the sunshine?" she laughed joyously.

Madb thought her vain, she hated dressing up and much preferred her work clothes. Luigsech couldn't disguise the fact that she was waiting for Maedoc, Luain was making him a new sword and was bound to come this way eventually. She simply had to look her best, she was desperate for him to notice her, besides, she was no longer the girl she had been the previous season.

"Are you going to help gather wood later?" Madb called out over her shoulder.

She knew that being reminded of the task would annoy Luigsech. "We have to sort the sticks before weaving can begin on the wall panels." The panels were essential for the building of the new house.

Luigsech frowned, she knew that everyone was expected to help, but she also knew there would be no young men in attendance. Sorting sticks was a task for old women and children it was no place for her.

"Maybe," she said distantly. "I have to finish making pots first."

She was learning to be a potter, working under her mother's guidance

9

she helped turn clay dug from the riverbank into useful domestic items, sometimes she made pretty ornaments and offerings for the gods.

Madb continued on her way, leaving Luigsech to dream of Maedoc and all the other young warriors. The familiar sounds of the forge ringing through the trees excited her as she approached the clearing and she loved the smell of smoke from the fire. Parting the curtain that covered the doorway she stepped into the workshop.

"Madb, come in, welcome." Luain's face brightened as soon as he saw her.

"I have brought you food," she said holding up the package.

"Bless you Madb, set it down there." Sweeping his tools to one side he made a space on his workbench.

Madb eyed the blade that her uncle had been forging, she admired his work immensely.

"Can I weave the copper thread for the hilt?" she asked. Enthusiasm reflected in her youthful face and her eyes burned as bright as the coals in the fire.

She had not been working with her uncle for long but she had a natural flair for metalworking, her fingers were better suited for the finer tasks and he was glad because his eyesight was not as sharp as it had once been.

"Of course you can, but first I need you to make some copper rivets," he smiled nodding towards a length of rod that he'd drawn earlier.

All she had to do was cut the rivets to length then form a dome on one end it was a mundane task she had carried out many times before. She didn't mind, she could let her mind wander as she worked and then the time would pass more quickly. Luain was going to use them as fasteners to secure a hardened steel strip to the edge of a shield, this would stop the wood from splitting when repelling the force of sword blade or axe.

They worked together in silence, her fingers moving to the rhythm of Luain's hammer and when the sun had reached the highest point in the sky they stopped for something to eat. Madb boiled water from the river before adding dried herbs which she kept in a pouch hanging from her belt. Stirring the mixture in the pot, she infused a refreshing brew and in companionable silence they shared the fragrant liquid.

When they had finished, Madb continued forming the rivets but before long a sound from beyond the door interrupted them. Putting her work to one side she looked up as Luain parted the curtain and she watched silently as he stepped out to confront three horsemen.

"Are you Luain Mac Lanis?" one of them called.

Madb crept closer to the door but remained alert and out of sight, hiding amongst the shadows her hand never far from the hilt of her knife.

"I am." Luain nodded.

The men were not from her village and from the condition of their horses they must have travelled some distance, mud was clinging to the horses' legs staining their flanks.

"We come from across the afon," the man continued using the old word which meant river. "We are here to discuss a commission."

Madb eyed him with suspicion, he was not much older than herself, but exuded a confidence which could have been misinterpreted as arrogance.

All three men were well dressed and their weapons were of the finest quality. They wore their hair swept back, braided and lime washed, combed to give the appearance of a horse's mane, they were clearly warriors. Two of the men had long moustaches which drooped over their upper lips but the spokesman was cleanly shaven. Madb's eyes darted quickly between them as she summed them up. From their body language, it was clear that her uncle was in no immediate danger, the men seemed friendly enough so she relaxed a little and began searching for clues to their identity.

All three men wore trousers made from dyed wool, the two in the background kept their cloaks wrapped tightly around them whilst the third, who was talking with her uncle, swept his aside revealing a fine linen shirt. It was obvious to Madb that they were all high born.

"Your skills as a metalworker are legendary," the young man began, "your ability to shape precious metal into fine items of jewellery has not escaped our notice." His voice was laced with an edge of flattery which Madb found a little condescending. Her uncle didn't seem to mind, he remained impassive he had the measure of them.

"You are requested to wrought a Torc which will be the finest ever seen."

Luain nodded and casually folded his thick arms across his chest.

"And where am I to find the raw material for the finest Torc ever seen?" He grinned.

The young warrior snapped his fingers and one of his companions stepped forward and Madb was drawn closer to the doorway. Although her uncle remained relaxed, she watched their every move.

The warrior laid the leather bag that he was carrying on the ground at Luain's feet then with a flourish peeled back the wrapping to reveal a block of white metal. Its irregular surface catching the light dazzled them all with its brilliance. Luain stepped closer and crouching down for a better look was momentarily speechless, he wondered at the type of metal it was and running his fingers expertly over the rich surface he smiled, it was warm to his touch.

"As you see, we have thought of that," Luain nodded and continued to study the material in silence.

Madb, holding her breath stared at the white metal. She was accustomed to working in copper or the much rarer yellow ore which the high born preferred to wear next to their skin, but she had never seen anything like this before.

"May I?" Luain asked once the spell had been broken.

"Of course," the warrior nodded.

Luain knew that it was something special as soon as he picked it up, the vibrations running through it excited him, it was charged with energy and in his mind he could already see an image of the finished Torc.

"We have weighed the metal and when the task is complete we expect to receive the same weight returned."

Luain nodded not taking his eyes from it. His mind working feverishly, he wondered why he had been chosen to make a Torc then he began to consider the consequences of such a request. The metal could not have come from around these parts and the thought worried him.

"It's from across the sea," the warrior whispered, anticipating his question.

Luain realised that the people of Hibernia would not have let such a treasure leave their shores without putting up a fight, how much blood had been spilt obtaining it?

"I guess that your request comes from Ban Mac Faelan," Luain watched the young warrior carefully.

Momentarily startled, he covered it well and recovering his composure he nodded. Ban Mac Faelan was the most powerful chieftain in the district, his influence was felt by every village in the area. He commanded vast armies from his fort which rose up out of the forest on the highest hilltop. Luain dared not refuse such a man but he did question his choice.

"There must be other men who can craft such a Torc," he said eyeing the man suspiciously.

"This is true, but my father wants the best." It was Luain's turn to hide his surprise.

"My name is Alma Mac Ban, I was told not to reveal my identity until you had accepted the task, but as you have already guessed I see no harm in giving you my name."

Luain nodded.

"I understand you know my father."

"Like you I was once a warrior," Luain explained. "I fought beside your father in some of the wildest battles."

Alma realised that his father had been liberal with the facts and he wondered why that was. He had of course told him that he was acquainted with Luain Mac Lanis but failed to mention just how close they had once been, if it was true what the metal smith said, then he and his father must have been battle brothers.

Luain had not always been a metal smith, he was once a warrior, but the passing of time had turned him grey, his reflexes had slowed and as the years advanced he turned his hand to a different skill. Now he gave his allegiance to Goibniu, the god associated with his new trade.

"I will of course undertake this task but it will take many moons to complete."

Alma nodded then with a sudden movement mounted his horse. Turning their mounts skilfully all three men rode away without another word.

Madb stepped from the workshop and stood beside her uncle, they watched in silence as the warriors rode away, their thoughts taking very different paths.

"So who were they?" Luigsech asked excitedly as she straightened up from her work.

Word had spread quickly through the village, now everyone knew that three strangers had been to see Luain Mac Lanis.

"Just warriors from the next village," Madb shrugged.

Luigsech was not satisfied, she had seen how finely dressed the men were, they couldn't have been just ordinary warriors.

"What did they want, what were they doing here?"

Her questions irritated Madb, she was under strict instructions from her uncle not to reveal the purpose of the visit it would be disastrous if word got out that there was such precious metal in the village. There were insufficient men to guard the forge or protect the lives of the people living there, it would be devastating if bandits discovered that they had something of value to steal.

"They want my uncle to make weapons," Madb lied convincingly.

Luigsech stopped and studied her. "Surely there are other metal smiths who would be willing to take on such work. Why did they decide to come here?"

"My uncle is the best," she said proudly.

Luigsech looked away and tossed her head. Madb was always boasting, she thought herself above everyone else and what's more Luigsech was certain that Madb had eyes for Maedoc. The more she thought about it the more furious she became.

She would show her, Maedoc would never look at Madb, she was far too plain, besides she did nothing about her appearance, Luigsech thought Madb resembled a boy. She smiled, satisfied with the thought. Luigsech was determined to have Maedoc for herself she had already consulted with a village elder who had given her a spell to ensure his love. Madb would not be expecting that, she thought with a smug grin. Madb was not telling the truth, she was certain of that and next time Maedoc made an appearance she would make sure he knew about the way Madb and her uncle were acting.

By nightfall most of the sticks had been sorted into piles, stacked by length and girth, they were now ready to be woven into panels which would be used to form the walls of the new house. The men had already selected heavy timbers for the roof and once the panels were in place, a mixture of clay, chalk, straw and animal hair would be blended into a paste and smeared over them, they would then be left to harden. This process sealed the panels giving them strength which would keep out the cold winds.

The light was fading and there was a chill in the air as Madb made her way to her uncle's house, she found him seated by the fire gnawing on a pork bone.

"Hello Madb," he waved the bone at her and made room on the bench.

Luain's housekeeper appeared and handed Madb a steaming bowl of hot stew. "You must be starved," Fedelmid said with a motherly smile.

Luain's wife had died two winters ago and Madb had taken on the task of housekeeper but once her training at the forge begun her uncle saw fit to engage a woman from the village. He knew Fedelmid very well and Madb was convinced that her duties went further than just house-keeper. At first she had been angry with this intrusion but as time went by she become accustomed to the woman whose kindly ways eventually won through.

Luain was silent he was brooding over the strange events of the day and could hardly believe that he had agreed to take on a job for Ban Mac Faelan. They had once been great friends, as inseparable as brothers, saving each other's lives many times over, but as the years slipped by circumstances overwhelmed them and they drifted apart. He grunted and shifted in his seat, that had been a long time ago and now things were very different, life had drawn him in another direction, he now had responsibilities. He frowned and wondered why Ban had sought him out after so many years. Ban could not know that it was Madb who created the jewellery; he carried on with the everyday work whilst she created the fine pieces. He smiled as thoughts of his niece filled him with joy, she was the ideal student, nothing was too much trouble for her and she was always willing to learn. He could not fault her work, he would entrust her with anything.

With regards to the Torc, Luain had no doubts that Madb would already have designs of her own worked out in her head he also knew that whatever he had to say on the matter would have little bearing, especially if she had already made up her mind. He glanced across at his niece, she had finished eating her stew and was now fully engrossed in watching the fire, it was as if she could see all kinds of omens in the flames as they danced around the hearth.

After a while the flames began to lower, the embers glowing red, now the heat was less fierce it no longer stung her face. At first it had been so warm that her eyes burned like pools against her skin, but now she was comfortable and feeling sleepy.

Suddenly Luain jerked awake beside her, he had been dozing.

"Relax Uncle, it's only me," moving closer she placed her hand gently on his shoulder.

"Why are you still awake?" he asked his voice thick with sleep.

"I can't sleep," she replied softly, feeding the fire with small dried sticks.

"So what's troubling you?"

"I know that you were once a warrior but I didn't know you and Ban Mac Faelan were friends."

"Ah," Luain grunted. Wide awake now he could sense her curiosity. "That was a very long time ago."

She studied him for a moment, waiting for him to continue.

"When we were young fools we were as close as brothers, we were inseparable and once old enough to fight without getting ourselves killed we became warriors. We went into the forest for our dream night under the same moon, we spoke to the same spirits and they decided to keep us safe." He smiled at this long forgotten memory, his eyes glistening with emotions.

Madb nodded, she knew how important it was to go into the forest and confront the spirits, she too had completed her own dream night and was still coming to terms with the experience. She had gone into the forest naked and alone, choosing to spend a long cold night beneath an ancient oak tree, she thought the spirit of the tree would protect her. Many spirits had confronted her that night but it was Madadh – alluidh, the wolf who finally appeared, he led her along the darkest paths. At first she had been terrified and it had taken all of her resolve to welcome him into her circle. He was an old and wise spirit, one that was cunning but strangely beguiling, he told her of the ancient ways, passing on many secrets and he promised to teach her many things. Eventually, he had curled up with her, keeping out the worst of the cold with his coarse hair, and they slept under the tree kept safe by the spirits. When Madb awoke she found herself alone.

It had not been so easy for Luain, many years before he'd struggled with the spirits for two days and three nights. Time had stood still, he had no concept of day or night whilst lost in the spirit world, the experience had almost driven him mad. Bel of the otherworld had never been far away during that time, but it was Nemain, the battle goddess who had saved him, she had plucked him from the edge of darkness and kept him safe until finally becaming his dream spirit.

16

"We were bound together Ban and I," he continued suddenly. He had no idea how long they had remained silent but he could feel the spirits drawing in close around them.

"We made a formidable pair."

"Why did you stop being a warrior, why did you become a metal smith?"

Luain thought for a moment before replying. "My sister, your dear mother, was always my favourite. Did she ever tell you of the times we sat together telling each other stories, scaring ourselves half to death with tales of spirits and ghosts?"

Madb smiled as the image of her mother's face appeared in the fire.

"When she asked me to take care of you I thought that she was mad and for the first time in our lives we argued, but as it turned out she was right. I had to stop fighting, my body needed to rest, I couldn't see it at the time, I was blinded by self-importance. I was becoming too old, your mother could see it, my body was slowing down. Of course I refused to believe her, I thought that I was invincible, oh the arrogance of youth." he grinned. "I didn't know it then but I was losing the edge, it would only have been a matter of time before someone younger came along to strike me down. Even though I had Ban to protect my back your mother still worried, her dream spirit had told her something that she refused to reveal, she had probably seen my death and Ban's as well I expect. Anyway, I did as she suggested and took up a trade," he smiled.

In the firelight Madb could see the wrinkles creasing his still handsome face and she was comforted by his warmth.

"It turned out that it was not only my death she had seen. She was becoming weaker as the season faded she knew that she was unlikely to survive the winter. So you see not only did she save my soul but she gave me yours to nurture."

"That's why you settled down then, because of me," Madb shuffled closer to the fire.

"I suppose so, for your mother too. I didn't want her going to the otherworld carrying such a heavy burden. I didn't know it then of course, but she had very little time left."

Madb studied him and could sense there was more, something in his past that he chose to keep to himself.

"We were precious to her," he continued unaware of her scrutiny. "She could rest more easily knowing that we would remain together."

They were silent for a while both caught up in their own thoughts and memories.

"I've been thinking about the task we have been given," Luain began. "I will need your help as I have many other jobs to complete."

Madb nodded, she was expecting as much, she had already decided how the Torc would look when it was finished. They discussed her ideas and Luain listened, but chose to make no suggestions. Madb fed the fire occasionally with dried sticks and before long the darkness of night began to recede giving way to a fresh new day.

When the sun had risen above the horizon, they made their way towards the forge where Luain cut and hammered the first of the metal. Drawing it into long strands he passed it to Madb who drew it even finer. He was amazed by her skill and the depth of her concentration and when it was to her satisfaction she began to weave a fine rope which was the best Luain had ever seen and pride swelled his chest. Once she had removed the oxide that formed on the surface as she worked, the rope shone like silver in the sunlight. There were other colours there too lying just under the surface, copper and gold and sometimes she thought she could see a pink hue.

Day after day they worked and the rope became longer, Madb continued to weave until it became as thick as her thumb. She worked as if in a trance, her hands guided by the spirits, her fingers becoming red and chafed, but not once did she complain. Luain made the tools that she would need to complete her work, tools that Madb would use to carve and shape the solid ends and drawing deeply on her imagination she was guided by her dreams and the Torc gradually began to take shape.

Never, during her work, did she wonder where the raw material had come from, Luain on the other hand worried constantly about its history. It unnerved him to know that it had come directly from Ban Mac Faelan. He consulted the spirits but they refused to help, he knew from handling the material that it was filled with negative forces and he prayed that once Madb had finished turning it into something beautiful only the positive energy from her youthful hands would remain.

The day was fast approaching when the job would be complete and he was happy with that. Alma Mac Ban could then take delivery of the Torc and the dark clouds looming over the forge would be gone.

IV

Maedoc arrived as they were putting their tools away. Madb was just returning the Torc to its soft leather bag as he walked into the workshop.

"Maedoc, welcome," Luain said stepping away from his workbench and holding out his hand in a gesture of friendship. He moved towards their visitor, this gave Madb time to hide the bag.

The young warrior smiled and nodded as Madb came forward to stand beside her uncle. Maedoc had been measured for his sword some time ago, but this was the first opportunity he had to call in. Luain had finished working on the weapon leaving Madb to put the final touches to its decoration before wrapping it in an oiled cloth, it was now standing against the wall.

"Come in, take a look," Luain said enthusiastically as he moved across the workshop.

Madb smiled, she could hardly tell which of the men was more excited. Picking up the blade, Luain held it out towards Maedoc. Unwrapping the cloth he gripped the copper wired hilt in his fist testing it for weight and balance. He began moving it from left to right then nodded, it was perfect in his grip. Like an extension to his arm, it felt natural and running his finger along the razor sharp edge he admired the workmanship. The blade had been engraved with a horse's head and there were swirling patterns etched along its length.

"This is a very fine weapon," Maedoc said moving towards Luain who shook his hand with an iron grip.

Maedoc had no idea that it was Madb who had engraved the blade, it was her own design. She had carefully plaited the copper strands, winding it tightly around the hilt to give it a sure grip the bright copper would soon turn a pleasing shade of green, oxidised by the moisture from his hand.

"It will have to be blessed, taste the salt of blood," Luain's eyes burned fiercely. "I'm sure there will be an opportunity for that soon enough." He alluded to the unrest between the settlements which always spiralled out of control at this time of year.

Maedoc nodded, he was pleased with his sword and as an accomplished swordsman recognised its quality. Madb studied him in silence, she admired his confidence, he was a fine young man but she regarded him very differently from her friend Luigsech. Madb considered him an equal, he was a man she felt comfortable with and would not hesitate to stand beside him in battle.

Luain helped Maedoc to wrap the sword in an oiled cloth, he then carried it out for him holding onto it as Maedoc mounted his horse.

"You are a good man Luain Mac Lanis and I thank you," his eyes shone with admiration as he looked down at them both. "I hear that Ban Mac Faelon and his warriors are becoming restless," he said more soberly. "I hope this blade will not have to spill the blood of his men."

"I wonder what he wants," Luain frowned. The news disturbed him but he hid his feelings well.

"I also heard that he has recently returned from Hibernia, what could have possessed a man to risk the wrath of Manannan at this time of the year?"

Luain felt Madb stiffen when she heard the name of the sea god.

"I suppose we will have to wait for the answer to that question," Luain said.

Maedoc nodded and wheeling his horse round rode away leaving them staring after him.

The following day Luigsech was making pots outside her mother's house, she was bored the laborious task that her mother had set was beginning to wear her down.

She was told that she had to make at least five new pots for each household. Luigsech sighed and massaged the back of her neck. There were twelve houses in the enclosure and that to her reckoning was a lot of pots.

She looked up as Madb walked past. Luigsech guessed that she was on her way to her uncle's forge, she had no interest in Madb's occupation but at that moment any kind of distraction would be welcome. Wiping her hands on a cloth, she stood up and stretched out the stiffness from her muscles before going off in pursuit of Madb. She fully intended to call out to her friend and walk with her for a little way, but something held her back. Perhaps it was the way Madb was walking, head down she seemed distracted, this was most unlike her. Luigsech decided to follow her friend but held back, maintaining a safe distance, Madb didn't seem to notice.

When they arrived at the workshop Luigsech hid beside a tree and watched as Madb disappeared inside. Luain was obviously there judging from the noise coming from within. Placing her hand against the tree, Luigsech felt the undulations in the bark beneath her fingertips. It seemed strange to be hiding from her friend and she wondered what it was that had stopped her from following Madb into the workshop.

Suddenly the ringing from the forge ceased and Luain appeared at the doorway, pressing herself closer to the tree, Luigsech didn't want him to see her hiding there, but she watched as he called out to Madb. She couldn't make out what he said but holding her breath, she waited as Luain passed close by.

As soon as he had gone she crept closer to the workshop and pausing at the door summoned up the courage to peer in. The air was silent, nothing stirred it was as if the place was deserted but as Luigsech pushed the curtain aside she saw Madb hunched over a workbench. The atmosphere inside was gloomy the workshop was filled with smoke from the fire, resisting the urge to cough she waited as her eyes adjusted then she glanced quickly around. Madb was sitting at a workbench with her back towards the door she was engrossed in her work, bent over some object. Luigsech couldn't see what it was her friend was doing so moving stealthily forward she stepped around the fire until she had a better view. Madb suddenly moved and Luigsech froze, she dared not breathe, her heart was galloping like wild horses inside her chest. She was filled with excitement, spying on Madb was much more interesting than making boring pots. She knew it was wrong, Madb's uncle could return at any moment and the prospect of being caught filled her with alarm, but she had to find out what Madb was doing.

Madb turned and reached to the back of the workbench then Luigsech's eyes widened as she caught sight of it. White metal gleamed as it reflected light and in an instant she realised what the rope like metal was. She was stunned, she hardly dared to move. Madb turned back into position having picked something up from the back of the bench and Luigsech lost sight of the Torc. She could hardly believe what she had seen, surely Luain Mac Lanis was not capable of making such fine jewellery perhaps Madb was just cleaning it for someone. A Torc made of white metal, it must belong to an immensely important person, she wondered who that could be. Questions filled her head until she thought it would burst and it was as much as she could do to stop herself from rushing up to Madb and demanding answers.

Luigsech remained rooted to the spot she knew that if she were to move she would do something clumsy. At last she found the courage to move and backing away made her way to the door. Once outside she hurried across the clearing towards the trees where she stopped to think about what she had just seen. She couldn't get the image of the Torc out of her mind and filled with curiosity she had to discover who it belonged to. After a while, once she had time to recover, she slipped back to the village where she continued making pots. She made up her mind, she was going to confront Madb the moment she saw her, she was burning up with curiosity and could hardly remain still.

Madb spent the day cleaning and polishing the Torc, the marks that had been made during the manufacturing process needed filing away and she wouldn't be content until the last scratch had disappeared. She had completed the final piece the previous day, a decorative clasp which would secure the shining rope around the neck of Ban Mac Faelan. It wouldn't be a comfortable piece of jewellery to wear, it was heavy, but then of course the Torc would only be worn on important ceremonial occasions.

She was proud of her work and studying the clasp was happy with the results, it had been fashioned from a solid piece of metal which Luain had cut from the block. She had worked it into the shape of a horse's head before attaching it to a finely worked chain, each link had been individually crafted before being joined together to form a short chain, this she attached to the end of the Torc. The ends had been carved from solid metal one was shaped to look like the rising sun. Rays of light reaching up over the horizon were depicted by ridges which had been carefully filed into the metal. This was to represent the birth of a new day and was dedicated to the Sun God - Belenos. The other end had been shaped to resemble the moon, the shape of a hare had been carved into the face this was to honour the Goddess Eostra who represents abundance and good fortune. The horses head was for Epona, the Goddess of horses and when the clasp was fastened, Epona would sit between Eostra and Belenos. This pleased Madb, she was satisfied with her design, the three deities were those she revered most and the carefully woven rope gleamed like the scales on a serpent's back. Turning it between her fingers tiny points of light flashed from its surface and smiling with approval she wrapped the completed Torc in strips of soft leather before returning it to its bag.

She knew that she had created something very special she had felt the vibrations running through the raw material. At first this had disturbed her, the sensation felt wrong, these were negative forces, but now they had been tamed she was no longer concerned. It was as if the shaping of the metal had transformed them into something more positive, it remained clear however that the Torc still held strange powers, the bearer of this magnificent piece of jewellery would have to be strong enough to harness and control such forces.

Madb stood up from her workbench and stretched her arms luxuriously above her head, arching her back she rolled her shoulders gently working the stiffness from her muscles. Glancing quickly around the workshop, she knelt down then concealing the bag into its hiding place whispered a prayer to the gods for its safe keeping. Standing up she ran her foot over the flagstone smoothing out the dust around its edges to disguise that fact that it had been moved. The light was fading quickly and glancing around once more before she was satisfied Madb left the workshop then made her way back towards the village.

"Hello Madb," Luigsech called out the moment she came into view.

Madb looked up startled by the sound of her friend's voice.

"What have you been making today?" Luigsech asked hardly able to contain her excitement.

"Copper rivets," Madb answered, surprised at Luigsech's enthusiasm.

"What are they for?" She stopped in front of her, barring her way.

"To decorate a shield."

"Oh!"

Madb stepped around Luigsech leaving her standing in the middle of the path.

"Do you ever make anything else?" she asked hurrying after her friend.

"Of course, I help my Uncle make all kinds of different things."

"Like what?"

Madb knew that Luigsech had no interest in her work at the forge so there must be a very good reason for her sudden fascination.

"I was just wondering if you ever make items of jewellery."

Madb stopped and studied her closely, searching for clues as to why she was asking such questions.

"We make armbands for warriors."

"Yes I know that, but could you make something beautiful?"

"There is beauty in everything we do," Madb told her guardedly. "Do you not think that there is beauty in the things you make?"

"Some of the more decorated items," Luigsech agreed, "but most of my work is simple and functional. I rarely get the opportunity to create something of real beauty."

"Then why do you ask?" Madb stared at her.

Luigsech was certain that she was being made a fool of, Madb was not telling her everything and this made her angry. She was even more determined to find out about the Torc. If Madb was not willing to tell her then she would have to discover the answers for herself. Madb and her uncle were up to something and she would not rest until she knew what it was.

V

The following day Luigsech went to find Maedoc. He was up on top of the bank which surrounded the village making an inspection of the defences. Theirs was a small and insignificant village, an army would hardly waste its time attacking them, but there were warriors camped in the surrounding forest and it would be wise to take precautions.

"Maedoc," she called out as soon as she spotted him.

He stopped talking to a group of men and glanced in her direction. She was a sweet girl and he found her smile beguiling, he also couldn't help but notice that she was growing into a fine young woman.

"Hello Luigsech," he said pleasantly as he came down off the bank. "What brings you here this morning?"

"I have something to tell you," she began, full of importance. "It's about Madb and her Uncle."

"Luain Mac Lanis?" he frowned as he studied her.

Immediately she could sense the change in him, she would have to be careful she knew how highly Maedoc regarded the metal smith.

"There is something of great interest going on at the forge and you should know about it."

"Go on," he nodded.

"They have an item of great value," she withered under his scrutiny but went on quickly. "It could affect the safety of the whole village."

His expression changed, softening as he acknowledged his understanding.

"That is of no surprise, a metal smith would often be in possession of valuable materials, it's the nature of his business." She realised that what he said was true.

They began to walk slowly and he waited patiently for her to continue, he had a feeling there was more.

"I saw something that was unusual," she persisted, "not the kind of thing one would expect to see in a forge."

Maedoc took her arm and her heart quickened, the touch of his hand was warm against her skin, it excited her but the sensation soon passed.

"What is it that's troubling you?"

She looked up at him and chewed nervously at her bottom lip.

"You won't be in any trouble Luigsech, just tell me."

"I saw Madb working on a Torc." There, she had said it, but couldn't make eye contact with him.

"You saw Madb with a Torc?" he asked incredulously.

"It was a most magnificent thing," she nodded, "made of a metal I have never seen before, it was shining white."

He remained silent taking in what she had just said.

"How did you manage to see this Torc?"

"I was in the workshop with Madb when she was working on it." She didn't want him to know that Madb had been unaware of her presence that she was spying on her.

"And where was Luain?"

"I don't know, Madb was there on her own." She was not happy with his reaction, things were not going quite as planned and she was now beginning to wish that she had remained silent.

"What did Madb have to say about it?"

Her mind was reeling, she knew that he was going to ask that question and now she was struggling for a plausible answer.

"She would not discuss it with me, she refused to tell me anything."

"Why was she being so secretive?" he frowned.

"I don't know, she wouldn't say." Luigsech felt herself cornered by her own stupidity she was sinking further into untruths and didn't know how she was going to get herself out of it.

"Are you sure about what you saw?" Maedoc asked. "It could quite easily have been armbands for a warrior."

She could hear the doubt in his voice it was as if suddenly he was talking to a child. This made her angry she had made a mistake it was foolish to think he would believe her.

"I know what I saw," she said through clenched teeth.

Maedoc glanced over his shoulder, it was clear that he had already lost interest in what she was saying, he would much rather be up on the ramparts working with his men.

Whatever was going on between Luigsech and Madb was of no concern of his he had no time for their girlish squabbles, besides Luain would never leave an item of such value in his workshop unguarded.

For the rest of the day Luigsech sat alone and sulked, she could hardly believe the way Maedoc had treated her especially when she had told him about the Torc.

He obviously didn't believed a word she had said, but worst of all it hurt deeply having him treat her like a child. She was certain that he thought more of Madb than he did of her, she would show them both, she would come up with a plan to discredit Madb then Maedoc would think all the more of her. As she brooded on the problem a plan began to formulate in her head and she started to feel better.

Luain sent word to Alma Mac Ban that the Torc was ready for collection and now he was gathering up all the off cuts and shavings, wrapping them together before placing them in the bag along with the Torc. Madb had done a splendid job, she had surpassed herself, coming up with the design and forming the metal by herself. He had contributed very little to the job, all he could claim credit for was cutting and drawing the metal into manageable lengths which Madb had worked and refined before twisting them into a rope. He had of course made the tools that she needed to complete the task, tools for cutting and shaping her clever designs. He was incredibly proud of her, she was developing into a first class metal smith.

The metal itself had been pleasing to work with and being relatively soft it didn't become hard or brittle when worked. It seemed to possess similar characteristics to the precious yellow metal which he associated more readily with high status jewellery. He rarely had an opportunity to work with such fine material, he was more accustomed to working iron or copper and occasionally silver. As the daylight began to fade, it became impossible to work inside the workshop so they finished for the day and made their way home.

Luigsech watched secretly from under the cover of lengthening shadows and once they had passed she slipped away into the darkness. The workshop was a still and foreboding place for a young girl to be alone. She was accustomed to the sounds of the forge, but now as the day was drawing to a close Luigsech was beginning to have second thoughts. Chiding herself, she thought of Maedoc, he would be pleased once she presented him with the Torc. Spurred on by this thought and with a sudden burst of enthusiasm she crossed the clearing and went directly into the workshop.

Once inside she could feel the heat from the fire even though the coals had been dampened down. The heat laden air was heavy with toil and she wondered how Madb could shut herself away every day in such a gloomy place. Skirting around the hearth she made her way towards the place where Madb had been working the previous day. She had seen a leather bag on top of the bench and guessed that was where the Torc would be hidden. The workbench had been cleared so crouching down she began searching beneath it but discovered nothing more than piles of tools and sharp off cuts.

The smell of the workshop filled her nostrils, it made her feel nauseous and light headed, she was not used to such an unpleasant environment and wanted to leave as soon as possible. Looking around in the gloom she tried to imagine the shape of the bag but there was nothing like it hanging against a wall or laying on a shelf. Under foot, swarf and grit crunched sharply, she didn't like the unfamiliar sound, it frightened her leaving her nerves on edge and she realised just how much she hated it inside the forge. Setting aside her fears she organised her thoughts and tried to think logically, allowing herself to be guided by her instincts she searched every corner of the workshop. It seemed a hopeless task, Madb had hidden the bag out of sight and now she was becoming frustrated. Perhaps the Torc was no longer there, Madb could have taken it with her, but she hadn't been carrying a bag when they left the workshop. There had been no strangers through the village during the day so it couldn't have been collected, it must still be there.

Slowly Luigsech made her way around the workshop, even searching the thatch above her head then she stopped by the hearth and sighed. Soon it would be completely dark and she would have to abandon her search. As she turned a stone underfoot moved and dropping to her knees she ran her fingers around its edge. It was definitely loose, she was certain that it had been moved recently so working her fingers under the corners she managed to prise it up and slide it to one side. Forcing her hand into the depression that had been made in the soft earth her fingers touched leather and gripping it firmly she pulled it out from its hiding place. Climbing to her feet she placed it on a bench then pulling open the drawstrings felt inside. Curling her trembling fingers around the Torc she eased it out of the bag, her heart skipped madly as she unwrapped it, she could hardly contain her excitement. Holding it in her hands she could feel the energy flowing through it, it was as if the Torc was alive and fumbling with the clasp she couldn't resist slipping it around her neck. At first the metal was warm against her skin and the weight of it resting on her collar bones made her feel important. She was elated and danced with joy, the thought that it had been made for a high ranking chieftain or king did nothing to put her off and even the notion that the gods might be displeased did not dissuade her. She had never seen jewellery like this before and realising that she would never have the opportunity to hold or even wear such a piece again made her even more determined to make the most of it before taking it to Maedoc.

At first the vibrations were a soft fluttering against her skin but soon they intensified and before long she could feel the Torc beginning to pulsate and throb alarmingly. She danced around the workshop fuelled by its energy and filled with a strange euphoria she thought it a pity that the whole village could not join in. In her mind she could see Maedoc smiling, taking her into his arms, crushing her to his chest she then imagined the taste of his lips. Laughing out loud she pictured Madb staring at them, she could see the expression on her face it was satisfying to see her looking so resentful, Maedoc was now truly hers.

Driven to new heights she saw riches beyond her imagination and her head was crammed with images of what might have been if she were a princess of Hibernia.

Suddenly the face of a woman filled her vision, her hair was full and red and her eyes were a beautiful shade of green. Luigsech had never seen a woman so stunning before. Why had she thought of Hibernia? The notion overwhelmed her then the vision of beauty began to fade, something was very wrong and she was becoming frightened. Suddenly Luigsech went cold, the vibrations around her neck were changing, it was as if the Torc was crushing her throat and she found it difficult to breathe.

The red haired woman was there again but this time her soft green eyes were burning with rage. For the first time Luigsech sensed death and began to panic, she could hear the sound of laughing and began to suffocate under the weight of the metal around her neck. It was becoming heavier forcing her body down into the earth. Suddenly, the face of the red haired woman reared up in front of her and Luigsech screamed. She lost her footing and stumbled backwards striking her head against the corner of the stone which had been used to cover the hiding place, lights exploded inside her skull. She lay there dazed, fighting for breath as the red haired woman hovered above her, her face hidden by a mask of evil was the last thing Luigsech saw, for when the woman returned to the otherworld she took with her Luigsech's soul.

The following morning Luain made his way along the path towards his workshop, the sky was clear, ice blue and cold. Strangely there were no birds singing, the forest was still and he could smell the earth and the trees. There had been showers during the night and now mist lingered in the contours of the land, but once the sun rose higher into the sky these persistent pockets would disperse and it would be another fine day.

Arriving at the doorway he pushed aside the curtain and stepped over the threshold then he froze. Something was wrong, the atmosphere inside his workshop was charged, it was as if the god Teranis had been beating his hammer and the hairs on his arms stood erect. His hand dropped automatically to the knife in his belt and he called upon his dream spirit for guidance and protection.

Suddenly he saw the body of a young woman lying on the floor near the hearth. At first he didn't recognise her, her head was twisted at an awkward angle and her face was turned away. Luain moved quickly covering the distance between them and throwing himself down beside her he could see that it was Luigsech from the village. He glanced fearfully around searching for clues, it was obvious that she was dead, but then his eyes widened as he saw the Torc around her neck. An eerie light was playing softly against her pale skin, light reflecting mysteriously from the Torc. Backing away he made a sign of protection whilst calling on the gods again for guidance.

He took a deep breath in an effort to calm his nerves then he leaned over the body. Her eyes were like cold pools, wide and staring but seeing nothing, her lips slightly parted revealed small even teeth. Death sat ugly on her face, her once rosy features now white and drained of blood. Her expression was a tangle of wonder and terror, never before had he seen a mask like it, it filled him with dread. Questions to which there were no answers filled his head and he touched her hand as if the contact would tell him all he wanted to know, but there was nothing, her flesh was as cold as a winter's day.

Luain rocked back on his heels and stood up, he must decide what to do next. He had seen death many times before but nothing like this, a young girl from his village was lying dead on the floor of his workshop. It was his fault, her blood was on his hands and he was sure to be accused of the crime, he would never survive the scandal.

This was all before he could mourn the poor girl.

He needed a witness, someone he could trust, someone else must see the body just as he had found her. Madb, he thought, he must get Madb together they would decide what should be done. Luain hurried back towards the village, careful not to rouse suspicion.

"What are you doing back here?" Madb asked as soon as she saw her uncle.

Luckily she was alone Fedelmid was away on some errand.

"You must come with me now." She could see that he was agitated, this was quite unlike him, there had to be a very good reason for him to be acting this way.

"Tell me what has happened," she said firmly.

"We have a problem to deal with, I'll tell you on the way."

When they arrived at the workshop Madb was appalled at the sight of Luigsech. She had of course encountered death before and it was never a pleasant experience, but the shock of seeing one of the women from the village like this left her stunned.

Dropping to her knees she carefully removed the Torc from around Luigsech's neck and wrapping it quickly tucked it out of sight. She pushed the flagstone back into place and with a handful of ash from the hearth cleaned off the dried blood, then filling the cracks around the stone with dust it soon looked as if it had never been disturbed.

"Did you touch her?" Madb glanced up at her uncle.

"No," he shook his head, "yes." Suddenly he remembered touching her hand.

Madb grunted as she glanced around. She began checking every inch of the workshop searching for anything that might incriminate them. Luain stood back to give her more room. He realised that he should have taken charge, should have done more, but the shock of finding her like this had unnerved him more than he cared to admit.

Madb, calming her raw nerves slowed her breathing until her heart rate returned to normal, then filling her lungs she began to chant. She called to Madadh-alluidh, her dream spirit, the wolf.

Luain watched as suddenly Madb fell to her hands and knees, her back arching she moaned and her eyes rolled up into the back of her head. Her body shuddered alarmingly as powerful sensations rattled through her bones, her senses sharpened and she could smell her own scent, it was sweet and full of musk. Sniffing at the air sharply she allowed her brain time to adjust and only then could she begin to digest the information that came flooding in. Using heightened senses she began to see pictures, at first the information was confusing, she had to learn to become selective, focus on what was relevant, so moving slowly around the workshop she tilted her head and flared her nostrils, tasting the air. The scent of her uncle was everywhere, the trail was both old and new all mingled into one, it was a path too complicated to follow but in the confined space she could sense his fear and confusion. Turning away she caught another scent the thread that she sought but following it was like chasing a ribbon blown about by the wind, dancing this way and that it weaved around the workshop, painting an image of Luigsech's excitement. Slowly, Madb began to untangle the complicated web before constructing a picture in her mind.

The trance that gripped her became more intense and like a magnetic force drew her further into her dream spirit, she could feel the essence of Madadh-alluidh. It was all around her, he influenced her every thought until she became immersed in his wisdom.

Madb focussed her mind on the place where she had hidden the Torc, the chamber in the floor beside the hearth. The energy emanating from the ground disturbed her so turning away she concentrated on Luigsech and could feel the excitement that had engulfed her friend. The elation that she had felt when discovering the hiding place was almost overwhelming. Luigsech had taken the Torc from its bag and fastened it around her neck, she had experienced the euphoria that surrounded it and felt the power of the Torc. It may be a thing of beauty but it had become a malignant force of terror.

All of this became clear to Madb and she hardly felt the shudder that rocked her then she cried out in anguish. From the moment Luigsech had discovered the hiding place she was doomed. Madb could feel the evil essence of the red haired woman as she appeared in ghostly form and drawing back Madb howled. She was appalled, the moment Luigsech had died had been terrifying enough, but her soul had been stolen from her body and she would never be able to rest in peace, she would burn in the otherworld for eternity, her crime, vain curiosity.

Madb trembled as she stared around the workshop, it was as if she was seeing it for the first time and she shuddered. Her dream spirit had gone leaving her exhausted and her emotions raw, she heard herself mewing, a sad and heartfelt sound which could have been a lament for the death of her friend.

In her state of semi-consciousness, Madb sensed Maedoc and her eyes widened. At first she thought he had been there with Luigsech but then she realised the trail was old, nothing more than a memory. He had been there the previous day trying out his sword and his presence remained, so intense had been his excitement.

Madb staggered against the hearth, her heart hammering inside her chest, her breath coming in short gasps. She had to calm her nerves and return smoothly to the real world, there was nothing more she could do for her friend. Luain stepped forward and laid his hand on her shoulder, the human contact was a comfort which eased her transition and she was grateful for that.

"She was alone," Madb said her voice barely a whisper. Stunned by what she had seen she began to recount her experience and Luain listened without interrupting. Madb knew that there was more to the

Torc than her uncle realised but the implications were far too terrifying to contemplate.

They had to decide what to do next they could hardly leave Luigsech lying on the floor. Kneeling beside the body, Madb checked for marks but all she found was a deep wound to her head. She stared into the face of her friend, they had never been close and at times had not got on at all but Luigsech hardly deserved this.

"We must bury her in the forest," Madb said her voice full of regret. "We cannot afford a scandal no-one must know that she was here."

She glanced up at her uncle, she had never seen him like this before, she couldn't understand how an old warrior like him could be so affected by death.

"Better we keep quiet and say nothing, once she is missed her mother will think she was taken by the warriors who haunt the forest. Ban Mac Faelan and his men will probably take the blame."

Luain continued to stare and Madb thought he had not heard, but suddenly he nodded he didn't like the implications of her suggestion but there was no other way.

"That could start a war," he grumbled.

"Yes it could," she agreed and wondered how Maedoc would react when he found out.

Suddenly there was a noise from outside, a horse whinnied as it pulled up sharp. Luain reacted immediately pushing his burly frame into the doorway effectively blocking it to visitors.

Alma Mac Ban and his two companions were dismounting. Luain was shocked, he had not expected them so soon and looking back over his shoulder, he silently mouthed the name of their visitor to Madb. Moving away from Luigsech she began to paw at the ground lifting the stone to retrieve the leather bag, then scrambling to her feet she crossed the workshop and pushed the bag into her uncle's hand before melting back into the shadows.

"Greetings Alma Mac Ban," Luain said stepping out into the light.

Madb was surprised at how calm and sociable he sounded.

"News travels quickly," he continued, sounding even more good-humoured.

"My father grows impatient, he wants his Torc."

Luain nodded knowing how much that sounded like the Ban that he used to know. "Yes, I'm sure he does." Holding out the bag to his old friend's son he studied him before standing back. There was something familiar about him, he had noticed it before but thought it was because he was Ban's son, this time however he was not so sure. Shrugging off the moment he watched intently.

Carefully Alma pulled the Torc from the bag and holding it up marvelled at the intricate carvings etched expertly into the metal. Light dancing over its surface stunned him and for a moment he was speechless.

"It is truly magnificent," Alma whispered. "The workmanship is quite exquisite."

His fingers played over the clasp feeling the quality of the fine chain which held it in place then he saw the icons on the solid ends. The meaning of such powerful images was not lost on him.

"You have surpassed yourself." He was in awe of the metal smith and continued to shower him with compliments.

Luain hoped that Madb was listening such praise should be directed at her.

Alma slipped his hand into the bottom of the bag and felt for the off cuts. Luain was trustworthy he was certain of that but he felt obliged to allay his suspicions.

"I am satisfied that our contract is now complete," he grinned. "You will be rewarded for your work of course."

Luain nodded accepting the fact that he would be paid even though nothing had been agreed at the start. Heaving a sigh of relief, he was glad when the men mounted up and rode away. He was happy to be rid of the Torc, it had caused him more worries than he cared to admit.

They took Luigsech into the forest and buried her without ceremony. Madb sang a lament as she covered the body with earth and Luain called upon the gods, asking for their blessing he wished her easy passage into the otherworld, although he feared it was too late, her soul had already gone, stolen by darker forces than he could imagine.

VI

Ban Mac Faelan had lived for forty two summers and still he remained an impressive figure. Standing resplendent in his ceremonial robes, he had just finished giving a rousing speech to some of his closest friends and loyal followers, now he was preparing to address the crowd.

Families from the outlying villages had been pouring into the huge settlement throughout the morning and now there was a party like atmosphere on the air. Groups of men were enjoying the horse racing and families met in the market place to exchange gossip or sample the wares from the various stalls which had been set up for the occasion. This was the third celebration of the year; Lughnasadh marked the beginning of the harvest season, berries were ripening on the bushes in the forest and grain in the fields was almost ready to be gathered in. This was a crucial time in the calendar as winter stores had to be replenished in order to guarantee the survival of the village during the harsh months ahead.

Suddenly Ban cried out and those around him jumped back startled by his outburst. Alma watched as his father's eyes rolled back into his head and the big man shuddered, clutching at his chest. He groaned loudly and the air rasped from his lungs then his legs gave out and he collapsed to the ground. Gasping for breath, his face was pinched and deathly pale, pain swept through his chest in waves. Alma dropped to his father's side and the men around them crowded in.

"Give him some room," Alma growled, "can't you see, he needs air."

Drawing back the warriors were bewildered by the sudden change in their leader, they looked on helplessly as Alma did what he could to make his father comfortable. Some of his men became suspicious and began searching the faces in the crowd, convinced that an act of terrorism had taken place.

"He's been afflicted by a malevolent spirit," one of them cried.

Alma looked up and shot him a penetrating stare.

"Alma," his father's voice was weak, "take this from my throat." His fingers were struggling helplessly with the Torc.

He had been so proud to wear it earlier, it was the perfect opportunity to show it off, to demonstrate his power and wealth, but now it was as an unwelcomed weight around his neck.

35

"Take it off me," he struggled desperately. Suddenly his body arched as a massive spasm shot through him, the force driving Alma backwards.

Ban could see her coming towards him through the mist. Her red hair was magnificent but it seemed unreal, it danced like flames around her head and her huge green eyes smouldered as they bored into him. The pain in his chest was relentless, it consumed him in waves and he lost the feeling in his left arm, it was as if his throat was on fire and he cried out in both agony and fear. Ban faced the woman as he would an enemy in battle and it was then that he realised that he'd seen her before.

The red haired woman from Hibernia drew nearer until she hovered above him and drawing her long hair over him provocatively she grinned as she saw the flicker of recognition on his face.

He shuddered and tried to draw back but the ground was solid beneath him, he was helpless, he had nowhere to go. Her breath was hot against his face and her pale skin glowed eerily, the heat from her flaming hair consumed him, then Ban Mac Faelan cried out.

"Father," Alma laid his hand against his father's forehead, "lie still." Ban could neither see, nor hear his son.

"You wronged my people," the woman hissed into his ear. "You murdered me. Take from thy neighbour that which is not yours and thou shalt reap the consequences for all eternity."

With his final breath Ban cried out a blood curdling scream then his soul was torn from his body.

Alma stood back, he was trembling and the crowd around him were silent with shock. Their Chieftain, the great Ban Mac Faelan, had died in agony on the ground at their feet and they had no idea why.

Alma had been unable to remove the Torc from his father's neck but now as he lay still, he loosened the clasp and lifted it up so the crowd could see. He could feel a residue of evil that had coursed through his father's body and as the vibrations stimulated his fingers his eyes narrowed suspiciously.

"Luain Mac Lanis," he said his voice hardly more than a whisper. "He must be responsible for this." The men closed in around him and nodded their agreement.

"He will pay for his treachery," he said louder this time so everyone could hear.

He had no idea yet what form this retribution would take, but of one thing he was certain, Luain Mac Lanis would pay dearly for the life of Ban Mac Faelan.

News of his death travelled quickly, even the people of distant Elmet heard of Ban's passing. The period of mourning lasted for five days and whilst his father's body was prepared for its burial ceremony, Alma was kept busy overseeing the last minute preparations for his tomb. Ban had commissioned the construction of his burial place some months earlier, but he did not know then that he would be in need of it so soon.

Luain was shocked when he heard the news. Since the death of Luigsech he'd been uneasy it was as if some other catastrophe was waiting to happen and a deep depression engulfed him. His whole life had changed it was as if the spirits had abandoned him, chosen to remain silent, no longer willing to warn him of the trials to come. The circumstances of Ban's death upset him greatly it was not a fitting death for a warrior. A great man like Ban Mac Faelan who lived by his sword should have greeted Bel of the otherworld from the chaos of a battle field.

Luain was certain that some evil force was responsible for his friend's death and it bothered him enormously. Another thought which kept nagging at him was the unpleasant vibrations he'd felt flowing through the Torc, this must have had some bearing on his death. Of one thing he was certain, Ban's soul was not at peace.

Luain and Madb travelled across the river to the next village for the funeral, he was tight lipped as he watched the ceremony and Madb, standing silently beside him, could feel her uncle's unease. She was convinced that once this sad episode was over he would settle down and things would return to normal.

"Madb," Luain turned to face her, "promise me that you will never speak of the Torc, tell no-one that you made it." She was surprised by what he'd just said and as she looked up he held her stare, he didn't look away until she nodded.

Once the ceremony was over a druid sealed the entrance to the tomb and recited an incantation which would safeguard the body of the great warrior who was interred there. Without warning Luain found himself surrounded, the crowd around him drew back leaving him in the embrace of Alma's warriors. His knife was taken from his belt and his hands were secured behind his back.

Madb was shocked by the sudden show of force, it happened so quickly, there was no warning or time to react and now she found herself caught up in the crowd. Madadh-alluidh was responsible for her safety he was a devious spirit who watched over her at all times.

Any opportunity that she may have had to help her uncle was now gone and all she could do was watch as Alma Mac Ban approached him.

"Luain Mac Lanis," his voice was strong, "you are responsible for the death of my father."

The crowd murmured their approval as the druid demanded their support.

"Through your treachery we have lost more than just a good man. My father brought stability to this land and without him the gods have seen fit to forsake us."

He glanced around at his people in search of reassurance. "The gods have sent a blight to destroy our crops, even as the grain is in the fields it withers under the heat of the sun. Our animals have begun to die and milk from our cows is soured."

Luain pleaded his innocence but it was no good, the crowd was against him and all seemed lost. The druid began to shout incoherent words that were as mad as his dancing and his eyes bulged as spittle flew from his lips.

"You will answer for your crime," he said pointing a knurled finger at Luain.

Madb watched from the safety of the crowd, they were in full support of Alma and the druid, the situation was becoming desperate. She was in no doubts of her ability she would be able to take some of Alma's men down but in doing so would secure her own death.

"I have committed no crime," Luain insisted, "I have murdered no-one."

"You have murdered Ban Mac Faelan with your wizardry, as surely as if you had struck him down with your own blade." The druid shouted.

Alma became impatient, he had heard enough and ordering his men forward they forced Luain along the path. One of the men beat him savagely knocking him to his knees and he was left knowing that retaliation would not be tolerated.

Madb was outraged and frustrated at not being able to help her uncle. He had given her a sign, an instruction to stay out of sight and not become involved, now swept along by the crowd she was overlooked, no longer associated with the man who had been arrested. The people around her were exuberant and clearly expected the drama to unfold further.

Luain was taken to a secure compound where he was forced to spend several days in the ruins of a filthy roundhouse which had previously been used to house pigs prior to slaughter.

Madb was delighted when she discovered where her uncle was being held and with the help of her dream spirit used her powers of concealment to slip past the guards on the gate. She was dismayed when discovering the conditions in which he was being kept, no food had passed his lips during his confinement but at least water was plentiful. His stinking prison was as hot as a bread oven and when the sun was directly overhead it was overpowering. Madb was worried that he might succumb to some disease.

"You must not let them know you made the Torc," he repeated his warning.

Madb re-assured him but never questioned the reasoning behind his concern.

The weather was not as hot as the previous day but it was still warm, hazy and close. Luain seemed more lethargic than usual and Madb was becoming anxious, she began to wonder if he was being drugged, but before she had time to think it through a noise from beyond the compound roused her interest. A druid began to shout and as he called and chanted, people were drawn toward him. Madb glanced at her uncle, he was leaning against the wall dozing in the cloying heat, safe enough for the moment she thought, so she decided to go and take a look.

The druid was standing on a platform which was supported by stakes driven into the bed of the sacred swamp, his arms were outstretched and his head was thrown back as he called to the gods. Madb concealed herself amongst the crowd and made her way towards the waterside. The druid's voice carried towards them but she couldn't make out what he was saying, his words were lost amongst the grasses which grew in thick clumps at the edge of the swamp. Suddenly he was answered by the booming voice of Teranis, thunder rolled around the hills chasing a bolt of lightning which tore at the sky.

The crowd were hushed in awe of the druid's magic. The gods began to gather in the sky overhead and a cool breeze rippled the surface of the swamp as it rustled through the reeds.

Madb was uneasy, the air around her seemed charged, heavy with the presence of the gods and Teranis addressed the crowd once again, his voice rumbling deeply overhead. The people around her became restless and a woman half crazed with age, cackled alarmingly. She pushed up beside Madb who tried to move away but the old woman took hold of her arm and pointed with a crooked finger towards the spectacle that was about to unfold.

Alma Mac Ban appeared on the platform beside the druid and gestured for two of his men come forward. Madb breathed in sharply when she saw her uncle held between the warriors, they were dragging him roughly towards the water's edge, he was unsteady on his feet. His hands were bound loosely behind his back and he was dressed in a clean white robe. They came to a stop in front of the druid and Luain was forced to his knees. Taranis called out again as if pleased by the proceedings and the old woman shrieked.

"There is nothing you can do for him now Madadh-alluidh," she said looking up at Madb.

Madb was astounded, she had never been addressed by her dream spirit name before and turning toward the old woman she towered above her menacingly as the hag cringed. With eyes half blinded by cataracts and legs bent with age, she sucked at her tongue through a toothless grin and Madb was repelled by the odour which came up to greet her. Straightening up she shuffled to one side as the druid began to chant, her skin crawling as she turned her attention to the unfolding drama.

Her eyes widened as one of the men standing beside her uncle swayed to one side, in his hands he held an axe which he lifted slowly. Bringing it down sharply, he twisted the shaft at the last moment so that the flat of the axe struck Luain's head, knocking him sideward's. A sickening thud echoed around the swamp and the crowd gasped, then they watched as the second warrior moved in, he caught Luain with a chord which he twisted around his neck and as he tightened the garrotte Luain struggled and danced instinctively as he fought for breath.

Madb went rigid as she watched her uncle's life draining away, the sound of his struggling brought tears tumbling over her cheeks and she was sickened, there was nothing she could do but watch the horrible drama unfold.

Alma stepped forward and grabbing a handful of Luain's hair forced him into the water, there was not much of a struggle as he was held under. Weakened at having been knocked senseless by the blow of the axe and half strangled by the garrotte, he had no fight left. The drugs that poisoned his system had done their work and he embraced the fate that awaited him.

The crowd around Madb erupted, cheering and clapping their appreciation, they were convinced that now the gods would be satisfied, they had been given the ultimate gift, a human sacrifice. Madb stood open mouthed, frozen to the spot, she was unable to move, her whole body numb. The scene began to play over in her mind in slow motion and as Luain became still in the water she realised that he was wearing the Torc.

Luain Mac Lanis felt the sharp blow against the side of his head and his world exploded into a kaleidoscope of colours, the Torc around his neck came alive as it wriggled like a serpent, vibrating and burning into his skin. It became increasingly heavy and as it tightened around his throat he could no longer breathe. Darkness closed in around him and it was then he saw the woman, she was coming towards him on a cloud of mist, it was as if she was floating across the water and her red hair moving about her face resembled flaming vapours. The stare from her huge green eyes seemed to bore right into him. She smiled and gestured towards him, holding out her arms in an offer of embrace and as she came closer his pain lessened, his lungs no longer burned, the pain in his head dulled and nothing seemed to matter.

Suddenly he was standing beside his own body and he studied it curiously. The woman stood beside him and together they watched as slowly it disappeared into the murky water of the sacred swamp. He glanced back one more time towards the shore, the people had gone nothing remained not even Alma or the druid.

"No!" Madb sobbed and she thought her heart would break.

The crowd around her took no notice, they were too busy clapping and cheering their appreciation. Alma Mac Ban was their leader and he knew how to appease the gods.

"He's killed his own father, the young fool," the old woman screeched.

Turning sharply Madb lifted her off her feet and forced her back against a rock.

"What do you mean?" Madb hissed coldly.

The old woman's eyes bulged with fear and she didn't look quite as mad as she did a moment before. She frowned as if trying to remember a half forgotten thought then her face brightened.

"Luain Mac Lanis was his father, not Ban Mac Faelan," she howled, mad again with laughter.

"What do you mean, his father, how do you know?" Madb was confused.

"I was his wet nurse when I was a young woman, the young fool suckled on my teats," she screeched madly again, "I was once close to that family, privy to what went on."

She winked and when Madb let her go she dropped to the ground and scuttled away leaving her standing alone.

41

Part Two

The Goddess in her Mother Aspect

*The radiant Goddess of the moon shall rise up at night
and in her chariot ride across the sky*

VII

"The west coast of Ireland is steeped in Celtic history and is one of the last places in Europe where Celtic traditions, language and way of life has survived. This is mainly because the Romans never arrived."

Orlagh Gairne was summing up having addressed a group of local historians in the lecture theatre at the National Museum of Ireland.

"If there are any questions then please sing out or for the coy amongst you I will be here for a while longer, so just come up and see me."

Orlagh was one of the historians working at the museum, her specialism Celtic history. She was part of the research team and was often found wearing wellies and a raincoat in the middle of a muddy field somewhere, wielding a trowel.

Standing five foot four, she had an impressive head of red hair which was testament to her Celtic roots and her vivid green eyes, although exquisite, could be rather intimidating at times. She liked to keep herself fit, working out at the gym, but these sessions of activity were becoming increasingly less frequent.

Collecting up her notes, she retrieved her memory stick from her laptop, before shutting it down. Her presentation had been a success, her collection of photographs and diagrams had worked well complimenting her power point presentation. She was always conscious of making these evenings light and entertaining, the people who came to listen were often not academics but individuals who were interested in her work. Satisfied with her performance, Orlagh chatted happily with a group as she packed away her notes.

The organisation that she worked for encouraged their academic staff to practice their teaching skills, Orlagh didn't mind, she rather enjoyed her moments of glory in front of an audience. She had just completed a lengthy project cataloguing a cache of Celtic jewellery that had been unearthed earlier in the year in County Meath and was glad of the diversion.

"That was a very interesting talk Dr. Gairne."

Orlagh turned and found herself face to face with a young man who gave her the warmest of smiles. "You're welcome," she smiled back at him. She had seen him earlier sitting in the front row of the audience.

"I should introduce myself," he grinned confidently. "My name is Jerry Knowles."

"Hiya Jerry Knowles," she said holding out her hand.

"I'm a student here at Trinity." Taking her cool hand in his he held onto it.

"What are you studying?"

"Dusty old history," he made a face, "no seriously." He allowed her to take her hand back. "I'm writing a paper on Germanic mythology," he paused just long enough to study her reaction. "Well, to be truthful," he continued, "the distortion of Germanic mythology by the Nazi regime, Hitler's corruption of that noble northern spirit." He said, quoting J.R.R.Tolkein.

"Well, I'm impressed," she smiled again.

"The whole pre-history thing does it for me, the bronze and iron age in particular."

"So Jerry, why Dublin I guess from your accent that you are not from around these parts."

"No, you're quite right, I'm a Man of Kent and proud of it, more Saxon than Celtic of course, with a dash of Norman thrown in."

She eyed him quizzically, he had not yet fully answered her question.

"I needed to get away from home and London wasn't far enough. I wanted to study of course so after a little research narrowed it down to either Edinburgh or Dublin, the frozen North or the Emerald Isle?"

"I understand your wanting to get as far away from home as possible, but there are plenty of very good universities closer to London."

"True, but as you so perceptively point out I had to put distance between myself and my folks. I was finding living at home a little stifling, I'd outgrown them I suppose," he paused before going on, "I could have studied in Europe, but I wanted an English speaking environment."

She began to work around him, collecting up her notes.

"So what draws you to Celtic history in particular?" she asked glancing up.

"My interests in the period and Ireland are inbred I'm afraid. My great grandfather was Sir Geoffrey Knowles."

Orlagh stopped what she was doing, her beautiful green eyes becoming huge, shining like emeralds against her pale skin.

"Wow, you're kidding me! Not Sir Geoffrey Knowles the great Edwardian archaeologist who discovered the Belgae Torc?"

"The very same I'm afraid."

"Well, now I am impressed, of course I've read all his papers, he had some very interesting ideas and techniques, many of which have been substantiated by modern day methods."

"He was an amazingly talented man, I just wish I had half his aptitude."

Jerry moved towards a chair and lowering himself into it stretched out his long legs before looking up at her. She was a lot more attractive up close and he was glad that she was no longer hiding behind the rostrum.

"What I really want to know," he began, "was your take on Animal Allies."

Orlagh looked at him and frowned quizzically, taking her time to consider his question.

"In what context?" she asked before moving closer, her interest suddenly aroused. "Generally or do you have something more specific in mind?"

"Well, I have a theory which I won't share with you just yet, but I'm interested to see if what you had to say might have any impact on my thoughts."

"I see," she smiled and drawing up a chair sank gracefully into it before crossing her legs.

"I don't suppose you would rather continue this discussion at a pub?"

"Nice chat up line," she replied dryly, "let's just see how we get along first shall we?"

Orlagh studied him through half closed eyes, she thought him attractive enough, although he needed to scrub up a little. He looked a little ruffled, his jacket creased, his corduroy trousers and brogues a little worn, his mousey coloured hair unruly and there was a shadow across his rather masculine square jaw. He was a student after all, she smiled, who probably had a reputation to maintain, but he was a long way from living in the gutter. It was difficult to tell his age, he was brimming with self confidence but had an air of calm about him that could only come with maturity.

"Well," she began deciding to play along with his games, "as you are undoubtedly aware, Celtic people believed in individual Animal Allies or Spiritual helpers. Nearly all Shamanic cultures held this belief," she paused to see how she was doing. "These allies were based on ordinary animals, creatures that people would have been familiar with, there are however, exceptions to that rule, notably..."

"The Unicorn," he interrupted, "Briabhall; the mythical creature which had the body of a white horse, the legs of an antelope and the tail of a lion, oh and not forgetting the single horn on its head."

"You know all this already," she said, grinning at him.

"Of course, but please do continue."

45

She decided to try a different approach. "The Native Americans had their totem animals and the Celts displayed theirs on banners, as with the banners of the Fianna."

Jerry smiled, encouraging her to go on.

"Painting individual devices on their banners, shields and some-times even their bodies, historians believe that this may well have been the origin of the heraldic devices that became so popular throughout Europe."

"That's true," he took up the conversation. "Others throughout history have used such devices, the Norsemen, Saxons and Normans for example, but most people seem to think that it wasn't until medieval times that such a display of wealth and power was used."

"What then was the Belgae Torc if it wasn't a symbol of power?"

"Quite," he nodded in agreement, "but that's another matter." He balanced his elbows on the arms of the chair and made a steeple with his fingers before resting his chin thoughtfully on top. "We can only guess at how these people chose their Animal Allies, having no written evidence we can only make a reasonable assumption." He looked thoughtfully at her.

"Well, we know from relics that have been unearthed that they were very Spiritual, their culture supported polytheism just to mention one strand of their beliefs." She shifted in her chair before continuing. "It seems likely from the scant evidence that Animal Allies would have chosen the individual, not vice versa."

"Ah," Jerry said collapsing his steepled fingers so his hands fell into his lap. "Now we come to the crux of the matter, it's my belief that as children we make our own choices, we all have our favourite animal," he explained. "What's yours?"

Orlagh looked at him sceptically. "The deer as it happens."

"Yes," he said his brow furrowing with concentration. "Fiadh, the white doe. There is the stag of course, a male version, but these animals were a common guide from the Otherworld. The creature is often copied in other rituals."

"I'm not sure I agree with your theory," Orlagh said registering his insinuation. "Modern day kids have their favourite animal but their knowledge of these creatures would be far greater than their Celtic counterparts."

"Only the range of animals," he nodded, "but a Celtic child would have much closer links with animals and nature itself."

"True," she agreed, "but don't underestimate the modern day kid."

"Okay, but it's my belief that when our Celt entered the spirit world to seek his Animal Ally, his mind would already have been made up, influenced by his childhood preferences."

"I'm still not convinced," Orlagh made a face, "a good theory I grant you that."

Reaching for her briefcase she thumbed through some papers before she found what she was looking for.

"Here's something you might like to read." She said passing it to him.

"Finding your Animal Allies. A Vision Quest." He read from the opening lines. "I see you are the author," he grinned appreciatively as he found her name at the bottom of the page.

"It's an experiment based on a meditation technique that I was working on once."

He nodded so she continued. "Something like this may well have been used by the Celts, but who knows, this theory is based purely on logic, it doesn't involve drug inducement of any kind."

"Well, it may surprise you to know I've already tried it out," Jerry laughed.

"What, the drug inducement?"

"No of course not, the Vision Quest, or a similar technique."

They laughed together.

"Okay so which animal is your ally?" she asked becoming serious.

"Before I tell you, I am aware that it was common practice to have more than one Animal Ally, different guides for different situations, however, I seem to have only one."

Orlagh remained silent as he paused.

"My animal, as it happens, is also the deer."

"Go on! You're kidding me," she refused to believe him.

"No honestly, I kid you not. You telling me that your favourite animal is a deer had no influence over my answer," he looked at her earnestly.

"Okay," she held up her hands, "I believe you."

"So as your favourite animal is the deer can I also assume it's your Animal Ally?"

"Well as you say, many animals for different situations but I have to admit, my primary ally is the deer," she looked at her watch and her eyes flashed. "Lord, won't you just look at the time. Listen Jerry, it's been great talking with you but I must go now. We should do this again sometime."

Collecting up her notes she stuffed them into her briefcase then turning on her mobile phone she checked for messages, there were none. Flicking off the lights she left the theatre and made her way along the corridor.

Janet May, secretary to Peter O'Reilly, Orlagh's boss, was still at her desk.

"Hiya Janet, still at it?" Orlagh grinned at her little rhyme.

Janet made no comment, she had heard it a million times before. "Orlagh, how did it go?"

"It was great, in fact I really enjoyed myself."

"So who was that gorgeous man I just saw leaving the theatre, did you get a look at his bottom?"

"Janet!" she exclaimed with a grin. "Of course I didn't, believe it or not we were discussing Animal Allies."

"No, I don't believe it, I know what I would have been doing if I were alone with such a hunk in the theatre."

"Go on, you'll have me in a blush if you carry on like that."

They both laughed.

"Look Orlagh, seriously now, O'Reilly wants to speak with you urgently."

"Oh does he, did he say what it's about?"

"No, well you know what he's like, keeps his cards close to his chest. I may as well have signed the official secrets act rather than a contract of employment."

Orlagh grinned as Janet continued. "Of course he didn't tell me anything, he wants you to call him on his mobile the moment you're finished here."

Orlagh checked her watch. "Officially I finished work forty minutes ago so he can damn well wait until tomorrow. You shouldn't be here either."

Janet agreed, so grabbing her coat and bag they made their way along the corridor.

"Do you fancy doing some shots at O'Toole's?"

"I'll settle for a small Irish cider."

"Oh go on, one small cider indeed."

Orlagh smiled and said good night to the security man as he let them out of the building. She thought Janet May a scream, she was just the tonic she needed.

"So, are you going to tell me, what in the devils name is an Animal Ally?"

VIII

The following morning Orlagh went directly to see her boss. Striding boldly into his office she sat in the chair that was set up opposite his desk and watched him expectantly. She knew he would be annoyed at her for not telephoning the previous evening, but she also realised that he wouldn't make an issue out of it.

Peter O'Reilly, skipping the pleasantries, came straight to the point. "I want you to fly to Paris tomorrow morning."

Orlagh, taken completely by surprise, stared at him suspiciously. "Paris?" she said hoping he would confirm what he had just said.

"Yes," he nodded, "then you are to catch a train to Cherbourg."

"Okay," she began to wonder what other surprises he might have for her.

"A ship will be waiting for you in the harbour."

"A ship?" now she was curious.

Peter rummaged through the paperwork that was spreading alarmingly over his desktop, and finally found what he was looking for. "It's an American survey vessel called," he paused whilst he studied the paper. "The Sea Quest."

She stared at him, her green eyes fixing him steadily until he began to feel uneasy.

"You need to make contact with a man called Jack Harrington," he went on quickly.

"Why would I need to join an American survey ship?"

"Jack Harrington is amongst other things a salvage expert."

"Oh come on Peter," she shuffled around in her seat before crossing her legs. "You haven't answered my question."

"Harrington has located a ship called the Hudson Bay," he said holding his hand up in a placating gesture.

"I presume this is a sunken ship."

"Yes," he didn't have chance to continue.

"What does a sunken ship have to do with me?"

"Let me finish and I'll tell you," he murmured reproachfully. He reminded her of her father whenever he did that. "The Hudson Bay sank just after the Second World War; it was carrying a huge quantity of Nazi gold and plundered works of art."

She nodded but chose to remain silent.

49

"The ship's inventory includes an item which will interest you immensely."

Cruelly he fed her bits of information drawing out the suspense and all the time wondering how long it would take her to work it out.

"The Hudson Bay," she whispered, her green eyes flashing. "The Belgae Torc?"

O'Reilly shot her a silly grin allowing her a few moments to take it in.

"I don't believe it," she said at last.

"It's true. We know the Torc disappeared in the early 1930's. It was a mystery, no one seemed to know what happened to it. It was assumed that the Germans acquired it somehow, maybe it was stolen to order or found its way onto the black market, nothing can be proven of course, but it hardly matters now."

"How can you be sure it's on the ship?" Orlagh was still sceptical.

"At the end of the war, Europe was in tatters. A massive clear up was in operation jointly co-ordinated by the British and American governments," he took a deep breath before continuing. "Churchill wanted to stop the Russians from discovering too much, they had a massive force on the ground and could easily have walked off with all the Nazi treasure if they knew where to look."

She listened to him patiently, waiting for him to tell her something that she didn't already know.

"The British government knew it would cost them dearly to re-build France and Germany, so the plundered gold would come in very useful. The Hudson Bay was one of the ships used to get the treasure safely out from under the allies' noses, besides, it's not just gold we are talking about here."

"I know about the works of art and historical artefacts that were stolen from galleries and museums. Most of these treasures hidden away by Hitler's top ranking staff were considered perks of the job, additions to their private collections, pensions for after the war."

Peter nodded and waved a piece of paper in the air.

"This is a copy of the inventory, it clearly states that the Belgae Torc was loaded onto that ship."

"Was the ship heading for England?" she asked fishing for its location.

"No, this cargo was bound for America."

She raised her eyebrows quizzically. "Is it the Torc the Americans are interested in?"

"No, not as such, they are more concerned with the gold. It will be your job to ensure that the salvage operation is carried out sensitively

50

and all the ancient artefacts recovered are documented correctly."

"As it's essentially a salvage operation won't the Americans have salvage rights?"

"Not entirely, with my contacts in the States and the museum having sponsored part of the operation, the Americans have agreed that we should have our pick of the artefacts."

"So they have no idea how significant the Belgae Torc is to European Celtic history?"

"No, I don't suppose they do, but you see how useful your influence will be."

She thought for a moment. "So I'm to lie, cheat the American government?"

"Not exactly, just be a little economic with the truth, play down the value of the artefacts, as I said, the Americans are after the gold."

"What influence will I have over a bunch of gold diggers?"

"I'm confident that you will find a way to persuade them from blasting open the ship and scattering valuable pieces of history all over the sea bed."

Orlagh nodded, she was well aware that salvage engineers were not as sensitive as archaeologists.

"So what's this Jack Harrington like?"

"He's not quite the rough neck that you might imagine," he began. "He is in fact very well respected in his field of expertise, his methods might not be what you are used to but he is a man of integrity. He knows well enough that the museum is providing financial support for this operation and he is also aware that we want to see a return for our investment."

She could hardly believe what he was saying, the thought that the museum was spending public money on a treasure hunt appalled her.

"This is a more cost effective method obtaining artefacts for the nation rather than having to bid for them against private collectors once they are recovered."

"Okay," she nodded, seeing the sense in what he was saying.

"Recently, Harrington has been involved in digging an American bomber out of the Arctic ice, it was his team of surveyors who made the discovery in the first place. He salvaged the aircraft, transported the parts back to the States where he restored it to flying condition. Of course it remains the property of the United States Air Force. Before that he led his team along the Amazon in search of an aircraft which crashed in the jungle a couple of years ago. He managed to recover the black box which helped air crash investigators to understand the cause of the disaster, this has resulted in safer air travel," he continued reading from a file.

"Wow, he sounds like a regular Indiana Jones," she said when he had finished.

"With your knowledge of underwater diving, I thought this job would be perfect for you."

"So where did the Hudson Bay sink? Please tell me it's off the coast of Hawaii."

"No, it's off the coast of Portugal."

She thought for a moment. "That's the Atlantic, near the Bay of Biscay."

O'Reilly simply nodded but made no comment.

"What's it doing there? It's hardly a direct route to the U.S.A. from France."

"Therein lies the mystery," he said looking at her steadily.

Orlagh sat back in her chair, folding her arms across her chest she wondered if there was more to it than he was letting on, O'Reilly had a reputation for being economic with the facts especially when it suited him.

"You are sure it's there, you're not sending me on a wild goose chase?"

"As I told you, the Germans were the last people to see the Torc, we have documented evidence proving that it was part of Hitler's Nazi occultism ideal, it was a symbol of his power, an influence over his people. You know that the Nazi's nurtured a strong fascination for their pagan past, they were notorious for re-inventing their glorious history."

"German mythology," Orlagh whispered.

This was the second time the subject had come up in discussion in the last twenty four hours and she wondered if Jerry Knowles knew about the re-discovery of the Belgae Torc.

"Here are your travel documents," O'Reilly pushed a package across his desk.

"I've arranged for your current projects to be covered whilst you're away. I don't anticipate you being gone for more than two weeks but you know what it's like with operations of this kind."

When Orlagh left his office her head was full of questions but she didn't think he was the man to give her the answers. She was excited at the prospect of actually seeing the Torc for herself, she had of course worked with Torcs before, but they possessed none of the complexity or the beauty of the Belgae Torc. It would be like discovering Tutankhamen's tomb all over again. If she were to bring it back to Ireland then she would be remembered in history just like the men who had originally discovered it Lord Randolf Sevington-Smythe and Sir Geoffrey Knowles were like household names in her field of work.

Crossing the street she headed for her favourite coffee shop which was situated just off St. Stephen's Green. Little tables and chairs had been set up on the pavement outside and as the lunchtime rush had not yet begun she had her choice of seats. Orlagh tried to remain calm as she waited for a waitress to take her order, closing her eyes she took a deep breath and listened to a string quartet that had set up near the coffee shop, they were playing Pachelbel's Canon. She allowed her mind to drift with the music and riding the notes she eventually began to relax. The music played with her emotions and her spirit soared only to be saddened when eventually it came to an end. The group were very good and she was grateful to them for the short interlude.

Dropping a few Euros into the violin case which stood open on the pavement she wished them luck as they prepared to move along.

"Hello," a voice sounded from across the pavement.

She looked up and could hardly believe her eyes, Jerry was standing there beside her table.

"Hi, are you stalking me?" she grinned.

"Not at all, nothing as exotic as that I'm afraid I always pass by here at this time of day."

"Do you really?" Orlagh smiled. "I often have coffee here, and when the weather permits I like to sit at a table on the pavement."

"Then I must have passed you by on many occasions."

"I guess so, look, would you like to join me? I'm not staying long, just having coffee."

"I would love to," he shot her a smile then sat down.

The waitress arrived so they ordered their drinks before beginning a conversation.

"I have some news that you might find interesting," she began.

"Really, then in that case you have my undivided attention." His English accent seemed more pronounced today.

She studied him carefully from across the table, the shadow on his face was gone his skin now smooth, then she noticed his subtle tan it was as if he'd just returned from a warmer climate.

"The Belgae Torc has possibly been found," she said the moment she realised that she was staring at him.

"Really?" his eyes widened in surprise. "It's been lost for so many years I thought it might have disappeared into a private collection."

53

"It's at the bottom of the sea," she went on to tell him about the salvage attempt.

"So you're going out to recover it?"

"Yes I leave tomorrow morning."

Their coffee arrived giving him time to take in what she had just said.

"So," Orlagh said when the waitress had gone, "tell me more about Sir Geoffrey Knowles and his team."

"I'm sure you are familiar with the story."

"Yes of course, but hearing it from you, someone who has read Sir Geoffrey's journals, would be interesting. I'm sure there are many things you could tell me that I wouldn't read in a text book."

"Apart from my great grandfather the other notable members of his team were Sir Cecil Mountjoy and Lord Sevington-Smythe, but I'm sure you already know that."

She nodded as she reached for her coffee cup.

"Lord Sevington-Smythe financed the whole operation, he had been my great grandfather's benefactor for years, they were great friends. The journals catalogue a series of finds which substantiate the theory that they were excavating a sacred site."

"Yes I remember reading about it, the items found were typical of what one would expect as spiritual offerings, but many academics refuse to believe the claim."

"Well, of course, the Torc was found in Somerset. The area around Glastonbury known as the Somerset Levels, it used to flood regularly until the water was controlled. In early times the levels were a series of lakes and swamps, only drying out during the summer months."

"Hence the name Somerset," Orlagh nodded.

"It soon became obvious during the excavation that they were not dealing with a cemetery or burial place, besides, the finds dated from different periods. They couldn't be entirely sure at the time but since then many of the artefacts have been accurately dated."

"And then of course their luck changed significantly."

"Yes," he nodded, "the Belgae Man." He paused for long enough to swallow some coffee. "Discovering the remains so well preserved rather confirmed the fact that they were dealing with a sacred swamp."

"As you say, the whole area was covered in water, lakes and bogs; this would have been a perfect place for Celtic rituals to have taken place. Often a deep pool of water was a place which they held sacred. I suppose water was seen as a kind of window, a portal into the otherworld, a place where the spirits were strongest."

Jerry nodded before continuing. "The journal describes the remains in detail, it was a male of about forty years old, now this was unusual as most human sacrifices involve much younger men. My great grandfather was convinced that something odd had taken place there he wrote in his journal that he could feel it, but the others disagreed, besides, there was no tangible evidence to support his theory. Anyway, the victim was well nourished, he must have been some kind of manual worker as his shoulders and upper body was well developed. The injuries that he had suffered were a fractured skull and strangulation, the garrotte was still around his neck. It was made from leather and was drawn so tightly that it almost severed his head."

"Then he was pushed into the water and held face down until he drowned,"

Orlagh shuddered.

"Most probably," Jerry looked up.

"It sounds to me like a 'Three Fold Death.'"

Reaching for his cup Jerry leaned back in his chair and waited for her to continue.

"The 'Three Fold Death' is where the victim dies of three deaths at the same time. Archaeological evidence suggests that this was the case with the Lindow Man, the bog body from Lindow in England. The man also known as Pete Marsh was found in 1984, his body well preserved in a peat bog, much in the same way as the Belgae Man. Both victims seem to have suffered death by ritual they have the same type of injuries."

She sat back, satisfied at being able to deliver this piece of information. Jerry remained unmoved, he knew about the 'Three Fold Death', having studied ritual killings and sacrifices.

"The only difference with our man is that he was wearing a priceless piece of jewellery"

"The Belgae Torc," she nodded.

"It must have been some serious ceremony," he told her, "human sacrifice alone was the ultimate offering to the Gods, but to include something as significant as a Torc was very unusual indeed."

"There is no evidence to suggest that the man was a King or Chieftain," Orlagh agreed. "Besides, men of that standing would never have been subjected to such a death."

"Not unless he was the victim of a conquering army," Jerry nodded. "He could have been made an example of in order to subdue the local population and of course appease the gods at the same time."

"No," Orlagh shook her head, "there's no evidence to support that theory, besides, the man was a labourer; from the condition of his hands and fingernails he must have been a craftsman of some kind."

"He could also have been a captured leader, put to work for a period of time before being executed," Jerry continued to expand his theory.

"No I don't accept that, any conquering army would want rid of men of rank as soon as possible, this sacrificial killing was something else. I grant you, it had massive significance at the time but I'm afraid we'll never know the true reason for this man's untimely death."

"The Torc is unusual," Jerry changed tack. "It's made from white gold. I didn't think we started using white gold until just after the First World War."

"It is very unusual," Orlagh agreed. "Torcs were usually made from gold, silver or sometimes copper, but I have never come across one made from white gold. If it's true then we have a problem to solve was the metal a natural alloy of gold and silver or was it manufactured in some way? If we could prove it was alloyed by the Celts then we'll have to re-write the history books."

"There's no evidence to suggest that it was alloyed, nothing Celtic has ever been found made from this material before."

"That doesn't mean it's impossible," she said, "maybe we just haven't found it yet," Orlagh had finished her coffee but had no memory of drinking it, she was completely absorbed in their conversation, "The Lydian's used white gold, it was mined from a naturally occurring alloy of gold and silver, that was around 600BC. Could they have supplied our Celts with the material?"

"It's not impossible I suppose," Jerry nodded. He ordered more coffee as the waitress passed their table. "Trade across Europe was not uncommon, in those days the Kingdom of Lydia was situated in the Mediterranean."

"Yes," Orlagh agreed, "it's in modern day Turkey."

"So it's not as unlikely as we might think, civilisations were spreading right across Europe, so white gold could have found its way to Britain, providing of course the Torc was manufactured in Britain."

"It would have been quite a substantial lump of gold," Orlagh said, "the Belgae Torc is the largest piece of jewellery I've seen from our Celtic past. I can hardly wait to hold it myself."

"It seems that you may be lucky enough to do just that," he eyed her carefully. "And I use the word 'lucky' very loosely."

She had of course heard tales about the curse surrounding the Torc. "The curse of the Belgae Torc is probably a load of old blarney!" she said.

More coffee arrived and sitting back in her chair she brushed stray hair from her face with the back of her hand. She studied him silently as the waitress fussed around their table, she hadn't seen it before, but now as she looked more closely she thought he looked innocently boyish.

"I wouldn't be too quick to discount it as an old wives tale," he said, "I've seen what my great grandfather wrote on the subject."

"Oh come on Jerry," she looked at him incredulously. "Do you really think it had something to do with the deaths of Lord Sevington-Smythe and Sir Cecil Mountjoy?"

The tone of her voice left him in no doubt of what she thought about the subject.

"My great grandfather wrote about many things," he said quickly, "most of which were never published. He had a reputation as a scientist to maintain, but the curse of the Torc would remain with him for the rest of his life."

"Okay," she tossed her head, "convince me."

"Well, in the case of Lord Sevington-Smythe, he was killed in an automobile accident."

This was nothing new, she had read about it.

"He was leaving the site at the end of the day when a bull charged out of a field, it slammed into the side of his car pushing it into a gulley where it rolled over killing him and injuring his driver."

"Yes," she nodded, "I know all this."

"Ah, but what you don't know is what was never reported. My great grandfather wrote an account of the freak accident in his journal, he said that Lord Sevinton-Smythe was wearing the Torc at the time of his death."

"Wearing the Torc?" she gasped.

"Apparently so, the journal goes on to say that his Lordship was so taken with the Torc that after it was cleaned he wanted to show it to his wife. As it was such a valuable item, he thought the safest place for it was around his neck."

"Did he really?" she eyed him suspiciously. "Or maybe it was because the man liked to act out the part of a rich and powerful leader."

"Well, I don't know about that, of course the thing about him wearing the Torc never made it into the papers."

"Surely it's a case of pure coincidence," Orlagh said. "I grant you, it was an unusual way to die. Of course, it could have been the noise from the car which startled the beast, I guess they didn't get many cars around the Somerset Levels in 1912."

His eyes narrowed as he frowned, but he had to agree with her reasoning.

"Sir Cecil Mountjoy was killed by a freak bolt of lightning." Orlagh stated.

"Yes he was."

"I suppose you are about to tell me that he was struck down by Taranis, the god of thunder."

"Well, funny you should say that," he grinned before going on. "Sir Mountjoy was killed in a thunder storm, but by all accounts he too was wearing the Torc at the time of his death."

"You're kidding me!" she put her cup down on the table and leaned towards him.

"Well, according to the journal, Sir Mountjoy didn't take my great grandfather's warning seriously. Like you he was sceptical, my great grandfather was convinced it was cursed but Sir Mountjoy would hear none of it, to settle the matter he agreed to wear the Torc for the day whilst working on the site. Apparently there was not a cloud in the sky when the lightning struck, it killed Sir Mountjoy instantly, but again the details of his death were kept out of the papers. My great grandfather couldn't afford the hysteria that would have followed such a report he needed his force of workers to complete the dig."

For a moment Orlagh remained speechless. "Of course with that amount of metal around his neck it was sure to attract lightning, it must have acted like a conductor rail on top of a tall building."

"That may be true during a raging storm, but that wasn't the case, there was only a single bolt and what are the chances of being hit by that? Anyhow, it had a profound and lasting effect on my great grandfather. He wrote about feeling strange vibrations whenever he handled the Torc, besides, many other people have confirmed his claims over the years."

"Surely you don't believe it was a curse?"

"I'm only going on what I've read in his journals and the comments handed down by my family. As part of my research I'm looking into other strange deaths which may have occurred with subsequent owners of the Torc, but it's proving near impossible, there are not many records. The Torc seems to disappear for long periods only to turn up in the most unlikely of places. After it was discovered in Somerset it was sent to London with all the other finds where it remained until the early 1920s, then it disappeared for ten years only to emerge in Suffolk as part of a private collection. By the mid 1930s it had gone again, I suspect by then it was in German hands."

"I can't understand why it didn't remain in the British Museum."

"I don't suppose there was any chance of that, there are a lot of unscrupulous dealers out there who recognise the value of objects like the Belgae Torc."

Orlagh checked her watch, they had been chatting for almost an hour and she had a lot to do before her early morning departure.

"Look Jerry, I would love to stay and talk with you all afternoon but I really must go," she rummaged in her bag and found one of her cards which she pushed towards him across the table.

"So I don't get your personal number then?" he eyed her business card.

"You've got my mobile number there," she grinned. "Let me know how you get on with your research." Getting to her feet she swung her bag over her shoulder.

"Hey, let's meet up as soon as you're back," he called after her.

"Sure, ring me."

He watched as she walked away and then she was gone, blending in with the crowd. He sat there for a while thinking about what she had said, he could hardly believe that there was a chance to recover the Torc. It seemed to him from reading his great grandfather's journals that the bottom of the sea was the best place for it he just hoped that she wouldn't be tempted to try it on.

When she returned home Orlagh ran up the short flight of stairs leading to her front door then fumbled in her bag for her keys. Before she had bought the flat, it had been a squalid bolt hole, neglected for years by a series of tenants looking for a cheap place to rent. It had been run down and the building in poor condition but Orlagh had seen its potential. Finally she managed to talk the landlord into selling and over the last eighteen months had turned it into a beautiful home.

The flat had once been part of a grand Edwardian property situated on the outskirts of Dublin and influenced by her grandmother who had a wealth of knowledge it now boasted many original features. Her grandmother had impeccable tastes and insisted that the work be carried out to the highest standards. Orlagh was overjoyed with the results her only regret was that her grandmother had not lived long enough to see it completed.

Going into her bedroom, she began pulling clothes out of the cupboards making a mental list of what she would need to take with her. Of course, this time was different it wasn't like any other archaeological dig where she would need nothing more than jeans, jumpers and a pair of wellington boots. The Sea Quest was no cruise liner but she thought she might need something a little more formal to wear when not working.

Once she had packed her travel bag she settled down for the evening, she was going to relax in a hot bath she always found travelling tiring so was determined to get an early night.

IX

Jack Harrington was standing on the bridge of the Sea Quest talking to Paul Seymour, the Captain of the ship. At six foot two Jack towered above his old friend who was grinning like a school boy. Through the window they watched as a group of young women clad in skimpy shorts and bikini tops made their way along the quay towards a small pleasure boat that was moored beside them in the harbour.

"Oh Lord, don't you just love the French," Paul said.

He had never been to Cherbourg before and was looking forward to going into town, most of the crew were ashore leaving only a handful of maintenance staff on board.

The Sea Quest was essentially a survey vessel, specifically designed for inspection, repair or maintenance work but Jack had made a few modifications and now the ship was mainly used for underwater salvage operations. At 113 metres long she was capable of carrying 90 persons although there was rarely more than 30 on board at any time, this included the ship's crew, maintenance engineers and salvage experts, but on this trip there would also be an archaeologist.

Jack turned his attention to the Sikorsky S-92 helicopter which was sitting on the forward deck. He was particularly fond of flying and was tempted to take the bird up for a view of Cherbourg from the air. Two engineers were busy fussing around the helicopter having just fitted a replacement communications system.

"Bird to bridge," the radio transmitter blared out loudly.

"You don't have to shout!" Jack replied, talking into the comm's system.

"Sorry boss, how's that?" the engineer adjusted the settings on the state of the art digital radio.

"That's better, you're coming over loud and clear."

The engineer popped his head out of the cockpit side window and raised his thumb towards the bridge.

"Dr. Gairne should be arriving at 15:30," Jack said turning towards Paul.

"Let's hope she's on time, we get underway at 17:00."

Paul was studying the screen on a small console unit and using a key board began typing in GPS co-ordinates.

"So what does she look like this Dr. Gairne?" he asked without looking up.

"I've no idea, all I know is she's an archaeologist," Jack sighed. "My guess is she'll be nothing but trouble."

"Unnecessary academic baggage," Paul mumbled as he concentrated on the screen.

"Well, as the Irish are paying a good proportion of our salary, I guess they have the right to send someone along."

"We'll just have to put up with her, stick her in the lab, we'll pick up some old relic from the wreck, that'll keep her busy." Paul finished what he was doing and leaned back against the control panel.

"I wonder if it will be as easy as that," Jack rubbed his chin and eyed his old friend thoughtfully.

Jack had been sent a report from his headquarters in New York informing him that Dr. Gairne was interested in only one item. It was listed on the original itinerary as The Belgae Torc, he had no-idea what that was so he had carried out a little research on the internet. He was curious enough to discover that the name of the Torc was taken from the Celtic tribe who once lived in the South West of England some two thousand years ago. The Torc was an item of jewellery, he just hoped they could find it or her journey would be a waste of time and money. He was more interested in the Nazi treasure, his main objective was to recover it from the wreck, the report suggested that it consisted of a huge quantity of gold bars and jewellery.

"Should be a straightforward job," Paul said as if he were reading Jack's mind.

Punching his arm playfully Jack nodded towards the girls who were now standing on the deck of their boat laughing and screeching, having fun.

Orlagh stepped from the taxi which had collected her from the train station and was now standing on the quayside scanning the harbour looking for the Sea Quest. She spotted the ship at once, it was brightly painted in orange and white livery and shielding her eyes from the glare that was skipping up from the surface of the water she managed to read the name stencilled boldly in black lettering along her bow. She was surprised, the Sea Quest was much larger than she had expected, it even had its own helicopter.

Shrugging her rucksack over her shoulder she picked up her sports bag and made her way along the harbour wall. It was a busy place with lots of small boats moving between larger ones or just sitting serenely in the water tied up to pontoons. She had been to Cherbourg once before at the end of the first leg of the Tall Ships race in 2005. Her adventure had taken her from Waterford in Ireland around the coast of southern England and across the channel to Cherbourg. The journey had taken five days sailing on a three masted ketch and once in France she had spent a memorable weekend whilst waiting to be collected by a support vehicle.

A party was in full swing on one of the small boats, the sound of music and laughter drifted noisily across the harbour. The afternoon sun was hot and the sky a cloudless Mediterranean blue, it was a perfect day for a party especially on a boat.

Orlagh loved the atmosphere of France, the combination of water, music and the smell of the sea lifted her spirit. She was glad to be away from her life in Dublin and at least for the next couple of weeks she could be someone else, do something completely different. She quickened her step, eager to join the ship and meet the people aboard.

Jack swung himself up into the pilot's seat and checked out the work which had been carried out on the helicopters flight deck. The radio transmitter looked no different from the one it had replaced but was much more powerful and had a clarity which far outstripped the old set. As he peered out of the cockpit window a red haired woman caught his attention, she was making her way towards the ship and instinctively he knew this was Dr. Gairne. She was nothing like he had imagined, stylishly dressed in a grey trouser suit she looked cool her thick red hair lifting lightly on the breeze as she moved and although the sunlight was bright she wore her sunglasses on top of her head.

"Heads up!" he spoke into the transmitter and Paul Seymour glanced up from checking the instruments on the bridge.

"Ahoy there!" he heard a shout. "Permission to come aboard."

Orlagh smiled and stepped onto the ramp linking the ship to shore then she made her way up onto the deck.

"Dr. Gairne," Jack hurried along the upper deck and down an open stairway. "Welcome aboard."

She dropped her bags and took his outstretched hand.

"I'm Jack Harrington."

"Hi, Orlagh Gairne."

He grinned, her rich Irish accent sounded strange to his ear and he could have sworn she had just said her name was 'All Again'.

Orlagh could feel the cool confidence which he exuded and was pleasantly surprised by his appearance, he was much younger than she had expected.

"Did you have a good trip?" he asked holding on to her hand.

"Oh you know," she shrugged, momentarily lost for words.

"Yeah," he nodded. "Would you like to follow me and I'll get you settled in."

He led her through the ship and she couldn't help but notice his broad shoulders and narrow waist. She let her eyes wander lower and as she gazed at his tight bottom she wondered what Janet would think of her now.

"Do we get underway soon?" Was all she could think to ask.

"Yes, but you have time to freshen up if you wish and grab some coffee before we say goodbye to France."

"Now that does sound civilised."

Her accent intrigued him, the sound of her voice was pleasing, he didn't imagine Dr. Gairne to be anything like this. The mental picture he had of her did nothing to prepare him for her appearance and he couldn't wait to get up to the bridge. Paul would be speechless, he was going to make it his business to be there when the good captain met Dr. Gairne.

Her cabin was not at all what she expected, it was spacious and bright with a large single bed set against one wall. The cabin was also equipped with an en-suite shower that wouldn't have been out of place in a good hotel, she was overjoyed to find a traditional port hole set into the wall, sunlight flooding in made the room feel warm and welcoming.

"Where's the balcony?" she joked.

"It's hardly a state cabin but you should be comfortable here. Don't be afraid to make use of the shower, there's always plenty of hot water."

She nodded as her eyes explored.

"When you're ready," he turned to lean against the doorframe, "make your way forward and up to the ward room, coffee will be served there."

Closing the door he left her standing in the middle of the floor and for the first time in years she felt like an awkward teenager.

"Orlagh Gairne," she chastised herself, "pull yourself together woman!"

First impressions were always important and Jack Harrington had struck her as being a very capable man, of course, she knew all about him having read the file Peter O'Reilly had given her. It contained details of the ship and his business affairs, but the photograph of Jack was nothing like the man himself. Not many men had the ability to unnerve her, but occasionally one would come along who would distract her unashamedly.

Once she was showered and changed out of her travelling clothes she made her way forward to find the ward room.

Jack Harrington was talking to a tall black man, another good looking guy, Orlagh thought as she stepped through the open door.

"Dr. Gairne," Jack looked up the moment she appeared, "come in. Let me introduce you to Captain Seymour."

"Paul," he said, correcting Jack as he moved forward to take her hand.

Jack watched as his friend's smile broadened across his face.

"Dr. Gairne, welcome aboard the Sea Quest." Paul quickly recovered his composure. "I hope your cabin is acceptable and you have everything you need."

"Oh yes, thank you Captain Seymour. It's surprisingly adequate." She liked him Immediately, his rich deep voice was soothing and his wide smile and dark smoky eyes welcoming.

"Would you prefer tea or coffee?" he asked sweeping her across the room. "I could get you some fresh coffee but it's not bad from the machine."

"Coffee from the machine will be fine, no sugar but a dash of milk please."

Jack grinned as he watched Paul pouring coffee into a mug.

"Please call me Orlagh." Jack heard her say then they laughed over something that he didn't catch.

There were a few other men in the room, sitting at tables or lounging by the windows, so Paul took her around introducing them in turn.

"This is the crew room," he explained. "We don't have separate rooms for the officers, we don't stand on ceremony on this ship."

Orlagh smiled and sipped her coffee, it was really quite good.

"Fresh coffee indeed!" Jack whispered into Paul's ear as soon as he was close enough.

"We'll be making way in fifteen minutes Orlagh," Paul said ignoring Jacks remark. His familiar use of her Christian name was not lost on Jack.

"Ah Dr. Gairne," Jack stepped up beside her. "Can I introduce you to the only other woman aboard."

A short stocky woman dressed casually in a pair of dark blue overalls had just walked into the room and at a glance Orlagh would not have realised that she was a woman.

"This is Rosamund Stacey, one of our electricians."

"Roz," she corrected him. "Hi Dr. Gairne." Her hand delivered a firm grip.

"Please call me Orlagh."

Roz nodded then moved away. She helped herself to coffee and standing alone, made no effort to join in with the other members of the crew.

"We'll go up on deck, wave goodbye to France, enjoy your coffee first." Jack guided her towards a table as Paul made his way to the bridge.

Orlagh found the friendly chatter which filled the room comforting, the camaraderie among the crew was firmly established, they had obviously known one and other for some time. She had been made to feel welcome and now, after her long journey, was able to relax. Maybe a couple of weeks on a ship was what she needed, she thought, it would be completely different to her life in Dublin.

The engines started rumbling from somewhere deep inside the ship and the Rolls Royce turbines sent vibrations running through the deck. Orlagh could sense the mounting excitement as cups on the table began to rattle and the bright orange hull inched away from the harbour wall. Side thrusters nudged the bow and the ship swung effortlessly into the middle of the harbour.

"Let's go out on deck," Jack said enthusiastically as he stood up.

The breeze on deck lifted her hair the moment she emerged from the doorway she wasn't expecting it to be so strong so raising her hand held it back from her eyes.

The upper deck was situated just aft of the bridge and communications station, a huge pylon-like structure towering above them, and as Orlagh looked up she could see a collection of satellite dishes all pointing in different directions. She had no idea what all the equipment was for but she did recognise a radar beacon.

Jack, standing at the railing, casually peered down on the group of girls who were now waving frantically at him from the deck of their little boat, he called out something which made them giggle and Orlagh smiled.

The breeze became stronger as they approached open water but the sea was flat and calm, the water inviting as it sparkled jewel-like beneath a clear sky. Orlagh was glad of her sunglasses and pulling them down over her eyes continued to hold her hair in place. She could hardly believe this was happening, only yesterday she had been working in Dublin, delivering her lecture with no idea that O'Reilly was about to send her on an adventure. She thought of Jerry and how nice it would be if he was there too, besides, the Torc was his great grandfather's discovery.

Orlagh travelled well at sea and was confident that she would soon find her sea legs. She peered around the deck, it was a wide open space which was longer by at least a third of its width and as she strolled along the railing she watched Cherbourg receding lazily into the distance. Water churned madly at the stern, whipped up by twin propellers and as Orlagh glanced down at the lower deck she could see a huge yellow crane. It dominated the space below, its superstructure folded back neatly on itself, the whole thing secured to a metal frame which was bolted to the deck.

"We are standing above the main workshops," Jack appeared by her side. "I'll give you a guided tour later, show you the ROVs and the moon pool." Glancing sideways he caught the scent of her hair, mixed with the fresh sea spray it reminded him of a sweet smelling plant he had once found in the Arizona desert.

"We have a number of Remotely Operated Vehicles on board and when we arrive over the spot where the Hudson Bay went down you'll see them in action."

"Is the Hudson Bay a long way down?" she asked looking up at him.

"No, about forty metres, it appears to be on top of an underwater hill, the seabed rises up sharply at that point but the area around it is much deeper so we'll free dive on her once we've surveyed the bottom. I like to have a complete picture before we dive."

"I once dived on a ship which sank in the Red Sea," she confided in him. "I can't remember it's name but she was carrying a cargo of bathroom suites, there were bath tubs and toilets strewn all over the seabed," she grinned at the memory. "I have photographs of myself taking a bath on the bottom of the sea."

"You'll be surprised what you can find under the sea," he nodded. "You dive then?"

"Oh yes, I'm a fully paid up member of the local scuba diving club, in fact I'm expecting to dive on the Hudson Bay."

"Only if it's safe, have you dived on many wrecks?"

"A few," she said turning to face him. "I've never been inside one though, all the ships I've seen have been so badly damaged that anything of interest lay strewn around. Most of my work has involved sifting through debris trails or running my fingers through silt."

"I didn't realise that you were involved in marine archaeology."

"Strictly speaking I'm not, my speciality often has me running around muddy fields or digging in peat bogs."

"I see," he nodded thoughtfully. He could hardly imagine her up to her knees in mud, she looked far too academic, but the image that remained was her in a bath tub on the bottom of the sea.

"Well, I'm going inside, I have things to take care of. See you at dinner."

Orlagh watched as he pushed himself away from the railing and loped across the deck.

"Twenty hundred hours, in the ward room," he called out over his shoulder before disappearing into a passageway.

There was a glorious sunset and they seemed to have the whole ocean to themselves. Orange, gold and violet streaks had appeared in the sky making the horizon look as if it were on fire and Orlagh was completely absorbed in the moment.

She was surprised at being offered a drink before dinner and clutching her tall glass of gin and tonic she looked up as Rosamund Stacey stepped out onto the deck.

"Hello Roz," Orlagh beckoned her towards the rail.

"Hi," she nodded, "beautiful isn't it?" she stared into the sky.

"Breathtaking," Orlagh sighed. "How far is it to the horizon? I've no idea of distance, there's nothing out there to make a comparison with."

"It's about seven miles," Roz said dreamily. "It depends how high you are above sea level."

They stood in companionable silence both women lost in their own thoughts.

"How long have you been working on this ship?" Orlagh asked eventually.

"This is my second voyage, the first lasted for six months."

"Wow, as long as that. Did you go somewhere exotic?"

Orlagh studied Roz over the rim of her glass. She guessed that Roz was about her own age, her hair was straight, short and black. She wore no make-up and Orlagh got the impression that she was not the kind of girl to make the best of her looks. She was wearing flat shoes and a baggy jumper over men's trousers.

"If you call the frozen north exotic," Roz shrugged before taking a mouthful of beer from a large glass.

"What were you doing up there?"

"Jack was digging up a World War Two bomber, it was frozen in the ice and we were there in support. I remained on the ship as part of the maintenance crew. As the parts came up they were loaded onto specially designed barges, we then hauled them aboard for restoration and repair."

"Did you do much of the restoration on board?"

"Oh yes, most of it in fact, it was my job to overhaul the electrical systems on the engines. Pretty basic stuff though, 1940's electronics is not exactly cutting edge technology."

"Wow, exciting stuff all the same. Do you get the opportunity to do much of that kind of work?"

"I do what I'm told," she glanced at Orlagh. "My duties are to the ship, I look after the electrical systems, radar, D.P. systems, ROVs."

"Okay," Orlagh laughed, "I've no idea what you're talking about!"

"Dinner is served ladies." Someone called from across the deck.

They entered the ward room and Roz made her way to her own table leaving Orlagh standing by herself. As she watched her go, Orlagh wondered what part of America she was from, she couldn't place her accent.

"Dr. Gairne," Captain Seymour called out above the noise, "you can sit beside me."

The ward room was now full of the aroma of food and it appeared completely different from before, tables had been set up in rows and there was enough room to accommodate the entire crew. She took her seat between Captain Seymour and Jack Harrington.

"Rose between two thorns!" she grinned as she sat down.

Captain Seymour led them in grace before they began their meal.

Orlagh was famished, she didn't realise how hungry she was until the mouth watering scents began to drift up from her plate. She looked towards the chef and his staff who were standing along a wall, it was as if they were waiting to be dismissed.

"They always hang around for a bit," Jack explained when he saw where she was looking. "They are listening for any complaints."

"This is really great, I didn't expect anything like this."

"I assure you," Paul chipped in, "we are quite civilised, the hard biscuits and weevils are served afterwards with the coffee."

The men around them laughed.

X

On an island in the Mediterranean off the coast of Africa, a submarine slipped its moorings. It was a World War Two German U-Boat type XXIII which in the 1940s was one of the most advanced submarines of its kind. With continuously welded seams it was the world's first single hull design. It had been simply designed with a pleasing streamlined form and apart from a relatively small bridge and a hump on its back which once housed the diesel engine exhaust silencer, there was a complete absence of clutter on the upper deck.

Originally there had been no forward hydroplanes but these had been added later, other than that the boat was in its original condition. Inside however, it had been modified beyond all recognition, the 1940s technology making way for state of the art equipment reduced the number of crew from fourteen to just four.

Other improvements made to the engine and electrical propulsion systems coupled with a reduction in living quarters meant that there were now valuable working and storage areas within the boat. The submarine was originally designed to carry two forward firing torpedoes, but was now capable of carrying more, on this trip however, it had four. Both speed and range had been significantly improved but the boat maintained its original dimensions and crush depth of 180 metres.

As it cleared the small harbour it disappeared below the surface then powerful electric motors kicked in sending it cutting silently through the water at almost twenty five knots and using a satellite navigation system, the captain set a course for the North Atlantic, a position just off the coast of Portugal.

The Bay of Biscay was as flat and as expansive as a salt plain and Orlagh was astonished. The last time she had been in these waters the sea had been a succession of angry peaks and deep troughs which tormented the ship relentlessly. Strong winds had also hampered their passage from the south coast of England to northern Spain. Pushing these unwelcome memories aside she shuddered, that trip had been far too uncomfortable.

Sitting on the edge of the deckchair that she had discovered beneath a stairway, she smoothed a high factor sun block over her skin and adjusted her sunglasses before pulling on a floppy hat, then she lounged back and sighed contentedly. With nothing better to do she was going to make the most of her free time and settling down, reached for her book. She had no idea that it would be like this, the ship was no cruise liner but it was comfortable enough, the only things she found lacking were an endless supply of cocktails and company, everyone else on board were going about their business. The ship was immaculately kept, there were never any tools or equipment left lying around, everything was in its place. Earlier that day she had wandered up to the bridge where Jack, Paul and an officer were pouring over a chart, not one of them noticed her, so quietly she had crept back to her place on the deck.

Orlagh removed her hat and shook out her hair before pushing her sunglasses up on top of her head, then putting her book aside she applied more sun block to her legs. Being fair skinned she burned easily under the sun but once a tan had been established her delicate skin became a little more resilient to the effects of harmful rays. Standing up she stretched her arms luxuriously above her head before leaning forward against the railings. The water was boiling along the side of the ship the sound of it pounding rhythmically against the hull was sooth-ing. The movement of the waves with curling white caps against the deep blue and grey of the sea intrigued her, and she found the soft spray and scented sea air refreshing. Earlier that morning she had spotted a basking shark making the most of the ideal conditions, she had been told to watch out for dolphins but, as yet, none had appeared.

At times there was traffic, large container ships would appear then slip silently along the horizon only to disappear having never got any closer. She would never grow tired of watching the sea, the colour of the water was constantly changing. For the most part it echoed the colour of the sky but when she looked closer she could see a myriad of shades, greens streaked grey with flecks of white or silver. It was a living thing, an evolving carpet which refused to remain still.

Turning away from the rail Orlagh made her way across the deck towards the ward room. The coffee machine was also a living thing, a never ending dispenser of dark aromatic liquid which was popular amongst the crew. This was their favourite meeting place. She also discovered a well stocked refrigerator, apart from cream and milk, there was an array of fresh fruit juices and bottles of chilled water.

Captain Seymour, making his way from the bridge, almost collided with her as he pushed the door aside.

"Dr. Gairne!" he said surprised to see her standing there.

"Orlagh," she corrected him.

71

"Sure, forgive me Orlagh," he grinned. "I hope I didn't startle you, I didn't see you behind the door."

"It's such a glorious day, how did you manage to arrange that?"

The sound of his rich laughter pleased her. "I'm in desperate need of caffeine," she admitted moving towards the machine. "Would you care to join me?"

"How could I refuse?" he said flirting with her. "It's not every day I get an offer like that."

Orlagh poured two mugs of coffee and they settled at a table by a window.

"So," he began, "where in Ireland do you come from Orlagh?"

"Dublin," she answered immediately. "Well, that's where I live now but originally I'm from Cork."

His knowledge of Ireland was shockingly limited, he knew it was divided into northern and southern parts and he also knew the south was known as Eire, but he knew nothing of its history or politics.

"And you, what part of the United States are you from?"

"St.Louis, Missouri."

"The Mississippi," she replied with a grin.

"Ole man river!" he chuckled. "Grew up on the river, lived on a boat with my parents and brothers. My father used to work the river."

"Wow," she studied him, "yours must have been an exciting childhood. Do you have any sisters?"

"No, I'm one of seven sons."

"You're kidding me!" she said in disbelief, "you have six brothers?"

"Sure do," he nodded, "what about you?"

"No brothers of sisters, I'm afraid I'm an only child, a fully paid up spoilt brat!"

"I'm sure that's not true," he said, his eyes lighting up.

"I spent a lot of time with my grandmother when I was a child." Talking to him was easy, she felt that she could tell him anything. "My parents were both academics, they had very little time for me."

"How sad." The space between his eyebrows furrowed.

"Don't get me wrong, I have no regrets, my childhood was idyllic," she smiled enthusiastically, her head filling up with happy memories. "My grandmother saw to that, she was the most wonderful person I've ever known, she was my best friend."

"Is she no longer with us?"

"I'm afraid not, she died about eighteen months ago."

"Sorry to hear that."

Orlagh sipped her coffee and discreetly studied him. He was a good looking man, it was impossible to tell his age, she guessed that he must be in his early forties but there were no clues hiding in his features. His cheek bones were characteristically high, his nose wide and his smile even wider, but it was his eyes which she found most alluring. Like rich dark pools of amber they were set wide apart and she liked the way they laughed whenever he smiled. She was convinced they hid many secrets.

"So, is there a Mrs Seymour?" the question escaped the moment it had formed inside her head.

"No," he grinned, the soft skin around his eyes creasing. "Not much time for a woman in my life. Busy schedule you see and before you ask, there are no ladies waiting for me in every port."

They laughed together and took a moment to enjoy their coffee and Orlagh summed him up. He was intelligent and interesting, a man who exuded confidence but in quite a different way to Jack Harrington.

"What's it like working with Jack?" she sat back in her chair and crossed her legs under the table.

"Jack, why he's not so bad, does have some stupid ideas sometimes though. Can't blame him for that I suppose, gotten me into some tight scrapes, I can tell you."

"I can imagine," she said softly, reading the messages in his face. She looked away and focussed on the deckchair standing out on the deck.

"When will we be arriving at the location where the Hudson Bay sank?"

"Day after tomorrow," he said with some certainty, "about two o'clock in the morning. We'll start work at first light."

"Oh, as long as that, I didn't realise it was so far."

"About two and a half days out of Cherbourg at twelve knots. We could get there sooner but this is our most economic cruising speed, besides, there's no rush."

"I suppose the Hudson Bay isn't going anywhere."

"I guess you want to get your hands on that necklace," he grinned.

"Oh, it's not a necklace, it's a Celtic Torc," she could tell that he was none the wiser so she described it in detail.

"Sounds like an impressive piece of jewellery."

"It's much more than that," she slipped comfortably into lecturing mode. "The Torc is a symbol of wealth and power, something a chieftain or a king would have worn to underpin his potency. The Belgae Torc is a particularly fine artefact, in fact, it's a very important piece of Celtic history."

"Why is it called the Belgae Torc?" he asked.

"Well, at the time it was made the Celtic population had spread right across Europe, including Britain and Ireland. They lived in settlements, some not much more than extended families. A collection of these settlements or villages would make up a tribe; each tribe was identified by a collective name, for example, the Belgae tribe was from an area in Somerset, in the south west of England."

"I see," Paul nodded, "a bit like the North American Indians. The only Celt I've heard of is Boadicea."

"Yes," Orlagh said, "she was the queen of the Iceni tribe who were located in the east of England. We call her Boudicca now, that's her Latin name. Boadicea seems to have been a misinterpretation made by the Victorians, anyway she was from a much later period than our Torc."

"How much later, didn't the Roman's invade in 54AD.?"

"Yes that's right. The Belgae Torc dates from about 50BC, years before Boudicca or the Roman invasion."

Orlagh went on to tell him about the preserved body that was found with the Torc. "Of course, they didn't call themselves Celts, that's a label the Victorians came up with, it's derived from the Greek word Keltoi. In the academic world they are known as Ancient Britons, well those from Britain that is," she grinned, "it's all a bit confusing because they were spread all over Europe, hence the neat Victorian label which covers the lot."

"Surely that's a good thing, Celt sounds rather cool."

"I suppose so," she remained unconvinced. "The period in which they lived covers the Bronze age through the Iron age, it's a development which took hundreds of years. The Stone age became the Bronze age with the discovery of copper and tin, then the Iron age followed when working and purifying iron ore became possible."

"I guess you could say we are still living in the Iron age." Paul grinned.

"Technically I suppose we are now in the silicon age, what with modern materials and computers."

They laughed before finishing their coffee.

"Well, I guess I'd better be getting along," he said more seriously.

"Shouldn't you be steering the ship or something?" she grinned.

"Don't worry Orlagh, the ship is equipped with the latest Sat.Nav. system. It works a bit like auto-pilot on an aircraft, as long as we have someone on watch the ship will steer itself."

"I see," she nodded.

"There are various locations on board from where I can override the auto-pilot and take control, I don't have to be on the bridge but I can assure you the bridge is manned at all times."

"Okay," she nodded again. "I would love to see the bridge, see how it works."

"That can be arranged," he told her. "Jack intends giving you a guided tour but that will have to wait until tomorrow, he's much too busy today."

The following day Orlagh followed Jack through the tangled passage-ways which made up the interior of the ship. They passed through so many steel doors that it took her a while to work out if she were forward or aft, she had no idea which way the ship was travelling when she was below deck.

The workshop area was impressive and Orlagh was amazed at how such a relatively compact space could be made to look so huge. It was a very useful area which was kept spotlessly clean and clutter free, there was of course the usual collection of tools and equipment together with the smells of oil and grease.

"This place is usually a hive of activity and once the work begins you won't be able to move," his voice echoed around the void. "When we start lifting, the items will come up onto the deck over there." He indicated towards the huge crane which was standing idle on the open deck at the rear of the ship. "First we'll catalogue everything then the items will be moved into here for cleaning and stabilising."

Orlagh nodded and turned slowly through 360° taking in every detail.

"How many people do you have working in here?" she asked.

"It depends on what needs doing but there could be as many as fifteen engineers. There is a rule however which states that there must be a minimum of two people working in here, health and safety doesn't allow for solitary working in this workshop."

Nodding, she could understand why, looking at some of the heavy machinery standing against the wall.

They left the workshop and made their way towards the laboratory, this was familiar territory for Orlagh, gone was the aroma of industry, replaced by the clean antiseptic air of the lab. Jack watched as she wandered around the workspace, he could imagine her working here dressed in a long white coat and safety spectacles. Opening a bright yellow steel cabinet she recognised most of the chemicals and cleaning fluids that were stored on the shelves and she ran her fingers lightly over the labels.

The lab was situated deep within the ship, there were no windows in the stark white walls, but it was brilliantly lit by tiny spotlights that were situated in the false ceiling. Fresh air was channelled in by a series of fans and ducts having first been passed through filters to remove any dust particles, this was to prevent any contamination reaching the delicate work which was carried out here. Orlagh was impressed, the facilities available were as good as she had ever seen.

"The hospital is next door," he told her.

"Wow, you have a hospital?"

"Yes, it's pretty well kitted out, we can cope with most emergencies, one of the officers is a qualified doctor."

"Now I am impressed, I had no idea."

"Come on," he nodded, "let's go and see the moon pool."

Leading the way he took her deeper into the ship.

"All the diving gear is stored in these lockers," he indicated towards steel cabinets that were fixed along a bulkhead.

Jack pulled a handle and another steel door slipped silently open and they stepped into a large darkened space. Lights activated by a microswitch came on automatically as they entered and once again she was amazed by what she saw. What appeared to be a swimming pool with steep sides was sunk into the deck.

"There are changing rooms and shower facilities there," he pointed towards a collection of modules that housed the amenities he had described.

The temperature here was constant and comfortable, allowing for short sleeve working.

"There are huge doors beneath the ship which are kept closed whilst we are moving," he explained.

"I didn't realise it would be so big it's just like a swimming pool."

The moon pool was full of clear water which beckoned to her invitingly. The lights were bright and everything looked clean and new, she could hardly believe that she was deep inside a ship.

"We do use it sometimes for bathing, it's salt water of course but it can be heated."

She studied him closely, wondering if he was telling her the truth.

"There's a filter system which cleans the water. We can also pump it out completely, use it as a dry dock or simply for storage."

"Are we below sea water level here?" she asked eyeing the curve in the steel walls.

"No, that's the outside water level," he nodded towards the pool. "The sides are steep enough to act like a diving bell. The only way the level can rise once the doors are open is if we take on more weight and settle lower into the water."

"I see," she said moving closer to the edge, "will we dive through here?"

"Maybe," he stepped up beside her, "it depends on the weather conditions. If it's rough up top, it's safer to exit through the bottom."

"So you don't always use it then."

"No, we usually go over the side but sometimes it's easier to bring things on board this way."

"How do you get the heavy lifting equipment down here?" She looked up at the overhead rails running the length of the chamber.

"There are lifts connecting us to the workshop above, they enable us to bring down the ROV's or send things up to the workshops."

Orlagh nodded, it all seemed so well designed she would never have thought facilities like this would exist on a ship, but then she had not been aboard a ship like the Sea Quest before.

XI

During the early hours the Sea Quest arrived on station. Its engines idled and the dynamic positioning system held the ship stationary, precisely over the spot where the Hudson Bay lay forty metres below.

When Orlagh entered the ward room it seemed as if the whole crew had gathered for breakfast at the same time, the air was alive with excitement, male voices rising and falling like the ocean waves. She picked up a tray of toast and coffee and moved towards Roz who was sitting alone at a table.

"Good morning. Do you mind if I join you?"

"Hi, sure help yourself." Roz nodded towards an empty chair.

"It all seems very exciting," Orlagh said over the din.

"It's always like this," Roz smiled, "like kids on Christmas Morning."

They were silent for a while and Orlagh had an opportunity to study the woman up close. Rosamund Stacey was a misplaced soul who gave off an air of aloofness, she seemed cold and distant and Orlagh wondered how she managed to fit in with the rest of the crew. She didn't doubt for a moment her ability as an engineer, if she wasn't at the top of her field she would not have been on Jack's payroll. Orlagh peered at her from beneath lowered eyelashes and thought that Roz could do a lot more with her appearance, it was as if she deliberately made herself look plain and uninteresting, almost like she was hiding behind a shield.

"So what happens now we have arrived?" Orlagh asked.

Putting her cup down she reached for a slice of buttered toast, waiting as Roz finished her mouthful.

"We send down the Eyeball," she said glancing up at Orlagh.

"Eyeball?"

"Yeah, a mini ROV. We'll drop it down and do a survey, make sure it's all there and safe before we decide what to do next."

"So we're not diving then?"

"Oh hell no," Roz said with a frown, "that's what the ROVs are for."

Orlagh couldn't hide her disappointment.

"You want to dive eh?"

"Well yes, I was hoping to. Jack said we probably would."

"There you are then, if that's what Jack said."

78

The conversation could have ended there but Orlagh was determined to get closer to the woman.

"I'm surprised to see everyone here this morning, yesterday this place was deserted. Where have they all been?"

"They know that when work begins there might not be an opportunity to stop until this evening so they are making the most of food time."

"I thought they might work shifts."

"Yeah they will when it's all settled down but everyone wants to be in on it at the beginning, give it a day or two and it'll work out. Depends on what comes up of course."

Orlagh nodded, she could understand that, it was just like an archaeological dig when everyone gathered in excitement waiting for the spade to open up the ground and expose the history that lay hidden beneath.

"So these ROVs," Orlagh began, "I assume they are fitted with manipulators of some description so they can recover items from the bottom."

"Yes," Roz nodded, "but the Eyeball is tiny, it's fitted with a camera and powerful searchlights. It will give us an idea of where to start then we can send in the bigger ones; the work class ROVs have all the equipment."

"So they will bring up the artefacts?"

"Possibly, it won't be as easy as that, never is. Anything lying around the wreck can be scooped up but I guess we'll have to blast the side out of the ship in order to gain access to the hold."

Orlagh froze, her hand holding toast hovered half way to her mouth.

"What do you mean blast open the ship?"

"We'll have to use explosives or at least a thermal cutting process in order to get inside. There won't be an open doorway with an illuminated sign above it saying welcome aboard."

"I didn't realise it would be so brutal," she said. "I hope the contents of the ship will be safe."

"There's always a risk but I'm sure it'll be fine. Jack knows what he's doing, besides he wants the Nazi gold."

Orlagh remained silent, her stomach churning like a bag of eels. She didn't care much for the gold but the possibility of destroying the Torc or losing it forever had not crossed her mind. She imagined the Hudson Bay to be a mass of buckled plates and rivets with the sea bed around it strewn with treasure. The thought that the Torc might still be hidden deep within the ship was not an option she had explored.

"Maybe the Eyeball will find what you're looking for." Roz was surprised by Orlagh's reaction and the tone of her voice softened. "Jack will probably send the Eyeball into the ship, survey the damage from the inside.

He might even order a dive, he won't decide to use aggressive methods until he has a complete picture."

Orlagh nodded.

"Would you like some more coffee?" Roz asked.

Orlagh nodded again.

She was standing in a completely alien world, a small control room that was situated on the upper deck just behind the bridge. This was where the ROVs and other underwater activities were controlled. Banks of computer screens, key boards, joysticks and unfamiliar controls were crammed into every available space; it was like something out of a science fiction movie.

Earlier Orlagh had watched the engineers fussing around a tiny box-like frame which stood on the deck. The Eyeball was a mini ROV which had one dark eye protruding from beneath a protective shield and there was a bank of powerful lights mounted on the bright yellow tubular frame which made up the body of the ROV. It was equipped with various sampling devices and detectors, many of which were unique, having been developed here on the ship by the Lab technicians and engineering scientists. Some were experimental components designed to work in the extreme environment beneath the sea. The Eyeball carried no manipulator arms, it was far too light for lifting work. At fifteen kilos it was fitted with a highly accurate subsea navigation system and even if it became detached from its umbilical cord it was still capable of sending out a signal so it could be located and retrieved.

"Standing by to launch ROV," a loud voice came over the communication system, filling the control room.

"Roger that, you may go for launch." Mark, the ROV pilot was at the controls, his fingers delicately caressing the various micro-switches.

"Sending the ROV down for a look see," came the reply.

Orlagh was fascinated, her eyes fixed on the screen which remained frustratingly blank.

"We won't see anything, not until 'Kitty' is completely submerged and on her way." Kitty was the name he had christened the Eyeball, he had affectionate names for all the ROVs.

Mark flicked a switch and the screen above his head came alive with a distorted image. To Orlagh it looked as if she was watching a storm of bubbles swirling around a finger of light. The light only added to the illusion by probing the darkness and slipping away into perspective.

"Bottom coming up," Mark spoke calmly into the microphone as he studied the instruments that were arranged around him.

"Roger that, standing by."

It was as if he were talking to crew members aboard the ROV, but Orlagh knew that was impossible, the men on the other end of the communication system were on the deck just below them.

Suddenly the image on the screen changed and as Mark eased back on the controls a great storm of swirling sediment fused with bubbles made it impossible to see anything. Orientating the ROV through 90°, Mark raised it up off the bottom and began to steer into clearer water. Digital numbers on the screen in front of him counted down and in the top left hand corner was a direction indicator which kept him on course. With a delicate flick of his wrist the indicator twitched before becoming stable then he set off on another course.

"Ah ha," he said suddenly, "what have we here?"

At first Orlagh could see nothing, she moved closer and watched. Suddenly a brightly coloured object lying on the sea bed came into view and the ROV stopped, hovering above it like a helicopter. The image blurred as Mark adjusted the controls, but then it became clear.

"Oh Lordie!" he breathed out sharply, "it's an ingot, a block of solid gold."

Orlagh stared at the screen in silence.

"Are you getting this Jack?"

Jack Harrington was on the bridge watching his own monitor.

"Sure am," he replied, "mark the spot will you."

"Roger that." Mark typed a command into the computer and made some more fine adjustments to the controls.

Lights began to flash as the computer went to work recording the co-ordinates that Mark typed in.

"What's etched on the bar?" he said to himself.

The camera zoomed in and a clear image filled the screen, a swastika and a date confirmed that it was Nazi gold, the ingot having been cast in 1944.

"Got it all recorded Jack," he said anticipating Jack's next question.

Moving the joystick forward he pushed the ROV onwards slowly monitoring and recording the debris field that was spread widely over the sea bed.

"Wow, the yellow brick road!" Mark said as he followed a golden pathway leading towards the ship.

Orlagh was amazed by the amount of debris; the sea bed was strewn with ingots and domestic items such as dinner plates, cups and bottles, there was even an old leather bag almost hidden in the silt.

"The wreck must have broken up," Mark explained. "The debris field is typical of a ship sinking, spewing its contents as it went."

She was relieved to hear that, maybe Jack won't need to blast the ship open after all.

Suddenly a huge shadow filled the screen and pulling back on the joystick, Mark lifted the ROV up slowing its momentum, then he re-focussed the camera as the ROV hovered in the water.

The aft end of the Hudson Bay came into view appearing right there in front of them on the screen. The ship was lying on its side embedded in the sea floor, Orlagh could make out one of the propellers and the huge rudder.

Slowly the ROV crept forward, inching its way along the hull as deck plates and rivets came into view. The hull looked in remarkably good condition, but about half way along they came across a massive hole. Steel plates were missing from this section and around the edges of the gaping hole plates were peeled back resembling sharp teeth.

"Looks as if it's been blown out," Mark mumbled surprised by what they had found. He concentrated on manoeuvring the ROV closer without snagging the umbilical cord on the jagged metal.

"Would you take a look at that," he said incredulously.

"What does it mean?" Orlagh asked.

"Are you thinking what I'm thinking Jack?"

"Yeah, looks like an explosion."

Orlagh held her breath, waiting for an explanation.

"Just look at those steel plates," Mark angled the camera exposing more of the cavernous hole.

"It looks as if the explosion came from inside," Jack confirmed what he was thinking.

"Yeah, must have been a big one looking at the damage. It goes from just under the waterline, right up to the railings."

"Some explosion, could easily have blown her in half."

"Yeah, must have been awesome, wonder how it happened."

"They could have been carrying explosives, certainly looks like a huge amount to have done that kind of damage." Jack couldn't remember reading about a cargo of explosives on the ship's inventory.

Mark inched the ROV even closer, its lights illuminating the interior until they could see into the hold but visibility was not good. "I could take Kitty in for a look."

82

"Negative." Came the response. "Do not enter the ship, not yet."

"Okay Jack, nothing much to see anyway, most of the cargo's spread all over the floor."

"So if the ship didn't break up as it was sinking," Orlagh began, "it must have been the explosion which caused such a wide debris field." She was trying to make sense of what she had just seen.

"Yeah, that's right, as the ship fills with water it displaces the cargo out through the hole. Anything from the deck not bolted down would also have been blown or swept away."

Her eyes widened in alarm as she thought about the Torc.

"Let's continue on, see what else we can find." Jack's voice filled the little control room, it was as if he was there beside them.

Orlagh was fascinated, the rest of the ship looked untouched, it was in very good condition and it was hard to believe that it had been lying at the bottom of the sea for more than 60 years. There was very little vegetation growing on or around the ship and there was not much decay.

Mark brought the ROV over the bow of the ship then turned back to look at the superstructure. This side of the ship looked strange it was like looking at a building that had fallen over onto its side. Half buried in the mud, the lozenge shaped windows which made up the bridge were dark and eerie, the bridge section now a vertical structure with the starboard wing rising up over the hull. All around this side of the wreckage lay bits of machinery half buried or sticking up out of the mud, the whole scene resembled a cemetery of cast iron head stones. Mark was careful to steer around these items and slowly the ROV travelled along the side of the ship and over the cliff-like deck.

Kitty was equipped with all kinds of equipment and was constantly recording its surroundings. Water samples were taken, temperatures and current flows also recorded and the extent of oil and fuel contamination was being calculated, then suddenly Mark saw something extraordinary.

"Have you notice the unexpected radiation recording Jack?"

"Yeah, just seen it myself, wonder what the guys wearing white coats will make of it."

Orlagh realised that the scientists in the labs must be watching their own screens and instruments as information was sent to their computers.

"It can't be anything from the ship, there must be another reason."

"Guess we'll have to wait for the lab reports. It won't do any harm to get some more water samples especially from the area around the hole."

"Roger that Jack," Mark said as he steered the ROV over the hull.

"So you think it was an explosion that sunk the Hudson Bay?" Orlagh asked.

"Looks that way."

"Who would want to sink her?"

"Well that's a mystery we might never be able to solve," Mark glanced up.

"We are here to salvage the cargo, not play detective by trying to discover the reason for her sinking." Jack's voice was loud and clear.

"It's always been thought that the ship hit a mine," Mark told her, covering the microphone with his hand so Jack couldn't hear. "If that were true then the blast would have gone inwards, not out."

Orlagh was puzzled, she couldn't understand why the Hudson Bay was off the coast of Portugal. If the war was over then surely the threat of U-boats in the Atlantic had gone, it wasn't as if the ship was having to make a detour in order to avoid being attacked and now to make matters worse, she had just discovered that the explosion which sank the ship had almost certainly come from within.

"Stand by for ROV recovery." Mark warned the deck crew that Kitty would soon be re-surfacing. Jack appeared at the door.

"Well, what do you make of all that?" Mark looked over his shoulder as Jack stepped in.

"It sure is a mystery, never expected to find that, especially the radiation readings. Anyway, we'd better prepare Jasper, send him down to do some prospecting."

Jasper was the name given to a work class ROV, a much heavier machine than Kitty. Fitted with two manipulator arms, Jasper was used to collect items from the sea bed, these would then be loaded into nets attached by wires to the light cranes that were situated along the side of the Sea Quest. When the nets were full the cranes would haul them up.

Mark piloted Jasper down to the sea bed and Orlagh remained in the control room long enough to see the first of the ingots going into the net. It was tedious work and once the operation got under way Orlagh left Mark to it and went to the upper deck to wait for the first net to be hauled up.

Orlagh thought about what she had just seen, it was a marvellous opportunity to see an underwater operation from the safety of a control room. The technology was amazing she had never seen anything like it before. She had imagined the Hudson Bay to be encrusted with sea life after being so long on the bottom, but there was a complete lack of life around the wreck. The more she thought about it the more she realised that something was odd, other wrecks that she had dived on were living communities of sea life, conger eels and other fish should have been abundant but here there was nothing. Jack had mentioned something about oil and water contamination so maybe that was the reason. She was going to check with the lab as soon as the samples had been analysed.

By the end of the day two loads had been recovered from the sea bed and now the gold bars were stacked on pallets in the workshop. Some of the gold had been taken to the lab to be analysed but Orlagh was yet to hear the results.

The following day a Roman short sword was discovered lying in the silt, a treasure that had been pilfered from a museum collection by a conquering army that had rampaged across Europe more than half a century ago.

Mark had used the ROV's motors to strip away layers of silt before carefully lifting it using the manipulator arm and now Orlagh was sitting in the lab dressed in a white coat complete with safety glasses. Carefully she worked on the short sword, cleaning away the oxidation and ingrained silt. The weapon was made of bronze, inlaid with a gold filigree design around the hilt and encrusted in semi-precious stones.

"Everything okay here?" Jack appeared at the door pulling on a pair of white disposable overalls and over shoes before entering the lab.

"Good morning Jack, this is a remarkable find," she smiled.

"Roman isn't it?"

"Yes you're right. I think it was intended as a dress sword, look."

He moved closer to peer over her shoulder.

"There are no marks along the edges of the blade so clearly it has never been used as a weapon."

"The Germans loved antiquities of this kind."

"They liked to take ideas from ancient cultures and use them as their own. I wonder where they got it from," she replied, glancing up at him. He was standing very close and she was thrilled by his presence.

"Nazi archaeology was rarely conducted with an eye to real, pure research, it was a propaganda tool designed to both generate nationalistic pride in Germans and provide scientific excuses for conquest."

"Wow," she exclaimed and stopping what she was doing turned to face him.

"I'm impressed, you should meet a friend of mine, Jerry Knowles; he's into German mythology." It pleased her to think that maybe he was interested in archaeology and was not just a gold digger.

"The distortion of Germanic mythology by the Nazi regime," he continued.

"Hitler's corruption of that noble northern spirit," she finished off his quote.

"J.R.R.Tolkein." he said grinning like a schoolboy.

"Yes I know, Jerry quoted the same passage to me recently. Why are you so interested in German mythology?"

"I'm not really, but what I do find interesting is what the Nazi's did to generate nationalistic pride, surely it couldn't have been a bad thing."

"Why do you say that?" she frowned and studied him more intently. "It was all based on a lie."

"I agree in part, some of it had to be true though, Germany has a glorious history just like any other European country. They took hold of certain aspects of history or mythology and blew it out of all proportion, twisting the historical facts to suit themselves."

"You must be kidding me, the whole thing was based on untruths and invention."

"Oh come on Orlagh," he said his voice full of emotion. "You must remember, Germany was digging itself out of a huge hole, the allies had stitched them up at the end of the First World War with the Treaty of Versailles. The oppressed German people were desperate to grab any nationalistic pride they could get their hands on and it was the Nazis who had all the answers at the right time, besides their claims were backed up by eminent scientists and historical thinkers."

Orlagh wondered why he was being so defensive, what interests did he have in the Nazi regime?

"Don't get me wrong," he read her perfectly, "I'm not saying I agree totally with what they did."

"Well, I'm glad to hear that."

"You have to admit though, what they tried to create was the best thing for Germany at that time."

"Even if it was corruption, force fed to the population by the Nazi regime. Come on Jack, the ordinary people of Germany were being brain washed, groomed to support another war in Europe, it was all part of the Nazi master plan."

"Yeah, I know my history," he growled.

Their conversation came to an abrupt end and Orlagh watched as he left the lab.

She wondered about his past, she knew that a lot of Americans had their roots in Germany just like many of them do in Ireland, but there was no evidence in his name to suggest German ancestry. He looked European, even Aryan, with his piercing blue eyes and fair hair she thought it more likely his history was firmly rooted in English soil. She was certain that his genes had been influenced by Saxons, when they settled in the south of England once the Romans had left.

XII

"We're still getting some unusual radiation readings from the area around the wreck." Mark said as Jack entered the control room.

"Okay Mark, maybe we should take a closer look inside the ship." Jack slumped into a chair and wiped his hand over his face.

"Any word from the lab?"

"Yeah, but it's nothing to worry about, they agree there is a raised level, especially from the samples taken closest to the ship, but it's no more than one would expect from a nuclear power plant."

"But don't you think it odd?" Mark said as he swung round in his chair. "The wreck's not a power station, hell, it doesn't even have a nuclear reactor, so where's the radiation coming from?"

"Well, unfortunately I don't have the answers, that's why we need to get inside that ship." Jack hauled himself up out of the chair. "I'll go get the engineers to make the Eyeball ready." He was as concerned as Mark he'd even checked the ships inventory again just to make certain that nothing had been missed.

Orlagh realised that something was going on when she saw the increased activity around the tiny ROV. With her curiosity aroused she made her way up to the control room where she found Jack and Mark.

"Hi, come in," Jack said. "We're going to send Kitty inside the Hudson Bay."

"Looks like I've arrived just in time," she said squeezing in between them.

Once the Eyeball ROV was hovering above the hole in the side of the ship, Mark focused his full attention on the delicate manoeuvring operation. Both his hands were busy working the controls and very slowly he inched Kitty down into the darkness.

"We have to be careful," Jack explained in hushed tones. "Although the hole is large enough for Kitty to get through the space inside tightens up rapidly. There is also the added complication of razor sharp edges from the jagged steel, we don't want to snag the umbilical cord."

Orlagh nodded drawing close to his side so she could hear him more clearly. The control room was just large enough for two ROV pilots to work in relative comfort. Sitting back to back they worked at control panels that were set along the wall, this way two ROVs could be manipulated simultaneously. It was sometimes beneficial to have two machines working together under water.

Jack watched the operation from his own screen and Orlagh was pressed up against him. She was painfully aware of him, he smelt good, a fresh mixture of spices that blended perfectly with his natural musk. It was not at all unpleasant and it was all she could do to focus her attention on the screen.

Light cast by the spotlights fitted to the Eyeball's sub-frame chased away the shadows from within the ship and as Mark piloted Kitty deeper into the narrowing space they could see for the first time the full extent of the damage caused by the explosion.

At first Orlagh could hardly make out what she was looking at, it was an alien world where everything was turned on its side. Doorways were horizontally situated and staircases went from left to right instead of up and down.

Gliding into a stairwell, Mark squeezed Kitty skilfully between a mangled railing.

"This is the end of the road," he said, bringing Kitty to a standstill up against a wall of solid steel.

"Looks like an internal bulkhead," Jack said. "There shouldn't be one there."

Mark turned Kitty slowly, searching for a way ahead. "This is the only way in, but for now the journey ends here."

Jack leaned forward and rubbed his hand over his chin. Orlagh, watching him closely, could hear the rough sound his fingers made as they brushed against his stubble.

"We'll have to cut our way in," he said frowning.

"There's a small gap between these two plates." Mark tapped the screen with his finger. "If we lay a small charge here, the blast should be sufficient to deflect off this one and with a bit of luck shove this one aside."

"It should work," Jack said after a moment, "be quicker than using thermal cutting equipment."

"I'll take some measurements and do the maths," Mark nodded.

Orlagh glanced between the two men.

"How will you plant enough explosives to do a job like that?" she asked.

"We'll dive, do it manually."

"Won't that be dangerous?"

"No, it's not what you think, we're not planning to use sticks of dynamite and light a fuse." Glancing at her Jack grinned. "We use modern plastic explosives these days with remote fuses that are harmless, nothing will happen until an electrical signal sets off the detonators, we'll do that from up here."

"It won't do too much damage then?" she worried, not certain about using such extreme methods.

"No, not if we get it right." He realised that she wasn't happy about using explosives so he explained the technique in more detail.

There had been no sign of the Torc and hopes that they would find it in the debris field were beginning to fade, she began to think that it was still somewhere inside the ship, maybe inside the hold. She worried that Jack would not spend much time looking for it. It wasn't in his interest to risk the lives of divers going through the ship on a fruitless search besides, his primary objective was to recover the Nazi gold.

Mark completed his survey and was now feeding information into the computer. "What you need will be coming out of the printer at any moment Jack."

Whilst they waited Mark piloted Kitty out of the hole.

"Right," Jack said as he snatched the paper out of the printer tray, "let's get ready for a dive."

The weather was beginning to turn nasty and the angry sea had the Sea Quest dancing to its tune. It wasn't uncomfortable yet but Jack thought it safer to dive through the moon pool instead of going over the side. There were two other divers waiting in the small briefing room when Orlagh and Jack arrived, these men were underwater explosives experts. Kitty had already strung a line from the wreck to a buoy for the divers to use as a guide and now it was bobbing in the waves just off the starboard side.

"We'll have just twenty minutes on the bottom," Jack began his brief. "There is enough air in our tanks for about an hour but I don't anticipate staying down that long.

That means two safety stops on the way up, allow for five minutes each stop, we won't be carrying pony cylinders so stick to the plan and we'll get back safely."

They were all experienced divers but Jack felt obliged to go through the safety margins. Diving on a wreck can be fraught with danger especially where explosives were concerned. He was also aware that Orlagh might be tempted to go off on her own and search for the Torc. Kitty had already indicated where some interesting looking shapes were lying in the silt close beside the ship, and he was intending to take a look.

The water in the moon pool was alive it reminded Orlagh of a wave machine in a swimming pool. Standing on the edge she looked down into the water, the doors in the hull were open but she couldn't see the bottom, it was like looking through a window which opened out onto a strange dark world. The water was grey and cold, nothing like the clear warm water of the Red Sea. The divers stood in line beside the pool checking each other's equipment and Jack appreciated the way the tight suit clung to Orlagh's curves. Her thick red hair was tucked under a hood and her delicate features stood out making her look younger and incredibly vulnerable. He checked her suit, running his hands lightly over her body, he scrutinised every seam and hose connection until he was satisfied that everything was where it should be.

"Ready?" he asked as she turned her face towards him. She nodded then they moved towards the edge of the pool.

The other divers each carried an extra piece of equipment, their packs containing explosives and detonators. They moved confidently giving the impression that this was just another day at work. Once in the water, Orlagh washed the lens of her mask before pulling it over her head, she had already adjusted the straps so now it made a water-tight seal around her face, then calmly she began to breathe the gas mixture from the cylinder strapped to her back. When she was learning to dive things had been very different, she had found it difficult to breathe underwater, automatically holding her breath whenever she went under, it had taken all of her resolve to learn the technique of breathing air from the tank. She had no trouble now though as she waited for the men to give her the thumbs up signal which would begin their descent onto the Hudson Bay.

Sinking below the surface Orlagh followed the others as they drifted out from the bottom of the Sea Quest. She was amazed by the size of the ship and glancing up, it loomed above her, its shadow blocking out most of the light, the rectangular hole in the hull looked like a strange lozenge shaped eye which stared coldly back at them. Kicking off after the others the ship disappeared into the gloom. It was much darker than she expected under the water and as they descended further she remained close to Jack. It hadn't looked so daunting watching Kitty on the screen from the safety of the control room, but now she could feel the tension building around her.

As they went deeper the water seemed to become thicker, it was much colder here than she imagined and they hadn't gone far before they had to use their lights which were strapped to the front of their suits. They also wore a light attached their head so wherever they looked light would be projected forward. Orlagh found it nothing like her previous dives, visibility in the Red Sea had been excellent and she didn't have to wear a full diving suit to protect her from the numbing cold. She thought about the ship, remembering every detail as she hovered above it. Things had been very different then, today they weren't diving to such a depth but visibility was poor and she was not able to see the ship until she was almost upon it.

They came to a halt in a line, strung out above the hole which loomed black and foreboding below them and suddenly Orlagh didn't want to go into the wreck. The ship was larger than she had imagined and although she couldn't see it all at once, she could feel its huge mass crowding in around her. Struggling with her fears she pushed her negative thoughts to one side and focussed on the men in front of her.

Jack signalled to the other divers and they disappeared, head first into the hole.

He remained beside her, hovering like a strange puppet held up by invisible strings, then he made a signal with his hands and she responded positively. They were going to take a look at some objects lying close to the ship and if they had time they would enter the wreck. Orlagh had never dived into a wreck before and the prospect of doing so now filled her with dread.

The items turned out to be nothing more than fragments of dinner plates and a few glass bottles, so with Jack leading the way they went hand over hand gliding effortlessly up the side of the ship. At the top he disappeared without hesitation through an opening into the bridge section and once inside their lights cast eerie shadows which danced against the bulkhead. Orlagh was disorientated, it was a strange sensation being inside a ship that was on its side, the equipment was at odd angles and there was nothing that she recognised. Her heart was racing and her breathing erratic, she had to remain calm, to have a panic attack now would be disastrous. Blinking hard she managed to focus on Jack who was making his way around the bridge inspecting the antiquated machinery. She remained hovering by the opening not fully committed to entering the ship and as she struggled with her emotions she wasn't aware that he had come up beside her. Startled by his sudden appearance she couldn't see his face through his mask, but she knew he was grinning. He indicated to his watch and pointed upwards, their time was

92

almost up and cursing herself for not having made the most of the time she followed him back the way they had come.

The other divers were waiting and with hand gestures confirmed that their job was done, then in line they began to make their way towards the surface. Orlagh was both relieved and disappointed that their time on the bottom had come to an end, she was surprised by her reluctance to go inside the wreck. Jack had warned her that she might become uneasy it was common to feel this way when diving into a wreck for the first time.

She felt much better after a warming shower and as soon as she was comfortably dressed in warm clothes, they made their way up to the control room. The Sea Quest was moving more fiercely now, rolling on the waves as the weather deteriorated. Paul sent a message to the control room from the bridge warning Jack that it was going to get worse over the next twelve hours.

"Okay Paul," Jack said responding to his message. "It'll be dark soon anyway, the charges are set so we're ready to blast."

"Roger that," came the reply, "blast away."

Jack pointed to a button on the control panel inviting Orlagh to do the honours.

"Would you like to set off the charge?"

She nodded, but before pressing the button, worried about the devastation she was about to unleash inside the Hudson Bay. There was no blast, no rumble, not even a tremor and she wondered if it had actually gone off.

"Has anything happened?" she asked.

"Oh yes, you can rest assured, you caused quite a bang. We'll see in the morning, Kitty will go and have a look."

The following day the storm had passed leaving the sea moderately calm and as Orlagh left her cabin she could hear men talking loudly further along the narrow corridor.

"Well I think she's a lesbian."

She stopped and frowned, wondering who it was they were talking about.

"Dr. Gairne had better watch out."

"Might be what she's looking for."

"I doubt it, have you seen that woman, Jack has his eye on her."

"Could be she's a frigid bitch!"

Orlagh gasped, then she began to make her way along the corridor, the men were still hidden from view but she could hear their remarks clearly.

"Not Dr. Gairne, Stacey." It was Roz they were talking about.

"Geoff tried to hit on her last trip but she wasn't interested."

"Well if he couldn't manage it then I agree, she must be a lesbo."

Orlagh had heard enough. "Good morning to you guys," she said coming up behind them.

"Dr. Gairne. Good morning." Both men were shocked when they saw her.

Orlagh was well aware of their discomfort and this pleased her, she was going to make them suffer for just a bit longer.

"Well boys, that's no way to talk about your colleagues, Roz would be devastated if she heard what you were saying about her, us girls like to be fancied." Pushing between them she continued on her way leaving them to drown in their embarrassment. She couldn't help grinning, the look on their faces had been priceless.

Jack was already in the control room and Kitty was just disappearing into the Hudson Bay so quietly Orlagh slipped in beside him just in time to witness the results of the blast. The heavy steel plates had been pushed aside as if they were made of paper and now there was enough room for Kitty to pass through. The area beyond was huge, a darkened cavern which held all kinds of secrets. Kitty's probing spotlights were swallowed up by the impenetrable gloom but Mark cautiously urged the Eyeball on, feeling his way around the debris. The hold was in partial devastation with gold bars strewn about like confetti at a wedding and there were upturned pallets and crates half submerged in silt.

"Wow, it's like Aladdin's cave in here," Mark said counting five pallets of gold bars that were still intact.

Jack studied the screen in silence, scrutinising every detail as Kitty revolved slowly through 360°. Even though the spotlights were having little effect, suddenly something caught his eye.

"Can you move in on that?" he pointed towards a shadow on the screen and the camera revealed what seemed to be a steel cabinet which had been thrown onto its side. Orlagh had no idea of the scale inside the ship, she found the blurred images on the screen confusing to follow.

"What do you make of it?"

"It's a substantial box," Mark whispered, "what do you think it's made of?"

"Metal of some kind, could be steel."

"Look how thick it is."

There was a gash in the metal which started at one corner and continued back along the side of the box. It had broken its moorings and was wedged on its end, pushed up against the bulkhead. Twisted metal lay strewn around and where silt had built up over time piles of unidentified objects were buried beneath it.

"Move around the other side," Jack said, his eyes never leaving the screen.

"What would be in a container as substantial as that?" Orlagh asked.

Jack remained silent and from the look on his face she wasn't sure she wanted to know.

"It can't be!" he said softly, his voice full of disbelief.

"What is it Jack?" Paul's voice sounded over the communication system. He was on the bridge listening to every word.

"Stand by Paul." Jack mumbled.

Mark steered Kitty around the box as phantoms of silt rose up, stirred by the eyeball's propulsion system.

"There's a symbol just there I think," Jack said pointing at the screen.

Orlagh could feel the tension mounting inside the tiny room.

"Are you thinking the same as me Jack?" Paul's voice sounded again. He was following the images on his monitor.

"Yeah, most probably."

"Will someone tell me what it is!" Orlagh was becoming impatient.

"I think it's an explosive device," Paul said.

"Oh no, not another one, the place isn't booby trapped is it?"

"No, nothing like that," Jack assured her.

"But the German's never developed a nuclear device."

"What do you mean a nuclear device?" Orlagh glanced up at Jack.

"Just stay calm," he smiled, "it's probably nothing, just an old steel trunk. We'll have to get a camera inside to find out."

Mark was already backing Kitty out of the hold, preparing to bring the Eyeball up, he spoke into the microphone telling the engineers on deck what equipment he wanted fitted as soon as Kitty reached the surface.

"But the Germans never developed a nuclear device," Orlagh continued, her eyes wide with shock.

"You're right," Jack said turning to face her, "look it's just a wild hunch, it's probably nothing but we've got to find out before sending anyone in there."

"Let's not get carried away folks," Paul's voice was calm over the communication system. "Jack's right, I want a full report before we even think of going in there."

"It's always been thought that the Germans were working on a nuclear device."

Jack began. "Hitler was determined that Germany would dominate the world with a monopoly of atomic bombs. They were already years ahead of the game by developing a delivery system, their V1 rockets were perfect for carrying nuclear warheads, they just had to develop a reliable guidance system."

Orlagh knew about the development of rocket power by the Germans, but she knew nothing about how close they were to having a nuclear device in the 1940s.

"Einstein warned American politicians more than once during the early part of 1940, but at the time the U.S. wasn't caught up in the war in Europe, so he wasn't taken seriously."

"But it was the Americans who developed the atomic bomb."

"Yes," Jack nodded, "with help from European scientists, those who escaped persecution and looked towards America for asylum during the 1930s."

"It's ironic don't you think that the bomb could easily have been developed by the Germans if they had not forced these people out of their own countries," Paul began, "the first atomic weapon might have fallen on London or New York instead of Hiroshima and Nagasaki."

"So you honestly believe that a nuclear device was developed successfully in Europe before the end of the Second World War?" Orlagh shuddered at the thought.

"That's the story we've heard," Mark nodded. "Fortunately, before it could be used France was overrun by the allies."

"But that's appalling," Orlagh said as she considered the implications of such an attack.

"Control room, Kitty is ready to roll." An engineer's voice came over the communication system.

"Roger that," Mark replied, "stand by to deploy the Eyeball."

Kitty was lowered carefully into the water by a winch man operating one of the small cranes and another crewman played out the umbilical at the same time.

"We are good to go, skip," Mark said giving Paul the heads up.

"Roger that Mark, she's yours to fly."

He grinned and punched the switch which set Kitty free; this was a routine he and Paul liked to maintain.

When Kitty reached the wreck, Mark wasted no time with sightseeing, he steered the Eyeball skilfully into the hole nursing it along the narrowing corridor leading to the hold. The steel box loomed ominously ahead and Orlagh held her breath as she watched it growing larger on the screen. The next few moments would be crucial, history books might have to re-written. She was a reluctant witness to the bizarre events which had overtaken the whole operation and she wondered what Jerry would make of it.

Mark used the computer keyboard punching in several commands and the tiny arm like manipulator carrying a fibre optic camera began to move, this was the type of equipment used by surgeons for keyhole surgery. Once he had passed it through the hole in the corner of the box, the 'optical lace', as Mark called it began sending pictures back to the control room. A microscopic but powerful lamp illuminated the interior of the box allowing the camera to pick up clear images. Orlagh could make nothing out of the shadows moving across the screen, occasionally light would be reflected back off some shiny surface, but again she had no idea what she was looking at.

"It's not like a 'Fat Boy' which was dropped on Nagasaki," Mark said, his voice almost a whisper.

"No, what we're looking at here is more like a conventional warhead."

"It's way ahead of its time." Mark nodded.

"Don't forget, this baby was designed to sit on top a V1."

"Look at the damage to the coupling."

"Must have been done when the ship was blown up, luckily the steel box is substantial."

"I wonder how powerful it is."

"It would have been designed to take out a city like London but you must remember it was experimental, nothing like this had ever been tried before."

"Do you think it's as simple as the uranium device dropped on Hiroshima or the plutonium implosion type dropped on Nagasaki?" Mark glanced at Jack.

"Most likely plutonium. The Germans wanted to wipe out the population and spare the buildings, but I guess this baby would have reduced London to a smouldering hole in the ground."

"Look at the damage to the casing, can you see the crack running down the nose cone?"

Jack looked closer at the screen, "yeah, that would explain the radiation readings."

"Is that thing safe?" Orlagh asked as she realised with horror what they were looking at.

97

"It's not going to go off anytime soon," Jack said.

"How can you be sure?"

"Well, for one it could have exploded when the box was thrown into the air by the blast which sank the Hudson Bay and secondly who in their right minds would carry a nuclear device in the hold of a ship complete with detonator?"

"But you think the detonator is on the ship?"

"Yeah, sure it is, maybe it's in the hold with the warhead but in a separate and secure container."

"What are your intentions Jack?" Paul asked from the bridge.

"Well, I'm sure not going to fish this baby out, it can stay put on the Hudson Bay, hell knows what condition it's in after more than sixty years on the sea bed. We'll have to salvage the gold though, but we'll need to send divers in for that."

"Okay Jack, but let's consider all our options first."

"Sure but one thing's for certain, we won't get a work class ROV in there unless we burn a hole in the side of the ship."

"I'm not keen on that idea, not with the possibility of an unstable nuclear device in the way."

"Don't worry Paul, we'll handle the job with kid gloves."

XIII

The U-Boat came up to periscope depth as it moved slowly through the shallow water, the captain, glancing at the depth gauge, was confident that the seabed would drop away beneath the keel. Turning his attention towards the Sea Quest, he began assessing the direction and distance to the survey ship. Both torpedo tubes were loaded and tension inside the boat was running high, not since the Second World War had a German U-Boat fired on another ship and the gravity of the situation was not lost on the small crew.

As the submarine crept closer one of the torpedo tube doors slipped silently open and trapped air bubbles escaped undetected to the surface. The captain was satisfied that at this distance his boat would remain unseen, besides, who would be expecting a U-Boat attack?

"Fire," he said calmly and with a hiss of compressed air a slim fish-like cylinder streaked towards its target.

Orlagh was on her way to the laboratory, one of the technicians had asked her to take a look at a hoard of semi-precious stones that he was cleaning, he was unable to tell if they were of Roman or Celtic origin. Suddenly an explosion ripped through the ship and Orlagh was thrown against the wall. As she fell to the floor the corridor was plunged into darkness as the lights went out and dust filled the air around her. Her ears were ringing as the noise ran through the ship and whilst she struggled to catch her breath the emergency lighting came on. Slowly she got to her feet and leaning against the wall for support checked herself out, there were no broken bones but her heart was beating wildly. With a series of deep breaths she made an attempt to calm her shattered nerves then on trembling legs made her way slowly along the corridor.

On the bridge the control panel which monitored the Sea Quest's vital functions suddenly lit up. Alarms sounded all over the ship and Captain Seymour, climbing to his feet, stumbled back onto the bridge. He was out on the starboard wing when the explosion occurred but now he was scanning the control panel trying to work out what had gone wrong. The ship had been stationary in the water, held steady by the dynamic positioning system but now it was in motion, broad siding stern first through the water.

"This cannot be happening," he muttered to himself.

"Paul, do you copy?" Jack's voice sounded over the communication system.

"Yeah Jack, what gives?"

"I'm looking aft at the moment, take a look back along the port side."

Throwing himself out onto the port wing Paul stared back in utter disbelief at the carnage below. The huge crane that towered over the stern rail was a tangled mess of scrap iron and a whole section of railing was missing. Deck plates were buckled and smoke was pouring from the engine room. The bright orange hull seemed to be damaged beneath the water line and it was clear that the ship was settling by the stern, it was then that Jack arrived on the bridge.

"Better get the helicopter started," Paul said calmly. "I want everyone to leave the ship immediately, have the crew launch a lifeboat."

Officers began to arrive and Paul issued his orders, once he was satisfied that he could do no more he went calmly to the radio and sent out a distress signal.

Engineers were already on the heli-pad preparing the helicopter. The Sikorsky S-92 was a four bladed twin engine medium lift helicopter, built for the military and civil market. It was capable of carrying twenty two people but Jack was confident that he could cram all thirty one souls onboard into its cabin and still make a clean take off, he had flown the Sikorsky overloaded before. At a cruising speed of 150 knots it had a range of just over 500 nautical miles, more than enough to reach the coast of Portugal.

One of the two lifeboats was being launched, this could accommodate ninety people, this was enough space for the whole crew, so Paul was happy that everyone on board would have the opportunity to escape before the Sea Quest sank.

The helicopter rotor blades were turning rapidly, chopping through the air with a deep and regular thud, one of the engineers was on the flight deck acting as co-pilot calmly going through the pre-flight checks. Jack ran across the heli-pad and dived into the cockpit.

"How are you doing?" he asked the engineer as he buckled himself in.

"Just about finished here boss, she's almost ready to go."

The ship was lower in the water, settling by the stern and now the helicopter was sitting at an angle on the deck. Jack was not unduly worried, this would not affect its ability to take off and even if the ship was to roll, he could leave immediately, hover in the air and use the winch to lift crew members to safety. At least half a dozen men were already in the lifeboat and as Jack peered through the side window he could see it manoeuvring close to the port side, this would allow more of the crew to transfer safely across.

Paul was still on the bridge, he was in communication with both the Sikorsky and the lifeboat and was receiving updates on the situation. There were now at least fifteen people on the helicopter and almost as many in the lifeboat so taking one last look around the bridge he left his station and made his way steadily across the heli-pad.

"Better get this baby airborne," he shouted the moment he arrived, then a shudder ran through the ship. "I want to take a look at the damage from the air."

Jack nodded and the pitch of the engines increased as the helicopter left the deck rising gracefully into the air. From above, the working area on the lower deck looked devastated, they could see a gaping hole in the side of the ship just below the waterline and Paul wondered how long his ship would remain afloat.

"What the hell caused that?" Jack said looking back at Paul.

Letting the helicopter drift slowly along the side of the ship he lifted it up over the upper deck avoiding the communications pylon rising up over the bridge. Suddenly there was a commotion in the back.

"What the hell's going on?" Jack shouted. Holding the machine steady he watched as Roz landed nimbly on the deck below, she had used a rope attached to the underside of the helicopter.

"Dr. Gairne is missing," someone shouted.

Roz made her way quickly towards the workshop at the rear of the ship but it was no good, she couldn't gain entry to the lower deck so slipping around to the other side she went in through a side door. Glancing around, she was shocked by the devastation, water was pouring onto the deck and the ship was heaving in the slight swell. Something caught her eye and peering out through the twisted doorway she could hardly believe what she saw. Clambering over the twisted deck plates, she stared out over the waves and wide eyed with shock, realised that she was looking at a submarine. It was still quite a way off the port side and obviously it wasn't there to offer them assistance. It looked menacing and as it turned towards the Sea Quest a plume of water erupted from its bow and a silver trail began racing towards the ship.

"Hell!" Paul shouted as soon as he spotted the submarine, "it's fired a torpedo."

Roz, reaching for the control panel, punched in a code overriding the automatic system then pushing the thrusters forward the engines began to turn over faster. The deck vibrated horribly as she used the little joy stick to turn the ship, then with the side thrusters straining the bow came round until the Sea Quest was facing the oncoming torpedo. She realised there was little time, it would only take a few seconds for the torpedo to cover the distance separating them, but by turning the ship she had effectively reduced the target area and at the same time set it on a direct course with the submarine.

Jack looked on helplessly as the torpedo plunged headlong into the ship. The impact sent a huge plume of water up over the bow but it failed to explode, glancing along the side of the ship it scraped paint from the hull as it went.

Orlagh pushed against the laboratory door just as the second torpedo struck, the noise of the impact was not as loud as the first but still the sound was terrifying and she cried out as the ship lurched drunkenly. Leaning harder against the door, it still wouldn't budge, so she pushed her face up against the window and peered in. The laboratory was dimly lit by red lights and as her eyes adjusted she could see a tide of water pouring in across the floor. Tables and chairs were smashed and equipment was floating on the surface, the devastation was shocking, it was then she saw the body. One of the Lab technicians was face down in the water, his arms splayed out. Orlagh, smashing her fist frantically against the glass cried out, it was no use the man didn't move. She looked away in horror, he was unconscious or dead and there was nothing she could do to help him. She backed away and re-traced her steps along the passageway, the door at the end had shut automatically when the alarm went off and now it was jammed, putting her shoulder to it was no good it wouldn't budge.

Roz pushed against the door from the other side and called out but it was immovable, turning away she made her way back towards the workshop area. Orlagh gave up and continued along the corridor which took her deeper into the ship. Vibrations ran through the deck as the engines strained, the ship was becoming heavy as it took on more water its centre of balance upset causing it to wallow drunkenly. Orlagh could hardly believe this was happening; it was her fear of drowning which spurred her on and images of the Hudson Bay lying on the sea floor filled her with horror. She moved quickly along the length of the ship passing cabins and little storerooms but still she couldn't find an exit. At a junction she hesitated, she had no idea which way to go, she had never been in this part of the ship before and in her panic to find a way out she turned left instead of going right and went deeper into the ship. Charging down a flight of steps she discovered another door at the bottom, this one opened easily as she pulled the lever and stepping through it closed behind her. She had read somewhere that ships were fitted with watertight doors, these were supposed to close in emergencies and prevent them from sinking.

She continued quickly along the passageway which was identical to the one she had just left, at the end was another staircase, this time there was no choice but to follow it down. At the bottom she stopped to get her breath, she was confused and terrified and swallowing down her frustration realised that this part of the ship was exactly like all the other places on board. This was her worst nightmare, trapped in a steel clad labyrinth from which there was no escape.

Turning on the spot she searched desperately for a familiar sign, something with which to get her bearings. Jack had brought her this way before, she was sure of it, the way ahead must lead to the moon pool. Cursing herself, she realised that she was in the bottom of the ship this was no place to be considering that it was sinking. Suddenly Roz was there beside her.

"There you are," she said breathlessly jumping down the last of the steps. "We have to get out of here."

"Sure we do but which way do we go?" Orlagh was breathless, her voice was raised in panic and her eyes wide with shock, she looked a mess.

"Just calm down, it's okay." Roz did her best to sound convincing.

"How do we get out, is it this way?" Orlagh said jumping up onto the step.

Roz took hold of her arm and held her back. "No, not that way, there isn't time, I have an idea, but you'll have to trust me."

Orlagh didn't like the sound of that. "Why can't we just go up?"

"It's too late, the ship is sinking we won't have time to make it up to the deck, go over the side and get clear before it goes down taking us with it."

"Dear God!" Orlagh was wide eyed with shock. "What will we do?"

"Follow me." Roz took her to the end of the passageway where she pushed open another heavy door, this one opened up into the diving area where the moon pool was situated.

"Put on the breathing equipment," Roz said quickly, "don't bother with a diving suit just the cylinder and a pair of fins, we'll need to get as far away as we can once we're off the ship."

Orlagh looked around searching for the equipment they would need. "Are you suggesting we wait for the ship to sink then swim out?"

"No not exactly, I'm going to open the moon pool doors, we'll get out through the bottom."

"But won't that let more water in?"

"It won't be pleasant," Roz agreed, "the water will come in as soon as I open the doors, we are well below the waterline because the ship is sinking. The pool works by maintaining the outside water level," she explained. "The sides are steep but water will burst over the top and start flooding this chamber, we'll have to wait for an equalisation of pressure before we can swim out."

"Holy shite!" Orlagh blasphemed. She was now feeling nauseous.

"Look, once you have your breathing gear on get up onto that locker and hold on tight, you won't be able to swim against the incoming flow so just wait for my command."

Orlagh's hands were shaking as she fumbled with the cylinder hoses.

"Oh and one more thing," Roz said, "we only have these small pony cylinders, they will only last for about fifteen minutes so breathe normally, you don't want to use it up too soon."

Roz gave Orlagh just enough time to get herself prepared before operating the mechanism which opened the doors in the bottom of the ship. At first the water rose steadily up the sides of the pool but as it began to surge over the top it became an angry torrent of grey foaming spray. Within seconds the room was flooding, water cascading along the walkways swept everything that wasn't fixed down ahead of it and the noise terrified Orlagh. The air in the room was beginning to move, she could feel it against her face, the pressure as it was forced through the vents in the ceiling sounded like demons moaning. Orlagh shuddered, it was almost too much to bear, her heart was racing inside her chest and she cried out. Clinging white knuckled to the top of the locker, she almost fell off as something solid crashed into the steel doors and vibrations ran up through her body. The noise was becoming deafening as cold grey water rushed up to meet her and she stared wide eyed as reality struck home, she was going to have to get in and swim for her life. She had not yet pulled on her mask, she was going to wait until the last moment not wanting to use up precious air from the little auxiliary cylinder.

"When you put on your mask don't forget to open the valve," Roz shouted over the din.

The small pony cylinders were used by divers in emergencies, they were usually carried strapped to their diving suits or left strung out along lines at various depths. Divers who had been down on the bottom for any length of time could use them if they needed extra breathing gas at decompression stops.

The water level was now two thirds of the way up the locker but the sheer volume of it was beginning to hold back the initial surge. Orlagh glanced across at Roz and wondered how she managed to remain so calm. Roz was already wearing her face mask and indicated to Orlagh to pull hers on. Turning on the gas valve she took deep breaths before following Roz into the water.

The captain of the U-Boat realised his error, he should never have surfaced.

He had considered the survey ship to be harmless it couldn't possibly present a danger to his boat. He was standing on the platform in the coning tower watching with growing concern as the Sea Quest began to turn, it wasn't until the strickened ship picked up speed that his apprehension began to increase. He was convinced that everyone had got off, he had seen the lifeboat loading and watched as the helicopter lifted off the deck but still the ship performed an outrageous manoeuvre. He was now going to have to take evasive action to avoid being run down. This he found frustrating, he liked to be in control, but now his carefully planned mission was going desperately wrong.

The submarine could crash dive in under nine seconds, more than enough time to avoid a collision. Shouting orders into a speaking tube, he dropped down the short ladder landing in the control room, then slamming down the hatch he secured the boat before giving the order to turn away sharply and dive.

At thirty four metres long the submarine could not crash dive safely in such shallow water. The bathymetric chart, an underwater equivalent to a topographical map, indicated that the seabed dropped sharply away and with the increase in depth they might just get away with it. The boat began to submerge and he watched the depth gauge anxiously. If he could get it right they would skim the bottom gently, following the angle of the sea bed into deeper water, it was a tricky manoeuvre but he was confident that it would work. The hydroplanes moved, pushing the nose of the submarine deeper and as the coning tower submerged he could hear the sound of the approaching ship, its propellers sending percussion waves radiating through the water. In his head he counted off the seconds, the ship would soon be passing overhead, it was going to be close.

When the impact came he was thrown across the control room and the sound of steel grating against steel filled his ears. The deck rolled to an unbelievable angle and the boat groaned under the weight of the ship riding on its back. The bull nose of the Sea Quest struck the submarine just after the coning tower where the hump which once housed the diesel exhaust silencer was situated. The submarine was pushed over onto its side by the force of the impact and plates in the pressure hull began to buckle. The helmsman pulled back on the hydroplanes in a desperate attempt to stop the boat from nose diving into the seabed, but it was no use.

Water was pouring into the control room and the captain picked himself up, he realised that he would have to secure the compartment, the hull had been fractured so he must act quickly if he was to prevent the boat from drowning. The bow was angled down and would soon make contact with the bottom, there was nothing he could do about that now, he was a passenger and he didn't like it one bit. He had no idea of the extent of the damage but at least for now they were still in one piece, all he could do was brace for impact and pray that the boat didn't break up. He glanced up wishing that he could see through the steel skin, they must be clear of the survey ship because he could no longer hear the sound of grinding metal. Suddenly they struck the bottom and the lights went out.

"Reverse engines," he shouted into the communication system, but before the order could be carried out the electrical system failed and the engines wound down.

"Blow the ballast tanks, let's get to the surface." His orders were in vain, with the loss of the electric motors the boat was helpless, all he could do was check out the damage before attempting any repairs to the power supply.

Orlagh followed Roz into the freezing water, the shock of it took her breath away, she didn't appreciate how much a diving suit insulated the body against the cold. Swimming down through the moon pool was a terrifying experience it was as if at any moment the ship would sink and crush them into the seabed. Kicking as fast as she could the fins on her feet propelled her through the water, she lost sight of Roz almost immediately but instinctively knew which way to go. Once clear of the doors she turned sharply and kicked away from the ship. The huge vessel looming above them cast a shadow over the whole area and filled her with a desperate urge to get as far away as possible, panic surged through her until she thought her racing heart would burst.

In the helicopter Jack watched as the submarine began to turn away from the ship, it was diving surprisingly quickly and for a moment looked as if it might get away. The shadow it cast beneath the surface was clear enough and then he saw the Sea Quest tremble as the two vessels came together, the force of the impact stopped the ship and it rolled slightly to port.

There was no sign of Orlagh or Roz and the Sea Quest was now very low in the water, they would have to get clear before it disappeared completely. He could only wait another two minutes and circling over the area scanned the water desperately searching for survivors. He could no longer see the submarine and could only guess at the damage that it had sustained.

The two minutes were up and he could wait no longer, he had a duty to the survivors on the helicopter, he had to get them away to safety. The lifeboat carrying the rest of the crew was steadily making its way towards Portugal, it only carried a limited amount of fuel and supplies so could hardly wait around especially with darkness just a few hours away.

From the cockpit of the Sikorsky, Jack could see no other ships in the area, if Orlagh and Roz were still alive they would have to survive alone for some time before help arrived. He glanced at his ship one last time before swinging the helicopter away, he could do no more.

XIV

When Orlagh came to the surface she was desperate to be rid of her face mask, certain that she was about to drown she filled her lungs with fresh air before hearing the sound of helicopter blades. At first she was filled with relief but then realised that the aircraft was receding into the distance and suddenly her eyes filled with tears. Fortunately the sea was calm and treading water, she managed to recover her frayed emotions before glancing around searching for something to use as a float. Roz surfaced a little way to her left.

"Orlagh," she cried, ripping off her mask, "are you okay?"

"I've had better days," she grinned, her teeth chattering from the cold.

Roz helped her to release the pony cylinder so she could stay afloat more easily and then they took stock of their situation. The Sea Quest was nowhere to be seen and they were alone in the water. They had no life jackets and treading water would use up precious energy, Orlagh was already struggling to stay afloat even without the weight of the cylinder strapped to her back.

"Relax," Roz said, "don't fight it, put your head back."

Orlagh did as she was told, she should know better, she was after all a competent swimmer but the stress and panic of the last hour had exhausted her and the air from the pony cylinder left her feeling nauseous. The muscles in her arms and legs were beginning to complain with the cold and with a huge effort she tried to relax and go with the motion of the sea.

"Look, don't worry," Roz said, desperate to reassure her. "There's sure to be a buoyancy aid from the ship, debris will soon start coming up." Roz sounded confident, it was as if she had done this kind of thing before and although Orlagh was terrified, she drew strength from her companion.

Roz was more than concerned but she disguised her anxiety well. There was nothing left of the Sea Quest and they were in the Atlantic Ocean with no life jackets, it would also soon be dark, the light was already fading along with their chances of survival. They couldn't possibly last the night exposed to the elements and if the sea was to become rough then that would be the end. If she didn't think of something soon they would be dead in just a few hours.

Suddenly there was a loud noise and something broke the surface.

Orlagh stared in disbelief as a bright orange lifeboat popped up like a giant cork beside them.

"Hell, I prayed for flotsam not a lifeboat," Roz cried out in astonishment. They swam towards it and hauling themselves aboard collapsed on the deck.

Roz took a few moments going over in her mind just how fortunate they were, more than once during the last hour they could easily have perished. Opening the moon pool doors had been fraught with danger, they could have drowned when the chamber filled with water or the ship might have plunged to the bottom carrying them with it. They had been very lucky to get out unscathed and now their luck seemed to be holding out.

"The ship has automatic release systems which are activated by water pressure," she explained. "I'm surprised the life rafts haven't surfaced yet."

"What caused the explosion?"

Roz remained silent she wasn't sure if the submarine was still close by and didn't want to alarm Orlagh further. After a while she rose to her knees and looked out over the side. Standing up she checked the horizon, there was no sign of ships and the other lifeboat had already disappeared, they were completely alone.

"I'm going to see what supplies we have."

The lifeboat was stocked with food and water but there were no dry clothes. In the cabin she found a locker filled with sets of waterproofs and blankets, so stripping off she pulled on the waterproofs before laying her things out on top of the cabin to dry.

Orlagh was sitting up wringing water from her hair running her fingers through the wet tangles. A warm breeze caressing her skin lifted her spirits and it wasn't long before she began to feel much better. The sun was hanging motionless just above the horizon, drenching the sea and the sky in the most amazing pastel colours. Shading her eyes Orlagh stared out in wonder, it was impossible to distinguish the point where the sun merged with the sea but the colours were utterly breathtaking.

"We should get the stove going and make a hot drink." Roz appeared from behind the cabin door.

"Are there any dry clothes for me?" Orlagh asked, "I'll catch my death if I hang around in these for much longer."

The lifeboat was much larger than she imagined, benches in the cabin were arranged into rows reminding her of a river cruiser, the area was cramped but the facilities were beyond her expectations.

"You finish off here," Roz said as she went towards the doorway, "I'll go see if I can get this thing going."

Orlagh changed out of her wet clothes and soon had a kettle of water boiling, grabbing two mugs she brewed tea then went out to find Roz.

"Must have gotten water in the fuel system," she said leaning over an access hatch. "I'll have to check it out."

Orlagh peered into the compartment, it was a dark alien world, she knew nothing about engines.

"Before I get too involved with that I'll see if we can raise someone on the radio."

Taking the mug that Orlagh held out to her she ducked into the cabin.

Orlagh watched as Roz pushed buttons on the control panel, she handled the equipment expertly leaving Orlagh feeling utterly inadequate. She was completely dependent on Roz and had no idea how to work the systems on the lifeboat. After a moment the hiss of white noise came over the speakers.

"Jack, do you read me?" Roz spoke clearly into the radio transmitter. She knew he would be flying the helicopter and was sure to be listening out on the emergency channel. He would probably be in contact with the other lifeboat.

"Roz, reading you loud and clear, do you have dry feet?" Jack's voice filled the cabin. He sounded relieved.

"Yeah, Dr. Gairne is here with me too, she's okay."

"That's good news. I take it you're on the other lifeboat."

"Yeah and as soon as I get the engine started we'll be making our way towards dry land."

Jack gave her some co-ordinates which she fed into the Sat.Nav. system and they talked for a few moments longer before signing off.

"Jack has us on his radar screen, we have a beacon which is sending out our position."

Orlagh was relieved, they were no longer alone.

"Don't worry, I'll soon have the engine running then we can go home." Roz made it all sound so simple and finished her tea before going back out on deck.

"You didn't answer my question," Orlagh said. "What caused the Sea Quest to sink?"

Roz hesitated then bent down to pick up a bag of tools. She wasn't ready to tell Orlagh about the submarine, besides she still didn't have it straight in her own mind.

"I really don't know," she answered, "I was working on an electrical system in the control room at the time so I didn't see anything."

"We were so lucky to get off the ship."

"Don't dwell on it, we did what we had to do, we survived."

Orlagh shuddered as she remembered the lab technician floating face down in the water.

"Do you think everyone got off?"

"Most of the crew made it to the helicopter, the rest went off in the other lifeboat."

Orlagh told her what she had seen in the lab.

"Don't think about it, there was nothing you could do."

Jack headed for a little used airfield that was situated to the north of Porto in Portugal. Here few questions would be asked, he wanted to avoid publicity, the media would go in to melt down if they got hold of their story. He could see the headlines now, '*Survey ship sunk by phantom U-Boat.*' Before it got out he had to discover what was going on, the welfare of the crew was paramount, he must ensure the safety of the lifeboats that were still out in the ocean.

The Sikorsky landed beside a cluster of ancient buildings putting up a dust storm raised by its down draft, proof that nothing had touched down on the runway for some time. As soon as the rotor blades stopped turning the crew were ushered into one of the buildings huddled around a tall structure that was used as a control tower.

"So what happens next?" Paul asked.

Jack remained in the pilot's seat scanning the instrument panel as he shut down the systems. The journey had taken a little under an hour and there was plenty of fuel left in the tanks. He studied the screen, looking at the two little red dots which indicated the positions of the lifeboats, one was a few miles ahead of the other and he smiled, all was as well as could be expected.

"At least they got out," he smiled.

"Roz deserves a medal for what she did," Paul nodded referring to her quick thinking and brave actions. "Once this is over I'm going to see she gets the recognition she deserves."

Jack agreed and finally switched off the Automatic Identification System monitor leaving the flight deck lifeless. It was almost dark as they made their way across the concrete apron towards the building where their men could be found. Officials were checking documents, not many of the crew had stopped to collect their passports when the signal to abandon ship had been given so a list of names was being compiled. The American Embassy in Lisbon had been contacted and news of their sinking was being hushed up. Officials at the Embassy would rather avoid any embarrassing questions regarding the loss of an American ship until all the facts were known. The crew were to remain isolated until the investigation got under way.

Commander Emilio Fernandez was the man in charge, he ran the air base, it was his job to handle the operation until the American officials arrived. He smiled broadly as Jack and Paul arrived and shook their hands warmly.

"Welcome to Portugal," he said as if addressing a group of tourists. His English was perfect but Jack had to listen closely as his accent was thick and could be deceiving. "Your Embassy has been contacted as you requested and arrangements have been made for your men to be transferred to somewhere more comfortable."

"We're not to remain here?" Paul asked.

"No Senhor the facilities here are far from adequate. I have been in contact with a small hotel not far from here, it is quiet the owners are very discreet," he grinned. The conditions were shabby in the sparsely furnished room. "Your Embassy staff will be arriving within the hour and by then we will be ready to move your men to their accommodation."

Jack nodded his head full of questions. He realised that none of them would be allowed to leave Portugal until officials were satisfied, so they would remain illegal immigrants having entered the country with no documentation.

Forty minutes had passed since the collision and now the submarine was laying at a slight angle on the seabed. The damage to the hull had caused a short circuit in the electrical system which meant a total loss of power to the underwater propulsion system. On the surface the submarine could use its diesel engines, exhausting the fumes into the atmosphere, but underwater it relied on electric motors which gave off no toxic fumes.

The control room was already ankle deep in water and both the captain and helmsman were working on restoring the power supply. It was crucial to get the pumps working, stem the flow of water into the boat, but it soon became obvious that the damage was too severe.

There were two other members of the crew, engineers who were stationed in the forward compartment. Nothing had been heard from these men since the submarine had been rammed.

"This is a hopeless task," the captain said. "Get to the rear hatch and find the emergency escape kits."

The kits consisted of a hood, worn over the head then sealed. It was inflated using a cylinder of breathing gas which served two functions, the wearer could breathe the gas mixture and the increase in pressure kept the water out, it also acted as a buoyancy aid, lifting the wearer to the surface.

The captain made his way through the control room, the water was rising steadily and he would soon have to seal off this section of the boat. This would effectively cut off the forward section, but first he must find out what had happened to the two engineers.

One of the men was lying on the deck in agony his face the colour of snow, his leg shattered.

"Günter," Schiffer gasped as he stepped through the hatch, "what happened here?"

"Captain," he said through gritted teeth, "Kirt is dead."

A torpedo had jumped off its rack when the boat was rammed and he was killed instantly.

"Can you get up?" Schiffer was uncertain of the damage to the front end of the boat. The torpedo tubes could be used as an escape route, but if the doors were damaged then exiting that way would be impossible. Looking down at his colleague he weighed up the possibilities, Günter was unlikely to survive an ascent from the rear escape hatch, besides, getting him through the ship would not be feasible.

Günter groaned and almost blacked out as he attempted to move, he was not going to make it off the boat and slumping down against the bulkhead he looked up. He knew it was a hopeless situation and silently his captain pressed a pistol into his fist before leaving him alone.

When Schiffer opened the control room hatch water poured out over the step. He glanced back over his shoulder, Günter was holding the pistol tightly in his fist his eyes huge like dark pools against his ashen face, after a moment's hesitation Schiffer slammed the hatch shut sealing off the forward compartment. Wading through the freezing water he made his way to the other end of the control room where he stepped through the hatch then he sealed off the compartment for the last time.

"Where are Kirt and Günter?" the helmsman asked when Schiffer arrived at the escape hatch.

"Both dead," he grunted as he pulled an emergency escape kit out of the locker.

The escape hatch was a cylindrical chamber which had watertight doors at each end, it was large enough to accommodate only one crewman at a time. It had its own power supply, huge batteries which were connected to a control panel, but the hatches were controlled by the main hydraulic system.

Schiffer crawled into the cramped space, he was going to be the first off the boat. Securing the inner hatch he pulled the hood over his head before inflating it then he checked the breathing hoses. When he was satisfied, he opened a valve allowing seawater to flood into the chamber and as soon as it was full the pressure equalised, then reaching up he pulled a hydraulic lever which opened the outer hatch. Kicking upwards he floated out of the chamber, then regulating his rate of ascent by gradually deflating the hood, he rose towards the surface.

The automatic system on board the submarine closed and sealed the outer hatch allowing the helmsman to activate the pump, as soon as it was empty he opened the inner hatch and the process began all over again.

Roz got the engine running and climbing from the cramped compartment she wiped oil from her hands with a rag. It was still daylight but the sun had almost disappeared below the horizon and the sky was no longer as spectacular as it had been.

"What's that?" Orlagh said pointing out to sea.

Roz stared to where she indicated and chewed at her bottom lip. "It's probably something from the ship."

"Wait a minute, I think it's moving."

Roz looked more carefully, there was something brightly coloured floating on the surface. "You're right," she said, reaching for a pair of binoculars, "it's a man." Focussing the lenses she took her time in making her assessment.

"Someone must have been left on the ship," Orlagh said moving to the side rail.

Roz remained silent, she was certain that everyone had got off the Sea Quest. The man in the water was pulling something up over his head, it was some kind of breathing equipment, Roz had never seen anything like it before.

"Come on let's go and help him," Orlagh urged.

"He's not from our ship," Roz lowered her binoculars and stared at Orlagh. "I don't recognise him."

"What do you mean, he's not from our ship?"

"The Sea Quest was sunk by a submarine," Roz said. "It fired a torpedo into us."

114

Orlagh froze and stared at Roz, she was horrified. "I don't understand, what do you mean a torpedo?"

"A submarine is responsible for sinking us."

Orlagh took a step back she thought Roz had lost her mind.

"Look Orlagh," Roz said reading her expression. "I don't imagine for one moment that you believe me but I didn't dream this up. You must have heard the second torpedo scraping along the side of the ship. I managed to get the engines going and using the side thrusters turned the bow into its path, then the ship rammed the submarine. I guess it was damaged and sank, so this man must be one of the survivors," she was talking rapidly the pitch of her voice raised by stress.

Shaking her head Orlagh didn't know what to think, she stared at Roz, why would she say such a thing if it wasn't true? She had felt the ship lurch just before a terrible metallic sound ran along the side of the ship.

"Why would a submarine want to sink us?"

"I've no idea but what I'm telling you is the truth."

"Okay, let's assume for a moment that it is," Orlagh said, "we must still help that man."

"No," Roz said shaking her head.

"What do you mean no?" Orlagh was horrified. "We have a moral obligation to help him, we can't just leave him out there."

"Orlagh," Roz attempted to reason with her. "He tried to kill us."

"How do you know it was him? He could have simply been following orders, besides he must have been part of a crew, he can't be held personally responsible, he may even be injured."

"We can't possibly help him, how can we protect ourselves, we haven't even got any weapons."

"He will die if we leave him out there, I won't be responsible for the death of another human being, we have to help him."

Roz remained silent, she was torn apart, she didn't like the idea of helping someone who had tried so hard to kill them, she thought it was a terrible mistake to bring him aboard their boat.

"Please Roz, help me," Orlagh was trying to steer the boat and get the engine to work. It was idling, the propeller hardly turning, they were stationary in the water.

The man had seen the lifeboat and was already swimming towards them. Every few moments he would stop, lift his head and wave. Roz glanced in his direction, he was still a long way off but she could hear him calling. It was almost dark and if they didn't act now they would lose sight of him in the shadows. Stepping forward she took control, pushing the throttle lever forward the engine revs picked up and the bow lifted sending the lifeboat cutting through the water.

"Go forward," she said, "guide me to where he is. Don't take your eyes off him for a moment, just point the way so I can steer towards him."

Günter took a final look towards his dead companion. The atmosphere inside the compartment was fast becoming hot and humid, the stale air almost impossible to breathe. He grimaced as he lifted the pistol, it was heavy in his grip and he couldn't stop the barrel from wavering. He winced as he pushed the ugly weapon against his head then closing his eyes he squeezed the trigger. A hardnosed bullet entered just above his right ear, tearing upwards through his brain and exiting through the top of his head. It continued up into the overhead pipe- work shattering the main hydraulic feed.

The helmsman entered the escape chamber sealing the inner hatch behind him, working quickly he pulled the hood over his head before inflating it with breathing gas. Once that was done he opened the valve allowing seawater to flood the chamber. He waited for a few moments as the water gushed in and when completely submerged he turned another valve which equalised the pressure. He then activated the hydraulic mechanism and the hatch in the pressure hull began to move. He was breathing hard and trying not to panic in the claustrophobic space, then he glanced up in utter disbelief as the hatch jammed.

The gap between the hatch and the sealing ring was hardly enough to get his head through, this small gap represented freedom, his only chance of survival. Bracing his shoulders against the hatch he pushed with his legs, his breath coming in short gasps as he strained. His heart began to pound uncomfortably inside his chest, but it was useless, the hatch wouldn't budge. He had to control himself, at this rate he would use up all his breathing gas in just a few minutes. In desperation he attempted to close the hatch but it still wouldn't move there was no manual override system and now with it partly open he couldn't even pump the water out. He was trapped with only a few minutes left to live. Frantically he tried to open the hatch leading back into the submarine but the safety system wouldn't allow it to move because the chamber was full of water. His last thoughts were for his wife and daughter.

The man was exhausted but they finally managed to haul him onboard just as the daylight faded completely then an eerie silence settled around

116

them. Roz went to turn on the lights. When she was gone, Orlagh helped the man to sit up, he was breathing heavily and was frozen so rubbing his back vigorously she attempted to get some warmth into his body.

The man was in his late forties, there was a few days stubble on his chin and his skin was pale under the light which now flooded out from the cabin. When he glanced up Orlagh looked into his eyes, they were an intense shade of blue.

"Thank you," he wheezed.

She detected an accent. "Who are you?" she asked stepping back.

"My name is Erich Schiffer, Captain Erich Schiffer," he said climbing stiffly to his feet. His accent was faint and he was very well spoken. From the sound of his name she thought he must be German.

"Why did you sink our ship?" Roz asked.

He spun round to face her. "And to whom do I owe gratitude for saving my life?" he grinned ignoring her question.

"Are you going to answer me or do we throw you back in?"

"You are American I see from your accent," he said his expression hardening.

"And you are German, you are from the U-Boat which sank our ship."

"A U-Boat?" he mocked, "I think you must be mistaken, the war finished a lifetime ago."

Orlagh could sense the hostility rising between them and she began to feel uncomfortable. "I'm Dr. Gairne," she said in an attempt to defuse the situation, "Orlagh Gairne."

"Ah Dr.Gairne," he said turning to look at her. An expression of shock clung to his face, it was as if he was seeing her for the first time but quickly he recovered his composure.

"Thank you doctor for saving me, but unfortunately I have no injuries for you to administer the first aid."

"I'm not that kind of doctor," she told him. "I'm an archaeologist."

"Is that so?" he nodded thoughtfully. He knew she was Irish, her melodious accent gave her away, her thick red hair and vivid green eyes pleased him and he found it difficult not to stare openly.

"What period of history is your speciality?" he asked, but was sure he knew the answer.

"Celtic history, iron age is my particular interest especially Celtic art and jewellery."

His eyes narrowed as he thought about the Torc.

Roz continued to stare menacingly, he realised that she would be a threat and he must take control of the situation. He was certain that

117

there was no-one else on the boat and had already begun to formulate a plan.

"I'm going to get us out of here," Roz said suddenly. Turning on her heel she disappeared into the cabin and as the engine picked up they got underway.

"You must get out of those wet clothes we have some warm blankets inside." Orlagh led the way into the cabin.

The man grinned and slowly reached into his pocket, when she returned with a blanket he pulled out a pistol and pointed it at her. Orlagh froze as cold tendrils of fear spread throughout her abdomen. Roz had been right they had clearly done the wrong thing in rescuing Captain Schiffer.

"Just sit down Dr.Gairne, I won't hurt you."

Roz could see what was going on from across the cabin and she reacted by looking for a weapon.

"Come over here, quickly," he shouted, swinging his pistol round until it was pointing at her. He watched carefully as Roz made her way towards him. "Do you have any rope?"

She didn't answer. Swinging his pistol, it made contact with her head and falling to the deck she was stunned but didn't lose consciousness.

"Do you have any rope?" this time he asked Orlagh who simply nodded her eyes wide with disbelief. "Then get it," he said, thrusting his pistol against Roz. "We shall await your return."

Orlagh was shocked she could hardly believe what had just happened. Slowly her mind began to function and she thought about using the radio to call for help, but she had no idea how to operate the equipment, besides, what could anyone do to help them? She found the rope then returned to the cabin.

Jack left Paul to deal with Captain Fernandez and the welfare of his crew.

He stepped outside breathing in the warm, dusty air. The sky was now completely black and apart from a few clusters of early stars nothing was visible. If he smoked he would have lit a cigarette to help calm his nerves.

Going over the events in his mind again, he pictured the moment he had spotted the submarine, he could still see the trail left by the torpedo as it streaked towards his ship. There was something puzzling about that submarine, it was small and compact probably no more than a hundred feet long, his first impressions were that he was looking at a German U-Boat, the type used in the Second World War. He allowed his thoughts to run with that notion as he walked slowly towards the helicopter then climbing into the cockpit he powered up the computer and looked up U-Boats.

There was more information than he could absorb so revising his enquiry he clicked on 'images' and the screen changed from text to pictures. Most of the photographs were black and white, the type taken during the 1940s. There were diagrams and other technical information on the screen and scrolling down an image caught his eye. He double clicked the mouse and the screen filled with information about a German U-Boat Type XXIII.

'The type XXIII coastal boat was one of the most advanced submarine designs of World War Two.' Quickly he scanned the information certain that he'd found the boat which had torpedoed his ship. It seemed impossible, there were no German U-Boats operating in the ocean today, he must be mistaken. He took another look at the picture, the more he studied it the more convinced he became, there was a U-Boat Type XXIII operating in the Atlantic Ocean.

Rubbing his fingers over his chin he began to make connections. If there was an organisation operating a U-Boat in the area they could only be after one thing, the location of the Hudson Bay. They must want the vast quantity of gold that was on the ship but Jack had made another discovery. Nobody knew about the nuclear device, it wasn't even recorded on the ships inventory, there must have been a cover up when the ship was loaded, the Americans keeping it under wraps. At the time they were desperate for atomic technology. His mind ran wild as he contemplated the whole idea. Whoever had sunk the Sea Quest must know about the secret, it seemed obvious that they had been disposed of before they could extract the atomic device.

He stared through the windscreen at the darkness. The submarine must have been deployed to protect the wreck until whoever was behind this had an opportunity to get their hands on the cargo, but why would someone want an antiquated device which was most probably unstable? It had just spent the last six decades on the seabed. Suddenly his eyes widened, it wasn't the device itself or the technology it had to be what it contained. Their equipment had detected radiation the moment they arrived over the wreck, the crate carrying the device had been damaged, causing a radiation leak.

Nuclear weapons of this era were known as Atomic bombs or A bombs, the energy coming specifically from the nucleus of the atom which was contained within the weapon. It was the mass of enriched uranium or plutonium that the submarine was protecting. Jack frowned then turning on the radar scanning equipment checked the screen. Immediately he saw that one of the red lights was missing and as he made adjustments to the controls his anxiety began to rise. Reaching for the radio transmitter he switched it on.

"Roz, do you read me over? Roz, this is Jack, do you hear me?" There was no reply, the airwaves were empty. He continued to call for the next ten minutes but the result was the same, Roz and Orlagh had gone. There must have been a malfunction with the transmitting system. He considered ordering the other lifeboat to turn around and begin a search but there was no point in having them miss their rendezvous with the British ship that had kindly agreed to pick them up. He was tempted to take off and fly a search pattern over their last reported position but he knew it would be useless. He would never be able to detect a small boat against the vastness of a black sea even if it was showing running lights, it would still be incredibly difficult to locate in the darkness, he would have to wait until dawn.

XV

Schiffer smirked as he pulled the rope tighter around Roz' ankles. Her eyes were smouldering with hatred and the bruises on the side of her face where he had hit her were turning ugly, there was also swelling around her eye. She was angry with herself for allowing Orlagh to talk her into pulling him onto their boat, but there was nothing she could do about that now.

Schiffer was in command, it was a position he felt at ease with and the first thing he did was to disable the Automatic Identification System which gave away their location, then turning off the running lights the lifeboat disappeared. With that done he left the cabin and went to check the fuel situation. The gauge on the tank was reading full and strapped inside a locker he found two jerry cans full of diesel, more than enough for what he had in mind. Returning to the cabin he went to the control panel where he made a course correction, then pushing the throttle lever all the way forward, the engine ran up to full power and they began to cut through the water.

The document locker was situated in this part of the cabin and searching through it he found what he was looking for. Spreading the chart out over the tiny table he studied it for a few moments then, when he was satisfied, he programmed the satellite navigation system. When that was done he engaged the automatic steering device and waited for a moment as the computerised system kicked in. Reaching for a pair of binoculars he grinned with satisfaction, he could now relax, every-thing was under control, then making his way forward he went to keep a lookout for ships or aircraft.

Jack used his mobile phone to contact Paul, he asked him to join him in the Sikorsky.

Paul wanted answers he was also a man who liked to be in control, his neatly ordered life had been turned upside down. Not only had he lost his ship, which was unthinkable in itself, but half his crew were adrift in the Atlantic Ocean. Hauling himself into the cockpit, he settled into the co-pilot's seat. Jack was talking to the British cruise liner who had agreed to rendezvous with the lifeboats, he was informing them of the possibility that now there would be only one.

"Roz and Orlagh have disappeared," Jack said as soon as he had finished on the radio.

"What do you mean disappeared?"

"They are no longer sending out a distress signal."

"That could mean their AIS has failed."

"True but I can't raise them on the radio either."

"They have to be out there somewhere, you spoke to Roz earlier."

Jack nodded but remained silent. He didn't need to remind Paul that the lifeboat was practically unsinkable and even with a complete power failure, or the loss of the radio mast, they would still be transmitting a distress signal. The only possible explanation was that the boat had been completely destroyed.

"I've already worked out a flight plan," he said. "As soon as it's daylight we'll work grid patterns starting with their last known position."

Paul nodded and glanced at his watch, dawn was at least six hours away.

"I've also been doing a bit of research and I think you should see this," turning towards the computer screen Jack pulled up an image of a German U-Boat Type XXIII. "I'm convinced this is the type of sub that attacked us."

Paul studied the screen for a moment before making a face, he wasn't convinced.

"You saw the torpedo trail," Jack insisted.

"Yes I saw the sub too but we have no evidence to back up our claim." Paul ran his hand over his face, he was exhausted the strain of the last few hours was beginning to tell. "Why would some lunatic in a submarine want to sink us?"

"I've given that some thought," Jack went on quickly. "The obvious reason is to get their hands on the Nazi gold."

Paul nodded, encouraging him to continue.

"I also believe it has something to do with that nuclear device."

"Why didn't they wait until we had retrieved it?" he didn't need to say more.

"Why indeed," Jack nodded. "It's my guess they don't want the rest of the world to know, they obviously want it kept secret."

"What would they want with an ancient atomic bomb? There are modern devices available on the black market that are infinitely more powerful."

"True," Jack nodded, "I don't think it's the war head they are after, they want the stuff that's inside."

Paul's eyes widened as he realised the implications of what Jack had just said. "Who are these people?" he looked from Jack to the computer screen.

Jack outlined his theory.

"So you're suggesting that we are dealing with a bunch of Nazi fanatics."

"That's what I think," Jack nodded. "Based on what we know, you have to admit that someone is going to a lot of trouble and expense to refurbish or build a replica Second World War U-Boat. Why didn't they just use a modern sub? That kind of behaviour is surely fanaticism." Jack was animated and Paul realised he was about to get a lecture.

"I believe we are dealing with a sect of some kind, a mysterious group of people who are not only in possession of a German U-Boat stuffed full of torpedoes, but also want the Nazi gold from the Hudson Bay. It's my guess that they need the plutonium or uranium from the warhead and I don't have to spell out the implications of that."

"They must be developing a nuclear weapon," Paul nodded thoughtfully.

"Whoever is behind this must have been watching us very closely because two months ago no one knew the whereabouts of the Hudson Bay. We only chanced upon it when surveying the area."

"Do you think Dr. Gairne is somehow involved?"

"No I don't think so," Jack shook his head. "I didn't discuss the subject with her but she did tell me about her student friend who's studying German mythology."

"You think he might have some answers?"

"No, it's probably just a coincidence," Jack said thoughtfully. "Orlagh is after the Torc, she or her organisation are not interested in anything else on board that ship. The only connection here is that the Nazi's want the same thing."

"Why that Torc in particular?" Paul asked. "I know they were into collecting historical artefacts."

"Orlagh told me that the Nazis had possession of the Torc during the 1930s and '40s, it seems they were fascinated with their historical past. Anyway, I did some digging around on the internet and discovered that it's shrouded in mystery. Apparently whoever wears the thing dies very suddenly, it appears to have some kind of supernatural power."

"You don't believe in all that mystical horse crap?" Paul sneered.

"No of course not, but there is documented evidence of people having touched the Torc meeting with premature deaths, it's a bit like the curse of Tutankhamen's tomb. Howard Carter died a few months after the tomb's discovery, his death was said to have been brought on by a curse."

"Didn't he die from some kind of insect bite?" Paul said, raising his eyebrows.

Jack sighed Paul had obviously missed the point. "Well let's just suppose the Torc has the same kind of power over life and death, it's just the kind of thing the Nazis would have been after."

"And you think our fanatical friends are searching for it too?"

"Probably not," Jack said after a moment's pause. "If I had to guess, I would say they are after the bomb. The Torc is a link with Orlagh but I think she's an innocent bystander in all this."

"You don't think the organisation she works for knows something that we don't?"

Jack looked up as light from the instrument panel illuminated Paul's face. "No I don't think so, if they did they would have told her, she's as much in the dark as we are, it's nothing more than a coincidence, the link with her has to be the Torc not the device."

"This is all pure conjecture after all," Paul said stretching his arms up above his head. "Before we get carried away with all this we have to find Roz and Dr. Gairne, so if it's wheels up at first light, I'm going to get some shut eye. It's been one hell of a day," he yawned.

Jack watched thoughtfully as Paul made his way across the concrete helipad.

There was less swell and the boat settled into the rhythm of the ocean. Orlagh was lying on the floor with her hands tied behind her back, it was an uncomfortable position, the rope was painfully tight and her fingers were cold and numb. Roz was propped up beside her with her back against a bench. Her mouth was sealed with tape because during the night she had given Schiffer a hard time, now her eyes were closed and she appeared to be asleep.

Orlagh struggled to sit up and finally managed to rest her back against the bench. Roz opened her eyes and after a moment murmured something through the tape, it was clear that she wanted it removed. Orlagh nodded her understanding and manoeuvred herself onto her knees then turning her back towards Roz, craned her neck so she could see and when in position Roz lowered her head until her face was level with Orlagh's hands. Slowly, with reduced feeling in her fingers, Orlagh managed to pick away at the corner of the tape lifting a flap before gripping it tightly. Roz pulled back and the tape came away then she inhaled deeply.

"Thank goodness for that," she said, "I thought I was about to suffocate."

"Where are we?" Orlagh glanced across the cabin. The windows were covered with a curtain of mist which obscured their view.

Schiffer was still on deck and they were alone in the cabin but still they talked in muffled tones.

"The boat's not wallowing anymore so I guess we're in shallow water," Roz began. "We must be somewhere off the Portuguese coast."

"We have been motoring all night," Orlagh nodded.

The engine was still on full power, its steady beat reassuring, but it didn't tell them where they were.

"It's no use speculating," Roz said, anticipating Orlagh's thoughts, "we could be anywhere."

It was barely daylight when Jack was at the controls of the Sikorsky. At 150 knots and just a few feet above the ocean, his eyes darted back and forth between the instrument panel and the horizon. Paul Seymour sat beside him in the co-pilot's seat, his eyes fixed to a pair of binoculars as he scanned the water ahead. The thin covering of mist that swirled over the coast seemed to be thicker further to the south, but out at sea visibility was good. Systematically Jack flew the grid, contacting ships that had passed through the area during the night, but none of them reported seeing anything of the little lifeboat.

"They can't have sunk," Paul said stating the obvious, "those lifeboats are unsinkable they even have the ability to right themselves automatically if they capsize."

Jack was aware of this. "If they were shot to pieces we would have found some evidence," he continued, thinking about the U-Boat. "The sub could have surfaced, kidnapped the women then destroyed the lifeboat."

"Why would they do that?"

"Cleaning up I guess."

"If we can't spot a disaster then it can only mean good news." Jack realised that if there was no mechanical failure and they had motored all night they would have reached landfall by now. He had notified the authorities, requesting they keep a look out, but the coastline covered hundreds of miles and with limited resources it was unlikely that the coastguards would be able to remain active all around the coast.

The Embassy in Lisbon had not yet contacted their people in Ireland so it was not confirmed that Orlagh was missing. As far as they knew she was safely on board one of the lifeboats; Jack was yet to inform them of her disappearance. He was banking on it being a simple case of systems failure and they would soon locate the women.

"I'll try the next sector," Jack spoke into the microphone, the sound of his voice coming clearly over the noise of the engines. As the helicopter changed course his eyes scanned the radar screen.

"If there had been an equipment failure wouldn't Roz have fixed it by now?" Paul asked.

"I've been having the same thoughts," Jack replied. "In the unlikely event of anything untoward happening they could have used flares, surely that would have attracted a ship."

Paul nodded, Jack had a point, there had been plenty of ships passing through this sector during the night. He sighed loudly before sending out yet another radio message.

Captain Schiffer ignored the women as he stepped into the cabin, going directly to the control panel he pulled back on the throttle reducing the boat's speed. The fog was beginning to clear and as Orlagh stared out of the window she could make out the ghostly form of bridge supports as they passed underneath, then she saw a small river boat moored against a buoy. It was not clear enough for her to see as far the banks but she got the impression they were in the mouth of a large river. She knew very little about the geography of Portugal and even less about the area of the Atlantic where they had been stationed over the Hudson Bay.

"How far off the coast of Portugal were we?" she whispered to Roz.

"About eighty miles."

"I'm trying to work out where we are exactly."

Roz remained silent, her knowledge of this part of the world was even less than Orlagh's.

Schiffer stayed inside the cabin, he was now steering the boat manually having disengaged the satellite navigation system. Turning to the radio set he carefully tuned into a frequency then he began to speak in German. He sent out a message that neither Orlagh nor Roz could understand and after a few moments a reply came back. The only words Orlagh could make out were 'Pheonix Legion', she had no idea what the message was about. Schiffer repeated the word 'Regua' before ending the conversation.

Orlagh was exhausted, settling down next to Roz she wished that she had a greater knowledge of Europe. She had visited France and Holland many times before but never Spain or Portugal. The first time she went to France was as a child with her parents, the huge standing stones and dolmans of Carnac in Brittany had inspired her and it was then she made up her mind to become a historian. The history of Europe fascinated her and studying the movements of ancient tribes especially the migration of people across the continents had formed the basis for her studies whilst at university.

The Romans intrigued her, she had plotted the development of Iron Age people and their conflict with the Romans who were spreading across Europe. In Britain the druids had been persecuted, they were hated by the invading armies, they were seen as trouble makers, inciting the ancient tribes to resist and rise up against the Roman legions. Eventually they had been slaughtered and over a period of many years the wild people were tamed, beaten and subdued by the conquerors, but a few strongholds remained mainly to the west and across the Welsh Marches. Here the ancient people of Britain retained some of their lifestyle and heritage.

"The mist is clearing I can see river cruisers on the water," Roz invaded her thoughts.

Orlagh got to her knees quietly, not wanting to attract attention she peered across the cabin towards the windows. The mist was still clinging to the glass like a spider's web making it difficult to see clearly but at least now the sun was beginning to peep through. They passed a river cruiser that was moored beside a jetty and Orlagh could make out a string of traditional looking boats moving in their wake. These were called 'rabelo' and had once been used to transport barrels of port wine from upstream. Suddenly she knew where they were.

"I think we're near Porto," she said. "This must be the river Douro. The source of the river is found near Duruelo de la Sierra, in northern Spain, and forms part of the national border between Spain and Portugal. The name Douro may have come from the Celtic root *dubro,* in modern Welsh *drw* is 'water' and *"dobhar"* in Irish," Orlagh whispered. This much she knew from reading the labels on port bottles. Roz nodded but remained silent.

"We are heading up river so we must be stopping soon at one of the towns."

Roz didn't share her optimism they would more likely be heading towards some remote area of Portugal. The Douro valley was a sparsely populated area of granite hillside, where tranquil lakes had been formed by dams that were built in the 1950s and '60s. There are five dams on the Portuguese Douro, functioning to make the flow of water uniform and to provide hydro-electric power to the region. With increasing interest in the production of Port wine a prosperous tourist industry had developed based on river excursions from Porto to points along the upper Douro valley. Boats pass through the dams by way of locks.

Once they were past the industrial riverfront of Porto the scenery began to change. Immaculately sculptured terraces where little white farm houses nestling between vines formed an idyllic landscape in one of the world's prettiest wine regions. Occasionally Orlagh saw famous Port wine company signs and logos which were placed on huge placards on the hillside and an old railway line, running beside the river, appeared every now and then as it followed the curves in the landscape. It was early in the morning and the river was not yet awake, it would be hours yet before the first tourists took to the water in one of the many cruise boats. They travelled further inland and the landscape began to turn wild. There was still agriculture but not on the same scale as lower down in the valley.

Jack and Paul had covered a huge area in the Sikorsky but their search had been in vain, they were no closer to solving the mystery of the disappearing lifeboat.

"At least they haven't been destroyed, there would be some evidence of that."

"So where are they?" Paul groaned as he glanced sideways at Jack. His eyes were raw from scanning the horizon and his brain began to play tricks on him, he kept on seeing shapes that were not really there, it was like looking at a mirage in a desert.

"We had better start heading back," Jack said glancing at the fuel gauge.

Pushing the throttles forward the nose lifted and they began to rise up into the air, it was then that something quite unexpected happened.

The river was beginning to come to life as the first pleasure cruisers took to the water. Schiffer kept to the centre of the river not wanting to promote unwanted interest, it must have been an unusual sight, a bright orange lifeboat cruising along.

The landscape continued to change and the further they went the more remote it became. By mid morning they had passed a couple of towns without stopping or rousing much curiosity.

"Can you untie me?" Roz called out suddenly. She had been fidgeting for a while and could stand it no longer. "Please, I need to use the bathroom."

128

Schiffer glanced up and nodded his head. Easing back on the throttle he slowed the boat then checked the way ahead before locking the rudder. When he was satisfied, he made his way across the cabin towards them.

"One at a time," he said. First he loosened her legs and helped her up then as she turned her back he untied her wrists. "Don't think about doing anything stupid," he hissed then pulling a pistol from his pocket waved it under her nose. "You have two minutes," he stared at her coldly before checking his watch.

Roz limped across the cabin her legs as stiff as dried leather. As she passed the control panel she glanced at the AIS, she was determined to activate it and reveal their position.

Her two minutes were almost up and stepping from the tiny cubicle that held the chemical toilet she looked towards Orlagh, Schiffer was there beside her. "Come here quickly," he demanded.

Doing as he said, her opportunity was lost, she got nowhere near the control panel.

"Untie your friend," he gestured with the pistol then standing back he watched them carefully.

With her hands free, Orlagh cried out as the blood rushed back into her fingers, Roz, taking hold of them, gently rubbed her wrists massaging the life back into them.

"Enough," Schiffer snapped, "tie her."

Orlagh picked up the rope and slowly wound it around Roz' wrists.

"Quickly," he demanded. Muttering something under his breath he left them and returned to the control panel where he took control of the boat.

Glancing forward Orlagh realised that Schiffer would be occupied for a few moments so as she worked Roz instructed her on how to operate the AIS. "You must activate the system Jack will pick up the signal," she whispered.

When she had finished tying the ropes, Orlagh made her way across the cabin. She locked herself in the toilet cubicle and worried about how she was going to get near the system without being seen. She didn't like the look of Schiffer's gun and felt sure he wouldn't hesitate use it.

Once she was finished she opened the narrow door and stepped silently into the cabin. Schiffer was no longer at the controls, he was checking the ropes that secured Roz, apparently not happy with one of the knots he was intent on making it tighter.

Seizing the opportunity Orlagh quickly located the panel which activated the AIS. There were no sounds to give her away as she pushed a series of buttons, the system was silent, it was as if nothing had happened and filled with relief she made her way across the cabin to where Schiffer was waiting.

The Sikorsky completed its climbing turn then settled onto a course which would bring it back over the airbase then suddenly the Automatic Identification System on the flight deck began to squawk. The VHF signal was activated by an identification code and a tiny red light began to flash on the screen.

"Roz," Paul said in astonishment.

Jack glanced up. "Where are they?" he frowned.

"But that's impossible," Paul said after a moment. "The signal is coming from inland."

"They must be on a river," Jack peered at the screen and unconsciously his brain began making calculations based on the information he was receiving. "The nearest big river is the Duoro."

"But that's miles away," Paul stared at him.

"True, reading the screen they are seventy miles upriver. As the crow flies they are at least two hundred nautical miles from our current location and we don't have the fuel to cover that distance."

"How long will it take to refuel this thing?" Paul grumbled.

Under normal circumstances it would take about forty minutes but Jack had no idea if fuel was readily available at the airbase.

"I had better call ahead and order some," Jack said. He didn't need to remind Paul that the return flight would take about an hour, then at least another ninety minutes before they arrived at Roz' location. That didn't allow for refuelling, so it would be hours before they could possibly reach them.

"Why haven't they contacted us by radio?" Paul asked.

"Maybe it's not operational, we've been through that before, it's no use speculating, at least now we have a signal."

"But what are they doing there?"

"I have no idea," Jack was as surprised as Paul, "I'm guessing it has something to do with that submarine."

The river suddenly widened into a huge lake, Schiffer had taken them through a series of locks which lifted them up to the top of a dam and steering close to shore he seemed to be looking for something. Orlagh was amazed by the scenery; terraces of vines sweeping inland covered the landscape for as far as she could see. The hillside seemed to be carpeted in velvet and then she saw another huge board advertising a famous Port wine company. In amongst the carefully laid out vines sheltered small white buildings, these were houses where farm workers lived, their lives seemingly idyllic to the tourists who cruised the river in luxurious boats.

The sound of the engine changed as the boat slowed, he had found what he was looking for and steered towards land. Turning into a narrow channel that was thick with vegetation the boat disappeared and as the water became shallow it scraped along the bottom, but it wasn't long before the channel widened and the water deepened. Throttling back even more, Schiffer brought the boat to a standstill, letting it nudge gently against the bank.

Jhorge, a dark haired ten year old boy, worked on his father's estate. Today he was responsible for a small herd of goats which he brought down to the water's edge to drink. He was bored, this was a job he'd done hundreds of times before and throwing pebbles into the water he skimmed them expertly off the surface, it was then he noticed a strange bright orange boat. It was nothing like the boats he was accustomed to seeing, there were no passengers onboard, no one to wave at him from the windows or from behind the lens of a camera. As it drew closer he heard the beat of the engine change and he watched as it turned into one of the irrigation channels. Something was wrong, he had never witnessed a boat coming so close to the edge of the lake before and he wondered what it wanted, what business did it have coming onto their land?

Rounding up his goats he climbed back along the path. He felt vulnerable out in the open but as he could no longer see the boat, those on board were unlikely to see him, even so he wouldn't feel safe until he had gained the cover of the vines. Crouching down he let the goats run along the path, they wouldn't stop until they were back in the yard and when the last of them had disappeared he made his way towards the irrigation channel in search of the mysterious boat.

A man appeared on deck shading his eyes against the glare of the sun.

Jhorge crouched lower and watched as the stranger turned towards him, holding his breath he dared not move. He didn't like the look of this man, there was something about him that made his skin crawl. Suddenly he turned and went back into the cabin then after a few moments two women appeared. The first one was tall and slim, she had thick red hair, the second one was smaller and had much shorter dark hair, she also seemed to have bruising to her face and she didn't look happy. His eyes widened when he realised they both had their hands tied behind their backs. The dark haired woman turned and said something to the man who was standing behind her, he couldn't hear what had been said but the man pushed her hard and she fell down. Jhorge stiffened, he didn't like what he'd seen, he had no idea what the women had done but he thought very little of the man's disrespectful behaviour; he'd never seen a man strike a woman before.

Leaving the boat they made their way along the path towards him. Jhorge had to move quickly, he slipped silently through the undergrowth wriggling under the wire which supported the vines then he crawled onto a neighbouring pathway. Holding his breath, he watched as the strangers passed close by and when they were gone he straightened up. Jhorge made up his mind, he would follow them, discover where they were going before running to tell his father.

XVI

Peter O'Reilly was sitting at the desk in his office at the National Museum of Ireland when the call came in. A representative from the American Embassy in Lisbon was about to give him some very disturbing news, his manner was brisk and his straight talking was impersonal and to the point. He told him that Orlagh was missing, having taken to a lifeboat when the survey ship Sea Quest sank in mysterious circumstances. The American refused to comment further when asked to clarify the situation. O'Reilly was told to remain by the phone he would be updated as soon as the details became available.

He was stunned, unable to move or think straight, his mind was momentarily blank. He couldn't understand how a tragedy like this could have happened, modern ships didn't just sink, there had to be more to it than that. This kind of news was the last thing he had expected, Orlagh was supposed to contact him when she had discovered the Torc and was on her way home. Running his hand over his face he breathed in deeply, it was as if he had just been slapped by a giant hand and he was numb. The prospect of the assignment being dangerous had never occurred to him, there were of course risks when free diving especially on a wreck, but Orlagh was a competent scuba diver, besides she was working with a team of underwater experts. The fact that the ship could sink was something that he would never have imagined.

O'Reilly took another deep breath in an attempt to slow his racing heart, his hands were shaking and he could feel his blood pressure beginning to rise. Forcing his mind to work he reached for the telephone on his desk.

"Janet, can you come in here please."

After a few moments she appeared at his door carrying her shorthand pad and a pen.

"Sit down," he gestured to a chair opposite his desk.

Doing as she was told Janet could sense that something was wrong, O'Reilly's face was bloodless and he looked unwell.

"I've just had a call from the American Embassy in Portugal," he began gravely.

She knew this already, having taken the call she had put it through to his office. Briefly he outlined his conversation and she could hardly believe what he was saying.

"Are the rest of the crew safe?" she asked. "Do we know how this happened?"

"I have no idea, they told me nothing more, we can only hope and pray that Orlagh's safe."

Janet nodded in agreement.

"Is there anyone we should contact? I haven't a clue about Orlagh's private life." He looked at her helplessly.

"I don't think there is anyone, she lives alone and has never mentioned her parents or other close family members. I will of course check in the personnel records."

O'Reilly nodded hating himself for knowing so little about his staff.

"Why are the Americans being so vague?"

"I have no idea Janet, none at all."

He looked as vulnerable as a child and all she wanted to do was wrap him up in her arms and comfort him but she remained firmly in her chair.

"You mustn't worry Peter, Orlagh is a very resourceful young woman. I'm quite sure she'll get through this."

Glancing up at her he smiled weakly.

Orlagh was hot and her stress levels were soaring. Schiffer was merciless, he had set off at a ruthless pace and now she was exhausted and irritable. Roz remained silent, having said nothing since leaving the boat, the heat made her light headed and she was stumbling more frequently.

"Can we stop?" Orlagh pleaded.

After a moment's hesitation Schiffer nodded and they slumped down gratefully in whatever shade they could find. He glanced at the women, they were both pale with exhaustion and he cursed himself for underestimating both the severity of the heat and the distance they had to travel. He had led them into a dangerous situation, they were ill provisioned and in no condition to undertake such a long trek. They had no water and were beginning to suffer the effects of heat and dehydration. He could still see the lake in the distance and on more than one occasion had considered turning back. Delaying their progress, however, was something that he could not allow, he had to rendezvous with the others and time was running out fast.

Suddenly something in the distance caught his eye and he scrambled to his feet.

Beyond the terraces where the ground became wild and melted into the hillside someone was sending out a signal using a heliograph. Small pinpoints of reflected sunlight flashed into the valley. Orlagh had seen it too, the signal came every fifteen seconds for two minutes then it stopped. It was obviously a message meant for Schiffer and as she studied him he moved towards them.

"Get up," he growled. Then they continued to climb the hillside.

Jhorge was trailing along behind watching carefully as they rested, he had also seen the signal. He realised then that the strangers were passing through his father's land and it pleased him to think that they would not be staying. Looking in the direction they were going he began to calculate time and distance. It would take them until dusk to reach the spot from where the signal had come and glancing up at the sun he reckoned that would be about two hours. He decided to return home if these people were just passing through he didn't need to follow them any further. Once they were off his father's land they would be in the National Park across the border in Spain.

The fuel bowser finally arrived. It had taken a long time to bring it up from a nearby military installation and Jack was beginning to wish he'd flown the Sikorsky there instead of waiting at the air base. Whilst the fuel was being loaded he filed a flight plan and got permission from the air authority to fly through Portuguese air space. It was late in the afternoon before they managed to get airborne and it would be dark by the time they reached the lifeboat. Pushing the throttles all the way forward Jack urged the Sikorsky to full speed.

The sun dipped closer to the horizon sending elongated shadows across the rocks and then the bandits appeared out of the landscape. They were filthy, their uniforms streaked with sweat and dust, evidence that they had been living rough for some time. Schiffer was relieved to make contact with his countrymen and he spoke loudly in his native tongue. He was first to drink water from the canteen.

"There's no need to keep them trussed up like pigs," one of the men said as soon as he saw Orlagh and Roz with their hands tied behind their backs. Moving towards them he drew a knife from his belt.

"You speak English," Orlagh said as he cut her free.

"Of course, my name is Rudi Mayer." Rudi was a tall man whose fair hair was cropped close to his scalp, he looked smart in his uniform even though it was desperately in need of a wash. Orlagh noticed that all the other men were dressed in the same type of uniform.

"You must be Dr. Gairne."

Orlagh was surprised by his cordial formality he was quite unlike

135

Schiffer, his blue eyes warm and friendly. "We have been waiting for you for quite some time," he continued and she wondered how long they had been on the hillside.

"You don't have time for formal pleasantries give them some water and something to eat." Obviously Schiffer outranked the men and he began organising them into groups before assigning a man to watch over them.

Jack took the Sikorsky in low over the dam skimming the surface of the lake. The high curtain wall holding back the water was a monument to man's ingenuity and command over the landscape. He checked the AIS, the little red light was still flashing steadily on the screen and he made a slight course correction which would bring the helicopter in over the top of the lifeboat.

"There it is," Paul said as he spotted the irrigation channel.

The light was fading fast but the bright orange boat stood out clearly amongst the tall grass and reeds. It looked abandoned, there seemed to be nobody on board. The down draft churned up the water as the helicopter hovered overhead and the grasses waved as if shaken by a giant hand. Jack searched for a clearing, a safe place to land, but there were trees dotted around the lake and the terraces began almost at the water's edge. Suddenly a small boy appeared from along one of the paths, his face turned towards them he waved his arms urgently.

"Is he trying to tell us something?" Paul said as the boy continued to gesticulate wildly towards the path.

Jack kept the helicopter steady, hovering over the boat. "Well I'll be damned, I think you're right."

Turning the Sikorsky in the direction the boy was pointing, Jack eased gently back on the cyclic and the helicopter began to rise. The boy was still waving as they searched the horizon but there was nothing to see amongst the neat terraces.

"Why would they want to go that way?" Paul muttered. "It doesn't make sense, surely they would have stayed with the boat."

"Not according to our little friend." Jack waved his hand out of the side window and eased the hovering machine forward in the direction of the distant hills. "You'd better keep a look out they could be anywhere down there."

They followed the pathway which ran as straight as a railway line between the vines and maintaining an altitude of fifty feet gradually the land beneath them began to rise. Paul was not convinced they had come this way, the landscape was becoming increasingly wild and inhospitable and as they passed over the hilltop they rolled into the valley beyond.

Schiffer saw them coming and had his men spread out across the clearing, they waited in silence their weapons trained skyward as the big orange and white helicopter came towards them. Jack coaxed the machine into a climbing turn and they sailed majestically across the sky. The shadows below were lengthening and it would soon be dark but as they made their return pass Paul saw something.

"What have we here?"

Jack pushed the anti-torque pedals with his feet and the nose came round giving them a better view. "You're right, there's something down there."

They were almost hovering now side slipping slowly along the ridge and Schiffer knew it wouldn't be long before his hiding place was discovered. He glanced at the pile of equipment that had been left in the centre of the open ground and cursed, how could they have been so careless? He wasn't expecting an attack from the air and couldn't understand how they had been located, both women were clean there was no evidence of them carrying a tracking device.

Hidden amongst the rocks his men waited for the order to open fire, the helicopter was unarmed so would be an easy kill, it was designed to carry passengers. The crew on board might have small arms but they would be ineffectual against the hidden ground force. Schiffer was more worried about the possibility of a radio message being sent giving away their position. He waited as the helicopter edged closer.

"Stand by to open fire," he shouted over the increasing noise.

Orlagh was horrified when he gave the order, he had spoken in English. Roz shuffled closer and crouching beside her watched intently as the drama began to unfold. She didn't like the idea of a dozen semi-automatic weapons pointing at her colleagues in the sky, Jack would have no idea what was about to hit him and there was nothing she could do to stop the attack. The helicopter was almost directly overhead and the noise was deafening. The down draft created by the rotor blades caused a mini tornado amongst the rocks sending dust and small stones thrashing against them, they held their breaths and waited. Orlagh covered her ears with her hands as a stream of hot exhaust gasses blasted over them.

"Fire," Schiffer screamed.

From inside the cockpit Paul could hardly comprehend what was happening, hundreds of tiny lights flashed from the darkness between

137

the rocks and as the first rounds began to strike he felt vibrations passing through the soles of his boots. A side window suddenly exploded showering him with fragments of glass, the round continued past his head burying itself in the bulkhead.

"Jesus!" he shouted, "they're shooting at us."

At the same moment Jack responded by throwing the helicopter onto its side, it plunged into the valley. Easing gently back on the cyclic he coaxed the nose up and at the same time pushed the throttles forward. There was a sharp smell of hot oil, something had ruptured but the machine was still responding to the controls. Pushing his foot down on the anti-torque pedal he put the helicopter into a climbing turn then craning his neck for a better view looked back at the hillside. There was movement near the summit but he couldn't identify the force on the ground.

One of the men moved forward from behind a rock and Orlagh watched in horror as he shouldered a long tube-like weapon. She had no idea what it was but he was aiming it at the helicopter. Roz watched as a tiny red light began to flash on a panel beside the man's thumb. He was tracking the helicopter's flight path and her stomach tightened as she saw the little red light change to green, then his fingers tightened around the pistol grip. Flinging herself across the clearing she slammed into him just as he fired the weapon. A bright flash lit up the surrounding area and a missile streaked away into the sky but his aim was spoiled and as they sprawled into the dust the weapon rolled away. Orlagh, frozen with shock looked on, she was unable to move as Roz wrestled with the man.

In the cockpit an alarm sounded and Jack responded immediately as a bright light came speeding up towards them. He just had time to roll away, push the nose down into a steep dive, but the helicopter bucked wildly as the missile found its mark. The force of the impact tore the machine apart and they were thrown around in their seats, the nose lifted as they spiralled out of control. Jack fought desperately with the controls but there was little he could do, the noise inside the cockpit was appalling and the sudden rate of climb pushed them back into their seats. They were now passengers and as the strickened aircraft reached the zenith of its climb it began its death roll back towards earth. With the tail section gone Jack had no yaw control, as the rotor blades turned the cabin went into a contra-spin, so, pushing the throttle controls as far forward as they would go he prayed for extra power. He hoped this would slow their rate of descent and lessen the force of impact.

"Brace yourself Paul," he shouted.

The flight deck was a mass of warning lights and alarms, there was no time to send out a distress signal. It was as much as Paul could do to remain in his seat, he braced his legs, pushing hard against the control panel and gripping the safety harness with both hands as he waited for the impact. He was glad to be wearing a safety helmet his head was bouncing off the bulkhead behind his seat. Suddenly the helicopter slammed into the ground and metal crumpled like paper as it rolled down the hillside. The cockpit began to disintegrate around them and as the windscreen shattered earth poured in as the nose attempted to bury itself into the ground. Spinning rotor blades ploughed into the earth, torn away by the impact splinters bounced over rocks before ripping into the terraces. Grape vines were shredded before the remains of the helicopter came to rest in a smoking heap of scrap metal.

Pain shot through his body as Paul hung in his straps and the silence after the noise was deafening. Hot metal began to creak, expanding with the heat then he heard Jack moving. The helicopter was on its side and before Jack released his harness he braced himself against the flight deck, free of the restraints he worked his way down beside Paul. The cabin had imploded around them and Paul was covered in shards of glass. There was nothing left of the instrument panel, but what worried Jack more was the smell of burning vapours that were escaping from the ruptured fuel lines, the air inside the ruined cockpit was becoming toxic, they had to get out. He fumbled with the harness which held Paul in his seat and with the sudden movement Paul groaned, his face contorting with pain.

"Where are you hurt?"

"Shoulder," Paul managed through gritted teeth. "Probably dislo-cated."

Quickly Jack removed the belt from his trousers then passing it around Paul's chest he managed to immobilise his arm before reaching above his head to release the door. Heaving himself up, he climbed out onto the side of the cockpit, then reaching back in he took hold of Paul and hoisted him up. Paul cried out in agony as they fell to the ground and Jack urged him on until they were a safe distance away from the smoking wreckage, he then glanced back over his shoulder.

They had rolled down the hill having crashed on the edge of the first terrace. The damage to the vines was enormous but at least it had been a relatively soft landing, thankfully they had missed the rocks. The rotor blades had done most of the damage churning up the earth with their motion before breaking up and spinning away in every direction.

Jack reaching down, grasped Paul by his good shoulder and helped him up, he was semi-consciousness and in considerable pain.

"We have to get away from here," Jack told him. "We must move, the scum that shot us down might just come down here looking for souvenirs." He urged Paul along the narrow pathway that ran between the vines the going was easy, they were heading downhill. Glancing back over his shoulder again Jack could see no movement from the hilltop, when it was daylight he was going to go up there but for now they had to find cover.

Suddenly there was a huge explosion and they were thrown forward onto their faces, the vines offered some protection as burning gases swirled around their heads then hot fragments of metal began to rain down. Jack was fearful that the explosion would start a series of fires, the vineyard was as dry as a tinderbox and there was no water nearby.

"Jesus, first the ship now the Sikorsky, our insurance premium will be sky high." Paul tried humour in an effort to reduce his discomfort.

From the hilltop Schiffer watched as the remains of the helicopter exploded.

The night sky lit up momentarily as a huge tongue of yellow flames leapt high into the air and he stared in fascination as the helicopter broke up. When at last the sound of the crash subsided he watched the wreckage burn satisfied that no-one could have survived such carnage. If it wasn't for the American bitch the missile would have vaporised the machine in mid air. He looked down at Roz who was lying curled up at his feet. She had taken a beating and had fought back valiantly, but she was no match for the heavier soldier. Orlagh hated herself for not helping Roz, she had remained hidden unable to take in what was happening around her. She could have done nothing anyway, cursing her gender and size she was startled when Schiffer appeared beside her.

"Go to your friend," he snapped, tossing her a canteen of water.

Jack and Paul remained where they had fallen. Paul's shoulder was throbbing mercilessly, a hot stabbing pain which became worse by the minute. The initial endomorphine rush was now beginning to fade, the body's natural reaction for dealing with pain and shock was failing with every beat of his heart. He was delirious and lying face down, his cheek pressed against the warm soil, the fresh smell of vines rose up on the air around him. Strangely he found this comforting but every now and then the breeze would change direction bringing with it the stench of burning rubber, aviation fuel and reality.

Jack was relieved that the explosion had not set off any more fires and the inferno surrounding the helicopter had almost burnt itself out. The vines in the immediate vicinity were destroyed and lumps of scrap metal and helicopter parts were spread over a wide area, there would be a huge cleanup operation for the hapless farmer in the morning. It was now completely dark, the only light coming from an impressive display of stars overhead. With no light pollution Jack could see constellation after constellation, it was a beautiful sight and laying there on his back, hidden between the vines, he could almost believe he was home on a camping trip.

"You okay buddy?" he whispered not wanting to disturb the silence.

"Thought you would never ask, I'm in agony here, daren't move a muscle."

Jack got to his knees and studied his friend. Gently he ran his hand over Paul's shoulder exploring and probing in an attempt to establish the extent of his injury. "Sorry old pal but if its dislocated I'm going to have to pop it back in." He knew a dislocation was one of the most painful injuries, he was also aware that once it was back in place relief would be instant but first he had to discover what kind of injury he was dealing with. An anterior dislocation would be easy to deal with providing there were no complications with torn tissue or damage to the bone socket.

"Can you feel your fingers?"

"Yes, I have a little too much feeling in this arm at the moment."

That was a good sign, at least there was no damage to nerves or blood vessels.

Jack continued probing, feeling for lumps but fortunately there were none and he was relieved not to be dealing with a more complicated posterior dislocation. That kind of injury almost always required surgery to re-align the bones.

"It looks to me like you have an anterior dislocation," Jack began.

"Okay nurse Harrington, spare me the bloody lecture, just do what you have to do and be quick about it."

Jack outlined the procedure for re-aligning the bones and carefully he removed the belt that supported his arm, Paul winced as Jack took hold of his wrist. Jack didn't want to cause him any more pain but once the procedure was over Paul would hopefully be as good as new. With a sudden movement Jack manipulated the arm and felt the bones pop satisfyingly back into place, Paul groaned and almost blacked out.

Jack laid Paul's arm carefully across his chest and using his belt again as a sling took the weight off the shoulder. He wished he had some NSAIDS, ibuprofen would help ease the discomfort and inflammation but the first aid kit had gone up with the helicopter.

The following morning Jack went to check the burnt out wreckage he studied the structural damage caused by the missile strike. The entire tail section was missing, there was a huge hole just behind the passenger compartment and he didn't want to think about what would have happened if the missile had scored a direct hit. There wasn't much left to salvage and this part of the vineyard was a mess, he would be facing a hefty compensation claim.

Turning towards the hilltop he studied the route. He would have to go up there, whoever had done this might have left some clues as to their identity, maybe he would find evidence that Roz and Orlagh had passed this way. It still puzzled him as to the reason why they left the lifeboat. He sighed loudly then made his way back to where he had left Paul.

"No breakfast I'm afraid," he grinned.

"I take it there's no pain relief either."

"The first aid box has been destroyed along with everything else."

"Never mind," Paul sighed. "It's much better today, you did a good job, it's just stiff and a bit tender." He made a face as he moved his arm out of the improvised sling.

"Don't go calling me nurse Harrington again it almost put me off, you were very lucky, I could have caused you some real pain."

"Did I really call you that?" Paul grinned. "I don't remember, I must have been in a right state."

Their light hearted banter went on for a few minutes longer, it was a good antidote and stress reliever.

"I'm going to check out that hillside," Jack nodded towards the point where the vines stopped and the rocks began.

"Surely you mean we are going to check it out, you're not thinking of leaving me out of your little adventure."

"I don't want to put you out, you do have a sore arm."

"I've had a lot worse, let's get going."

It took them forty minutes to reach the spot where Schiffer and his men had been camped. The area was a perfect lookout post the view across the valley towards the lake was uninterrupted, idyllic, especially in the early morning light. In the centre of the open space they found

142

evidence of a fight and where the dusty earth was churned up there were traces of dried blood. Jack knelt down and ran his fingers lightly over the area then something caught his eye. Half buried in the dust was a silver button and, turning it over between his fingers, he discovered an emblem embossed into its face. It looked like a giant bird of some kind rising up out of flames and underneath he read the words 'Phoenix Legion'. Paul appeared from behind the rocks.

"Look what I've found," he passed a handful of cartridge cases to Jack.

"Standard Military issue, hardnosed," he said and Paul nodded in agreement, then Jack showed him the button.

"Who are the 'Phoenix Legion'?" Paul asked.

"Presumably the guys who shot up our transport."

"Do you think Roz and Dr. Gairne are with them?"

"Maybe," Jack said thoughtfully.

"At least they left us some refreshments." Paul held up a canteen of water and grinned as he took the stopper out then he sniffed at the contents cautiously before taking a mouthful.

The trek back to the lifeboat took them over two hours, it was pointless hurrying, besides Paul was exhausted and still in considerable discomfort. When they arrived on board Jack powered up the radio set and made contact with Ed Potterton. Ed, one of his trusted friends and colleagues was in charge of a ship that was making its way along the coast of Portugal. They had just completed an operation in the Mediterranean.

"If I can locate some fuel we'll meet you in Porto later today," Jack told him.

"Roger that," came the reply.

As soon as he'd signed off Jack went to check the fuel situation. The main tank was almost empty and both the jerry cans were missing. Returning to the cabin he studied the chart that was still laid out on the table and reaching for a pen he began to calculate distances and fuel consumption.

"We don't have enough fuel to make it back," he told Paul when he appeared.

"Can we be sure to get some on the way back to Porto?"

"No, we don't know if that's possible. I've no idea where the river boats operate from, besides, the farmer here must have a supply of diesel, maybe we can buy some from him."

"Well I'm sure not going to ask him, look at what we've done to his grapes."

"I always thought you had a yellow streak running through you," Jack teased.

"In the meantime we have coffee and some emergency rations, so let's have breakfast," popping a pain relief tablet into his mouth Paul went to make coffee.

XVII

News that Archaeologist Dr. Orlagh Gairne from the National Museum of Ireland was missing became a headline story. Released by the American Embassy in Lisbon to the world media, it informed them that both Rosamund Stacey, the ship's electrical engineer, and Dr. Gairne had been kidnapped. The report failed to include the sinking of the Sea Quest or any other details regarding the disaster, however, it did imply that they had been travelling together in Portugal. No radical group as yet had come forward to be linked with the crime. The item went out that evening on the World News and when Jerry Knowles heard he was astonished. He wanted to know more, but it was too late to contact the museum where she worked. Naturally he assumed that her colleagues would have more information.

Going over the story in his mind he knew of no factions or political groups currently operating in that part of the world, besides, what would they want with an archaeologist and an electrical engineer? He wondered how they had come to be travelling together, it didn't make sense, Orlagh was supposed to be working on a ship anchored off the coast of Portugal. He wanted to know if her disappearance had anything to do with the Torc, he was well aware of the disastrous effect it had on people's lives. Perhaps they were the victims of a robbery someone might have discovered they were travelling with such a valuable item.

He sighed loudly, chastising himself for allowing his mind to run away with him.

His ridiculous scenarios were a waste of effort, besides it was a pointless exercise trying to speculate on the reason behind their disappearance. He would have to wait until morning before contacting the museum.

Jack and Paul made it all the way back to Porto with fuel to spare. The farmer who owned the vines they had destroyed turned out to be amazingly reasonable and businesslike. He realised that he could make a legitimate claim for compensation and he also knew the value of his fuel. Jack furnished him with details of his company in America and promised to organise a cleanup operation, he was going to send in a salvage team to recover the remains of the Sikorsky.

Ed Potterton was a huge lumberjack of a man who could easily pass as a world class wrestler.

"Welcome aboard," he said enthusiastically pumping Jack's hand as he stepped onto his ship. He treated Paul somewhat differently, gently grasping him by his good shoulder he grinned. "Still sore eh?"

The Nautical Explorer was the sister ship to Sea Quest, she was identical in every way. Ed took Jack to the ward room whilst a group of men on the lower deck made preparations to bring the lifeboat aboard. Paul went straight to the ship's hospital where an attractive female doctor lavished sympathy on him whilst prescribing more pain killers and an X-ray.

"Sorry to hear about your ship Jack," Ed began. "What the hell have you gotten yourself into?"

Jack told him about the Hudson Bay and the discovery of the atomic warhead he also filled him in with details concerning the sinking of his ship.

"A genuine World War Two sub, you're kidding me Jack!"

"I know how it must sound," Jack sat back in his chair and studied his friend.

"Well, if I'm going to be salvaging the Sea Quest I'll need protection from the Navy."

"I've already spoken to the guys at the Embassy and they agree."

Potterton asked about Orlagh and her role aboard the ship, they also discussed Jack's theory regarding the atomic device. Ed thought him a little crazy especially when Jack shared his thoughts on German Mythology and a group of Nazis called the 'Phoenix Legion'.

The Nautical Explorer got underway just after sundown. Jack was going to remain on board until they reached the spot in the Atlantic where the Sea Quest had gone down. He'd already arranged with the American authority for a naval ship with Anti-Submarine Warfare Combat Systems to be on station, they didn't want to lose another ship.

Early the following morning they spotted the warship and were given the all clear. The Navy had done a sweep of the sea bed, there were no submarines lurking there. The sensitive equipment aboard the Nautical Explorer picked up the sunken Sea Quest, they identified the Hudson Bay but there was also another mass resting on the bottom.

"You didn't tell me there were three wrecks down there," Ed said turning to Jack.

"Let me see," Jack studied the screen. "Can you enhance that mass and give me a report?" he tasked the operator.

The man at the screen began working and after a few moments turned towards Jack.

"It's smaller than both the other hits, about 100 feet long. It's narrow and cylindrical in shape."

"Could it be a submarine?" Jack asked as he glanced at Ed.

"Yes Sir, I can make out a single structure on the deck, it could be a coning tower."

"Could it have been sunk by the Sea Quest?" Ed asked.

Jack had no idea what happened after the torpedo stuck his ship, he was too busy flying the helicopter, he thought he saw the Sea Quest strike the submarine but he couldn't be sure.

"Obviously something went wrong. Ask the Navy to confirm that its dead, our instruments are not sensitive enough to pick up sound coming from that thing."

After a few minutes the report came back confirming that nothing was being emitted by the sub, it appeared to be inert. They were also informed that the sub was lying over at an angle and it appeared to have sustained damage to its bow. They were given the all clear and could go to work as planned.

"We'll check it out when we dive on your ship Jack," Ed told him.

Jack would have liked to have stayed longer, dive on the sub himself, but he had another job to do which didn't involve getting his feet wet.

"Is the helicopter ready to ferry me inland?"

"Ready when you are Jack."

He'd arranged to be dropped off at an airport in Portugal from there he would catch a flight to London then a connecting flight to Dublin. His schedule was tight so he had to get going as soon as possible.

Jerry Knowles wanted answers. Orlagh was missing, he knew that she was on an assignment to recover the Torc from the sea bed and considering his family connections he felt responsible for her. He also thought that the media were not giving out the full story he had to know if she was in possession of the Torc.

"Honestly Jerry we don't have any more information."

Janet thought him a very attractive young man and regretted the fact that there was at least twenty years between them. Orlagh didn't know how lucky she was to have him fussing over her like this.

"There must be more to it, are you certain O'Reilly isn't holding anything back?"

"No," she shook her head, "he wouldn't do such a thing, I understand your concern but we don't have anything else to tell you." She could see how anxious he was and couldn't help feeling sorry for him.

Jerry frowned, she didn't understand, he thought she was obviously unaware of the curse surrounding the Torc. He was worried that Orlagh had been somehow caught up in it. Suddenly O'Reilly appeared from his office and approached the reception area.

"Oh Mr O'Reilly," Janet gasped.

He glanced from his secretary to her visitor.

"This is Mr Knowles," she began, "he's a friend of Orlagh's and he's enquiring after her. I'm just explaining that we have no more information."

"No that's right, we can't help you," he said knowing the recent news broadcast did not match the report he'd been given by the Embassy.

"Did Dr Gairne discover the Torc? Jerry asked loudly.

O'Reilly froze and looked at him quizzically. He wondered what he knew about Orlagh's assignment and why should he be so interested?

"It was my great grandfather who discovered it in the first place," Jerry felt obliged to explain. He would use his ancestor's reputation to his advantage.

"Ah, the famous Sir Geoffrey Knowles," O'Reilly said with a nod, his frown softening. "You're his great grandson eh, why are you here?"

"I'm a student at Trinity, I sat in on one of Dr Gairne's lectures recently."

"I see," O'Reilly said. He wondered how much of what the young man was telling him was true. After the shocking news about Orlagh and the way the Embassy were handling it, he was feeling a little paranoid.

Janet stared at him, she was embarrassed at the way O'Reilly was behaving, he was clearly suspicious of Jerry but she couldn't think why.

"Please forgive me Mr Knowles I'm a little upset by all this at the moment." He saw the way Janet was looking at him and suddenly felt he owed the young man an explanation.

"You haven't answered my question yet," Jerry nodded.

"The answer is that I'm not sure. Dr Gairne was going to inform me once she had discovered the Torc but as yet I've not received that call."

"So she hasn't been in touch with you?"

"I'm afraid not," he shook his head. "I've no idea if she has located it or not. I would have thought it a little too soon anyway she wouldn't have had time to complete her search." It was the first time he had realised that fact and now he was beginning to calm down he discovered that he could think a little clearer.

"It's been a pleasure meeting you Mr Knowles but really I must go.

Leave your details with Janet and we'll contact you as soon as we have more news." He nodded towards Janet before leaving the building. She knew that he would be gone for a couple of hours, he was on his way to meet Jack Harrington at Dublin airport, this piece of information she decided to keep to herself.

Jack Harrington stepped off the flight from London and glanced around the busy airport, this was his first visit to Ireland and he was impressed by what he saw. O'Reilly was waiting for him outside the terminal building and even though Jack had never seen the man before he instinctively knew the tall, middle aged man dressed in a dark blue suit was Orlagh's boss.

"O'Reilly," he said, "Harrington, Jack Harrington." Jack hurried towards him with his hand outstretched.

"Good to meet you Jack, welcome to Ireland".

It was a short drive into the city and on the way they exchanged the usual pleasantries that strangers meeting for the first time often do. Jack learnt that O'Reilly was married to Niamh and both their children now lived in England. It wasn't until they were outside the hotel where Jack would be staying that they actually got down to business.

"We found no sign of the Torc on board the Hudson Bay, but we had only just started excavating inside the ship."

"I guessed as much, Orlagh told me she had been down on the wreck and her work was about to begin in earnest."

"Did she give you any details about what we discovered?" Jack wanted to find out if O'Reilly knew anything about the warhead.

"No, Orlagh didn't go into details, why were there any other antiquities on board?"

"Yes, we found a Roman short sword and a cache of precious stones. Orlagh was going to verify the period from which they came but unfortunately she didn't get the opportunity." He obviously had no idea about what they had found.

"What caused your ship to sink Jack?"

He wondered when he would be asked that question and took his time to consider his answer. "We think it was espionage, probably a deliberate attempt to stop us from salvaging the gold on that ship."

"Why would anyone want to do that?" O'Reilly scrutinised him closely.

"I have no idea at this time, but naturally I assume there's something on board someone doesn't want us to find."

"The Torc?"

"Maybe."

"Well, it doesn't sound possible," O'Reilly shook his head. "Have you any ideas regarding the identity of the organisation behind such an atrocity?" He found it hard to believe that someone would go to such extreme measures.

"I've given that question some serious thought," Jack said, searching for a plausible answer. He wasn't about to tell the man what he really thought or indeed what had actually happened. "It's quite possible that the company who owned the Hudson Bay think they have a greater claim on her than us," Jack frowned, his answer sounded a bit thin even to his own ears so he went on quickly, "it could also be one of our competitors who think they should have the salvaging rights, besides, there's a considerable sum in Nazi gold lying on the sea bed."

"But to sink your ship and risk the lives of your crew," O'Reilly stared at him incredulously.

"Well that's the business we're in I'm afraid. Maybe they only wanted to damage my ship, put us out of action for a while, but the operation went wrong."

"Does this kind of thing happen often in your line of work?" O'Reilly found what Jack was telling him quite unbelievable.

"Let me get you a drink," Jack said. "You look as if you could do with one."

He decided to steer away from this line of questioning.

Jack registered at reception and had his bags taken up to his room, then they went into the bar. He insisted that O'Reilly find a place to sit whilst he ordered some drinks. It was not busy and the atmosphere inside the bar was relaxing. Jack carried two large Irish whiskeys to where O'Reilly was installed and put them down on the low table.

"Now where were we?"

"Espionage and competitors," O'Reilly said helping himself to one of the whiskeys.

"Oh yes, well you have to remember that the gold alone on the Hudson Bay must be worth many millions of dollars and there are also untold ancient artefacts, the Belgae Torc for one. We had only just begun to lift the gold which was lying around the wreck, and in just a couple of days we had recovered over two tons of bullion."

"I see, I had no idea there would be such a vast quantity."

Jack smiled O'Reilly was beginning to accept his story. It was true enough but he wasn't prepared to give him the full facts, besides, he knew very little himself.

"So what happens now?" O'Reilly took a sip of his drink and holding it in his mouth savoured the rich malty flavours.

"I already have another ship on station it will start salvaging the Sea Quest and at the same time continue recovering gold from the Hudson Bay." He kept quiet about the submarine and the Navy warship.

"What about Dr Gairne, any further developments?"

Jack was aware that O'Reilly knew about Orlagh taking to a lifeboat, he couldn't lie about that.

"We discovered the lifeboat about a hundred miles up the River Douro in Portugal."

"What the Devil is she doing there?" O'Reilly raised his voice.

"I have no idea," Jack left out the bit about being attacked and shot down. "We found evidence to suggest that Dr Gairne and a member of my crew had probably been taken against their will across the border and into Spain."

"So the story about them being kidnapped is true then?"

"I'm afraid so," Jack nodded.

"What's the American Embassy doing about it?"

"I guess they have been in contact with the authority in Spain. I expect to have people on the ground in less than twenty four hours."

O'Reilly nodded and took another mouthful of his drink.

"We'll be working in conjunction with the Spanish authorities, I'm hopeful to turn something up quickly. If they have been kidnapped then we'll hear soon enough, there's sure to be a demand of some kind."

"Will your men be starting from where you found the lifeboat?"

"Yes, I assure you we have one of the most experienced trackers in the world on the job if they're out there he will find them."

"What kind of a demand do you anticipate?" O'Reilly asked thinking about a ransom figure.

"It's sure to be connected with the Hudson Bay, so I guess it will be all the gold on the wreck or something along those lines."

O'Reilly nodded his head spinning as he tried to imagine the wealth on board the wreck.

"Why exactly are you here Jack?" Again his mind began to function more clearly.

Jack picked up his drink before answering. "Well, for one, I thought it courteous to report to you in person, given the circumstances. I want to re-assure you and Dr. Gairne's family that everything is being done to locate her and bring about her safe return. Secondly, to let you know that we will continue our search for the Torc and the third reason I've come to Ireland is to talk to someone called Jerry Knowles. Dr. Gairne mentioned him I believe he and I share a common interest."

"I see," O'Reilly studied him. "My secretary Janet might be able to help you there, she should have Mr Knowles details. I'll have her pass them on to you."

"I would be much obliged," Jack grinned.

XVIII

Jack arrived at the museum the following morning. He intended to be there early but the sights and sounds of Dublin were irresistible, so he spent a couple of hours sightseeing, wandering about the city talking to the local people and soaking up the wonderful Gaelic culture. Janet looked up the moment he arrived and she flushed at the sight of him.

"Hi," he said as he breezed casually into the museum, "you must be Janet."

Oh my goodness! she thought. He knows my name.

His fair hair was thick and brushed stylishly back, the stubble on his chin suitably designer and she felt herself going weak at the knees as she drowned in his deep blue gaze. Words from a slushy novel filled her head. Jack was amused by the effect he was having, she looked as startled as a cat, so he waited for her to arrange her emotions.

"Yes but how do you know....," then she remembered, Peter had told her earlier that Jack Harrington would probably be calling in to see her today and cursing under her breath she settled a pleasant smile on her face.

"Welcome to Ireland Mr Harrington," she almost dropped her smile, she sounded so corny.

"Jack," he smiled, "please call me Jack, all my friends do." He almost winked but at the last moment stopped himself, clearly the poor woman was struggling to remain composed as it was.

"Okay Jack." The muscles in her face twitch as she smiled. "I understand you want Jerry Knowles' details."

"That's right I need to talk with him."

"Any news of Orlagh?" She didn't think there would be but she just had to keep him talking, the sound of his voice and his wonderful accent was driving her wild.

"I'm afraid not but I do have people out there looking for her, I'm hoping Mr Knowles will be able to help."

Janet frowned and wondered how he could possibly help, Orlagh hardly knew him.

"Orlagh didn't find the Torc then?"

"No, I'm afraid not," he smiled.

"Would you like to see some?"

"How can I refuse?"

Janet was even more flustered and she felt like an inexperienced teenager. Jack was obviously younger than her but the age gap was not as large as that between her and Jerry Knowles. What was she thinking? She had to get a grip of her tumbling emotions.

"If you would like to follow me," she said a little too quickly.

Janet found him surprisingly knowledgeable he asked well formulated questions about many of the artefacts they had on display. He stopped to marvel at the Book of Kells remarking on the beauty of the illuminations.

"Here is our collection of Celtic Torcs, as you can see there are many different styles," she waved her hand over the arrangement. It was an impressive collection and Janet went through the exhibits explaining that the Torcs on display were discovered all over Ireland.

"That doesn't mean to say they had all been made here," she said. "Some scholars believe that many of the Torcs were made in Britain or component parts could have come from Europe and assembled here, finished off by Irish craftsmen."

"Now that one has to be my favourite," Jack indicated to an elegantly crafted piece.

"That's a first century buffer Torc," Janet leaned towards him until they were just inches apart. "It was discovered in Broighter in 1896 along with several other gold objects."

They studied the Torc in silence and Jack was amazed at the complexity of its design.

"The Belgae Torc is similar than this one, it's made from fine strands of gold weaved together to form a rope-like band."

"Yes," he nodded. "Orlagh showed me a picture it's truly a magnificent piece of jewellery."

"Oh yes," she agreed. "But it's so much more than a simple piece of jewellery."

"Yes I know, I understand the significance of a symbolic piece like this."

She began to feel foolish going on about the objects, what did she know anyway? She wasn't an academic like Orlagh, but then Jack didn't know that. She just hoped he wouldn't catch her out by asking too many awkward questions.

"I had better not take up anymore of your time you must be a busy man."

"Not at all," he lied. "I'm most grateful to you for allowing me to see such wonderful things. You are so lucky to work surrounded by so many beautiful objects and just look at this building." He waved his hand airily above his head.

"Oh yes indeed, I'm privileged alright," she smiled. "Let's get you Jerry Knowles' details."

When they arrived back at the reception area she handed him a slip of paper on which she had written the information, she was tempted to include her telephone number but thought better of it. He thanked her, holding onto her hand as they said goodbye, then she watched him walk away and she thought her heart might break.

"You're an old fool Janet May," she told herself and turning away attempted to gather up the threads of her morning.

It was almost midday when Jack left the museum. Pulling his mobile phone from his jacket pocket he punched in the number Janet had given him. Jerry had just left a lecture at Trinity College and was now making his way into town. He'd been unable to concentrate on his work, there was too much going on in his mind and he was desperately worried about Orlagh.

"Hello, Jerry Knowles," he spoke into his phone as it started to ring.

Jack explained who he was and that Orlagh had spoken about him.

"Is Orlagh okay, have you found her?"

"No, I'm afraid not. I'm in Dublin and would like to meet up with you. Orlagh told me we should get together as we share similar interests."

"Okay," Jerry said with a frown, "I'm almost at St. Stephen's Green, that's near the museum where Orlagh works."

"So am I," Jack said glancing around at the people passing by.

Jerry noticed a tall lean man dressed in jeans, cowboy boots and a smart jacket speaking into his mobile phone, it had to be Jack Harrington and as he called out the man turned around.

"Jerry?" he said his eyes wide with amazement.

"Dublin's a small place."

"Well I'll be damned," Jack smiled as he held out his hand. "It's good to meet you at last Orlagh speaks very highly of you."

Jerry was amused, surely the man was exaggerating Orlagh hardly knew him.

"How about we find somewhere for a spot of lunch," Jerry suggested, his English accent in total contrast to the backdrop of Dublin.

"Sure, sounds great. How about one of those traditional Irish pubs, I've not yet had the opportunity to sample the local brew."

Jerry led him into town and installed him in a suitably Irish pub. He knew the landlord, it was a favourite haunt for students, the food was good and reasonably priced and the happy hour seemed to last all evening.

"What's your connection with Orlagh?" Jerry asked as soon as they were settled at a table and nursing a couple of beers.

"She was on my ship, we worked together."

"So you're the captain of the Sea Quest?"

"No, you've got it wrong," Jack lifted his glass and held it to his lips. Pushing his nose through the pure white cap he found the rich black beer. "I'm not the captain, I owned the ship," he said after tasting the ice cold brew.

"I see," Jerry nodded as he placed his glass carefully on the table. "What happened, how was Orlagh kidnapped? She was supposed to be on your ship."

"Well that's a long story," Jack replied. Sitting back in his chair he studied him carefully and wondered just how much he should tell him about the situation and the mystery surrounding Orlagh.

"Did she discover the Torc?"

"No, I'm afraid we didn't have enough time to excavate the wreck. Did she tell you about the Hudson Bay?"

"Yes of course, we discussed the fact that the Torc was part of the Nazi hoard on board that ship."

Jack nodded, satisfied to be steering the conversation in the right direction. Then Jerry told him about how his great grandfather had discovered the Torc and something of the mystery surrounding the tragic deaths of some of the people who handled it.

"Well I can assure you that Orlagh has not suffered a similar fate, as I told you, we didn't get a chance to find the Torc."

Jerry smiled, relieved that she had not become yet another victim of the curse.

"So, tell me Jack, what happened?"

"Before I decide just how much I can tell you, could you tell me something first?"

Slowly Jerry picked up his glass and took a few mouthfuls, his eyes never leaving Jack he wondered what he meant. Like two boxers before a bout they summed each other up, then after a few moments he made his decision.

"What do you want to know Jack?"

"Tell me about German Mysticism," he began. "I know all about the German fascination with history and their glorious past. I'm also aware that much of it was fabricated by the Nazi regime to heighten patriotism amongst the German population during the Second World War."

"German Mysticism eh?" Jerry was surprised by his request, he didn't see that coming. Taking his time he lifted his glass and took another mouthful of beer before continuing. "Neo-Paganism is I think what you mean but it's not restricted to the people of Germany, it has evolved in all the industrial countries in particular the United States and Britain."

"But the Nazis were great fans of Neo-Paganism," he insisted.

"Yes I agree but you can also include most of Continental Europe to that fan base; German-speaking Europe, Scandinavia, Slavic Europe, Latin Europe and elsewhere. It's even big in Canada."

"I see," Jack said wondering if that were true of the 1930s and 40s. "That pretty much includes all of Europe then."

"The largest Neo-Pagan religion is known as Wicca, though other significantly sized Neo-Pagan faiths include Neo-Druidism, Germanic Neo-Paganism and Slavic Neo-Paganism."

"So quite a diverse religious movement then?"

"Indeed," Jerry nodded enthusiastically. "With wide ranging beliefs, these include for example, Polytheism, Animism and Pantheism just to name a few. Many Neo-Pagans practice a spirituality that is entirely modern in origin whilst others attempt to accurately reconstruct or revive indigenous, ethnic religions as found in historical and folk law sources."

"Would you lads be wanting a refill?" the landlord called out from behind the bar. The men were deep in conversation, but it bothered him to see them nursing empty glasses so he dispatched a barmaid to their table with two fresh pints of Guinness.

"The word 'Pagan,'" Jerry continued once she had gone, "comes from the Latin *Paganus,* this means 'rustic' or 'from the country' and later was also used as 'civilian.'"

"The Christian religion, as I understand it," Jack frowned, "turned the meaning of the word into a derogatory term."

"Yes," Jerry nodded, "you're right. From about the 4th century the word increasingly became to mean 'uneducated non Christian', but it wasn't until the 19th century that the term Neo-Pagan was coined."

"People throughout history who held these beliefs were persecuted and accused of heresy, perpetrators of evil as seen through the eyes of those with Christian beliefs."

"Yes true," Jerry said, "but in modern times thinking has changed, we don't burn witches these days." He paused to enjoy another mouthful of his beer and absentmindedly fingered the menu which was propped up on their table. "Neo-Pagan religions respect the concept of an Earth or Mother Goddess. There are male counterparts such as the Green Man and the Horned God. These Duotheistic philosophies tend to emphasise the god and goddess genders being analogous to that of Yin and Yan in ancient Chinese philosophy."

"So you mean women are held in high esteem?"

"Yes," Jerry agreed, "the complimentary opposites. Many Oriental philosophies equate weakness with femininity and strength with masculinity, but this is not the prevailing attitude in Neo-Paganism Wicca."

"Many Celtic deities were female," Jack said.

"True and of course women could rule, look at Boudicca and Cartimundua for example, they were both very strong female leaders."

"They of course followed the old religion, worshipping natural things like the Mother Earth, the provider and sustainer of life. Women in those times were also druids representing the female philosophy of their beliefs." Jack was caught up in Jerry's way of thinking. He found himself enjoying every moment of their conversation and the beer was good too.

"Of course some claims of continuity between Neo-Paganism and older forms of Paganism have been shown to be spurious, or outright false. Many ideas put forward by the Nazis to inspire the population have since been proven to be pure fabrication or at least only half truths encouraged by leaders to dupe the people into going along with their proposals for war."

"I'm aware of that," Jack said, "it was done in a very clever way, I still find it hard to believe that only a handful of carefully selected men could have had such a hold over so many people."

"You have to understand that Germany at that time hungered for change, they had to break free from the crippling restrictions imposed on them by the Versailles Treaty that had been put in place at the end of the First World War. They thought the only way they could develop as a nation was to conquer Europe but unfortunately once they created the monster, the monster took over. It soon became clear that there was no going back but by restoring the people with their glorious past the Nazi regime could paper over the cracks that were beginning to appear in their rationale."

Jack studied him, digesting what he had just said and Jerry paused before continuing.

"The Nazi leaders were masters at conducting psychological games, they played on their history, twisting and turning it into something far grander than it was. They added bits which were used to convince the people that they were doing the right thing.

Take the Aryans for example, they were supposedly a superior race, demigods built in the image of man, pure Germans, a race designed to lead them to greatness, they were supposed to last for a thousand years."

"The Third Reich, the Nazi ambition to revive the Holy Roman Empire."

"Yes," Jerry nodded. "The Roman Empire was considered to be the First Reich and the German Empire the Second. The Third Reich succeeded the Weimar Republic and ended with Germanys defeat in World War Two." Jerry reached for his glass but it was empty again.

"What was the Weimar Republic?" Jack asked before ordering more Guinness.

"Weimar was the cultural centre of Germany in the late 18th and 19th centuries. It was the capital of the grand duchy of Saxe-Weimar-Eisenach." Their beers arrived and Jerry continued. "In 1918 the German National Assembly met in the city and drew up the constitution of the new Weimar Republic, but eventually after facing constant political and economic crisis it was overthrown by Hitler."

"Could it have possibly continued after the war?"

"The Third Reich?"

"Yes, is it possible that some kind of breakaway party rescued their ideals from the confusion at the end of the war?"

Jerry considered his answer as he picked up his glass. What was Jack getting at, was this the reason for his visit? "I guess it's a possibility, some groups tried to keep the ideals alive, but you have to understand, at the end of the war Germany was totally defeated and in terrible economic crisis. Without the backing of the people everything they stood for was virtually worthless."

Jack nodded and reaching into his pocket produced the button that he'd found on the hillside in Portugal. "What do you make of this?"

Jerry studied it for a few moments, turning it over in his hand. "The Phoenix Legion," he said with a frown.

"I picked it up recently," he told Jerry about his trip to the terraced vineyard in Portugal but left out the part about the destruction of his Sikorsky.

"So you think Orlagh has been taken across the Portuguese border into Spain?"

"Yes I do and I think the group who has kidnapped her along with a member of my crew are connected with a continuing Third Reich."

Jerry looked up at him.

"Rising from the flames, quite poignant don't you think?" Jack continued.

"It was supposed to last for a thousand years but it collapsed after only twelve, by the end of 1945 it was all over. Why do you think Orlagh has been kidnapped by this faction?"

Jack told him about the Nazi gold on the Hudson Bay but left out details regarding the atom bomb and the fact that the Sea Quest had been sunk by a German U-Boat.

"To answer your question about a continued Third Reich," Jerry said, "there could be a group out there who believe in what the Nazis started. There are groups such as the Aryan Brotherhood, a Nazi prison organisation, there is also the Wolf pack Brotherhood somewhere in Scandinavia. There are hundreds of groups who believe they are keeping the old ideals alive."

"I believe that the 'Phoenix Legion' is another one and I'm convinced they have Orlagh but at the moment I've no idea why."

"Could it be that this organisation is after the Torc? If what you say is true and they are a continuation of the wartime faction, then they must be aware of the Torc, it was a coveted possession of the Nazi regime. Maybe they think Orlagh has access to it, perhaps they aim to use her as a bargaining tool, the ransom could be the Torc."

"I hope that's not the case as I have no idea where it is, neither does Orlagh."

"Would you lads like to order some food?" the landlord called to them from behind the bar.

Twelve hours later a crack team of mercenaries were landing on a hillside above the site of the crashed Sikorsky. They were made up of ex-servicemen from both sides of the Atlantic who worked and trained together to the highest standards. Dropping from helicopters that hovered above the hilltop they merged with the landscape the moment they hit the ground. Jack employed these men for a multitude of tasks, each one a specialist in his field, not only were they used as muscle but Jack exploited their individual talents. There were explosive experts amongst them, communications and I.T. specialists all hand-picked by Jack and recently they had all been trained to dive and fight underwater using the most up to date equipment. Sometimes they were called on to provide personal protection services and were occasionally hired by both the British and U.S. governments. Special operations were what they were good at and Bob Sharpe, known as 'Razor' was leading the team. Razor was an explosives expert who had served twenty two years in the British Army. He had spent most of his career in a Parachute regiment but before that had trained as a Royal Engineer, specialising in steel fabrication and welding, before going into Ordinance and Explosive Devices. It was in O.E.D. that he learnt to manufacture and deal with all kinds explosives.

Jack had briefed his men by video link so they were fully aware of the situation.

It was their task to seek out and secure the group who had not only destroyed his Sikorsky but were also suspected of kidnapping the women from his crew.

The sun had just emerged from below the horizon as the last of the helicopters delivering their cargo disappeared from view. Razor organised his men and gathering up his equipment Joe MacLeod sniffed around the perimeter of the enclosure like a bloodhound. He was searching for clues about the men who had previously held this location. Joe was one of Jack's most trusted friends they had known each other since childhood and never missed the chance to go off fishing and hunting together.

Joe was a native North American Indian, his tracking skills were second to none and he could live off the land as easily as shopping at a supermarket. His skills were not however restricted to outdoor pursuits, he was a highly talented I.T. expert who had designed and built many of the computer programs used in government offices and other high profile businesses. It was one of his jobs to head up the team of computer experts employed at head office in New York.

He was not a big man but he was all Red Indian. When standing tall he barely reached five feet, his long straight hair was as black as the night sky and his intelligent eyes were equally as dark. He was strangely eccentric, which could easily have been mistaken for madness, sometimes he could be moody and difficult, but he was generally popular with everyone who knew him. His great grandfather was responsible for his name. Arthur James MacLeod had left the shores of his homeland for America during the first gold rush, but unfortunately his prospecting yielded very little in the way of wealth. The work was arduous often taking place under the most difficult of circumstances, so MacLeod found distraction by taking a Native Indian bride this was closely followed by the arrival of a child. The immigrant from Scotland had been a huge bear of a man but Joe inherited none of his genes, all he had to show for his Scottish lineage was a penchant for wearing a MacLeod tartan kilt and his great grandfather's sporran. Christened by his comrades 'Little Big Mac', he was more commonly known simply as Mac.

Mac was rummaging amongst the rocks and now had a pretty good idea of what had taken place here a couple of days earlier, after consulting with his spirit guide Mac appraised Razor with the details.

"The group we are seeking consists of thirteen men and two women," he began, "twelve of the men were camped here for two days then a man and two women joined them."

Razor listened without interruption, his eyebrows rising slowly as the drama unfolded. It always amazed him at how detailed and animated Mac became when delivering his narratives. He sometimes wondered if the little Indian used embellishment for his own pleasure or did he really see every detail.

"The helicopter would have been totally destroyed if it wasn't for one of the women; she risked her own life to disrupt the launching of the missile."

"What do you mean Mac?"

He led Razor to the spot where the man with the launcher had crouched to take aim. "This is where they fought," he waved his hand over the area of disturbed earth,

"Jack also stopped here." Crouching down he ran his fingers lightly over the boot prints in the dust. "He did this," Mac glanced up at Razor then he stood up rubbing his hands together.

"Jack told me he found a button which had most likely been torn from a uniform."

"The woman was beaten here, there are traces of blood in the earth."

Razor took a closer look but was unable to see any marks that could be attributed to blood.

"She lay here for a long time, many hours, probably all night but this is where her companion waited," he indicated to a boulder which conveniently made a natural seat.

"Okay Mac, so the women were here. Which way did they go?"

"South East," he nodded towards a path winding down into the valley.

Razor scanned the horizon and frowned. "That way leads to the Spanish border."

"Yes," Mac nodded. "Los Arribes del Duero Natural Park," his accent was flawless.

The region separating Portugal from Spain was wild and isolated, a perfect place in which to disappear.

"Why head towards Spain?" Razor asked, peering into the wilderness.

"Why not?" Mac shrugged. "Perhaps they have allies there."

Razor nodded but remained silent.

"The men we seek may be meeting someone who could make them become invisible."

Razor looked at him. "Explain," he said.

"They have something which doesn't belong to them so it's natural to assume that someone will come looking for them."

"True, but haven't they already destroyed the search party?" Razor said nodding towards the wrecked Sikorsky.

"They know the crew survived, they found no bodies," he continued. "Maybe they are thinking a radio message could have been transmitted before it crashed."

"True but we are speculating, we don't know for sure what they are thinking."

"Put yourself in their situation, would you take a chance on them not sending out a signal?"

Razor nodded but said nothing, Mac was right, he would want to get as far away from this place as possible.

"They left here before sunrise and went at speed."

"Then lead on," Razor gave the order to move out.

Jack was on the next flight out of Dublin. As the aircraft levelled off at the top of its climb he relaxed and loosened his seat belt, he was sorry to be leaving Ireland so soon but he had to get back to Spain. Getting a seat on a flight to Santiago de Compostela was easy enough he also managed to arrange for one of his helicopters to pick him up from the airport. It would ferry him to rendezvous with Bob Sharpe and his team. He didn't really need to be in on the ground, he could very easily have run the operation from the control room on the Nautical Explorer, but he wanted to be part of the action. He felt responsible for Roz and Orlagh, they had been lost on his watch, besides, he had to get even with the bandits who destroyed his Sikorsky.

His conversation the previous day with Jerry Knowles had proven very useful and now many of the gaps in his knowledge had been filled. He had also questioned Jerry about the 'Phoenix Legion' and other fanatical groups but he seemed to have little knowledge of groups that could be operating in northern Spain. He also discovered that he liked Jerry very much, he could learn a great deal from the young man. He was the type of person he liked to employ in his organisation and as soon as he worked out where the lad might fit in he was going to offer him a job. Jack was sure that having had his interest aroused Jerry would dig deeper.

Jack allowed his thoughts to drift back to the sights and sounds of Dublin, once this was over and he'd found Orlagh, he promised himself that he would return to Ireland for an extended visit.

They had cleared the valley and were now making their way up over the next range of hills. Suddenly Mac halted, he was not happy. Going forward alone he became as cautious as a sniffer dog as he made his way along the narrow track. Razor allowed the rest of his men to relax and take a comfort break. Mac inched slowly forward his eyes darting from rock to rock, the hairs on the back of his neck erect, this was a clear indication that all was not well.

Straining his eyes he searched the distance but could see nothing out of the ordinary. This wasn't good sniper country, there was too much cover and the pathway winding its way around the rocks allowed few opportunities for a clear shot. He didn't think they were about to be attacked, the area was not ideal for an ambush either, but mines and booby traps could easily have been laid along the track. A whole number of anti-personnel devices could be employed and Mac was determined to check out the way ahead. As he walked cautiously forward he spotted a trap, he was right, there was an almost invisible nylon wire stretched between the rocks on either side of the path. In the darkness it would

164

have been impossible to spot and once tripped would set off an explosion that was not designed to kill but to maim. It would be sufficient to tear off a lower leg or an arm just enough damage to incapacitate a man, the unfortunate victim would then require immediate medical attention which would tie up at least another man thus removing two men from the group. This was an old ploy designed to weaken a force, slow up its progress, it could even stop an army from moving forward by destroying its morale. This type of guerrilla tactics were to be expected, Mac knew that eventually they would run into a trap, the only thing he was not sure of was the complexity of the device, he was just about to discover what kind of a group they were up against.

He whistled sharply, the warbling sound of an alarmed bird. Razor heard the signal and knew that something was wrong so ordering his men to take cover amongst the surrounding rocks he went forward. He was not yet sure what they were up against but at least his men would be ready to respond if they were needed.

"What is it?" he whispered as he came up beside Mac.

Mac was crouching beside a huge rock, his weapon still slung across his shoulder.

"Booby trap," he pointed towards the fine line that was pulled tight across the path.

At first Razor could see nothing. Straining his eyes he scanned the way ahead and eventually found what Mac had seen.

"Got it," he whispered.

The line was attached to a small green box which had been secured to a rock by cable ties.

"Just large enough to rip away a calf muscle or knee cap," Razor said. Carefully he withdrew his knife and made the device safe.

"Crude but effective," Mac nodded. They would have to be careful, there was sure to be more.

Continuing on at a slower pace, the group spread out line astern so if there was an explosion only one of them would be caught in the blast. By midday they had cleared the hill having discovered two more devices, now they were in open country and now Mac was worried about snipers. The men remained spread out and were silent as they moved quickly over the rough terrain they were still several miles from where they expected to meet Jack. Suddenly there was a sharp crack and a huge piece of rock erupted from a boulder. One of the men cried out in agony, his elbow shattered by the explosion, then in a choreographed movement they all dropped flat to the ground.

"Did anyone see a muzzle flash?" Razor called out.

The attack came as a complete surprise none of them had seen a thing. Mac was a few metres ahead of the others this put him in an exposed position. For the moment his best chance of avoiding detection was to remain completely still but he knew this was only a temporary respite because the sniper was sure to pick him out.

Although they were pinned down, there had been no other shots so Mac concluded that the sniper must be operating alone from a position some distance away.

Ahead lay an open area of scrubland which was strewn with rocks and very little vegetation, it ran level for about a mile before rising up into the hillside which was covered by a thin layer of green. Stunted trees and bushes clinging to the poor soil offered the sniper scant cover.

"I'm going to move forward," Mac shouted back over his shoulder. He wanted to reach the cover of two large rocks which lay a few metres ahead, but in order to achieve that he would have to draw attention to himself, he was about to became the primary target.

"Watch for a muzzle flash, I intend doing this only once."

He would have to be quick the sniper was using a .50 calibre rifle which was capable of rapid fire. If hit by an incoming round there wouldn't be much left to send back to his poor old ma. Suddenly with the agility of an Olympic sprinter, Mac launched himself forward and a heavy calibre shot rang out. The impact of the round was like a mini explosion and the rock in front of him disintegrated into shards like cut glass. Diving for cover, Mac was able to avoid most of the splinters, but his heart was hammering against his ribs. He thrived on the adrenalin rush and turning his head he grinned back at Razor. No one had seen a flash, the sunlight was too bright and the hillside too distant.

Mac peering between the stones lay on his stomach and carefully surveyed the damage caused by the incoming round. His computer like brain began making calculations, his eyes darting between their position and the distant hillside. He pulled a pair of binoculars from his back pack and scrutinised the way ahead but it was no good, there were hundreds of places in which a sniper could remain concealed. They had to locate his position, they couldn't afford to stay pinned down for long, the men they were chasing were already many hours ahead. Razor was also searching the skyline, he knew they stood little chance of locating the sniper using binoculars, he would have to fire his weapon again, only then would they stand a chance of finding his hiding place.

Daniel Minogue, known as Kylie, sensibly kept his head down as he rummaged through his back pack. He pulled out an egg shaped object and laid it down carefully on the ground in front of him then he produced a mini joystick which he connected to a laptop. Arranging these things around him, he flipped open the laptop and booted it up before reaching for the fist sized egg. Running his fingers lovingly over the smooth surface he felt for the button which activated a tiny motor then as the shell opened a tiny dragon fly drone was revealed. Lifting it carefully from its protective casing he held it in the palm of his hand taking in every detail. The drone was his own design, constructed specifically for surveillance and delicate spying missions. The lens built into the bug eye was the latest in micro camera technology and there was also a tiny but highly sensitive microphone which he could use to listen in on conversations. It was capable of picking up sounds from a considerable distance. The screen on his laptop was now activated and running his fingers over the keys, Kylie tuned into the frequency that was being transmitted by the drone. With the forward facing camera now activated he made a few adjustments sharpening up the resolution before gripping the joystick and then the drone came alive.

Unfolding like an insect stirring from hibernation it flexed its body, its wings becoming a blur, then after a few moments it lifted effortlessly into the air. There was hardly a sound as it hovered a few feet above Kylie's head. He glanced up and grinned as if acknowledging an old friend then with a flick of the joystick sent it out through the air towards Mac.

Mac looked up as the dragonfly buzzed around his head and he smiled before whispering co-ordinates which Kylie picked up on his earphones. Feeding the information into the laptop Kylie flew the drone out across the dusty plain vectoring in on the position that Mac had given him. The information was based on triangulating the flight path of the two incoming rounds this was a good starting point from which the drone could begin its search.

Bridget was a French Canadian who had spent much of his childhood living in New York. He had joined the Marines eighteen years earlier and had served on some of the largest ships in the U.S. Navy. His real name was Francois Bardot and he was a crack shot who had served his time in Iraq working with the army as a sniper. He had met Jack whilst in Iraq and when his tour of duty was over had joined Jack's company.

"Bridget," Razor called, "set up the AS50."

"Roger that," he didn't need to be told twice. The AS50 was British made and it was his favourite weapon, it enabled the operator to engage targets over long distances with pin point accuracy using explosive or incendiary ammunition. Bridget had the highly transportable rifle set up and ready for use in under three minutes, then peering through the optical sights targets over a mile away became clearly visible. He made some fine adjustments to the bipod which supported the weapon then leaning in against the butt waited for further instructions.

Kylie had the bug over the target area by the time Bridget was ready to fire but as yet he had been unable to locate the sniper. The drone began to fly circuits over the co-ordinates that Mac had given him and adjusting the lens on the tiny camera Kylie kept his eyes fixed on the computer screen.

The rest of the men waited patiently, they could do nothing they were effectively pinned down, anyone moving risked having an exploding shell fired at him and they were all well aware of the destructive capabilities of that unwelcome scenario.

Kylie manoeuvred the bug to the next sector of its search pattern then suddenly something caught his eye. Hovering forty feet above the ground he focussed the lens and zoomed in.

"Bingo," he muttered, "got him folks." He began tapping commands into the keyboard and a string of numbers appeared on the screen. Reading them out clearly Bridget dialled the information into his sight, making fine adjustments which positioned the AS50's barrel with digital accuracy. Carefully he peered through his optical sight but still could see nothing of the target so settling down he waited patiently for his eyes to become accustomed to the stillness.

"He's right there under the bush by the outcrop of rock, I can see him clearly from the air," Kylie told him.

Bridget focussed the high powered telescopic lens until finally he was able to identify the target. The man hiding in the bushes had no idea that he'd been spotted, the air around him was still and hot, there had been no movement from the target area for some time and he was becoming bored. They were playing the waiting game, he knew that eventually the men he had pinned down would have to make their move or at least wait until it was dark before breaking cover. What they didn't know was that he had thermal imaging capabilities so there would be no escape.

At that moment Bridget completed dialling in the parameters based on the information that the drone had sent back and was now preparing to fire. Exhaling calmly he steadied himself before stroking the trigger and moments later the man hidden in the distant bushes ceased to exist. The incoming round struck the barrel of his rifle and exploded, he was killed instantly.

Hovering forty feet above the scene the drone took it all in and transmitted spectacular pictures of the devastation, Kylie zoomed in closer to confirm the kill but it wasn't really necessary, there was little left to see. Bridget was up on his feet, the men around him following suit and a few seconds later Razor gave the order to move out. Kylie and Bridget were left to follow up the rear once they had packed their equipment away.

Twenty minutes later they arrived at the spot where the sniper had been hiding.

The men were more interested in the weapon than the remains of the gun man, but Razor took a closer look. The sniper was wearing a grey coloured uniform, his jacket adorned with silver buttons which were embossed with a bird rising up from the flames. Jack had already told him about the button he'd found on the hilltop along with everything he knew about the 'Phoenix Legion'.

Orlagh heard the shot which rumbled through the air like distant thunder, there was no mistaking this one. She thought she'd heard two earlier but couldn't be certain. They were holed up in a huge cave that was situated halfway up a hillside. It looked out over a valley that was flushed with water tumbling angrily over huge rocks, there wasn't much of a riverbed the white water simply crashed where it pleased, sending a fog like spray high into the air. Inside the cave the noise reminded Orlagh of a metro train approaching a station.

There were two entrances, a huge opening at the front which was accessed by the wide flat plateau and a smaller gap between the rocks at the back. They had been forced to climb up to the main opening from the valley floor below it had taken them the best part of an hour to reach it. The ascent had been hard work and now exhausted they were glad to rest. At the rear of the cave, where the rocks parted they had a view over the valley. The drop was sheer, a chasm which fell into the boiling cauldron below, the only way up to this opening was by scaling the rock face using climbing equipment. The cliff continued to soar dizzily upwards towards the summit which was lost against the backdrop of a brilliant sky and thick foliage.

Orlagh was fascinated when she discovered traces of ancient cave paintings etched into the walls. She would have liked to investigate further, but unfortunately most of the archaeological evidence had been destroyed by Schiffer and his men when they took up residence using the cave as some kind of storage facility.

Roz was hurting, the injuries to her face were sore and her head was

169

throbbing mercilessly. One of her eyes had swollen shut and she was still suffering from dizzy spells. Orlagh, full of concern, glanced at Roz who had collapsed with exhaustion onto a box with her back against the wall. An ugly bruise stained her cheek and was spreading over her neck, Orlagh worried that Roz might have suffered a fractured skull, from the look of her ashen face Orlagh felt sure that her cheek bone or eye socket was damaged beyond mere bruising.

Roz was lucky not to have suffered a broken jaw the beating she had taken for spoiling the aim of the missile launcher far outweighed the crime. At first Orlagh thought that Schiffer was going to finish her off, Roz slowed their progress and if it wasn't for a man offering his help, she was certain that Roz would have been left for dead. Orlagh knew that a helicopter had been ordered to pick them up she had overheard one of them talking into a radio set. He'd sent out a message in German but some of the words he used were English and with her limited knowledge of the language she had managed to put the message together. Orlagh had no idea how long it would be before the helicopter arrived. Roz had told her Jack would never leave them, she was convinced that he was already on his way. Orlagh wondered if that were true and would he get there in time. The shot they heard earlier seemed to confirm what Roz had said and from the way the men around them were reacting it seemed they were expecting trouble. Orlagh had no idea why this was happening, Schiffer and his men refused to answer any of her questions and the further they went into the wilderness the more concerned she became.

Razor and his men re-grouped at the base of the hill. Here the vegetation was scarce, the poor quality soil could only sustain the hardiest of plants and out on the plain it was as barren as the surface of the moon. They would have to go over the hill, but there was a larger one waiting for them on the other side, Razor felt sure that was where the kidnappers were holed up. They had about thirty six hours head start and calculating the distance as he studied the terrain, he pinpointed a location where he might expect to find them.

"We must go over the top," Mac said. "To go around will take too long."

"There is sure to be more traps waiting for us," Razor eyed the narrow pathway which seemed to dissolve amongst the rocks.

Mac was also expecting more traps it was an obvious scenario, one he would have set if the roles had been reversed.

"We must be careful."

"You're the one in front so if you happen to tread on a mine be sure to let the rest of us know about it," Kylie grinned.

"Up your kilt," Mac grumbled.

Their banter was in good humour every man in the group knew the dangers and accepted them without question. If any one of them were severely injured the likelihood of survival this far from civilisation would be slim, it would take a medevac helicopter team hours to reach them. They had all been in this situation many times before and were well aware of the risks.

"Right men, let's go," Razor gave the order to move out. He looked at the man with the shattered elbow and was met with grim determination the only way to keep this soldier from moving forward was to remove his legs.

The helicopter created a hellish storm of swirling gasses and dust particles as it came into land. Orlagh held her hands tightly over her ears and turned her face away, although they were inside the cave there was still the risk of being pebble dashed by small stones. As soon as the rotor blades stopped turning men went to work rolling drums of fuel towards the machine and loading supplies from the cave. Orlagh watched the activity going on around her, obviously this place was some kind of transition point. She wondered how Schiffer and his men had managed to get all the supplies to the cave, there was no obvious access from either the river or the valley below, the only way in was on foot or by air, the terrain was much too rough for trucks, besides it was a long way from the nearest road. She had no idea where they were going and every attempt at conversation with the men around her had been met with a stony silence. So much fuel was going into the helicopter that it didn't take a fool to work out that they were going on a long flight. She knew they were in northern Spain, so where next? Questions ran around inside her head, curiosity taunting her mercilessly.

Roz looked as if she were asleep she was still wearing the waterproofs she had taken from the lifeboat. Orlagh had found her set much too warm under the sun and had managed to exchange the fluorescent top for a grey jacket like the men wore. It was still hot beneath its rough weave but at least not as suffocating as the plastic brightly coloured waterproofs. Orlagh was worried that Roz had become dehydrated.

"Here," she passed Roz a water bottle. Roz drank deeply before wiping her mouth with the back of her hand. "What do you think will happen to us?" Orlagh asked.

Roz looked up at her, light coming from the mouth of the cave formed a halo around Orlagh's head, it made her appear ethereal and Roz had to blink hard in order to see her more clearly. "I have no idea," she lisped through swollen lips. "We just have to stay alive until Jack comes." She was confident that he was on his way but Orlagh didn't share her optimism.

"I guess once they have finished loading that thing we'll be taken out of here," Orlagh glanced towards the helicopter which stood beyond the entrance.

"Don't worry," Roz moved, groaning with the effort, her bruised muscles had stiffened. "He will be here, besides I get the impression they don't want to harm you."

Orlagh frowned and wondered what had made her say such a thing. "How can you be so sure Jack will come, didn't you see the way his helicopter crashed?"

Roz remained silent for a moment and closing her eyes willed herself to remain calm. She was as frightened as Orlagh but didn't want to show it.

"Didn't you hear those shots?"

"I think I heard one."

"There were three," Roz said positively. "This lot left a sniper at the bottom of the first hill, he fired two shots."

Orlagh looked up her eyes wide with concern, she had no idea that a trap had been set.

"Look, none of this matters, Jack will come and I don't think he's far away."

The helicopter was finally fuelled up and ready to go. Schiffer had his men clear the area of fuel drums and discarded equipment before having a final word with the pilot. When they were finished he strode confidently into the cave.

"Get up," he ordered.

Orlagh rose to her feet, she was terrified at what he might do. "Where are you taking us?"

"We are going for a little ride," he grinned. "Don't worry, I'm sure you will find our destination fascinating."

Roz remained silent as she considered the possibility of escape. They had been kept out of the way inside the cave and she was still dressed in brightly coloured clothing, there would be little chance of them simply walking away, she didn't blend in too well with her surroundings.

XX

Ed Potterton was sitting in the control room on board his ship the Nautical Explorer, his eyes fixed on the computer screen as an ROV approached the wreck of the Hudson Bay. The picture was grainy and of poor quality at first but as the ROV approached the wreck it became clearer. This was the first time Ed had seen the Hudson Bay and he was amazed to find the upper deck and bridge section in such remarkably good condition. It was hard to believe that the ship had lain on the bottom of the ocean for over seventy years.

As the ROV swept over the starboard side his eyes widened and he moved closer to the screen. There was a gaping hole in the side of the ship, Jack had told him to look out for blast damage but he didn't imagine he would encounter anything like this.

"This can't be right," he mumbled to himself. "How the hell could that have happened?"

The man at the controls kept the ROV stationary, hovering just above the damage its powerful lights hardly penetrating into the gloomy interior of the ship, clearly someone had been there before them.

"Take it in," Ed said. "We need to get a closer look."

It was as if the thick plates forming the hull had been sliced through with a hot knife. The edges were clean, each section peeled back like the skin of a banana. The damage could not have been caused by a blast it must have been made by using a process with infinitely more control. The rest of the hull and superstructure remained undamaged and Ed began to consider every underwater cutting process available in an attempt to solve the mystery.

"It can't have been done by a mechanical method," he said thinking aloud. "It would have taken some time and a lot of effort to cut a hole that size."

"Looks as though it's been lasered," the ROV pilot said.

Ed scratched his chin and thought for a moment before realising that his observation wasn't as farfetched as it had initially sounded. A thermal cutting process must be the answer.

The ROV descended slowly into the chasm and Ed was able to get a closer look at the smoothly cut edges. It was clear that whatever had cut its way into the ship hadn't stopped once they were through the hull, the bulkheads and corridors had also been sliced through resulting in a shaft going right into the heart of the ship. The ROV dropped slowly into the hold, its powerful spotlights illuminating the storage area.

"There's nothing there," the pilot murmured. "We're supposed to be looking at an atomic warhead."

Ed studied the screen in silence, his brow a deep furrow as he tried to make sense of what he was seeing. Glancing down at the photograph Jack had given him he could see a steel box that was strapped to a pallet, it was lying on its side propped up against the bulkhead. Ed had no idea how big it was, there was nothing by way of scale to compare it with, but it must have been quite a size judging by the hole cut into the side of the ship.

"There's nothing down here, the hold is empty."

"Someone's cleaned up pretty well," Ed nodded. "We had better document this, have a good snoop around, make sure the camera is running and get some shots of the damage to the hull. I'd like to know how they did that."

The ROV pilot nodded and began making adjustments to the controls. Ed made his way up to the communications room on the upper deck and put a call through to Jack.

Jack Harrington was on the ground at Santiago de Compostela airport in northern Spain. He had just stepped off a flight from Dublin and was heading across the concrete apron towards a waiting helicopter when his mobile phone began to ring.

"Hi Jack," he recognised Ed's voice instantly. "We've just gained access to the Hudson Bay and her hold is empty."

"What do you mean empty Ed?"

Ed began to explain what he'd found. "It looks like some kind of high tech cutting equipment was used, probably laser."

"Must have had some heavy lifting equipment too," Jack said. "They were damn quick we were only there a couple of days ago."

"We've seen nothing out of the ordinary, no large surface vessels scuttling away. I'll check with the Navy see if they picked anything up."

"What about the sub, have you checked her out yet?"

"Not yet Jack, I'll get the ROV over there as soon as we've finished in the Hudson Bay."

"Okay Ed, keep me informed on the sat phone I'll soon be out of range on the mobile."

Jerry Knowles had no lectures timetabled, which was a blessing because he could think of nothing else but the conversation he'd had with Jack Harrington.

Jack was convinced that Orlagh had been kidnapped by some kind of Neo-Nazi secret society but the whole idea sounded unreal. Opening his laptop he booted it up and went straight to Google where he typed in 'secret societies', then he clicked on the first link.

'The Nazis and Bolsheviks, British security forces, the founding fathers of America and the Vatican have all justified their actions, for the good or for the ill, by claiming the mystical ideals for secret societies.'

He flicked through a few more sites, many of which he'd seen before, but one caught his eye so he opened it up.

'Nazi archaeology was rarely conducted with an eye for real, pure research, but was a propaganda tool designed to both generate nationalistic pride in Germans and provide scientific excuses for conquest.'

This is what Jack had said, he'd got the impression that Jack knew a lot more than he was willing to let on. Clearly he wanted to expand his thinking by questioning and confirming his own ideas. Jerry had found this amusing at first, he was more than willing to indulge the American, but as the evening went on he became influenced by the idea that Orlagh had been kidnapped by a force much more dangerous than they had first thought.

Orlagh and Roz were pushed into the helicopter then the others crowded in around them. There was enough room for them all, but in the confined space Orlagh felt claustrophobic especially beside the unwashed men with their dusty, coarse uniforms. The helicopter shuddered as it rose up into the sky and the noise inside the cabin become unbearable as the pitch of the engines increased. Pushing her hands over her ears, Orlagh looked out of the window. She could see nothing at first as the dust storm caused by the down draft obliterated her view. They ascended into clearer air and she could make out the jagged peak of the hilltop and the vegetation cloaked plateau, but it was impossible to see the entrance of the cave from this angle.

They drifted slowly along the valley until the white water below turned into a wide river flowing gently through the Los Arribes del Duero Natural Park. She could now see the dam which had caused the river to back up and form a huge lake, then swooping down until they skimmed the surface, the helicopter turned onto a southerly course.

The men didn't talk much inside the cabin the noise of the rotors was much too loud, so they settled onto the benches with their equipment pushed under their feet. Some appeared to be asleep whilst others stared out of the windows and for the first time Orlagh realised that they were all fair haired, there wasn't a dark head of hair amongst them.

Roz found the movements of the helicopter hypnotic and resting her back against the bulkhead allowed the vibrations to run through her shoulders and along her spine, it wasn't long before her eyelids began to droop and the muscles in her face relaxed. Her head was still spinning but she let her mind go blank until the throbbing inside her skull began to subside.

A few hours' march from the cave, another helicopter was making its approach to a flat area of land. Bob Sharpe had his men clear and mark an area with coloured flares which helped to guide the helicopter in, as soon as its runners kissed the ground Jack Harrington jumped out and ran the few metres to where the men were standing. He had to shield his eyes from the swirling dust and keep his head bowed low.

"Jack," Bob called as he went forward, his hand outstretched.

"Bob, it's good to see you," both men straightened up and pumped each other's hand.

Jack had changed from his travelling clothes and was now dressed in something more suitable for the harsh conditions in which he found himself.

"How was your trip?" asked Bob

"No complaints, what about yours. How's your injured man?"

The man with the shattered elbow was going to be airlifted to hospital and as he moved forward to take Jack's place in the waiting helicopter he grinned and nodded.

"We are ready to move out," Bob said.

Moving away from the rotor blades Jack followed him to where the group of men were waiting and grinning widely, he spoke to those he knew.

"Mac you old scoundrel," he shook the man's hand. "How are you, you mad Scotsman?" Jack could never get used to seeing a Native American wearing a tartan kilt. The sleeves on Mac's army issue shirt were rolled up to the elbow and sweat marks stained his back.

"Mad Scotsman indeed," Mac's brow creased and his dark eyes rolled up into his head. "I suppose I must be mad to have agreed to this wild goose chase, I've almost been blown up twice and shot at by an annoying sniper."

"Surely that's much more entertaining than sitting at a desk in the I.T

176

suite back at base." Their banter was easy and it continued until finally they organised themselves into the fighting military group that they were, only then did they continue on their way, moving further into the wilderness.

Jerry Knowles had spent almost two hours surfing the internet but as yet had discovered nothing about the 'Phoenix Legion'. This was encouraging because the more he searched the more likely they were to exist, he knew they must be concealed somewhere inside the virtual world and given time he would find them.

At last Orlagh managed to doze she surrendered her body to the hypnotic effect of the engines. She had not slept properly since before the sinking of the Sea Quest, it had taken her a while to adjust to the unaccustomed surroundings of her cabin, she never slept well outside her own bed.

They had been in the air for just over four hours when she finally opened her eyes. Schiffer was staring at her, the weight of his gaze made her feel uncomfortable so shifting in her seat she turned her attention to the view from the window. They were flying low over water and looking down over a patchwork of blues and greens Orlagh wondered where they could be. She glanced at Roz who was slumped forward with her chin resting on her chest, she looked miserable but at least the swelling around her eye didn't seem so bad, it was no longer completely closed.

"How are you feeling Roz?" she spoke loudly as she shuffled closer.

"I'm okay, don't like flying much but I'll get over it.

"Have you any idea where we are?"

Roz blinked as she looked out of the window. "We must be over the Mediterranean," she glanced at Orlagh, "we've been going in a southerly direction for most of the time."

"Are we heading for Africa then?"

Before Roz could answer the helicopter began to descend and pressing their faces up against a window they searched the horizon but still there was nothing to see only water.

It took Jack and his team four hours to reach the plateau. Mac led them onto the flat area but stopped the men from wandering all over the scene before he had time to do a survey. Like an investigating officer at a crime scene, he didn't want them spoiling evidence that might have been left behind.

"Keep to the edges," he said, before moving carefully towards the indentations in the dust.

Circling the area it was clear that a helicopter had stood there for some time, but much of the evidence had been disturbed by the powerful down draught from the rotor blades on takeoff. In spite of this there were sufficient footprints around the entrance of the cave and over parts of the plateau for Mac to be able to form an opinion of what had taken place there.

"Be aware of booby traps inside the cave," he warned the men. They hardly needed reminding of the dangers, but this was simply Mac's way of saying they could move forward, he'd seen enough.

"What do we have here Mac?" Jack and Razor appeared beside him.

"A helicopter sat here for many hours," he indicated with the toe of his boot where deep ruts had left their marks in the ground. "See how they have been chiselled into the earth? This bird must have been a big one, it seems to have been serviced, it was re-fuelled and I'm sure there will be evidence of this inside the cave."

They moved towards the entrance where men were milling around in the shade, everyone was searching for explosive devices which may have been left behind but clearly they were not expected to penetrate this far so there were no nasty surprises.

Empty fuel drums littered the floor and there were marks in the ground where they had been moved. Fanning out the men began a detailed sweep of the area.

"The transport was re-fuelled here," Mac confirmed. "It was large enough to carry them all so it has the capability of long range, judging from the amount of fuel stored here its tanks have been filled so I'm guessing a range of at least 500 miles."

"Are there any indications that Roz and Dr. Gairne were here?"

"Yes," Mac nodded. "I have seen their marks, I can feel their presence."

Razor smiled as he shot Mac a sideways glance, he seemed to be following an invisible trail which led him deeper into the cave. Mac stopped when he reached the rocks that looked as if they had been sculpted into seats.

"This is where they rested."

Jack studied the area and moving carefully amongst the jumble of rocks he peered at the walls. Running his fingers over the ancient etchings that had fascinated Orlagh he said, "Razor, look at this."

Bob Sharpe stepped up smartly beside him and his eyes widened when he saw the crudely drawn cave paintings. Even though they looked as if they had been created by a child there was something magical in the way they had been made and when he scrutinised them more closely he realised that the animals in the picture didn't exist anymore. They had become extinct many thousands of years ago but here was evidence that once this unforgiving and dusty landscape was teeming with life, it was a place where humans had lived, probably in this very cave.

"There," the sound of Jack's voice startled him. He indicated to a place below the drawings and stepping forward Razor could make out words which had been scratched into the smooth rock. These were modern letters and had nothing to do with the cave drawing.

'Thirteen men armed with assault rifles, well provisioned. Dr Gairne unharmed, no idea where they are taking us.'

"Roz must have written that," Jack murmured.

"She must be an extraordinary young woman," Razor said appreciatively.

"At least we know they are still alive, or they were when she wrote this."

Mac found nothing more of interest, there was evidence that the group of men had been using this location for some time and as Jack paced around the smooth stone floor he digested the facts. He couldn't understand why such large amounts of aviation fuel and other supplies had been stored here, it didn't make any sense. It would have been impossible to move them in by any other method but by air, the operation must have been very costly. There was no mistaking the cave was an ideal place to hole up, but why here?

"This place seems to be a transition point," Razor said, moving up beside him.

"Yeah," Jack nodded, "but strategically placed between where?"

Kylie booted up his laptop and began loading the information Mac had given him.

By making a calculation of the amount of fuel that had been stored he was able to guess the type of helicopter that had been used to airlift the group away. He adjusted the parameters covering several angles before coming up with a plausible answer.

A map of the area flashed up on the screen with their current location at the centre, he then drew a circle the outer circumference representing the maximum distance a helicopter could fly based on the amount of fuel it had taken on. Jack and Razor, leaning over his shoulder, studied the screen.

"They wouldn't have gone west," Mac said, "unless they were intending to rendezvous with a ship." The Atlantic lay in that direction but it was the way they had come.

"Okay, so north would put them close to the border with Russia," Jack thought aloud.

"We can most likely rule that one out too," Razor glanced at Jack.

"South and east puts them into the Med," Mac said.

Jack moved closer to the screen. "They could be somewhere in Spain."

"But why so much fuel?" Razor looked puzzled.

"It's my guess they went south, they could just about reach North Africa."

They were silent for a moment before Razor nodded his head in agreement.

"They could have another fuel dump hidden somewhere along the way," Mac said throwing another idea into the mix.

"How much head start do you think they have?" Jack glanced at him.

"At least four hours, it's difficult to be precise."

"Well, as they have already flown the coop it's useless us remaining here," Razor said. "We'll stay for a brew then we head back to Portugal."

Jerry was getting warmer as he searched the internet. He followed a link which took him on a journey into the world of secret societies and societies with secrets then he found himself on a forum reading messages that were passing between members of a group called *The Brothers of the Sacred Whisper*.

The Brothers were a group consisting of people from all over northern Europe their membership seemed to stretch from southern Ireland in the west to Germany in the east, taking in the U.K., Norway and Sweden. The forum was conducted in English and was mostly made up of trivia and certain code words which occasionally sparked off a tirade of conversation.

Mad Max was from Berlin, he was talking to Pixie-Lee from Cork in Ireland, evidently the brotherhood extended its membership to sisters too. They were discussing the Dark Ages and the spread of Saxons across England once the Romans had left. Jerry read the messages with interest and after about fifteen minutes decided to cut in on their conversation.

'Hello Pixie-Lee and Mad Max, my name is Caradoc and I'm from Dublin.'

'Greetings Caradoc,' Mad Max typed.

Pixie-Lee remained silent.

'What do you do in Ireland?'

180

'I'm a student at Trinity, what about you?'

Jerry knew that it was important to set up a rapport with these people, he would have to gain their confidence if he was going to ask sensitive questions.

'I've just qualified as a Doctor,' Max told him.

'Wow, well done. What do you specialise in?'

Jerry kept up the banter keeping it light as he worked on Mad Max' confidence.

He told the man that he was studying history but didn't let on that his interest lay in German Mysticism and Neo-Nazi Paganism. Mad Max spoke about his own interest in history especially the migration of Saxons across Europe in the early part of the last millennium.

'I'm researching a specific organisation I'm hoping will be able to help me with my dissertation,' Jerry decided to creep a little closer to the topic he had in mind.

'What organisation?' Mad Max asked.

'The Phoenix Legion.'

There were a few moments of silence and Jerry thought he had frightened Mad Max away.

'Wow, that's one hot potato.'

'Why do you say that?'

'You don't want to know, believe me, don't go digging around there.'

'I can't seem to find out anything about them on the internet.'

'You won't, the only way to access their site is by using encrypted code words.'

'How do you know that?'

'I hear things. Here in Germany they are a revered group of socio-paths, their Nazi ideas are not relevant today.'

'So you know how to contact them?'

'No man, I didn't say that.'

Jerry could sense his discomfort and he could imagine Mad Max peering over his shoulder, looking out for Nazis hiding in the shadows.

It seemed that Mad Max had had enough, he was unwilling to discuss the subject further and Pixie-Lee chose to remain silent. Jerry wondered if she was still there eavesdropping on their conversation. As he watched the screen Jerry got the impression that the whole forum had been in on their conversation, the uncontrolled banter passing between those on line seemed to have stopped. It was as if the site was holding its breath, waiting for something unspeakable to happen. Jerry shuddered and signed off then he stared at the screen for a few moments, the research he was engaged in had thrown up more questions than answers. Why were people so reluctant to discuss the 'Phoenix Legion'?

He tried another forum but met with the same response, at least now he had proof that they existed and were obviously a force to be reckoned with. He logged off and shut down his computer realising that he would have to handle this subject very carefully in future.

Roz was squashed uncomfortably up against a bulkhead and as she opened her eyes the glare pierced her brain, swallowing down her nausea she held onto the wooden bench, waiting for the sensation to pass. After a few moments her eyesight began to clear and she was able to focus on the water that was flashing by beneath them then glancing up towards the horizon she thought she could see land.

The helicopter shuddered as it hit turbulent air and the noise inside the cabin intensified making her head throb even harder. Roz tried to ignore her discomfort by focussing on the scene from the window. It soon became obvious that they were heading towards two small islands which were separated by a narrow strip of water. One island was larger than the other and there was evidence of life, buildings were clustered around a tower. The second island was covered in foliage and as the helicopter swept over it she could make out another tower rising up out of the trees.

Flashing across the narrow channel they heading towards a short grass runway and Roz had a clear view of the towers and buildings. She couldn't see anyone on the ground, the little village seemed deserted and as the helicopter turned away to line up with the runway, she lost sight of it.

Orlagh had her face pressed up against a window she too had seen the large towers. She had also caught a fleeting glimpse of a circle of standing stones off in the distance and for a moment was convinced that she had seen a complete copy of Stonehenge. All the stones were standing and it looked as if it had been built recently, but as soon as it appeared the image was gone, lost against the landscape and she was left wondering if she had seen it at all.

The helicopter flared out and landed with a bump then its engines started to wind down. As the door came open the cabin was filled with a blast of warm air and Orlagh took a deep breath, she could smell the sunshine and the sea and it lifted her spirits. Schiffer's men poured out fluidly in military style and lined the way towards the nearest building.

"Right ladies, it's time for you to see your accommodation." Shepherding them out of their seats, he led them along the line of men and Orlagh though she could see a cluster of Iron Age roundhouses complete with smoke rising from their thatched roofs. Once inside the building they were welcomed by a committee consisting of six tall women all dressed in long white robes; they reminded Orlagh of druids.

"Welcome to the Island of Gog," one of them said as she stepped forward. She smiled warmly, holding out her hands in a gesture of welcome.

"Where are we?" Orlagh asked as she looked around the sparsely furnished room.

"You are on Gog, the largest of our islands."

"Gog," Orlagh grinned, "don't tell me, the other island is called Magog."

The woman smiled and simply nodded. "You are to come with us we will make you both comfortable."

Orlagh glanced at Roz who remained silent.

"I see your friend is in need of medical attention," the woman continued, "we will take good care of her," she addressed Orlagh it was as if Roz wasn't there at all. Drawing protectively around them, the women led them away and Schiffer standing back, watched them closely.

Outside the air was warm and scented with spices and wood smoke, it was a pleasant combination and once they were away from the airfield Orlagh was amazed to see people lining the path. Some of them were smiling and others had their heads bowed as if in silent prayer. She glanced enquiringly at Roz but could read nothing in her expression.

"A welcoming committee?" None of the women responded they were intent on moving along the pathway at a steady pace. "What is that large building?" Orlagh tried again.

"That is the temple of Gog," the woman who had spoken earlier responded.

It was by far the largest structure on the island, a plain rectangular construction it reminded her of a power station. The other buildings were the collection of simple roundhouses all neatly thatched, arranged amongst them were architectural styles borrowed from every period in history, nothing seemed to belong together but it was an interesting mix. There was an element of Roman style as well as Ancient Egyptian and Greek, the place was a cocktail of influences all married together to form an ageless collection of dwellings, some of which seemed to work whilst others looked totally out of place. They were hustled along a pathway then, ducking into one of the roundhouses, Orlagh was surprised to find herself in a small room which could have been part of any modern house. The air inside was cool and delicately perfumed, it reminded her of a health spa.

"You will be able to bathe and we have a change of clothing for you."

Roz was taken into an adjoining room where she received medical treatment for her injuries whilst Orlagh was attended by women from the escorting group. She was presented with an earthenware mug of wine which was chilled, dry and slightly spicy, it refreshed her and immediately she felt more relaxed.

Ceramic bowls decorated with intricate patterns were full of fruits, nuts and olives, these were scattered around the room. Orlagh wandered around taking in every detail and as she went she sampled some of the delicacies. After a few moments she was led into another room which was filled with scented steam and before she had an opportunity to object the women moved in and began to undress her. Once her dusty clothes were discarded she was led towards a huge bath tub filled with bubbling water. It was heavenly and sinking down she lay back and closed her eyes relaxing as the women washed her hair and once it was clean she was offered another mug of wine. After the discomfort of the last few days she was happy to remain in the bubbling water, like champagne against her skin not only did it wash away the grime but also her cares.

When they had finished Orlagh was led into a room where she was dried and oils were rubbed into her skin. The women worked their magic, massaging away her aches and pains and it didn't bother her at all. Not once did she feel uncomfortable or question the reason why she was being treated in such a way, she was determined to make the most of it.

When her hair was dry she slipped into a long white robe which was cool against her skin then she was allowed to rest on a soft leather sofa surrounded by cloud-like cushions. Orlagh sighed contentedly and after a while her thoughts began to drift, she wondered if Roz was also enjoying such luxurious treatment. The euphoria of the moment soon began to wear off and she began to feel a little apprehensive.

"Where is my friend?" she asked one of the women who was standing by the door.

"She will be joining you presently."

XXI

The Eyeball ROV approached the submarine which lay inert on the seabed and as it got closer the image of the ghostly shape sharpened until Ed could make out every detail. He was sitting in the control room on board the Nautical Explorer adjusting the lens on the camera when he sucked in his breath, he had never seen a World War Two sub in such good condition, it was as if it had just come out of the shipyard. The hull was painted grey and on the coning tower was some kind of emblem, moving closer to the screen he stared at the strange design. It was circular with dog legged spokes radiating out from its centre.

"Get a picture of that," he said. "I want to send it to Jack."

"Roger that," came the reply.

A printer began to hum and an A4 sheet of paper spilled out containing a clear image of the symbol. Reaching for it Ed frowned, it meant nothing to him and there was nothing more on the side of the sub, no numbers or letters to give it an identity, it remained an anonymous enigma at the bottom of the ocean. He had expected to find the sign of the 'Phoenix Legion' like the button Jack had shown him.

"Save this image in a file on the computer."

The Eyeball scanned the deck as it carefully inched its way along the submarine. There were two torpedo tubes at the bow, one of which had sustained damage when the sub slammed into the ocean floor, a thin stream of bubbles were rising steadily from the fractures in the pressure hull.

"She must be taking on water," the ROV pilot speculated.

Ed remained silent as the Eyeball turned and retraced its steps back along the deck. Beyond the coning tower they could see the devastation caused by the Sea Quest when it rammed into the exhaust silencer hump, orange paint from the ship's hull had scarred the buckled steel plates and it was obvious that the pressure hull had been ruptured here too.

"Must have been some impact," Ed muttered in awe.

"Looks like a lucky strike, I guess the sub was on a crash dive and the collision forced it into the sea bed."

"I guess so," Ed agreed, "I wonder what damage it caused inside."

"There must be some flooding, look at the gaps between the plates."

The holes were not large enough to allow the Eyeball access.

"We could send a Work Class ROV over to lift the lid in the coning tower," the pilot suggested.

"I don't want to risk divers, not until we know what we're dealing with." Ed was, however, quite happy to scrutinise the sub using automatic systems. The powerful manipulator arms on the larger ROV would be sufficient to lift the hatch, then the Eyeball could go in and their questions would be answered. Whilst the ROV was being prepared they continued to survey the boat.

"What do we have here?" the pilot muttered.

Ed was glued to the screen as the Eyeball crept its way slowly along the hull, it was clear that the emergency hatch had been activated but it was only partially open.

"Looks like someone tried to escape."

"Move in closer, get a light into that chamber."

The delicate arm of the Eyeball moved forward. It was fitted with the latest in micro-camera technology and as he passed the fibre-optic cable into the chamber the ROV pilot gasped.

"Oh my God!" Ed whispered. "There's someone trapped inside."

They could see the body of a man, he was wearing a hood over his head but it was not clear if he had suffocated or drowned. Ed felt chilled as he considered the man's final moments.

"He must have put up quite a fight, look at his hands." The knuckles raw, the skin was torn from his fingers.

"It looked as if he attempted to punch his way out of the steel chamber."

"Who can guess at how desperate you might be at the end," the pilot whispered.

"Pull the camera out of there."

The Work Class ROV arrived at the coning tower and the pilot steered it towards the hatch. The manipulator arm extended forward carefully until its finger like hooks gripped the wheel locking the hatch in place, it turned easily and as it opened a few bubbles escaped from the compartment.

"This section is flooded," Ed remarked.

Once the hatch was fully open the Eyeball ROV went in and descending beside the coning tower ladder it reached the control room, its powerful lights illuminating the interior, but it soon became clear that this was no ordinary submarine. Panels arranged along both sides of the cramped space were crammed with high tech equipment there was none of the valves and bulky machinery that Ed expected to find. The control room resembled a computer room similar to the one he was sitting in, screens lined the walls and state of the art electronics filled every available space.

"Wow, looks like the Star Ship Enterprise," the pilot said in awe.

"No need for a crew, this thing must have been capable of driving itself," Ed was amazed by the technology. "Can we hook up to one of the computers, see if we can learn something?"

The Eyeball nudged closer until it came level with a USB socket then slowly an arm extended and a cable was coupled with the submarine. The pilot, tapping the keys on his keyboard, began uploading information and after a few moments the computers started to communicate. "Looks like we need a password of some kind."

Ten seconds later there was a huge explosion as the interior of the sub disintegrated taking the Eyeball with it. The screens on the Nautical Explorer went blank as the computer shut down and it was some minutes before Ed had things back under control.

The work class ROV had not sustained much damage in the blast and the moment its camera had been re-activated it began sending pictures back to the control room. The coning tower was completely gone leaving a huge hole in the deck where the control room had been situated.

"It didn't like that," Ed said. "Were we able to download anything?"

"Not a chance, the system was far too sophisticated I didn't even get through the firewall before it destroyed itself."

"That sure is one way to hold onto your secrets," Ed was amazed by what had just happened. "Lucky the blast didn't take the Work Class with it."

"There seems to be some minor damage but I think I can recover it."

Jack was disappointed to be on his way back so soon, he'd hoped to join the chase, lead the team in to rescue Roz and Dr. Gairne. The Sikorsky from the Nautical Explorer was dispatched to collect them. The round trip from ship to cave and back was just within its range providing it wasn't pushed beyond its cruising speed and a few hours later Jack was on the deck of the ship, surveying the damage to the Work Class ROV.

"Must have been some blast, lucky you didn't have divers in there," he said turning towards Ed.

The other heavy duty ROV was being used to salvage vital and expensive equipment from the Sea Quest. They had already emptied the hold of gold bars which had previously been collected from the wreck of the Hudson Bay.

"It seems they didn't have time to booby trap your ship," Ed reassured him. "Once the heavy stuff is off I'll send divers in to reclaim some of the sensitive equipment."

Jack and Ed made their way towards the control room, Jack wanted to see the footage from both the Hudson Bay and the submarine.

"I want to send the image from the coning tower to Jerry Knowles, maybe he can tell us what it means."

Orlagh realised that she had been drugged, but the sensation was not at all unpleasant. She could remember everything that had happened and was now resting comfortably in a beautifully furnished room which was decorated with Iron Age designs. One of the 'Celtic' like spirals she recognised, four spirals intricately interlaced seemingly with no beginning and no end.

"The wheel of being," she whispered to herself.

This was used by druids in Celtic times as a peace symbol, the four spirals representing the conflicting elements, with the central spiral placed to create balance and harmony. The design was repeated on all four walls. Orlagh was fascinated, she wanted to know more about this place and rising from the comfort of her chair, she smoothed the long white robe around her legs pulling the plaited belt tighter around her waist. Her hair felt luxurious, free from dried sea salt and dust her skin shone vibrantly, she felt amazing.

There was a door located in one of the walls, at first she couldn't see it because it formed part of the wall design, then pushing her hand against it she stepped hesitantly into a smaller room. In the middle of the floor stood an earthenware bowl that was raised on a stone pedestal, smoke drifting up from it turned into dancing patterns which perfumed the air as it went. Crossing the room she opened another door which led into a room that was identical to her own. Roz was slumped in a chair supported by cushions. She was dressed in robes that were similar to Orlagh's, evidently she had been treated in the same way. The injuries to her face had faded and now there was some colour in her cheeks.

"Roz," Orlagh was beside her.

Roz opened her eyes and for the first time in days could see clearly, her head was no longer throbbing and there was hardly any pain.

"Orlagh, are you are okay?"

"Of course, I've been very well looked after."

"I thought they might have taken you away, locked you up or something."

"No, as you see. I can't believe it, it's just like being at a health spa."

"We've been drugged," Roz said as she stretched out the muscles in her shoulders.

Orlagh frowned and moving away studied the patterns on the wall. "Who are these people?"

"I've no idea, at least they don't appear to be hostile."

"Are the drugs to subdue us or administered as an aid to relaxation?"

"I guess a little of both," Roz said looking around her. "Don't suppose they wanted any hysterics."

"Well I for one don't intend doing anything to provoke whoever is running this place, I could do with more of this kind of treatment."

"Yeah but I would like to know what's going on."

"It's certainly a strange place, one of those women told me about the temples. They have one on each island, we saw them as we flew in."

"Temples!" Roz frowned, "Temples to what?"

"I have no idea, apart from the fact that she called them Gog and Magog."

"What the hell are they?"

"Historical literature tells us that Gog and Magog were two warring giants. They probably represented good and evil and the eternal turmoil between them," she glanced at Roz who appeared to be interested so she continued. "The Christian book of Revelation tells us that Gog and Magog rule the nations in the four quarters of the Earth, or the four corners of the world."

"They sound like super powers to me, the conflict between USA and the USSR during the cold war."

"True," Orlagh nodded. "But the prominent Muslim scholar, Javad Ahmed Ghamidi believes that Gog and Magog are descendants of Noah. They are supposed to come from the line of Japeth, one of Noah's sons."

"Communism and Capitalism more like," Roz looked sceptical.

"Well, that's what the woman said, the huge buildings are temples to Gog and Magog, that's also what she called the islands."

"That's weird," Roz said. "I've never come across islands with those names before."

Jack was in the control room studying the computer screen, he watched the footage shot by the Eyeball moments before it was destroyed in the explosion. They were still no closer to discovering what the symbol on the coning tower represented, it was a mystery that he was keen to understand. Using the computer keyboard he highlighted the symbol and saved it in a folder, then composing his message he attached the file before sending it as an e-mail to Jerry Knowles.

He sat back in his seat, he was tired but knew he would be unable to sleep, every time he tried his thoughts brought him back to Orlagh and Roz. There had been no word from the kidnappers and considering the hardware at their disposal he realised that they were not dealing with an ordinary kidnapping. His fingers tapped on the keyboard and the screen changed in front of him, he kept thinking about the fuel dump in the cave on the remote hillside in Spain. He had no idea what kind of helicopter had landed there but he knew it was a big one capable of a long distance flight. The average large helicopter on full tanks would cover about 450 nautical miles, he had a feeling that would put it somewhere in North Africa but he wanted to check out all the possibilities before agreeing with his instincts.

He studied a map of Europe which extended down as far southern Spain and the Mediterranean. France was not a likely destination and Italy was out of range, so moving south he looked at Spain more closely, but even that was unlikely. Letting his eyes wander over Gibraltar and across the short straits to Morocco he traced the African coastline east. The helicopter would have had just about enough range to get there. Zooming in on the area he followed the isolated coastline with his finger but he had no idea what he was looking for.

"What would they be doing in Morocco?" he grumbled. There seemed no obvious answer. It was possible to hole up somewhere along the coastline, it was a barren enough place there must be hundreds of suitable locations. The only thing he could think of was the proximity to the sea. If the group had a fully restored World War Two submarine, it was possible that they had access to other ships. The more Jack thought about it the more convinced he became North Africa had to be where they were taken. Leaning back in his chair he sighed loudly before hitting the print button.

Jerry Knowles was working on his computer when Jack's e-mail arrived.

He had almost finished the paper he was working on and the distraction was hardly welcome, but seeing as it was from Jack he opened it immediately. He knew what the symbol was the moment he saw it and immediately began to type his reply.

He headed up the message 'Black Sun', (occult symbol).

'The term Black Sun is also referred to as the Sonnenrad, (German for 'Sun

190

Wheel'). It's a symbol of esoteric or occult significance and was used in Nazi mysticism. It's also seen in other occult groups and Germanic neo-paganism.

It has very strong links with the German regime of the 1930s and 40s. The design has been linked with Nazi groups such as the Shutzstaffel (S.S.)'

Jerry paused for a moment before reaching for a file on his bookshelf. Flicking through his notes he found what he was looking for.

'The design can be seen on early Medieval Germanic brooches and is thought to be a variation of the Roman swastika fibula. Some Alemannic or Bavarian brooches incorporate a swastika symbol at the centre. The number of rays in the brooches varies from between five and twelve.'

The design Jack had sent was a Black Sun consisting of twelve rays. Jerry studied his computer screen, absentmindedly playing with the end of his pencil.

He flicked through his notes again wondering how much information to include in his reply. Reading over what he had written, he glanced back at Jack's message, all he wanted to know was what the symbol stands for and his views on the subject based on what they had previously discussed. Jerry believed that the symbol was a physical link to the Phoenix Legion, they were both convinced that the emblem was some kind of new world ideology based on resurrecting the idea that the Third Reich will last for a thousand years.

He continued typing.

'The Black Sun was a powerful symbol which can be found in a floor mosaic at the castle of Wewelsburgh, a Renaissance castle located in the north-west of North Rhine-Westfalia in Germany.'

Jerry remembered seeing it as a child when visiting the area with his father.

It was then that he'd discovered the castle was used by the highest ranking S.S. Generals during the war as a meeting place.

'The Black Sun or Sun Wheel is significant for the Germanic-light and sun mysticism which was propagated by the S.S. In their studies on sense characters, the sun was interpreted as 'the strongest and most visible expression of God'. Twelve was a significant number in their rituals.'

Jerry continued to read his notes, in his opinion this was significant proof that a society, up until now a secret society, was in existence. With the discovery of the Hudson Bay, something on board that ship had brought the organisation out of hibernation and Dr Gairne was innocently caught up in it. He wondered what they wanted with her.

Before he sent his reply Jerry added a final comment.

'The former S.S. member Wilhelm Landig of the Vienna Circle, coined the *idea of the Black Sun, a substitute swastika and mystical source of energy capable of re-generating the Aryan race.*

Orlagh looked up as three women entered the room, they bowed their heads courteously.

"Good morning my Lady," one of them said, her English heavy with accent.

"Where are we and why are we being held against our will?" Orlagh asked as she stood up.

"You are honoured guests and we are on the island of Gog in the Kingdom of Elmet."

"What are you talking about?" Orlagh snapped. "Elmet was a Celtic Kingdom in the north of England."

"That may be so but now it is here," the woman eyed her calmly. "Do you have everything you want?" She glanced around the room checking the bowls of fruit and other delicacies.

"Yes thank you, apart from our freedom of course."

"You are at liberty to leave this room if you wish but we will have to accompany you if you are planning to walk outside."

Orlagh glanced at Roz. "Then we shall walk outside," she said and turning to Roz helped her up out of her chair.

XXII

Jerry hit the send button and the e-mail icon on his computer screen confirmed that Jack had received his message. He sat for a few moments wrapped up in his own thoughts he was determined to find out more about the 'Phoenix Legion' and the group behind the Black Sun. His fingers danced over the keys and the words 'Brothers of the Sacred Whisper' appeared on the screen, then double clicking on the link he entered the website and joined the forum. He studied the line up for a few moments before finding Mad Max.

'Hello Caradoc,' Pixie-Lee had spotted him.

'Hello Pixie, how's the weather in Cork?' He cringed the moment he sent his reply, only the English would talk about the weather and it made him feel foolish.

'Wet, how about Dublin?'

Did she know that he was English? He didn't think so at least her response spared his feelings. They chatted for a while before Jerry steered their conversation towards more serious matters.

'Let's go private,' Pixie-Lee typed.

Leaving the open forum where anyone could join in on their conversation, they entered a 'side room' from where they could chat in private.

'I was talking to Mad Max the other day,' Jerry typed.

'Yes I know, you were asking some awkward questions. There's no way I would have talked to you as openly as he did.'

'What are you afraid of?'

'You've no idea what you are getting yourself into,' she began, 'you should be more careful.'

He thought for a moment before going on. 'I see, I didn't realise the subject is so sensitive. I'm studying German Mythology at Uni. and I'm researching for a paper I have to write.'

'Then you really do have to be careful, don't even think about publishing your work on the internet or otherwise.'

Now she was sounding paranoid, he had the impression that she knew a lot more than she was prepared to discuss.

'Do you know anything about the 'Phoenix Legion'?'

'Not much, only what Mad Max told you. Their influence hasn't spread as far as Ireland but in Europe, Germany especially, the Legion is beginning to attract members. It seems to me that they are a group of nasty individuals who have links with the underworld.'

'I see, so they exist then?'

'Of course they exist, rumour has it they are planning to become a lot bigger, spread their ideals.'

'How do you know that?' he asked.

'As Mad Max said, we hear things.' she remained silent for a moment, reluctant to tell him more, but then she made up her mind. 'Look Caradoc, I'll give you a lead but you also need some advice.'

'Okay Pixie, I'm listening.'

'Look up a website called 'Sonnenrad'.'

Jerry stared at the screen that was the second time within the hour he had come across that word. 'German for Sun Wheel,' he responded.

'You've heard of it?' she seemed surprised.

'Of course, as I said I'm studying the subject.'

She became silent again and as Jerry waited he could sense her reluctance to continue.

'You have to use a password to get into the site,' eventually she responded but there was another long pause. 'Once you are in you have to enter the word 'Wewelsburg'.'

The name of the castle in Germany, he was hardly surprised.

'And your advice?'

'If I were you I would leave well alone.'

Suddenly she was gone and he was left staring at an empty screen. Questions swam around inside his head, first Jack now Pixie-Lee, what had the symbol of the Black Sun got to do with anything? The answer to that question was obvious, the 'Phoenix Legion' must be a society who worshipped the symbol of the Black Sun. It made sense, the Nazis had done the same thing during the Second World War and from what Pixie had said the Legion was gaining momentum in Europe. Without another thought he entered the word 'Sonnenrad' into a search engine and was immediately directed to a website.

In the centre of the homepage he found the word 'enter' and clicking on the little box the screen changed colour then he was urged to use a password. Slowly he typed in 'Wewelsburg' and the image of a castle filled the screen, behind the illustration was a gigantic wheel which cast a shadow over the castle. Slowly a drawbridge lowered from the curtain wall and he was invited to cross the moat. It reminded him of a computer game and as he made his way across, a line of medieval knights dressed in black armour came smartly to attention. Once inside the castle he was drawn towards what appeared to be an altar. The screen changed again and he was left staring at the Sun Wheel, it was just like the real thing, a huge green mosaic wheel set into a marble floor. He waited for something to happen then suddenly choices began to appear on the screen, first he had to say which language he wished to proceed in and from a drop down menu he selected English. He was amazed at the extent of choice there must have been every language possible, the site was obviously available worldwide not just in Europe.

Outside it was a beautiful day and Orlagh was impressed by the building they were being kept in. The design was simple enough but it had a subtle grandness about it. The pure white walls were capped with a thatch of gold that was in complete contrast to the formal gardens and as Orlagh looked out over the splendid sight she sucked in her breath. The landscape that was laid out before her was a jumble of formal designs borrowed from many periods in history. She counted at least a dozen different influences but the garden was arranged in a symmetry that seemed to work. There were Egyptian columns carved to resemble huge lotus flowers, it was as if they had been plucked from an ancient temple and the avenue was filled with perfectly tended vines, then she noticed the Roman effect. Straight lines and order seemed to tame the natural growth of plants, keeping them neatly in their place.

Huge Grecian urns overflowed with pastel colours and classical sculptures were cleverly arranged to draw the eye, she was enchanted and as she turned her head she saw a huge ornamental pond which reminded her of another grand design. This one borrowed from the Palace of Versailles in France. Giant bronze dolphins were leaping from a lake and there were fountains of water cascading over pink and white lilies the size of dinner plates. Yet another section resembled the gardens of the Alhambra, this area was based on biblical influences that she thought must closely resemble the Garden of Eden. There were too many delights to take in at once, it was like staring at a huge painting, the more she looked the more she could see.

"Wow," Orlagh enthused. "I would never grow tired walking here just think of the work that must have gone into its creation."

Roz had to agree, but she was more interested in the bigger picture, she was trying to divorce herself from the hypnotic effect of the beautiful garden. From where they were standing they had a good view over the village. Out in the bay Roz could see the other island; the mysterious tall building appeared to be growing up amongst the thick jungle-like foliage which dominated the landscape. 'The temple of Magog,' she thought.

Drawing Orlagh along the path she was able to get a better view of their island. From the elevated walkway she looked down on the Iron Age village which was clustered around the huge Temple of Gog. Its smooth concrete sides seemed out of place amongst the pretty round-houses, their white walls and neatly thatched roofs were in stark contrast to the ugly walls of the tower. She studied the temple with suspicion and wondered what it could be used for. A building that size must play an important role in village life, she thought. It was a rectangular struc-ture, a storage silo of some kind, but she discounted that idea, it was much too large for storing grain. Perhaps the wealth of the village was housed there and that's why it was called a Temple, maybe the inhabit-ants worshipped their wealth as some kind of deity. Her thoughts were beginning to run wild but she realised that it wouldn't do to speculate. She liked to deal in facts, besides she wanted to see the harbour which must lie on the far side of the island.

They walked on a little further and Orlagh continued to admire the garden.

Roz was annoyed by her acceptance of their situation and could hardly believe that Orlagh could remain so relaxed and content. It was as if they had got to her somehow, influenced her mind with some kind of psychological treatment. She needed Orlagh's support, they had to work together if they were going to get away from this place.

Roz sighed with frustration and glanced back at the group of women who were following on behind.

The only other way off the island was by air, she had seen the light aircraft lined up along the grass runway when they had arrived but that way out was beyond them. She had no idea how to fly and was sure that Orlagh didn't posses those skills either.

Although Orlagh was standing beside Roz, her view of the island was completely different. She marvelled at the fascinating collection of roundhouses and the people who worked beside them. Not once did she consider why they were there or how they came to choose this way of life, it was as if they had forgotten all about modern techniques and facilities, they were like a lost civilisation.

The Iron Age reconstruction must be an experiment of some kind, she thought, people existing using old methods, and the more she looked the more she liked what she saw. The research possibilities excited her, this was a truly magnificent discovery. She began to think about funding

196

and what might be available to set up an expedition to study the inhabitants of this island.

There was a relaxed almost idyllic atmosphere surrounding the village, everyone she saw appeared to be happy and resolved to their lifestyle. Most of the people were fair haired with the exception of a few red heads and they were all dressed in traditional tartan and roughly woven cloth typical of the period. It seemed strange that they were all pale skinned, given their location she had expected to see darker skins from mainland Africa.

"Is this a commune of some kind, an experiment in ancient techniques?" Orlagh turned to one of the women in their group.

"These are the people of the kingdom of Elmet," she simply replied.

Roz, listening to the conversation frowned.

"What do they do here, how do they exist?" Orlagh continued to probe.

"We are guardians of the Temple of Gog, the gods provide for us."

Orlagh glanced at Roz who remained stony faced. Linking arms they continued along the path putting some distance between them and their chaperones.

"We have to get away from here," she spoke in lowered tones and gripped Orlagh's arm more tightly. "You have to help me plan our escape, we must work together on this, I can't do it by myself."

Orlagh glanced at Roz, she could feel her distress. The injuries to her face were healing and she wasn't as pale as she had been previously. Orlagh could see though how passionate Roz had become about escaping.

"If I could find a radio transmitter perhaps I could get a message to Jack." She was thinking about the buildings clustered around the landing strip, there must be a communication station there somewhere.

"What about Schiffer and his thugs?" Orlagh said.

"We haven't seen them since we arrived so I guess they have business elsewhere." The fact that they had not seen them bothered Roz, she was certain they had a major role to play in all this.

"There must be guards."

Roz nodded in agreement as she glanced back at the women following them.

"Where are we?" whispered Orlagh

A warm breeze bathed them in scent and Orlagh, stopping to admire a bloom, ran her fingertips gently over the brightly coloured petals. She was amazed by their delicacy.

"Have you ever seen such beautiful flowers?" Roz asked.

"No not in Ireland."

"I think we are off the coast of North Africa," she said confirming Orlagh's suspicions.

"So somewhere near Libya or Morocco?"

"Nearer Morocco I guess. I don't think the helicopter would have had enough fuel to fly as far east as Libya."

"So we must be close to Gibraltar then," Orlagh frowned.

"True but I think we are closer to Africa. If we could reach a boat we could make our way to the mainland and disappear before Schiffer and his cronies had a chance to find us."

Orlagh glanced at Roz and could see the determination in the young woman's face. There was no doubt in her mind that they could do it, escape from the island or make contact with Jack. Orlagh remained silent as they continued along the path. She was thinking about the implications of Roz' plans and marvelled at her resilience. If it wasn't for Roz she would have certainly perished by now, either drowned on the Sea Quest or lost in the ocean having survived the sinking. Suddenly the beauty of their surroundings were not as delightful as they had been a few minutes earlier, her thoughts became clouded with apprehension and uncertainty. What were they doing here and why were they being treated so cordially?

Jack was restless, the operation was taking far too long and he was still no closer to finding Roz and Orlagh. The information Jerry Knowles had sent was full of disturbing undercurrents, there were things he didn't understand or expect to be dealing with, but at least now he was beginning to discover what they were up against. There was still a lot more that he wanted to know, questions to which he had no answers bothered him and the lack of understanding was beginning to get him down. How could he possibly defeat these people if they didn't understand them, he also wanted to know where the atomic device from the Hudson Bay had gone.

"Hi Jack," Paul said. He had joined the Nautical Explorer earlier having spent time ashore enjoying a spot of rest and recuperation.

"Hello Paul old buddy," Jack smiled as he pumped his friend's hand.

"Another fine mess you've gotten me into!" Paul grinned as he glanced around.

He felt out of place on the Nautical Explorer, he should be standing on the bridge of his own ship.

"Tell me about it."

They were looking out over a smooth sea and light from the instrument panel illuminated their faces with ghostly hues.

"I understand there's been no word from the kidnappers."

"No," Jack shook his head.

"So what's the plan?"

Jack filled him in with the latest details. "I'm going with Razor and the men on a little shore leave. I can't stand this waiting around."

"I can understand that Jack."

"I've pulled some strings and called in favours with the British authorities.

I've managed to get us into the airport on Gibraltar, there's also a handy marina close by."

"RAF Gibraltar?" Paul eyed Jack sideways.

"Yeah, I reckon we'll have to fly out to North Africa before long and Gibraltar is a heck of lot closer than here."

Paul turned towards Jack and encouraged him to continue.

"I intend to start flying search patterns over the Med and the coast of Africa."

"The Libyans won't be too happy about that."

"We won't be that far east. I'm going to concentrate my search along the coast of Morocco." Jack outlined what he had discovered, he was certain that the people they were looking for had a base set up somewhere along the coast.

"You saw the sub," he continued. "There could be more where that came from."

Suddenly Paul didn't feel quite so happy to be standing on the deck of the Nautical Explorer.

"Coffee?" Jack asked. "You've gone a little pale old friend!"

It was true that they were being well cared for but Roz was full of concern.

She was certain they were being drugged, kept in an unnatural state where their senses were weakened, their fight or flight reflexes muted. She refused to drink the wine which was plentiful, it had a pleasant flowery aftertaste and contained very little alcohol, but she guessed it was responsible for holding them in a constant state of relaxation. The drink was addictive and she was convinced that Orlagh was taking it regularly. Questions nagged at her brain, she had not yet managed to locate the guards, in fact the only people they had contact with were

199

the six women who were acting as ladies in waiting. They showered Orlagh with attention it was strange the way they fussed around her. They seemed to hold her in very high esteem and Roz was beginning to feel uncomfortable, she was unused to all this kind of treatment. Orlagh didn't seem to mind, it was as if she had been treated this way all of her life, but Roz knew her mood was being influenced by the narcotics, if only she could stop Orlagh from drinking the wine. She sighed and walked around her room for the hundredth time. There were so many things she needed to know, she had to get out beyond the garden compound.

As soon as it was dark the women retired for the night and Roz lay on her bed listening to the silence planning what she was going to do next. Orlagh had talked excitedly throughout the evening mostly about what they had seen of the village and the people who lived in it. She viewed the whole thing from a historian's perspective, discussing her plans to set up a research grant and employ a team of archaeologists to study and observe the villagers. She wanted to find out what was going on, excavate some of the remote parts of the island. All Roz had seen were people struggling for a meagre existence using antiquated methods and machinery, she couldn't understand why anyone would choose to live that way.

Everything was still, the darkness complete and sliding her legs over the side of the bed her bare feet touched the cool floor tiles. The temperature had dropped slightly now the sun had set and the air was not so stifling. Roz crossed the room and pressed her ear up against the door, there were no sounds coming from the corridor beyond so cracking open the door slightly she listened and when satisfied that it was clear she slipped out of the room. The corridor was in complete darkness, she couldn't see a thing. The wall curved slightly with the shape of the house so moving forward, her hand against the smooth surface, her fingers felt the way.

Orlagh's room was situated further along the corridor, there was sure to be a woman stationed outside so Roz continued in the opposite direction. In her mind she pictured the route they had taken to the garden earlier, she would have to pass through two rooms, hopefully they wouldn't be locked.

The first room she negotiated with ease, but moments before opening the second door she heard a noise, there were people in the room beyond, their voices becoming louder so backing up quickly she just had time to press into a corner before the door opened. Two of the women guarding them appeared, they were carrying a candle or a lamp of some kind and as they crossed the room Roz was thankful that it cast only a feeble glow. When they were gone she went into the second room and made her way towards the door that opened directly onto the garden. Remaining flat against the wall she took a deep breath, her heart was beating rapidly inside her chest but she had to remain calm. Straining her ears she could hear nothing, the garden terrace seemed to be deserted so opening the door wider she slipped out of the house.

As silent as a prowling cat she made her way across the tiles, turning her head from side to side, watching for movement in the undergrowth. Suddenly the warm breeze kissed her skin, it lifted her hair and she smiled. The air was pleasantly perfumed with wood smoke and spices and occasionally a sweet scent would drift up from the garden. Pulling her long white robe tight between her legs she made her way quickly along the terrace and when she reached the far side of the garden she hauled herself up over the wall then lowered herself down into the long grass on the other side.

There was barely enough light to see, the moon had not yet risen, but silver threads of starlight touching the landscape were sufficient for her to make her way towards the village. She hadn't gone far before she discovered a sunken pathway. It had been impossible to see it earlier when they were standing on the terrace and she almost laughed out loud. It must be used by the villagers so the gentry couldn't see them as they made their way to and from the village.

Pausing in the darkness at the end of the pathway she studied the nearest houses. Nothing stirred, everything was eerily silent, she had expected to see people or at least animals moving about, but here there was nothing. Holding her breath in silent anticipation she considered her next move. The white from her robe stood out against the darkness and she wished that she was dressed in something more suitable. She made up her mind, at the first opportunity she would have to steal some trousers from a clothes line. Moving steadily between the houses she kept to the shadows looking out for anything that she might find useful. Here the houses were packed closely together, it was as if they were seeking comfort in each other's company and occasionally she could hear sounds coming from within, mainly it was people snoring but now and again she could pick out voices. The houses had no windows, one narrow doorway served as an entrance, this was covered by a thick curtain that could be tied back during the day. She guessed that the people living here enjoyed clement weather conditions, they were so close to Africa and would be unaccustomed to freezing mornings and frost, the worst they had to contend with was probably heavy rainfall.

Suddenly a strange sound stole through the darkness and she froze. The rhythm of her racing heart made her head throb and cursing under her breath she moved closer to one of the houses. Ducking under the low thatch she searched the way ahead in an attempt to locate the source of the noise. The low rumble sounded again, an eerie moan filling the night with demons, then grinning to herself she was filled with relief as she peered around the curve of the house. A huge animal lay stretched out in the shadows, it was obviously caught up in some nightmare and was becoming more vocal with each snore. She couldn't see it clearly but guessed it was a dog of some kind so creeping silently from her hiding place she made her way along the pathway.

The huge black shape which dominated the way ahead was the building known as the Temple of Gog, it blocked out the stars and cast an eerie shadow over the village. Up close the structure was a gigantic collection of concrete blocks which were square cut and seemed completely out of place in a village that was filled with roundhouses. Roz made her way around its perimeter keeping close to the walls. There seemed to be no entrance, if this place was a temple then surely people would have access. Glancing up she could just make out a number of small openings, gaps that had been left in the block work. These were not large enough to let in significant amounts of sunlight but as she looked closer it became obvious, each opening was covered by a grille which must provide ventilation for whatever was housed inside.

It wasn't her plan to gain access to the building, not tonight, she was more concerned with locating the harbour so leaving it behind she hurried towards the edge of the village. Here the houses were set further apart with wide pathways running between them. These were larger than the others so the residents here obviously enjoyed a higher status.

Still there was no one around, the place was silent. She thought that maybe the inhabitants were subjected to a curfew, she had expected to come across somebody, law enforcers perhaps, but there was no one and as far as she could tell there was no evidence of electronic surveillance equipment set up along the paths. No lights or alarms had been tripped so she continued on her way keeping to one side of the pathway, never straying far from the cover of the buildings.

Finally the moon showed over the horizon, it was in its first quarter and bright enough to cast a silvery glow over the Iron Age landscape.

The light magnified the fluorescence of her robe making her stand out like an angel amongst the shadows.

She had searched for some other clothing, trousers and a shirt would have been perfect, but there was nothing to be had amongst the buildings. Suddenly there was movement from up ahead and diving for cover she turned her head towards the sound.

The village was perched on an elevated position which jutted out into the ocean, a path plunged down to meet the sea before running parallel with the beach, and further around the headland she could just make out a harbour. It was sheltering in bay of deep water and was protected from the open sea by a huge wall and sea break. Keeping below the skyline Roz moved along the path before heading off at an angle, then using the long grasses which covered the headland she was able to make her way unseen towards the harbour.

The tall grass began to thin out and searching the way ahead she could make out a group of men who appeared to be working near to the harbour wall. From her hiding place she could see the layout of the harbour clearly. Jetties invisible in the darkness were now apparent and she could see fishing boats tied up to fenders which offered protection to their wooden hulls against the rough stone wall. There were more boats in the harbour than she imagined, fishing was obviously important to the survival of the villagers.

There were at least six men working along the wall, but they were too far away for Roz to see what they were doing. Suddenly one of them began to signal with a light, he was directing a powerful beam out to sea. Straining her eyes, Roz couldn't see a thing, there was insufficient light for her to see beyond the harbour, the ocean was in total darkness. For several minutes the man continued to send his signal, then he was rewarded with a tiny light that flashed far out to sea, the men continued to watch with growing excitement as the light drew nearer.

Whist she waited for something to happen Roz scrutinised the harbour. She was searching for a small speedboat, something in which they could make their escape, but there was nothing apart from basic fishing boats. None of these boats showed a light and they seemed to be of simple construction. Made of wood they each had a single mast, this was not what she had in mind, besides, she doubted her ability to sail such a craft especially in unfamiliar waters.

Out to sea a ship was beginning to take shape, it was moving slowly towards the harbour which seemed far too small to accommodate it, the low rumble of its diesel engines disturbed the air around her as it cut steadily through the water. With no lights showing apart from the signal it drew closer then suddenly moonlight began to play over its sides. Light danced along the smooth hull as the ship changed course, now the sea was boiling angrily as side thrusters kicked in sending vibrations running through the water. Roz was convinced that she was about to witness the ship smash into the harbour wall and holding her breath, she waited for the collision, but the ship simply vanished. Suddenly the harbour was empty, even the men who were there moments before had gone. She scanned the area thoroughly waiting a full ten minutes before moving then hitching up her robe she picked her way along the path following the curve of the cliff.

She had to discover where the ship had gone and approaching the centre of the cove it became clear what had happened. Cut into the cliff was a huge cave, Roz was amazed at the scale of the interior it was as if the whole hillside had been hollowed out. The ship was now docked against a harbour wall and she could make out movement as men and machinery began working feverishly to unload its cargo. The operation was impressive and drawn towards the entrance she had to find out what was going on, why the ship was hidden from view. She couldn't understand why these people had gone to such measures to create a secret harbour.

Roz slipped into the cave and made her way to a point where she could hide but also see what was going on. Her nerves were as taut as wire and she felt vulnerable dressed in only a thin, pure white robe.

XXIII

Jerry worked his way around the website and was amazed by its complexity. It appeared to be a hierarchal system and a series of codes were needed in order to gain access to the various levels. He was searching for a forum, somewhere to read comments or chat with others who were on the site but he had not yet reached that privileged level. To the casual visitor the site was ordinary enough, it was made up of interesting historical facts about the castle and other information regarding the Sun Wheel, but to get to the next level he had to enter another password. A box flashing in the centre of the screen invited him to input the secret code, only then could he proceed into the inner circle.

Straightening up in his chair he worked the stiffness out of his neck and shoulders. The hour was late and he desperately needed coffee, he had an early start in the morning but was determined to get to the next level, all he had to do was enter the correct word into the box. Pixie Lee had given him only one password, this got him into the website, but she had not told him how to progress through it. Turning away from his laptop he went to make himself a mug of coffee and ten minutes later he was still no closer to solving the problem. He thought about the Sun Wheel and the castle at Wewelsburgh; he knew about the Nazi link with the castle, the meeting place of the S.S., it was also supposed to be a stronghold where they could store historical treasures. He started listing them off in his head searching for a likely password, the Holy Grail, Spear of Destiny, the Ark of the Covenant, but none of these seemed to fit.

The box on his screen continued to flash, it seemed to be goading him into taking a chance. Like a game of Russian roulette it was a gamble that if he got wrong he would regret, there would only be one chance before the website closed down. Jerry suspected that here on the edge of the inner sanctum the security system protecting the website would probably be very sensitive.

Steering his mind back to the list of historical treasures all he could think of was biblical artefacts with religious connections, he was certain that the password would be based on one of those treasures. It could of course be an anagram of any of those words. He sighed and rubbed his forehead with the palm of his hand, he was going around in circles. Suddenly he had an idea, the Belgae Torc was another treasure that the Nazis were interested in, in fact, it was one of their prized possessions during the Second World War so almost certainly would have been kept there at the castle. The problem was that the Belgae Torc was a Celtic treasure, the odd one out on his list, all the rest were linked to Christianity. Slumping down in front of his laptop his fingers itched to type in the words but he held himself back, he had to be sure, he needed more time to consider his options. After a pause he realised there was no reason to wait, it had to be the password so he typed it in and suddenly the screen changed. Blocks of text appeared in front of his eyes, he had reached the next level and the website was revealing more of its secrets. He had to read quickly, the words coming in a never ending stream. There were references to the Third Reich and the Master Race but it didn't make any sense, it was such a jumbled mess that at first he thought it might be written in some kind of code, but after a while he began to understand some of the sentences then something caught his eye. Gog and Magog were two powerful opposing forces, it seemed they had formed an alliance and were working together against a common enemy. He began to read faster but found it difficult to keep up, the words scrolling up over the screen irritated his tired eyes until he found it impossible to take anymore in. He couldn't understand everything that he read anyway, the threads were too obscure, the ancient text confusing, the best he could do was to scan the text. There were, however, continued references to the Eagle and the Lion, clearly these represented enemies of the 'Phoenix Legion'. Sometime in the past they had been responsible for a gross injustice, this appeared to be the suppression of the Third Reich.

Jerry slumped back in his chair, he was exhausted, he yawned and rubbed his eyes with the palms of his hands, the intensity of the information was just too much and he was too tired to read any more. Suddenly he made a connection, the Eagle must be the U.S.A. and the Lion was Great Britain, the suppression of the Third Reich must be a reference to the end of the Second World War. He had no idea what Gog and Magog had to do with anything, but he had an overwhelming feeling that something unpleasant was about to happen against these two countries. This must be a reference to a terrorist plot of some kind, but he had no idea what it meant. There had been attacks on both America and Britain in the past, his head reeled at the possibilities but he had to remain calm. There was nothing that he could do about it now, besides it was unlikely that an atrocity would happen immediately. Reaching for his coffee he took a mouthful and grimaced, it had gone cold. He e-mailed Jack with what he'd discovered and included the web address along with the passwords.

Figures were swarming all over the ship, boxes were being unloaded by hand and larger crates were taken off by cranes, these were then placed on the concrete wall beside the ship where forklift trucks carried them away to be stored. Roz was amazed by the scale of the operation it was just like any other busy port in the world. This was the first time she had seen modern machines in use on the island and these men were dressed differently from the inhabitants of the village. They appeared to be military, some wearing black uniforms whilst others wore the drab grey she had seen amongst Schiffer's men. Still she couldn't understand why the ship was being unloaded under cover, why go to so much trouble to conceal the operation?

Roz shivered in the darkness, her flimsy robe was no protection against the cool damp air that was rising up from the water. She remained hidden in the shadows wishing that she'd stayed in her warm and comfortable bed. Pushing these thoughts aside she moved deeper into the cave, she couldn't see what was in the crates but she wanted to know where the forklift trucks were taking them. There were tunnels leading off the main chamber, each one well lit but it was not clear where they went, she was on the opposite side of the harbour and it was difficult to see much beyond the ship.

One thing was clear, the cave seemed to go on forever, running deep under the island. The workings must be vast and she wondered what else went on here. It was a completely different world from that on the surface, the latest equipment was being employed to tend to the ship whilst up above people were stuck in a time warp. Suddenly an alarm sounded and Roz froze, slumping down against the wall she hid from view amongst a pile of huge steel storage drums. Men appeared from one of the tunnels, they were dressed in some kind of protective clothing and the workers who had been alongside the ship moments before had disappeared. Slowly a crane began to move and Roz peered over a steel drum. A metal box strapped to a pallet was hoisted from the ship's hold and as it swung up into the air she could see that it was old, corrosion had eaten into its surface and where labels had once been there remained only faded stains. One corner of the box had been damaged, the steel plates deformed and peeled back. She couldn't see what was inside the box but the men dressed in protective clothing treated it with respect, they were handling it carefully and slowly lowered it from the ship onto a flat bed truck before it was moved into one of the tunnels. Once it had gone the original workforce returned to continue with their work.

She wondered what was inside the box, it was obviously some kind of hazardous substance, judging by the way the men were dressed and the care they had taken when unloading it, it had to be something very nasty. She had seen enough and could stand the cold no longer, rubbing her arms she shivered before retracing her steps back to the mouth of the cave.

"Halt!" a man suddenly shouted and Roz began to run. Glancing back over her shoulder she could see him on the other side of the harbour, there was no way for him to get across and there was no one on her side of the wall so she was in the clear. Her chilled muscles complained at being asked to work so hard, but running as fast as she could she managed to disappear into the darkness beyond the entrance. Slipping along the harbour wall she made her way back towards the path which would take her back to the top of the headland. Here the ground rose up sharply, it was hard going but by the time she reached the top she had left the sounds of the harbour far behind. The village was just a little way ahead, but as she began to veer off to one side heading towards the cover of the nearest building a shot sounded, as the round passed close overhead it made a sharp sound as it drilled through the air.

"Halt," someone shouted.

She froze and cried out in panic then glancing back over her shoulder she saw a group of men carrying weapons. She was shocked to see them so close, there was nothing she could do but remain still in the middle of the pathway, her chest heaving with the effort of running uphill. Men surrounded her and one of them lunged forward with his rifle, the end of the barrel scoring against her ribs. A sharp pain shot across her chest and she cried out as her legs gave way, she couldn't understand why he had done that and she hated him for it.

"Get up!" An officer grasped her roughly by her shoulders and hauled her to her feet. Unable to support herself she staggered against him.

"Stand up," he bellowed as he pushed her away. Turning towards his men he issued orders and they began to make their way back towards the harbour.

Gently Roz probed her ribs with her fingertips, nothing seemed to be broken and the heat from the initial pain was wearing off. They marched her quickly back down the hill and as they approached the harbour she realised where they had appeared from so quickly. Turning sharply off the path they headed away from the sea then in front of them the earth bank opened up into a doorway and she was hustled into a dimly lit corridor. The sound of the men's boots on the concrete floor was deafening in the confined space and as they pushed her along Roz could feel her apprehension rising. The air was becoming cold and stale and the further they went the worse it became.

She hated enclosed spaces, it was made worse by the men in close proximity, pressing their bodies up against her they made little effort to respect her personal space, then suddenly they halted beside a series of doors.

Roz tried to remain calm, running would do her no good, she was sandwiched between two lines of armed men. She didn't think they would fire their weapons in such an enclosed space but if she did try to escape she wouldn't get very far before one of them would be upon her. She had no idea how far underground they had come, the island must be a warren of passageways and caves. These tunnels had to be linked to the harbour she had seen earlier, the storerooms where the ship's cargo had been taken must be somewhere near.

"In here," the officer appeared from behind a door. He didn't follow her in, the door simply slammed shut behind her.

Sitting behind a huge desk was a small weasel of a man. He was wearing thick round steel rimmed glasses which made his eyes look huge and he was dressed in the black uniform of an S.S. Officer. He studied her impassively as if she was some kind of unpleasant specimen. The silence was almost unbearable as she waited for him to begin, but he simply leered at her and remained unmoved. His hands clasped tightly together were resting on top of his desk and he allowed the tension between them to thicken. Roz, sensing danger, backed away as he moved and her stomach began to tighten.

"So," he said loudly. "What were you doing in our compound?" His voice heavy with accent made him seem even more sinister.

"I was curious," she managed to sound calm and relatively confident.

"Curious eh?" he said and putting both hands flat on the top of his desk he levered himself up. "You are forbidden to leave your quarters after dark and you are especially forbidden to snoop around our facilities." Like a predator he slowly made his way towards her. "So I will ask you once more, what were you doing in our compound?"

Roz studied him nervously, he was not a big man but he exuded evil. "As I said, I was curious and I didn't realise there was a curfew."

He simply nodded and stood up straight. "Why did you choose to go snooping after dark?" he tried a different approach.

"I couldn't sleep and as it was such a lovely evening I thought I would go out for a walk. I didn't realise that I was a prisoner."

"You were caught in a prohibited area," his voice boomed loudly in the confines of the room.

"I disagree, I was on the edge of the village admiring the view over the bay."

He moved forward until he was just a step away. "Why admire the sea when it's so dark, there is nothing to see?" his eyes narrowed.

Her 'fight or flight' reflexes screamed 'flight' but there was nowhere for her to run. "The moonlight was nice on the surface of the water."

Suddenly he struck, the force of the blow snapping her head back she fell back against the door.

"I will ask you again, what were you doing in our compound?"

Roz gasped with shock, this man was clearly not going to let her off with a warning, what level of violence was he prepared to go to in order to get her confession?

"I saw a light flashing out to sea so naturally I was curious," she paused, waiting for him to respond.

"What did you see?"

"I saw a ship," she continued cautiously, "it entered the harbour."

"And you followed it into the compound."

It was no use lying he probably knew she was in there anyway.

"Yes," she nodded, slowly edging away.

"Stand still, I did not tell you to move."

She was appalled at the way she was being treated and was about to remind him about her human rights, that she was an American citizen, but she chose to remain silent. The side of her head was throbbing from where he had hit her and she didn't want any more of that kind of treatment.

"Well, what did you see?" he went on persistently.

"I saw your men off loading crates from the ship but that was all, I didn't stay there for long, it was too cold."

He eyed her through her flimsy robe before returning to his desk where he grunted before he sat down.

XXIV

Jack briefed Razor and the men on board the Nautical Explorer. He was worried about the information Jerry had sent. He had entered the web site using the code words he'd been given but could make very little out of what he saw, his historical knowledge wasn't up to deciphering the text but Jerry's report had spurred him into action.

"We leave this morning for a base in Gibraltar, wheels up at 10:00," he glanced around the room, studying the men's faces. "I believe the target to be situated somewhere along the Moroccan coast and I intend flying reconnaissance missions in order to locate their base."

"So we're not just looking for kidnappers then?" Razor posed the question.

"No Bob, things have moved on a little, let me explain. We are now dealing with a highly organised group of terrorists." He kept it simple the men didn't need to know about the Nazi styled faction.

"What is Dr.Gairne's link with a gang of terrorists?"

"I don't think there is one, I'm convinced that her kidnapping along with Roz Stacey, is simply an unfortunate turn of fate. Their surviving the sinking of the Sea Quest was a bonus to whoever took out the ship," he didn't mention the submarine or the fact that it was now lying on the bottom of the sea beside his ship.

"So what's changed?"

"Last night I received some intelligence about the group we are seeking. You all saw what they are capable of and the extent of their facilities, the evidence was in the cave," he paused and shot a glance at Razor. "I have reason to believe that these people are plotting something big against both the U.S.A. and the U.K."

The men shuffled in their seats.

"Do you have intel about specific targets?"

"No Mac, we have no information about where or when, but you can be sure an attack is imminent and it's not going to be pleasant. I for one want to make sure it never gets off the ground."

Consent rippled around the room.

"What do you expect to find along the coast of Morocco?"

"A naval base of some kind."

This time the men broke out into groans of disbelief.

"You don't have to worry," Jack held up his hand, "I don't expect the

Moroccan Government to be involved, in fact I would be surprised if they are even aware that terrorists are camped out along their shore."

The men in the room became silent.

"I have no intention of starting a war with an African country. If the Moroccans were involved then it would be up to the military to go in and sort it out, besides we have to remember that Dr Gairne and one of our people are involved. We are dealing with an independent group of terrorists."

"How can we be sure the hostages are there?" asked Mac.

"We can't, but we have to assume that is where the helicopter went after it took off from the cave in Portugal. I've made some calculations and believe that the area I intend to search is at the extent of the helicopter's range."

"What if it landed somewhere in Spain?" Mac continued his argument.

"I think it's highly unlikely, there has to be a remote hideout somewhere near the coast because we know the terrorists have ships which they wouldn't be able to hide in Spain. They are highly organised and our mission is to root them out, it won't be a simple task I can assure you of that."

"We have to locate them first," Mac nodded.

"We also have to remember that our primary objective remains the safe recovery of Roz and Dr Gairne."

"What do you want us to do whilst you're flying recon missions?"

"I want to talk to you about that Mac. I need you to set up computer sims, I want every scenario covered."

Razor stood up when Jack gave him the signal, he had come to the end of his brief and now he wanted to speak with Mac.

Jack left the room and Paul followed him out onto the deck. Standing in silence they watched an engineer on the deck below who was fussing around one of the ROVs.

"So the plot thickens," Paul shot Jack a worried glance.

"It doesn't get any easier," Jack agreed.

"We're not certain that Roz and Dr Gairne are still alive."

Jack told him about the message they had found scratched into the wall of the cave. "They were alive then and I feel certain they are now. Dr Gairne is somehow valuable to these people," he didn't have the same confidence about Roz.

"How did we come to be involved in all this?" Paul sighed as he leaned against the rail. "We were only supposed to be salvaging some gold bars from an old ship."

Jack studied his friend. "It's strange how these things happen. I had a feeling about the Hudson Bay, it was shrouded in secrecy at the end of the war in Europe and it remains a mystery now."

"Well who would have thought it would turn out to be carrying an atomic weapon."

"Someone knew what was on board that ship, the only thing they were unsure of was what happened to it. Unfortunately we opened a can of worms when we located that wreck."

"You can say that again," Paul glanced at Jack. "Tell me, if you knew there was something dodgy in what we were doing then why did you allow Dr Gairne to join the salvage operation?"

"It was partly to do with politics and funding," Jack admitted. "The National Museum of Ireland put a lot of money into the operation. It's all about the Belgae Torc, besides its good for our organisation to be seen working with our Irish cousins."

"When you take off this morning you're not thinking about leaving me behind?" Thrusting his chin forward Paul looked squarely at Jack.

"Not if you're up to it," Jack grinned. "I wouldn't dream of cutting you out of the action."

"Then I'd better go and pack."

Orlagh was alone in her room. The excitement and relief she had enjoyed since their arrival was beginning to fade and she had spent a sleepless night worrying about Roz. At first the thought of escaping horrified her, going out into the sea again in a small boat was the last thing she wanted to do. She felt safe here, they were being well cared for and after the ordeal of the last few days their treatment on the island was heavenly. It seemed incredible to Orlagh that they had been there for only a short time, it wasn't so long ago that she had joined the Sea Quest in Cherbourg and she would never have imagined the events that had overtaken her.

Roz was right of course, they must at least try to get a message to Jack or attempt an escape, they couldn't remain there indefinitely. She had responsibilities, people would be worried about her, she only had two weeks to find the Belgae Torc and make her way back to Ireland. There was not much chance of her achieving that objective now, the Torc was still on the wreck and she wondered if she would ever get another chance to recover it for the Museum. Sighing deeply she reached for her goblet of wine, the cool sweet liquid was refreshing and it made her feel better.

Roz had not shown up for breakfast, this was the first time Orlagh had been alone at a mealtime and she realised that she missed the American's company.

"Do you have everything you need Miss?" one of the women appeared at the door.

"Have you seen Roz this morning?"

"No, not yet."

"Would you mind finding out where she is please?"

"Of course Miss," the woman smiled before leaving the room.

Suddenly there was a noise from outside in the corridor, she heard raised voices then the door flew open.

"Stand up," a man dressed in a black uniform shouted.

"What is the meaning of this?" Orlagh, standing her ground, faced him.

"You are to come with us," he indicated towards the doorway.

"Why, where are you taking me?"

"My orders are to accompany you to the General."

The women gathered at the door, they would remain with Orlagh they were responsible for her wellbeing.

General Leopold Meyer was head of the SchulzStaffel and part of his job was to ensure the security of the islands. Roz had breached his well-organised system and now his superiors were demanding an explanation. He was in a foul mood because he had been ordered to look into the problem personally ordinarily he would have detailed one of his subordinates to deal with it.

Orlagh and her entourage were marched through the compound surrounding the garden. Apart from the huge roundhouse, where they were being kept, there were a number of other buildings. General Meyer had commandeered one and was waiting for Orlagh to arrive. The officer in charge knocked on the door and Mayer stood up as the women entered.

"You ladies can leave," he said curtly, "you must remain." He peered menacingly at Orlagh. One of the women began to protest, they were supposed to stay with her at all times.

"I will not repeat myself, either you leave or I will have my men physically remove you," he waited patiently as they filed out of the office.

"Dr Gairne," he began respectfully, "your companion has been apprehended trying to escape from my men. She had infiltrated a prohibited area."

"I see," Orlagh nodded not yet having grasped the implications of what he'd just said.

"Your friend was caught spying in an area which is sensitive to the security of this island."

"Spying?" she was appalled by the term he had used. "Roz isn't a spy."

"We take this kind of behaviour very seriously indeed," he continued.

"Where is she now?" Suddenly she feared for Roz' safety.

"She is being questioned by our experts."

Orlagh saw the satisfied expression spread across his face.

"When they have finished with her she will be dealt with."

"What do you mean dealt with?" she shuddered.

"We have our methods," he hissed. "You will remain confined to your quarters." It was clear from her reaction that she knew nothing about her friend's actions.

"Tomorrow you will attend a ceremony," he grinned. "I would think that with your professional historical interests you will find it very interesting."

Jerry hurried across St. Stephen's Green as soon as his lecture was over, he wanted to get back to his bedsit where he was going to continue researching the Sonnenrad website. He'd been exhausted the previous evening, but now with fresh eyes and a clear mind he felt sure he would have a greater understanding of the texts. He had to find out more about the two biblical Giants, Gog and Magog, and their connection with the 'Phoenix Legion'.

As soon as he arrived home Jerry turned on his laptop and once it had booted up logged onto the website. Entering the code words he went straight to the higher level where the texts began to scroll over the screen. This time he knew what to expect, reading quickly he grasped the meaning of the words but at the end of several pages he found something that had not been there before.

'In the Kingdom of Elmet where Gog and Magog lie slumbering, the final elements are being put in place and soon the giants will breathe life once more.

Together they will go forth to slay the enemy, the great Eagle and the Lion will be brought to their knees and the pure Aryan bloodline will govern those who remain.

All you of pure blood should heed this warning, when the moon represents the Goddess in her Mother aspect, the ceremonies will begin with the light of life and the Third Reich shall reign for a thousand years.'

He studied the text carefully reading it over again slowly. It was a warning of an atrocity that was about to happen, it seemed that the terrorists were preparing to strike. Jerry had no idea what to make of the Kingdom of Elmet. He knew of course that it had once been an ancient Kingdom located in central England, but it didn't seem likely that the terrorists were operating from there. It appeared that the two giants were about to wreak havoc, but in what form was this going to take?

Jerry stared at the last part of the text thoughtfully he didn't under-stand the reference to the moon. Perhaps he should locate Pixie Lee on the Brothers of the Sacred Whisper forum, maybe she could answer his questions, but then he realised it would be safer to leave her out of this. If it was as dangerous as she said then involving her could put her in an impossible situation.

Turning the problem over in his head, his fingers danced over the keys of his laptop and before he realised what he was doing he had Googled 'moon phases'. Several sites appeared on the screen and scrolling down the list he selected one which referred to Celtic moon cycles, he discov-ered that each cycle had a mystical name, some of which referred to seasons. The Strawberry moon was the name given to the full moon during the strawberry picking season and the harvest moon was an obvious title. Scrolling through the information he found what he was looking for.

'Celtic full moon. The full moon represents the Goddess in her Mother aspect and ceremonies that are held during this phase are Handfastings, (Wiccan weddings), and Coming of Age Rites.'

He studied the information in an effort to relate it to what he'd seen on the Sonnenrad site. The full moon represents the Goddess in her Mother aspect, that was what the text had said. It gave praise to Cerridwen, Isis and many other Mother Goddesses. Jerry realised that this could relate to re-birth and fertility, the text had mentioned ceremonies beginning with the light of life.

He continued to read from the screen and discovered that the period of the full moon lasts from about three days before to three days after the actual full moon. He frowned, not a very accurate time frame. The text had said, 'When the moon represents the Goddess in her Mother aspect.' That was clear enough this was undoubtedly a reference to the full moon.

'When the moon is at its zenith it forms a silvery sphere in the sky. This is the time for spells and invocation to lunar Goddesses. This is a time for strength, love and power.'

He stopped reading and paused for a moment before sitting back in his chair to think. Reaching for his diary he checked the moon's phase and discovered that the previous evening it had been in its first quarter. Flicking through the pages he found the date of the full moon then he stared at the screen. In six days from now the moon will be at its zenith. His mind whirling he read through the text again, there was still much to discover, but one thing was clear, a terrorist attack was imminent and he realised with growing frustration that he had no idea where it was going to take place. He also needed to know more about the mythical characters Gog and Magog. He needed to speak to Jack.

RAF Gibraltar is made up of a 2000 metre paved runway which is intersected by the main road that runs to the border with Spain. No military aircraft are currently based there but there are regular visits so the servicing facilities are excellent.

The station functions as a civil airport and Jack had been given permission to use its facilities. A helipad on the corner of a concrete concourse was put at his disposal and as the airport wasn't particularly busy he could fly in and out without having to complete huge amounts of paperwork. There was a marina close by where he could place boats if he needed them and his men were going to be stationed in a building on the outskirts of town that was just a few minutes from the airport. The location couldn't have been better with the coast of Morocco not far away.

Jack brought the Sikorsky in and set it down gently in the centre of the helipad. Remaining in his seat as the twin engines wound down he knew that the next few hours would be hectic so he stole a few moments to focus his mind.

It was early afternoon and a warm breeze was blowing in from the Mediterranean, climbing stiffly down from the cockpit, he followed his men across the concrete apron. His first task was to make contact with the RAF officials, there was paperwork to be done and he had to arrange passes for his men. He also needed to ensure that aviation fuel would be available over the next few days, he anticipated flying every day until he located the terrorists' camp.

Suddenly his mobile phone began to ring.

"Jack Harrington," he said loudly over the noise of the airport.

"Jack, its Jerry. I need to speak with you."

"Hi Jerry, listen, I've just got into Gibraltar and have a mountain of things to do. Can I call you back in a couple of hours?"

"Okay Jack, but you really need to hear what I have to say. It's no good me e-mailing you."

Jack briefly outlined his plans then promised to call him back as soon as he could.

Orlagh had no appetite for her evening meal she couldn't stop thinking about her friend. She knew that Roz was desperate to locate the harbour which she thought was on the other side of the island, but she didn't expect her to go searching for it so soon. From what General Meyer had said, it was clear that she had stumbled across something important and he was agitated enough to suggest that Roz was being treated harshly. Orlagh was desperate to know what was going on, but the women who fussed around her seemed reluctant to discuss anything that took place beyond their Iron Age world, it was as if nothing else mattered.

She paced anxiously around her room, her nerves on edge knowing that Roz could be in danger. Roz could be obstinate and annoying at times but it was inconceivable to think that she was suffering at the hands of these thugs. Orlagh shuddered, if only she had convinced her not to try anything foolish, they could have made a plan, maybe walk out in the village. Roz could then have got a look beyond the Temple of Gog and perhaps she would be safe now. Reaching for her goblet she took a mouthful of wine, this was becoming a habit, Orlagh didn't realise how reliant she was becoming on the cool, refreshing liquid.

Eventually Jack stopped and returned Jerry's call. Several hours had passed since they had last spoken and he was feeling guilty for making him wait so long.

"Jerry," he said as soon as the connection was made, "sorry pal, things have been mad here."

"Jack thanks for getting back to me. I have some rather disturbing information for you," he paused, "we don't have much time before the terrorists plan to strike."

Briefly he outlined his discovery.

"So you're telling me that this cryptic message is on the Sonnenrad site?"

"Yes Jack, it's there for all to see."

"They obviously have followers in both the USA and the UK. That's worrying especially if that's where the suspected targets are located."

"Clearly," Jerry agreed. "We can't be sure how many people are involved but according to my contacts recruitment has been ongoing, at least in Europe."

"I see," Jack stared at his feet and frowned. "From what you're saying I guess the terrorists plan to strike at the next full moon?"

"It seems so," Jerry confirmed, "it's all in the text, it said the ceremonies begin with the light of life."

"The light of life eh, I wonder what that means."

"I have no idea, I don't even know what Gog and Magog represent, but I must admit, I don't like the sound of it."

"Okay Jerry, I'll inform the US and the British Governments, at least they will be prepared," he paused for a moment before asking the question. "So Jerry, give me the bad news, when's the next full moon?"

"We have six days including today."

"Well, I hope I'm right in expecting the terrorists to be holed up somewhere in Morocco."

"Yes but that might not stop them, you need to locate the cell co-ordinating the attacks. We have no idea what form these atrocities will take, it's not as if we've heard of this group before so we don't know what we're dealing with."

"Calm down Jerry," Jack could hear the tension building in his voice, "I'm sure the Governments will do all they can to assist us and in the meantime try to find out about Gog and Magog, I'll be a little happier when I know what we're up against."

He needed Jerry to remain focussed, his input was invaluable and Jack was amazed at how much he'd managed to discover already.

"Listen Jerry, we'll talk again tomorrow. E-mail me the moment you have something and I'll keep you up to date with the search this end."

XXV

The following day Jack was in the air immediately after breakfast. He decided to eat before the flight because the previous night he'd missed dinner and had no idea when he would get the opportunity to eat again. Paul was beside him in the co-pilot's seat and together they set out to scan the beaches of Morocco.

"So you think their hideout is on the northern coast," Paul said as soon as they were in the air.

"I reckon so," Jack nodded as he scanned the instrument panel. "The Moroccan coastline is about 3000km long," he shot Paul a glance, "don't worry buddy we won't be searching all of it."

"The terrorists' transport could only make it as far as the northern shore."

"That's what I figured, so that narrows it down to about 500km."

Paul studied the computer screen which displayed a map of the area. Most of Morocco's coastline was on the western side, but unless the helicopter carrying Roz and Orlagh had re-fuelled on route, the hideout was unlikely to be on that side of the country. Looking to his left Paul could see a vast expanse of water known as the Alboran Sea. This was the westernmost part of the Mediterranean, lying between Spain to the north with Morocco and Algeria to the south. To his right was the Strait of Gibraltar, a narrow channel which connected the Mediterranean with the Atlantic Ocean. Ahead he could make out the coast of Africa with the Rif Mountains in the distance.

It was a clear day with very little haze but he knew that visibility was sure to deteriorate. As the warm air coming up from the continent meets the cooler air over Europe it would become hazy but at the height they were planning to fly it shouldn't be a problem.

Jack put the Sikorsky into a gentle turn and as the compass needle swung round he began their descent towards the coastline. They followed the curve of a huge bay flying at 150kmh. Their maximum range was 1000km and once they had covered the 500km trip to Algeria, they should just about have enough fuel for the return journey to RAF Gibraltar. Those figures were a little close to the mark but Jack was willing to take the risk Paul, however, was determined to ensure that they headed for home before the point of no return and hopefully have fuel to spare.

Roz had been drugged, she could feel the acid effects of the narcotics coursing through her body, her head was spinning alarmingly and her mouth was as dry as sand. All she could see through the haze were shadows, mere suggestions of people moving in the periphery of her vision. She groaned as a loud noise penetrated her skull then rough hands pulled her to her feet. All she wanted to do was lie down but the bodies pushing annoyingly around her held her upright. She had the impression that they were moving along a narrow passageway and in the distance could see a bright light which reminded her of the entrance to heaven.

Orlagh was seated on a raised dais-like platform, the crowds were still, seemingly held in some kind of silent anticipation. The ceremony was an interesting mix of Celtic music and ritualistic dance which had been going on for hours, she had never experienced anything like this before and was finding it fascinating.

Druids appeared on the stage dressed in long black robes and wearing some kind of strange headdress. They led the crowd in a Pagan ceremony and she could feel the tension rising from the crowd, it was as if something special was about to happen, then turning to face her, the druids raised their arms above their heads.

"You must stand and salute them," the woman beside her urged, "stand up and raise your arms."

Orlagh did as she was told and the crowd went mad, their voices rising up until the auditorium was filled with a thunderous sound. She could feel the small bones in her ears vibrating as the noise echoed from the walls around her.

Jack brought the Sikorsky into land then glanced across at Paul.

"I could do with some coffee," he grinned.

"That was close, have you seen the fuel gauges, we've been running on fumes for the last fifteen minutes."

"You worry too much, I told you I'd get you home."

Swinging down from the cockpit, Paul winced as pain shot through his stiff shoulder.

"Have you got some painkillers for that?" Jack asked glancing sideways at him.

"Yeah, once I get hold of a mug of coffee I'll swallow some."

"You sure you're up for this pal?"

"Don't even think about cutting me out," Paul replied firmly.

Jack let the matter drop he could see that Paul was in no mood to discuss his discomfort. He wanted the helicopter refuelled immediately, it had to be ready to go at a moment's notice; he was going to check out some of the coves they had seen earlier. It was now mid afternoon and he intended to be back in the air within the hour.

Inside the building they were using as a control centre, Mac had set up computer terminals and most of the men were going through virtual battle scenarios. This was a valuable part of their training where different operational patterns could be studied, the computers working out the success rate of every move. Accurate figures could be calculated regarding ammunition requirements based on the parameters that Mac fed into the system, it could even predict casualty rates this information was invaluable to the rapid response team.

Kylie was working on a table to one side of the room. He was making fine adjustments to one of his drones and as he studied his laptop his drone darted around the room infuriating the other members of the team. He saw Jack and Paul the moment they appeared and carefully landed his drone on Jack's shoulder.

"Good to see you boss." Kylie's voice was transmitted through the drone and Jack grinned.

"You bloody idiot," Jack called across the room.

"What did you find boss?" Mac sidled over.

"Loads of idyllic sandy coves with warm blue sea lapping gently over golden sands."

"Any flaxen haired, huge breasted beauties skinny dipping in the surf?" he grinned.

"No such luck Mac." Jack moved to the side of the room where the coffee machine was situated and filling two mugs passed one to Paul.

"Nothing stood out," Paul said in an attempt to sound serious but Mac eyed him with amusement.

"We are going to take a closer look at some of the likely spots," Jack confirmed, "some of the coves look interesting especially the ones with cliffs or headland."

Jack regarded Mac with interest he was impressed with the way the little Native American had got the men working.

"So how goes it here?" Jack asked glancing approvingly around the room.

"As you can see the boys are busy, we have every battle situation going on, we'll be ready," Mac sounded confident. "I assume we'll be facing the usual array of weapons with the occasional grenade thrown in."

"You can count on it," Jack nodded. "Has there been any news from Jerry Knowles?"

"No," Mac said, his fingers dancing over the computer keyboard. "Let's see how they deal with this." He programmed the machines with an ambush and the men reacted quickly to the simulated threat. Jack watched the monitor with critical interest noting the different ways in which the men responded to each problem. These games were important, valuable data was collected and time spent here would save lives. Later the group would re-visit the monitors to study their efforts, it will be their opportunity to discuss tactics and decide how best to deploy their skills when facing the terrorists.

Jack smiled, his father always used to say 'forewarned is forearmed', 'children who got burnt treat fire with respect'. His father had been full of idioms and sometimes they came back to haunt him.

Roz was pushed from the safety of the corridor and she stumbled into the light. At first she could see nothing, the light assaulting her eyes blinded her temporarily and strange noises filled her ears. As soon as she appeared the crowd rose and cheered with delight, it was as if she was the long awaited star of the show.

Orlagh, watching from the balcony, looked down on the stage. She could hardly believe her eyes, Roz was on her knees with her head hanging forward, she didn't seem to have the strength to stand. Two druids came up behind her and raised their arms above their heads this made the crowd cheer even louder. With her senses momentarily distorted and weakened by drugs, Roz struggled to gain her composure. She was aware of the large space around her and could hear people cheering, but as yet she had no idea why. Tears stung at the back of her eyes and there was a sharp stabbing sensation in her brain. With a huge effort she struggled to get to her feet but strong hands forced her back down to her knees, it was then she became aware of the druids who were standing close by. The crowd began to quieten and Roz sensed that something was about to happen.

Suddenly one of the druids grabbed the collar of her robe and in a single movement ripped it from her body. Roz gasped and was thrown forward by the force of the fabric tearing. The crowd rose to their feet and began to cheer loudly.

Orlagh cried out as she watched Roz sprawl onto the ground, her body appeared to be covered in a mass of bruises, obviously administered during her interrogation, but as she looked closer Orlagh realised that the markings were not bruises at all. Roz was covered with intricate Celtic swirls and designs, tattoos which must have taken some considerable time to complete. Roz would never have given permission for these patterns to be etched onto her skin so she must have been held down or drugged, Orlagh was horrified.

Roz was pulled roughly upright and made to face the crowd. She looked dreadful, her face pale with dark rings circling her eyes. Orlagh couldn't tell if these were bruises or the effects of drugs. The druids began chanting, softly at first but after a while their voices became louder and the crowd quietened. Between them they lifted Roz up, holding her like a doll above their heads they displayed her to the crowd. The people howled with delight as she was paraded in front of them, the druids moving slowly around the stage so everybody could see and once they had completed a circuit they forced Roz back down to her knees. Holding herself rigid in an attempt to stop from collapsing she rocked nervously back and forth and Orlagh could hear the sound of her sobbing.

Somewhere at the back of her mind Roz was aware of what was going on but she didn't have the strength to fight the druids. It was as if her body was not her own, it wouldn't respond to her will and through her humiliation she sobbed with frustration. She thought about Orlagh and wondered if she was somewhere in the crowd, consumed by dread she realised that Jack would not be in time to save her and instinctively knew that this was not going to end well. The drugs had robbed her of her strength, but slowly her mind was beginning to work. She had no idea how long she had been like this, kept in a drugged state, she could hardly remember the interrogation, but the pain and the indignity of it was lodged firmly in her mind. Not once did they touch her but the threat was there all the same. She had been terrified but in the end had found relief in the drug they had forced upon her.

Orlagh was equally as horrified she looked on helplessly as the scene unfolded in front of her. She could do nothing to help her friend, she was seated on a gilded throne high above the crowd and had a perfect view of the stage. For a while she had enjoyed being the centre of attention, it was as if she were a queen or goddess, it had been a strange sensation when the crowd rose up to cheer as she took her place on the dais.

The theatre was made of solid white stone the walls beautifully carved with Celtic designs, there were rows of impressive columns supporting the stands and balconies above the stage. As the sun began its journey towards the horizon the white stone took on pink and orange hues, the building carefully aligned to capture the last rays at the end of the day.

Movement on the stage caught Orlagh's attention as one of the druids appeared from behind a column. In his outstretched arms he carried a red velvet cushion and as he moved slowly towards Roz the crowd hummed rhythmically in tune with his steps, the strange sound filling the auditorium made Orlagh shudder. He stopped when he was close beside Roz who remained on her knees, Orlagh could no longer hear her sobbing, the voices of the crowd drowning out all other sounds.

Suddenly the druid held up his arms and the crowd became silent then slowly he lifted something from the cushion, holding it up in the air sunlight flashed off gold and Orlagh held her breath. She could hardly believe what she saw, the druid was holding the Belgea Torc, it was unmistakable she had seen enough photographs of it and could identify it at a glance. How did they get it off the ship? She hardly had time to confront her questions before the druid brought the Torc down until it touched the top of Roz' head, then with slow deliberate movements he slipped it around her neck. Orlagh was still holding her breath as she watched.

At first nothing seemed to happen, Roz held herself rigid as the druids backed away until she was alone in the centre of the stage. Excitement and anticipation rose up like a wave around the auditorium as the crowd waited.

Orlagh let out her breath, the shock of seeing the Torc was wearing off and now she realised the implications of the ceremony, throughout history whoever wore it had died and she was sickened by what she saw.

Roz could feel the weight of the Torc around her neck, it was warm resting against her skin and she was so tense that she could hardly breathe. Her heart was a hammer booming inside her chest but at least her eyesight was beginning to clear, the drug induced clouds receding into the background. In the distance she could see someone coming towards her, at first she was unable to make out the figure, but then she realised it was a woman, she could see her thick red hair and pale white skin. Roz sighed with relief, it was Orlagh.

The Torc around her neck was becoming heavy, the metal vibrating softly as if it was a live serpent encircling her throat. Roz tried to focus on Orlagh's face, but still the weight of the Torc bothered her. The vibrations were stronger now and she could feel the heat radiating from it, she remained uneasy, her stomach tightened with apprehension and although her brain was sending signals to her limbs they refused to move, she was frozen to the spot.

Orlagh seemed to be drifting over the ground, Roz couldn't see her feet beneath her long white robe which swirled like gossamer around her legs. Standing close, she cast no shadow and Roz realised that something was very wrong; the woman looming over her couldn't possibly be Orlagh. The breeze lifted the woman's red hair and as Roz looked into her huge dark eyes she was filled with dread. Someone had once said that the eyes were windows to the soul, but these eyes were lifeless, terrifying pools of darkness that were evil and foreboding. Roz, filled with horror, was unable to look away. The woman remained expressionless and slowly reached out towards Roz, the touch of her hand was like ice against her skin, it chilled her to the bone and Roz shuddered. Her head began to fill up with terrifying images and then the chanting began. She couldn't understand the words, the language was all wrong. Suddenly the Torc around her neck began to burn as it pulsed against her skin. The woman's fingers were moving like serpents against her scalp and pain seared through her brain like bolts of lightning, then Roz choked as she tried to draw in a breath. She was suffocating and her eyesight was beginning to fade, the pain in her head was almost too much to bear, it burned relentlessly into her soul. Still she couldn't move, not even in the moment of death was she able to throw off the paralysing force which held her firmly in its grip. Slowly darkness robbed her of her sight and her chest felt like it was on fire. Relief was slow to come and as a scream caught at the back of her throat she gasped, then it was all over.

Orlagh cried out as the vague outline of a ghostly figure standing over Roz evaporated into the air. She blinked, not certain that it had been there at all, but Roz was motionless her body slumped on the cold stone slabs, the Belgae Torc still around her neck shining magnificently in the dying rays of the sun.

The druids appeared again and slowly moved towards Roz, they gathered her up in their arms and presented her to the crowd. Holding her limp and naked body high above their heads they chanted, but this time the crowd didn't cheer, they moaned softly, a lament to the dead. It was as if their grief had been rehearsed and Orlagh hated them for it. She was stunned and could hardly believe what she had just seen, she felt nauseous and tears rolled unchecked over her cheeks. Her heart ached for her friend and trembling with shock she turned towards one of the women who was standing beside her. She too had been looking down on the stage, but her face displayed no emotion, she seemed coldly detached from the proceedings, it was as if she was disgusted by what she had seen but was too frightened to resist. Who were these people and what did they want from her? Roz had been right, she should have listened, she should have helped her to find a way off this island, maybe if she had then Roz would still be alive.

It was almost midnight and Jerry couldn't sleep. He was sitting at his desk poring over his notes trying desperately to understand the riddle he had discovered on the Sonnenrad website. It was obvious to him now that the terrorists were going to strike at targets in both the U.S.A. and the U.K. He also realised that they were dealing with dark forces that had lain dormant since the end of the Second World War, but now the beast was gaining strength and the time had almost come for it to rise up once again.

He was amazed at the references to pure Aryan blood and the Third Reich, these were terms that he thought had disappeared from Europe, there were also clear indications that this was all about retribution. He could hardly believe that in the modern world, especially within today's Europe, ideals driven by Nazism and the Occult could exist side by side. He was shocked, this small but growing band of fanatics were intending not to just overpower Europe, but also take on the world's most power-ful nation.

With a sigh he rubbed his hand over his face before reaching for his mug of coffee. He took a mouthful and grimaced, again it had gone cold he shuddered then put the mug down and focussed his mind on the facts. The terrorists were likely to make their attacks on the capital cities, that way they could maximise casualties and cause a lot of damage, once they had achieved that they could move in and take full advantage of the shock and horror. The obvious targets would be public places or maybe a seat of power. If the terrorist wanted to strike at the heart of the nation then the Houses of Parliament and the Pentagon would be the most likely targets, but it didn't make any sense, surely the terror-ist would strike when the Government buildings were full, destroying empty buildings at night would be a waste of effort.

Jerry knew about the atomic weapon that had been on board the Hudson Bay, he was also aware that it had disappeared. Drumming his fingers against the top of his desk he'd already made the terrifying connections and his blood ran cold, then snatching up the telephone he dialled Jack's number. Jack answered on the second ring.

"Jerry, it's good to hear from you buddy."

"Sorry to call so late."

"Don't worry about that pal, we're too busy to sleep, what have you discovered?"

Jerry outlined his theory and they discussed possible targets.

"That's what I figured," Jack sounded grim.

"Do the terrorists have access to long range submarines that are capable of firing nuclear missiles?"

Jerry's question bothered Jack. "They certainly have ships," he began. "The only sub we've seen so far is an old but heavily modified Type XXIII, but I guess we can rule nothing out. Why do you ask?"

"It's only a theory Jack but what if they are capable of using the atomic components from the warhead that went missing from the Hudson Bay. They could use that stuff to arm their missiles then fire them at our cities from the submarines."

"That's some theory," Jack said. "I was thinking that maybe the weapons would be carried in by suicide bombers or roadside bombs set up in vehicles packed with explosives. If they could get close enough they could do some real damage."

"True," Jerry agreed. "But they wouldn't have to get that close if they are using nuclear technology."

"Well, there's not much time for them to ship their devices out if the attack is going to take place at the next full moon, that's only a few days away."

"So if they were going to use submarines to transport their missiles they would already be at sea. They could of course be planning an air strike."

"Yeah, but even if that were true they still wouldn't have had time to utilise the material salvaged from the Hudson Bay."

"The text tells us that Gog and Magog lie slumbering in the Kingdom of Elmet, it goes on to say that the final elements will be put in place soon and the giants would breathe once again. That indicates to me given the timescale and the fact that they've just managed to get hold of the atomic warhead, the explosive devices have not yet been put in place."

"I see where you're coming from Jerry but we can't rule out the fact that the attacks won't happen in a few days time. I can't help thinking that the weapons have already been deployed and this whole thing with the atomic warhead is some kind of diversion."

"I'm not so sure about that Jack, why go to all that effort salvaging it if it wasn't part of the master plan?"

"Have you got any more information about the location of this Kingdom of Elmet?" Jack changed the subject.

Jerry told him what he knew about the historical Kingdom, but that was no help, there were no clues as to where they might find it. Jack was convinced that the terrorists' lair was somewhere along the Moroccan coast and he filled Jerry in with the events of the day.

"Have you had any communication from the terrorists regarding a ransom demand?" Jerry asked.

"No, it's unlikely that either Dr. Gairne or Roz Stacey will be ransomed, that's not what this is all about."

"Then why take them? They must want them for some purpose."

"I don't think so," Jack replied. "They were not targeted, they have no value. Roz and Dr. Gairne were simply in the wrong place at the wrong time. It's my guess that their kidnapping was pure chance," he went on. "We know that at least one man escaped from the crippled sub. I think the women were overcome when they were struggling to recover from their own ordeal, maybe they were already on board the lifeboat."

"It doesn't make any sense, if they have no value or connection with the terrorists why take them into captivity?"

"We don't know the answer to that Jerry but we do know they were alive when at the cave, we found evidence of that but it now appears that it won't be a simple hostage rescue mission after all. If you are right then there's a lot more at stake."

"You agree then, we know the likely targets and we think nuclear devices of some kind are going to be used?"

"I'm afraid I do Jerry," Jack said.

A brief silence followed as both men reflected upon the consequences of their reasoning.

"I have to say though Jerry, I like their style, naming their devices after two mythical giants, that's quite amusing."

XXVI

The shock of seeing Roz in the arena horrified Orlagh but still she couldn't fully accept what had happened. The druids, having produced the Torc, had changed everything but she was relieved to know that it was safe and not lost forever at the bottom of the Atlantic. Witnessing its dark powers first hand was beyond anything she could have imagined, she had read the reports regarding its past, Jerry had even told her about the entries in his great grandfather's journals, but still she refused to believe that Roz was dead.

Her attendants had not given her a moment's peace since the ritual they remained at her side monitoring her mood. As soon as they returned to their dwelling Orlagh was offered a cup of wine and a hot scented bath was drawn, she was happy to go along with whatever they suggested, she felt safe in their company and not a bit uncomfortable. Sipping the wine she began to feel more relaxed, she realised that it was drugged, Roz had warned her about it the moment they had arrived, but it was too late, she was becoming ever more reliant on its effects.

The bath was ready and a woman helped her to remove her gown and as Orlagh stepped into the warm scented water she sank down and laid back. The bubbles were heavenly against her skin and closing her eyes she sighed deeply. Someone began to massage her scalp lathering her hair with scented herbs, and it was all she could do to stop herself from falling asleep.

"How did the druids get hold of the Belgae Torc?" she asked no-one in particular.

"They have always had it," one of the women replied.

"But that's not possible," her eyes snapped open. "It was lost when the ship carrying it sank."

"No, it was not lost," the woman perched on the edge of the bath reassured her.

"But I don't understand, I was sent to the wreck to search for it."

"The Belgae Torc was never lost," she continued softly as if talking to a child. "It came to us in the 1940s, it's a story we all know well." She passed Orlagh another goblet of wine.

With the head massage complete the woman slipped her hands under the water and began to work the tension out of her shoulders. Orlagh's eyelids became heavy and she sighed contentedly.

"It's true the Torc was on the ship called the Hudson Bay," the woman continued, "when it sank a crewman managed to get away in a lifeboat, unfortunately he was the only survivor of the tragedy. He took with him many treasures including the Belgae Torc but he was a long way from shore and had very little in the way of provisions. Eventually after many days his lifeboat washed up in a bay but by then the man was dead. Ironically he was surrounded by treasures which, if he had survived, would have made him a very wealthy man."

"Did he die from exposure?" Orlagh asked sleepily.

"No, the man made a tragic mistake, he put the Torc around his neck, he was unable to resist its beauty he must have felt like a king wearing such a powerful symbol."

Orlagh's eyes shot open again, this was another reference to someone meeting their untimely death whilst wearing the Torc.

"How did it end up here?"

"The druids who discovered the lifeboat recognised it immediately, all the treasures were brought here but the Torc was coveted above all else. It belongs here amongst the druids and the pure blooded Aryans, it's our symbol of power, part of our heritage, it was made for us over two thousand years ago."

Orlagh frowned but remained silent. The news of the escaping crewman was never recorded, as far as everyone knew the Torc had been lost with the ship. Finally she let her thoughts go, it was easier to simply relax and allow the woman's hands to work their magic.

Jack and Paul were in the air again. This time their mission was to take a closer look at some of the locations they had picked out from yesterday's flight. Jack had worked through much of the night and together with Mac they had fed information into the computer which analysed the results. Mac had written a program that studied the data and made scientific calculations based on geographic statistics and tidal flows, it had come up with some startling results. The program was invaluable, it cut down on the time they would spend in the air and now they could focus their efforts on the most favourable sites. There were dozens of locations which fitted the terrorists' requirements and Jack was determined to make a thorough search of every one.

The helicopter flew out over the narrow channel which separated Europe from mainland Africa and as they went Jack told Paul about his conversation with Jerry Knowles.

"It doesn't sound good," Paul glanced across the cockpit when Jack had finished. "The clock is ticking and we have just a few days to find a group of madmen, two nuclear devices and get our people back."

"Should be a piece of cake," Jack grinned.

Paul was amazed by his relaxed attitude, nothing seemed to get Jack down, he had already lost one of his survey ships and a Sikorsky S92 helicopter, Paul was glad he wasn't footing the bill. He had known Jack for a long time and understood the way his mind worked. When Jack was committed to a mission nothing could stop him, his dogged determination never failed him Jack always got what he wanted. Jack believed that men made their own luck and whatever the situation he always managed to turn things to his advantage.

The first four locations on their list proved to be fruitless. They made a thorough search of the area, flying low over the beaches and headlands. At one point Jack almost flew the helicopter into a cave, but averting disaster Paul insisted they put down on the beach and survey the cave on foot. The following day was the same. Systematically they flew over possible locations working their way inland occasionally chasing a likely lead. Time was slipping away rapidly and Jack was beginning to think that maybe he was wrong. Perhaps the terrorists had taken on more fuel, travelled further than he had first thought. If that were true then their hideout could be on the Atlantic coast or even in one of the neighbouring countries.

They finished their daily search pattern and with the fuel tanks running low Jack set a course for home. Swinging the helicopter out over the Alboran Sea on an 'as the crow flies' course they left the coastline behind, it was then that Jack made a discovery.

"Hello, what do we have here?" the sound of his voice startled Paul.

Peering towards the horizon Paul could just make out two islands through the haze and with a frown he glanced at the computer screen, they didn't appear on any of the charts. Jack made a slight course correction and headed towards the nearest.

"Are those buildings?" Paul asked as tower like structures came into view.

"Looks like the islands are inhabited. Any information on the computer?" Paul checked the screen again.

"Nothing on the map, they must be too small."

"Strange, with people living there you would have thought someone would have mapped their location on a chart."

The island was covered in foliage and apart from the single tower which looked strangely out of place there was no other evidence of occupation. The Sikorsky flashed over the narrow channel which separated the two land masses and they looked down with growing interest. Laid out below was a village of thatched roundhouses that were grouped around a tower identical to the one they had just seen.

"Twin towers," Jack muttered.

There was a small grass landing strip on the southerly tip of the island where a collection of light aircraft were grouped together. The airfield was situated some way from the village and as they skimmed the grass, heading back towards the village, they passed over a circle of standing stones. A moment later they were back over the village, circling around the tower. Further on they discovered a natural harbour nestling in a cove that was surrounded by high cliffs. A wall acting as a sea break extended into deeper water and small fishing boats were tied up along one arm. Jack slipped the helicopter into a tight turn and it was then they saw the huge entrance cut into the cliff face.

"What do you make of that Paul?" Jack asked as they hovered just above the surface of the water.

"A clever and secure extension of the harbour I guess."

"Why would they want to hide their boats?"

"It's huge, large enough to hide a navy."

With the throttle all the way forward the Sikorsky went into a steep climb and circled over the cliff top before dropping back down again to sea level. Jack wanted to take another look at the cave and hovering opposite the entrance Paul activated the thermal imaging video camera.

The Forward Looking Infra Red, (FLIR), as it was more commonly known, was an essential piece of equipment which allowed them to produce images based on the heat values of targets within its view. Police helicopters were fitted with this type of equipment and Jack had it installed on his helicopters to help make surveying a little easier. Paul kept the camera running as they circled over the village.

"What do you make of that tower?"

"It's identical to the one on the other island." Paul said twisting around in his seat to get a better look.

"Just look at these huts, reminds me of an ancient village."

"Sure looks primitive apart from that collection over there." Paul nodded towards the group of buildings that were clustered around a large round house. The complex was bordered by gardens and Jack couldn't help being impressed by their formal symmetry.

"Someone sure spends a lot of time on that," he nodded. "Where is everyone?"

233

They could see no-one, the population had disappeared, Jack expected to see animals but there was nothing the whole place was deserted.

"I'll get some thermal images of those houses try to get some pictures of the interiors." Paul worked the turret which housed the camera and Jack held the machine steady, he then checked the computer screen to ensure that it was recording.

They were just a few metres above the houses, their down draft worrying the thatch on the roofs as clouds of dust billowed up from the pathways that crisscrossed the village. Jack was convinced they had found what they were looking for, the airfield and the harbour with its secret hideaway both needed further investigation but what intrigued him most were the towers.

"Get some shots of those towers," he didn't need to remind Paul but it made him feel better to issue the order.

They swept along the length of the island once more recording every inch and adding it to the computer memory, when they were finished they turned towards the other island. It needed only a cursory glance as it was mostly covered in foliage so there wasn't much to see. The only thing of interest was the tower rising up out of the trees and when they had finished Paul glanced at the fuel gauges as Jack set a course for home.

Orlagh was in the garden when the alarm went off it was a sound that she had heard in movies many times before as a child, the kind that warned of air raids. It lasted for several minutes.

"You have to come inside," one of the women called urgently from across the flower beds.

"What's going on?"

Orlagh was ushered into the building, her questions ignored until she was safely inside.

"Will someone tell me what's happening?" she demanded.

"There's an intruder."

The chopping sound of a helicopter was becoming louder as it drifted closer and looking at the other women Orlagh could see fear in their eyes. The walls of the house began to vibrate as the huge machine hovered overhead.

"Why is it necessary to hide?" Orlagh shouted above the noise.

"It could be hostile, perhaps a gun ship from Africa."

"But I don't understand."

"There are people out there who given the chance would take our islands away from us, they are bad men who do us harm. Sometimes they launch attacks on our village and if they catch us in the open they kill us with their guns."

Orlagh was horrified and she cowered amongst the women until eventually the helicopter moved away.

Deep beneath the island Storm Troopers raced along the passageways and once they reached their emplacements they turned their guns to face the intruder.

"Hold your fire," came the order, "they appear to be unarmed."

Men watched through binoculars as the helicopter hovered low over the deserted village. The people had taken shelter in their roundhouses along with their livestock, but the machine was so close they could see Jack and Paul at the controls. Slowly it gained height and began to drift out over the water, then picking up speed it disappeared towards the horizon.

When it was safe another alarm sounded the all clear and people began to move about the village again before returning to their work.

The Sikorsky joined the circuit flying around RAF Gibraltar before coming in to land. Paul had already sent the file containing the film to Mac's computer and before the rotor blades had stopped turning they were making their way towards the control room.

"Let's get some coffee then see what we have on the film."

Paul nodded in agreement as he massaged his shoulder discreetly, the vibrations from the helicopter had set it off again but he wouldn't admit to it.

Already the fuel bowser had arrived to fill up the tanks and Jack waved to the driver who jumped down from his cab.

"Hi Jack, Paul." Mac nodded as he met them at the door. "Sent the men out on an exercise, can't have them getting fat playing computer games."

"Good idea Mac." Jack grinned as he made his way across the deserted room towards the coffee machine. "I think we may have found the terrorists' lair."

"We've sent a file to your computer," Paul explained as he reached for the mug Jack was holding out to him.

"Let's take a look," Mac was already at his terminal, his fingers darting over the keys.

The file included a five minute video of their flight across the islands and over 100 stills, many of them taken with the infra red camera. They studied the video in silence before opening the other files.

"Let's have a look at the thermal images I'm sure there were people hiding in those roundhouses."

The first picture revealed an empty house but as they studied the others it became clear that they were occupied, heat signatures from human bodies and animals were showing up.

"I thought as much," Paul nodded, "get a close up of that one." He pointed at a doorway on the screen and as Mac zoomed in, the face of a child peering up at them materialised out of the gloom. "What did I tell you?" he grinned.

"Why hide?" Jack frowned. "I'm not too concerned about the village," he continued. "I would like to get a closer look at the cave in the harbour wall."

Mac found the stills of the harbour and clicking on one zoomed in until the cave entrance filled the screen.

"Not a lot to see." Paul muttered.

"What's that?" Jack pointed towards a smudge. "Can you clean that up a bit?"

Mac hit some keys and the image improved.

"What does that look like to you?" Jack glanced at Paul.

"There are pathways leading from the harbour wall into the cave, you can see them clearer on this side," he touched the screen with his finger. "I think this could be a docking area," he tapped the screen again, "looks like there are cases stacked up against the wall, can you see those cranes?" he turned towards Jack.

"Yeah, that's my thinking and just there you can make out the back end of a ship."

Paul looked closer and Mac did what he could to sharpen up the grainy image.

"Well I'll be, you're right Jack, that's definitely the stern of a ship."

"I wonder what it's doing in there and what's more, I'd like to know what else is hidden inside that cave." Jack glanced at the others, they were thinking the same. "What are those, can you zoom in there Mac?"

Jack nodded towards a number of grey outlines perched on top of the cliffs which had shown up on a wide angled shot. Mac switched to thermal imaging mode and zoomed in.

"What have we here?" Jack whispered.

"Looks like gun emplacements," Paul squinted at the image. "It would make sense, they are just where I would place my defences, they cover the harbour quite nicely."

Each emplacement appeared to be manned by two gunners.

"Heavy machine guns I would guess," Mac said running his hand over his chin.

"There are several dotted about," Paul agreed. "We'll have to get a definite count and mark them on a map."

"We had better make a start before the men get back," Jack said as he moved towards the printing machine. "Can you print off two aerials, one normal and one with thermal imaging?"

"Roger that." Mac replied and the printer began spitting out two large scale maps of the island.

Jack spread them over a table and the men moved in for a closer look then picking up a marker pen he began to pinpoint the locations of the harbour defences.

Paul took additional notes as Mac described what he could see on the screen, this would form the basis of an attack plan which would be invaluable when briefing the men.

"This is conclusive evidence, we've found the terrorists," Jack began. "We have a secret hidey hole just here," he indicated to the location of the underground harbour, tapping it with the end of his pencil, "we also have defensive bunkers here, here and here."

"There are bound to be more around the airfield." Paul nodded, turning his attention to the southern tip of the island, "That runway is far too short for anything larger than light aircraft unless they are operating STOL capabilities."

"Helicopters come under that heading and there are some serious aircraft out there capable of short takeoff and landing," Mac said.

Jack and Paul agreed although they had seen no evidence of helicopters at the airfield.

"What do you make of this tower Mac?" Jack asked. "The tower on the other island is just the same as this one."

Mac moved towards the computer and flashed up an image then he studied the video footage.

"Obviously a storage silo," he frowned. "What would they store in something so large?"

Jerry Knowles thinks the islands are called Gog and Magog," Jack told them, "those are also the names given to two mythical giants."

Both Paul and Mac nodded, they were familiar with the biblical tale.

"These could be launch towers," Mac said.

"What, missile launch towers?" Paul was shocked by Mac's remark.

"Some missile," Jack muttered, "they would have to be enormous, as large as a Saturn five, the rocket used to send Man to the moon."

"Surely not!" Paul glanced at Jack.

"You asked for my opinion," Mac shrugged. "For all I know they could be water towers."

XXVII

Orlagh was standing alone on the terrace overlooking the garden. She was enjoying the beds of exotic flowers which released their scent into the cool night air. The sun had just melted spectacularly over the horizon and now the sky was a rash of colour painted onto a web of lace which stretched across the heavens.

The silence around her was as heavy as her mood, the only sounds coming from small creatures rustling amongst the plants. Orlagh looked up and studied the sky searching for the moon which had not yet made an appearance. She knew it was going to be huge, tomorrow it would be full and she felt certain that the villagers would be practicing their lunar rituals and magic spells. She thought of moon struck hares, pagans believed that seeing a moon gazing hare would bring growth, re-birth and good fortune to their village. 'The hare is known to be sacred to the Goddess Eostre and eventually became known as the Easter Bunny.' Orlagh smiled as she remembered a paper she once wrote on the subject.

Creeping further along the pathway she was suddenly overcome with sadness. It was as if someone had just flicked a switch plunging her world into darkness surrounding her with an atmosphere of gloom. Just a few days ago she had walked this way with Roz but now her friend was gone. Orlagh missed her very much, a huge void had opened up in her life which left her feeling utterly alone, even the treatment she had come to rely on could do nothing to alleviate the loss which threatened to overcome her. Turning back towards the house she had lost the urge to walk, the gardens no longer held their appeal and now all she wanted to do was shut herself away in her room and take pleasure in a goblet of wine.

A few miles away Jack was staring up at the same piece of sky, tomorrow the prophecy of the 'Phoenix Legion' would be upon them and he would have to act. In less than twenty four hours his small team of men must go in hard if they were to prevent a national disaster. He thought about the events of the last two weeks and could hardly believe how a simple salvage job had turned into a deadly race against time. The lives of so many people weighed heavily upon him and still there was much uncertainty to overcome. All he had to go on was what Jerry Knowles had told him and of course what he had seen for himself on the Sonnenrad web site. Maybe they had got it wrong perhaps these people were just harmless fanatics, no threat to their countries after all. Jack sighed deeply and wondered why he couldn't believe that.

Suddenly his thoughts were shattered by a loud noise scratching against the sky, flashing lights came out of the stars and turned towards the end of the runway. He watched as the sleek and powerful shape of an RAF Tornado materialised from out of the darkness. It streaked past him jet engines howling, the noise and the thrill of the moment gripping him until he was overcome by an excitement that he hadn't experienced in years. The aircraft rapidly lost momentum and turned at the end of the runway before making its way back then it parked next to his Sikorsky.

Jack was grinning like a schoolboy as he watched the canopy slip silently open, starlight glistening like pearls against its reflective surface as the pilots climbed down. Shaking his head in admiration, Jack thrust his hands into his pockets as he wandered back towards the temporary control room.

The following morning he gathered his men for a briefing. Screens had been set up in the control room and these were now displaying detailed maps of the island, gun positions covering the harbour and other vital information.

"Tonight we are going to make a covert attack on this island," Jack tapped the screen with his finger and waited as excitement rippled around the room. "Paul and I have located the terrorist's stronghold," he continued. "We've discovered a secret harbour." Using a laser pointer he indicated to a position on the map. "It's heavily fortified and I suspect they have an early warning system in place because the guns were manned the moment we arrived. There are heavy machine gun placements here, here and here," he used the laser pointer again, marking the positions on the map. "As you can see their converging fire covers the harbour so we can't go in that way. Now, because of the early warning system and the noise, we won't be using the Sikorsky, but I've managed to locate two landing craft that were left here in storage by British Marines." He peered around the room in order to gauge their reaction. Razor was standing at the back making notes in a small writing pad then he glanced up.

"I intend to go in using these landing craft," Jack turned back towards the map. "One team will land near to the airfield that's situated on the southern tip of the island." The red laser point danced over the area. "The airfield is to be taken out, I don't want anything coming in or going out once we've arrived. The second group will come ashore fifteen minutes later about half a mile from the harbour." Again he marked the position. "The first team will make their way towards this village. Between the village and the airstrip is a ring of standing stones, I want to check it out on the way. The other team will go towards the harbour using this coastal path," he studied the men again.

"We have two objectives, number one, stop the terrorists from launching their attack and number two, locate and release our people."

He went on to tell them about the intelligence Jerry Knowles had supplied and the information he had got from the Sonnenrad website.

"Don't you think these devices would already be in place?" someone asked from the floor.

"That's possible, we can't rule out that fact. We are either going to discover a control room of some kind from where the bombings will be co-ordinated or if the devices have not yet been launched we have to discover and disarm whatever delivery system they have in place."

"What about resistance Jack, do you know the strength of the terrorist cell?" Razor asked the question.

"You can bet your life there will be stiff resistance, you all saw the cave on the mountain and the resources these people have at their disposal."

For the next thirty minutes Jack outlined his plan in minute detail before answering the many questions that arose. Contingency plans were discussed covering every eventuality.

"The Sikorsky will be on standby, it will provide us with a first class ticket off the island once we have achieved our objectives. One of the RAF pilots stationed here has agreed to fly it."

When he was done Jack left Razor to brief the men further then going out onto the concrete apron he watched a group of technicians fussing around the Tornado. He discovered that the aircraft was fully armed, it had been on a mission over Iraq when it developed a fault, but the technicians were now almost finished and it was due to leave later that evening.

Orlagh was being prepared for the Lunar Festival, she was dressed in a fine white robe that was trimmed with gold and on her feet she wore slippers of soft leather. One of the women was tidying her hair whilst humming a tune and Orlagh felt like a little girl again. She was unaware that the druids had increased the drug dose that she was being given, not only was it added to her wine but now also to her food, consequently Orlagh was feeling a little detached from reality. Her mind no longer her

241

own she forgot about Roz as she drifted in a world of their making, even her thoughts were being manipulated by the druids. She had fought valiantly against the forces that whirled around inside her head, but now her drug induced emotions were in freefall and there was nothing she could do to rein them in.

"Today is the celebration of the moon, the Goddess in her Mother aspect." The woman brushing her hair explained and Orlagh could hear the excitement in her voice.

"You must be as radiant as the Goddess herself."

Outside the sun was already making its way towards the horizon and the villagers were forming up along the route which had been marked out by the druids.

A channel from the beach ran in a straight line towards the auditorium where the stage was set. The auditorium had been decorated with flowers and lush green foliage this was supposed to represent a sacred grove.

A chariot of gold, pulled by two white stallions stood magnificently on the beach and people milling about were overawed by its power. This was a vehicle fit for a goddess and as the waves lapped gently up against its steel rimmed wheels children took their places youngest first increasing in age and size all along the route. Each child held a basket of petals which they would spread like confetti along the road, laying down a carpet as the chariot passed them by.

Orlagh was leading a procession which moved regally along the coastal path, the women surrounding her chanting as they went and Orlagh let the sound of their voices wash over her like the warm breeze drifting in off the sea. It was soothing, the natural rhythm helped to calm her nerves. Her heart was beating unnaturally fast, it was as if she had been running but she was not out of breath. In an effort to clear her blurred vision, she filled her lungs with fresh sea air and smiled contentedly, far out on the horizon the sun was beginning to set and the sky was filling up with a rainbow of colours.

Orlagh hardly noticed the druids flanking the procession, like shadows against the changing light they remained inscrutably silent. One of them climbed up onto the chariot and took his place on the driver's platform, holding the horses steady he watched over his shoulder as Orlagh was helped up on board then with a flick of the reins the horses began to move. Gilded wheels began to turn and Orlagh looked down at the children, their eager little faces all smiles and she was enchanted. Petals from their baskets created little puddles of colour on the road ahead and as Orlagh waved back the children squealed with delight, their voices soaring with her spirits.

The journey was painstakingly slow and incredibly uncomfortable. There was no suspension to soften the ride and as the chariot rode over stones and ruts she was thrown off balance. Orlagh was not used to travelling this way and had to use her legs as well as her arms to grip onto the wooden sides, it was a huge effort to avoid being tossed over the side. The druid gripped the reins tightly in both hands giving the horses little room to stray, and as Orlagh glanced ahead she could see the amphitheatre. Suddenly the tone of the horses' hooves changed and once they reached the smooth stone surface the chariot stopped pitching. She was relieved for the respite, her knees and elbows bruised from holding on so tightly, but now at least she was able to stand upright and enjoy the rest of the journey. The wheels rumbled pleasantly as they passed beneath the archway, this was the entrance to the theatre and the driver guided the horses skilfully between the vast stone columns which supported the seating and viewing platforms above.

As soon as they appeared the villagers already assembled cheered and the noise inside the auditorium became deafening. One of the horses threw its head up, startled by the sound, but with a string of expletives the druid managed to regain control and they rumbled on. He steered the chariot slowly around the vast stage giving everyone the opportunity to see Orlagh and joyfully she waved back at them. She felt like a queen, with one hand firmly on the grab rail and her feet spread wide apart she smiled enthusiastically enjoying the carnival-like atmosphere.

Finally they arrived at the raised dais in the centre of the stage and two men stepped forward. They were magnificently dressed in woollen trousers patterned with stripes which loosely resembled tartan, and their heavy cloaks were pinned at their throats. Their skin was tattooed with Celtic swirls and colourful designs and their hair was swept back, lime washed and braided creating the appearance of a horse's mane.

Clearly they were warriors of noble standing and Orlagh was almost overwhelmed, it was as if she were living in a dream. They lifted her down and accompanied her to the dais where a heavy golden throne, richly upholstered in bright red velvet, was waiting and once she had taken her place, the chariot moved away. The magnificent warriors remained in her peripheral vision, standing like body guards at her side, then her attention turned towards a group of druids who were emerging from a side tunnel. They marched solemnly onto the stage dressed in long black robes embroidered with silver thread, each one wearing some form of strange head dress.

The crowd became silent as they appeared and for the first time Orlagh realised that the druids were chanting. They made their way slowly across the stage before turning to face the setting sun and with their arms raised high above their heads, they sang until it disappeared completely over the edge of the earth.

'As the moon waxes and wanes and walks three nights in darkness, so the Goddess once spent three long nights in the Kingdom of Death.'

The sun tipped over the horizon but the sky remained bright in defiance of its passing. Slowly as the heaven grew pale torches were lit then the druids turned their faces towards the moon, their voices rising from a whisper they chanted.

'At this time the moon represents the Goddess in her Mother aspect, give praise to Cerridwen, Isis and all the other Mother Goddesses.'

The crowd murmured their response and the druids worked their magic with a mysterious dance. Giving thanks to the setting sun, they welcomed the rising moon.

Orlagh was drawn towards the moon, held captivated by its majesty she was amazed by the silver threads of light that rained down around her. She could feel its magic and magnified by the excitement of the crowd she could sense their mood, their life forces working in harmony with the lunar celebration.

Now she understood why it had gripped mankind from the beginning of time. The perfect disc hanging low in the sky had just cleared the horizon, it seemed almost close enough to touch and she was held in awe.

In the background the druids continued their chanting, their voices a drone of hypnotic rhythm which possessed all those who were near. They sang their secrets which were never clear their words whispered in an ancient tongue, a code understood only by the Gods. The spirits were there all around them, it was as if an invisible door or portal to the underworld had opened and the ancestors had emerged. Orlagh could feel them crowding in, eager to take part in the celebration. The druids worked the silver threads, weaving both the dead and the living together and as the spirits were drawn in the crowd held their breath, dizzy with anticipation. Suddenly the druids broke away and like demented demons began to spin and whirl, leaping into the air chanting their magical chorus.

The night sky in the west had darkened, the last of the sunlight growing weaker until it faded completely, this created room in the heavens for the first of the night stars. Jewels began to stir from their celestial slumber and Orlagh looked up in wonder. Turning towards the moon she could see the hare, she could make out its face, its ears and the attitude of its body all imprinted into the lunar surface. She had of course seen it before but never as clearly as this, perhaps it was the influence of the druids or the fact that the moon was so huge, larger than she could ever have imagined. Maybe it was the drugs circulating around her system.

Suddenly the crowd cheered louder and the druids performing their individual dances became still, their chests rising and falling from their exertion. One of them held up his arms and as he faced the moon his voice rang out clearly.

'Oh great Goddess in her Mother aspect, Cerridwen, Isis and all the Goddesses shine with a light so pure, a maiden filling the heaven,' he paused and the silence around them was palpable. 'Draw down the energy which this bountiful Goddess bestows on us, feel the fire and the power.'

Turning towards the crowd he made a signal and they wailed in response, Orlagh shuddered as the sound touched her soul.

'The magic tonight is strong, feel it charging through the air around you. The Goddess, she gives us strength to do what is just, we will take back what was stolen from us, subdue our enemies, smite their armies with our magic, they will be powerless to resist.'

The crowd roared in agreement and when finally they became still the druid continued.

'Gog and Magog will rise up out of the earth, go forth into the sky, lifted up by the hand of the Goddess, they will bring down flames onto the heads of our enemies and we shall reign for a thousand years.'

This time the crowd stood to roar their approval. Carried along with the moment Orlagh wanted to cheer too but something held her back, something terrifying, almost too frightening to contemplate. Slowly the crowd became calm and the moon continued its journey across the sky. Orlagh could feel the charge in the air, it was becoming oppressive, clawing at her with cold, lifeless hands. Glancing nervously about she shivered almost expecting to see the spirits crowding in around her.

The druids formed up into two columns, standing shoulder to shoulder, they faced each other to make a narrow pathway which stretched out across the stage.

One of them began to move along the line and in his arms he carried a cushion of soft red velvet, on this cushion was the Belgae Torc. Orlagh's eyes widened with shock; held fast by invisible hands she could feel panic beginning to rise up from deep inside her.

The druid moved closer and tiny fingers of silver light played over the Torc highlighting the twisted ore and the finely carved ends. Once he arrived at the edge of the dais he paused, then bending forward, placed the cushion on the step at her feet, he then glanced up and held her gaze, peering deeply into her soul. She could feel him inside her head and when the moment had passed he bent towards the Torc. Slowly he raised it up and presenting it to the crowd and the auditorium was filled with light. This time the light was ancient and cold, as mysterious as time itself; it fed their passion and Orlagh almost cried out. Startled by her emotions, her skin began to crawl and although stunned by its beauty, it was the forces surrounding the Torc that disturbed her most. Pushing these thoughts aside, she had to remain calm, remind herself that this was simply a magnificent treasure made for a king.

The druid turned slowly with the Torc held high above his head and the crowd waited patiently as time stood still. Moving forward he lowered his arms until the Torc touched her hair, she could feel its weight as he slipped it over her head then it brushed against her skin. She was stunned, to have something so valuable around her neck was shocking, this was an item of such huge historical importance and to be standing there wearing it was simply unthinkable. This was a moment made of dreams and she could hardly believe that it was happening.

The druid drew back leaving Orlagh astonished, she wondered what was going to happen next. Her heart skipped a beat and her breathing became rapid, then she began to feel the first of the vibrations rising up from deep within the metal. It was as if a butterfly had gently touched her skin with its wings. The Torc was alive, white gold glowing magnificently, it sent tremors through her body.

At the end of the avenue of druids a figure of a woman appeared, she was as beautiful as a goddess and as carefree as the breeze. With flame red hair floating around her head, her eyes were magnificently resplendent, shimmering shades of green just like her own. Orlagh made no sound, rising up out of her chair she was drawn to the edge of the dais. The Torc was now an oppressive band of heat around her neck resting heavily against her delicate bones, its vibrations worked steadily into her very soul. She wanted to cry out but the hand of fear held her tightly in its grip, and as realisation began to set in, she would have gladly given anything to be somewhere else.

246

The goddess was now standing close and Orlagh frowned, she could have been looking at her own reflection, the woman was the image of herself, the same green eyes, pale skin and thick mane of red hair. At first her expression was warm, the gleam in her eyes friendly, but after a while her face began to change as dark shadows slowly masked her beautiful features. From the corner of her vision Orlagh could see the darkness beginning to draw in. At first it was as ghostly as a mirage, subtle movements that were not really there, but held firmly by the woman's stare the magic was too strong, she couldn't find the strength to break free. In desperation she tried harder but it was no good, she could feel her life force beginning to drain away. The Torc tightened its grip around her neck, burning into her soul just like it had done with countless others over the course of time. The vibrations were unbearable now and she began to choke, then her legs gave way and she collapsed at the woman's feet.

Orlagh's vision was fading and as darkness closed in she thought she could hear voices, at first they were distant whispers, her brain playing tricks, starved of oxygen her thoughts ran riot, a fantasy designed to lessen the impact of death. The voices continued to push through the fog of suffocation and with her fingers grasping frantically at the Torc she pulled at it with the last of her strength. They were becoming irritatingly persistent, the whispers growing ever louder and turning her head she struggled to see where they were coming from. Standing close beside her she could see the ghostly figure of a young woman together with a magnificent stag and a wolf. Orlagh tried to blink, a vain effort to clear her vision, but her eyes refused to work. The stag moved closer, overwhelming her with its presence but she wasn't afraid, he was a friend that much was clear. His warmth crossing the divide, reached out towards her and suddenly she remembered a conversation with Jerry Knowles. It was as if the thought had been placed inside her brain as some kind of explanation.

"So which animal is your ally?" he asked. He was grinning but she was reluctant to say for fear of ridicule, when she finally told him that it was the Deer he confirmed it was his own too. At first she refused to believe him, but he spoke with such conviction that she had no choice but to accept what he said. She had shown him her published paper on Animal Allies it was a subject they discussed seriously.

The red haired woman was standing close now, reaching out she touched the Torc, her fingertips tracing along the intricate rope-work and the tiny horse's heads that were carved into the finials. Orlagh tried

247

to pull away but there was no strength left in her body, the burning sensation and the forces vibrating through the metal had become unbearable and she so desperately wanted it to end. The woman gripped the Torc, her frozen touch chilled Orlagh to the bone and as she moved closer her icy stare cut like a knife and Orlagh cried out. The wolf snarled and the stag bellowed a battle cry forcing the woman to draw back, then she began to hiss the words of an evil incantation. Starved of oxygen Orlagh no longer knew if this was reality or just a dream. She wanted the pain to go away, she was beyond caring, if death was a blessed release then she would welcome its cold embrace, but then a voice filled her with hope.

"I am Madb, daughter of the Belgae, creator of the Torc. At the forge of my uncle, Luain Mac Lanis, I drew the threads of gold from a solid ingot. The Torc was made as a symbol of wealth and great power but over time that power has become corrupt, it has taken the lives of many and with each life the Goddess of Hibernia grows stronger. Luain Mac Lanis was mistakenly thought to have made the Torc, he stood accused of creating the curse but that was not true, he paid the ultimate price, sacrificed for a crime he did not commit and his body cast into the sacred bog."

Orlagh understood every word and she choked with emotion. As she struggled with her final breath the stag and the wolf came up beside her, they stood in defiance against the evil surrounding her and the red haired woman snarled with rage.

"The ore belongs to the people of Hibernia. It was stolen by Ban Mac Faelan along with the lives of many of my people, he and his kind have paid the price for their treachery."

"And why do you want this woman?" Madb demanded.

"Her soul belongs to me, in my image she will sit beside me in the great hall and together we will wield much power."

"No," Orlagh screamed.

The crowd cheered and the druids chanted, they could see nothing of the spiritual struggle that was taking place. Orlagh's soul was snatched away by her Animal Allies. The red haired Goddess had no time to strike, Madb saw to that. Stepping forward she lifted her spear and thrust it deeply into her breast and her cries echoed through eternity. Only the druids knew the truth but they were helpless to intervene. Forbidden to cross the boundary that separated the two worlds they wailed in disbelief as their evil influence began to fade along with the red haired goddess.

The crowd were on their feet in praise of the Goddess in her Mother aspect and their song rang out for the spirit of the red haired woman who wore the Belgae Torc around her neck. At last the power was finally theirs and it would last for a thousand years.

XXVIII

J ack looked up at the huge silver disc which seemed to hang motionless in the sky. It reminded him of a huge Christmas tree decoration and he grinned as he remembered as a boy watching the first American astronauts as they walked on the surface of the moon. It was hard to believe now that this satellite continued to intrigue man. For thousands of generations humans had looked up into the night sky to stare in wonder at this mysteriously bright object. Myths and legends were born out of admiration for this our nearest celestial neighbour, but now its secrets have been realised and we live in a world where man has walked on the moon.

The landing craft gave a throaty roar as it coughed a cloud of diesel fumes that drifted across the surface of the dark water. Easing its way out of the marina it made its way towards the narrow channel separating two of the world's greatest continents. The journey to the islands would take just under an hour and during that time the men busied themselves with last minute equipment checks and focussing their minds on the mission ahead. Some of them simply rested their heads against the side of the boat and dozed, seemingly at ease, unperturbed by the strange circumstances in which they found themselves. Jack could never understand how they did that, the thought of a mission filled him with adrenalin; he wouldn't be able to relax until it was over. The second landing craft was on the water fifteen minutes behind them. Combined they were a small but effective force, each man handpicked for their particular specialism. They were well equipped, wearing body armour and carrying the latest lightweight assault rifles. Heavy calibre rifles, set up for rapid firing, had been mounted in the bow of each landing craft and they carried enough explosives to sink an armada.

"Radio check," Jack whispered into his short wave battle radio which was strapped to his shoulder. A cable running from an ear piece, passing under his collar was fixed by tape to prevent it from moving and a small microphone was secured to a button hole on the front of his combat jacket. Six pairs of eyes stared back at him and one by one the men nodded or gave the thumbs up signal then in turn they murmured their individual call signs.

"Five minutes to feet wet," he said checking the luminous face of his wrist watch. Jack knew they would be heavily outnumbered but his advantage was the element of surprise, no one on the island knew they were coming so he was confident that this operation would be a success. Glancing around at his men his faith in their abilities was immeasurable he would trust his life to anyone of them.

Paul nudged his elbow and grinned, he was having the same thoughts, the expression on Jack's face was one that he knew well.

"Two minutes," Jack spoke into his buttonhole then Paul throttled back on the engine. As the revs dropped the sound of the engine died away and with vibrations running through the hull the boat turned in towards the darkened shore line. Jack, lifting his pack, shrugged it onto his shoulder; it was full of explosives, more than enough to take out the landing strip. That was their first objective he had to be sure that the airfield could not be used as a spring board to launch an attack on their country or even as an escape route. Shingle grazed the underside of the boat as it shuddered to a halt, then the men became mobile, throwing themselves over the side into the surf before making their way silently up the beach and melting into the landscape.

Paul was breathless with excitement, he remained at Jack's side as they emerged from the water then running up the wet sand they threw themselves down and took stock of the situation. The only sound came from the sighing of the surf and as Paul glanced around he was amazed, he could see nothing of the men. He knew they were close but they may as well not exist, there was nothing to say a small force had just come ashore.

Jack peered ahead through a pair of powerful night vision binoculars and focused on the air strip. He could see a number of light aircraft parked on a hard standing, then he made a careful survey of the buildings. There were no lights showing at the windows and he could see no movement around the perimeter so he gave the order to close in. Keeping low to the ground they moved like spectres through the darkness, safe in the knowledge that working as a team they were covering each other and, when they arrived at the runway, Jack began pacing. As soon as he found the right spot they went to work digging out a shallow channel. Once it was deep enough they started laying their explosives, ramming soil in between the packages, the last item to go in was the detonator. When they were finished they made their way back towards their men.

"Counting down from five," Jack's voice was calm and measured then a few seconds later he pressed the button on the electronic detonator. A shock wave fanned out over their heads showering them with soil and with hardly a sound a huge crater appeared in the middle of the runway. Jack grinned with satisfaction then gave the order to move out.

Their next objective was to take a look at the circle of stones they had seen from the air and spreading out across the moonlit landscape made their way towards the great monoliths. Even from this distance the mysterious structure was impressive. It reminded Jack of Stonehenge, the famous Neolithic monument on Salisbury Plain in the south of England. His men were strung out in a line, individually they made small targets, a sniper could easily be holed up behind one of the huge stones. Jack was first in amongst the stones, in typical fashion he led from the front, there was nothing he would expect his men to do that he wouldn't do himself.

"Paul, on me," he commanded, "we have something here."

Paul appeared by his side and cautiously they approached an alter stone. Something was laid out on top and drawing closer they realised that it was a human form. Moving in quickly they covered each other before stopping to stare in disbelief.

"Roz Stacey." Paul said his eyes wide with shock.

Roz was laid out on the stone, her arms folded across her belly. Between her fingers she clutched a small bunch of yellow flowers and as they moved closer Jack could see that her body was covered in strange markings. At first he thought it was the onset of decomposition, but as the moonlight played over her skin he realised that she was covered in tattoos.

"She has a pulse," Paul said, his fingers pressing gently against her throat. "It's faint but she's alive."

"Medic, get in here quick," Jack spoke urgently into his microphone and almost immediately a man arrived. "See what can be done here," he said as he glanced at his watch. Time was his enemy and it was slipping away alarmingly. The other landing craft would be coming ashore further along the bay and he was painfully aware that he was working to a tight schedule. It was imperative he kept strictly to the plan, finding unconscious civilians was not part of that design, no contingencies had been made for this event. He had to make a decision and fast, he needed every man in his group, he couldn't afford to leave the medic here with Roz.

"You've got two minutes, do what you can then move out," he turned to glance at Paul and reassured him that they would return for Roz later.

The medic nodded and quickly rigged up a saline drip. Paul covered Roz with a space blanket, a thin lightweight material designed to retain heat, it might do something to help raise her temperature.

"Let's go." They moved out and continued their advance towards the village.

Paul remained silent, he was shocked to find Roz like that and he wondered what horrors she had been subjected to. He thought about Dr Orlagh Gairne and began to imagine all kinds of unpleasant scenarios, he also realised that they had probably arrived too late to save either of them.

Jack and his men entered the village only to find it deserted.

"Spread out," he whispered into his radio and they fanned out.

Moving cautiously, they slipped between the buildings checking each one in turn, but there was nothing left to see and soon Jack found himself up against the huge silo like building which dominated the centre of the village.

Further around the headland, the other team had beached their landing craft and were now making their way along the coastal path leading towards the harbour. Jack listened to the occasional communications coming from the other group and he smiled with satisfaction. He was happy to be doing something positive at last, now they had found the terrorists lair they could infiltrate their hiding place, their first objective was to take out the machine gun posts that were situated above the harbour.

Moonlight illuminated the sheer tower walls like a huge spotlight and standing back Jack craned his neck in order to see the top of the building. There were no windows and there seemed to be no way in. High up on the wall something caught his eye, a small grille of some kind stood out against the smooth drab surface.

"What do you make of that?" he nudged Paul then pointed upwards.

"Extract grilles," he confirmed.

"Kylie," Jack spoke into his radio, "can you see the grilles near the top of the building?"

"Yeah Jack," came the reply a few seconds later.

"Put a drone in through one of them."

"Roger Jack."

Within seconds Kylie had powered up his laptop and his drone was hovering above his head, its wings a blur of movement. He did a careful systems check before letting the little dragonfly go. Kylie watched its progress on his laptop as it passed between the horizontal blades which made up the grille then his camera began scanning the darkness. At first he could see nothing, it was like staring into a bottomless pit,

253

then pressing a button on the keyboard he focussed the night vision camera, only then could he begin to make sense of what was going on. A row of tiny red lights were glowing at the base of some kind of huge structure and as the drone descended deeper into the darkness it all became clear. The picture on his screen reminded him of the interior of an operating theatre, the red lights and pipe work resembling some kind of giant life support system. A huge cylinder filled the entire space and at various levels he could make out more cables and tubes running from electrical cabinets that were connected to the walls. As he neared the bottom he discovered four huge fin-like stabilisers, these were set at ninety degrees to each other then lower down he found a set of massive engine exhaust cones which looked exactly like space shuttle boosters.

"Jack, we've got some kind of rocket in here and it's huge, I would say this building is a giant missile launcher."

"Roger that Kylie, good work. Is there only one in there?"

"Yeah Jack, only room for one."

"Thanks, get your drone out of there." Jack, shrugging off his pack, began unloading explosives and Paul helped him to arrange them against the wall.

"If this is a rocket launcher then the building we saw on the other island must be the same."

"I know," Jack nodded but made no further comment.

They both realised there would be no time to get across to the other island and destroy the second missile.

"We'll have to find the launch control centre."

"That's some device," Paul nodded towards the wall as they continued laying their charge. Once they had finished they made their way back to where the men were waiting.

"Stand by for a big bang," Jack sent a warning over the radio then began counting down from three. He pressed the detonation button and a neat hole appeared in the wall and before the dust had settled they went forward.

"What's the plan Jack?" Paul asked as they pushed through the hole.

"We'll rig up enough explosives to knock it off course."

Paul was lost in the darkness as Jack glanced towards him. "Once it's launched we'll blast it out of the sky, it's too risky to destroy it on the ground." Jack couldn't see the expression of alarm creasing Paul's face but he could sense it. "Don't worry pal, we'll use a pressure fuse, set it to go off at above 10,000 feet."

Paul pretended to be unconcerned as he flashed his torchlight up against the side of the missile.

"Looks like something out of NASA."

"Let's be quick," Jack shuddered. "I don't want to be stuck in here when this baby decides to launch."

Paul looked up at the huge engine pods and nodded in agreement. The clock was running and they still had to get underground, find the central nervous system and take it out. Once they were done they retraced their steps returning to their men who were covering the area. The noise of the explosion might have given them away and Jack was taking no chances.

"All quiet here," was the report, then as if on cue they heard three explosions in quick succession.

"That'll be the gun emplacements," Jack grinned.

He spent a few moments in communication with Razor who confirmed that the targets had been destroyed, he also told Jack that they had met no resistance so far, but Jack had a feeling that was about to change.

"Move out," he told his men then they left the village.

The slope leading down towards the harbour was narrow and became increasingly steep as it went. As if sensing danger the men spread out, spilling onto the grass banks either side of the pathway, it was Jack who saw movement first and as he whispered a warning into his battle radio his men dissolved into the landscape.

Jack stopped and brought his weapon up to his shoulder then crouching low, his knees bent beneath him, he slipped off the safety catch. Peering through the night vision sight that was mounted on top of his assault rifle he counted ten men as they appeared out of the semi-darkness. Speaking calmly into his radio he assigned each of his men a target, this way it was guaranteed that seven of the enemy would be taken out on the first volley they could then pick off the remaining targets.

"It seems there's a doorway leading into the underworld," Paul whispered as he sighted his weapon. They had not yet been spotted, but as soon as they opened fire their advantage would be lost. Jack gave the order to fire and the silence exploded into a confusion of flashing lights and flying lead. Seven men died instantly and the remaining three vanished into the shadows.

From their elevated position it wasn't long before Jack's men eliminated the remaining targets and as soon as the job was done they moved out and continued on their way. As the path levelled out they discovered a steel doorway set into the bank, it led to a narrow passage-way going directly into the earth.

"What have we here?" Jack grinned as he peered in.

The dimly lit corridor was like something out of an old wartime movie, lined with concrete, there was just enough headroom for the tallest man. It ran for about twenty metres before turning sharply to the right. Jack had to make a decision, this could be a gateway leading into the underground complex or it could easily turn out to be nothing more than a subterra-nean bunker which housed a troop of guards. It made sense that this was part of the complex it seemed an ideal way to deploy troops rapidly around the headland between the village and the harbour.

Jack made his way along the tunnel and his suspicions were confirmed, this was no simple bunker, the passageway continued beneath the island, so abandoning his plan to follow Razor into the complex via the harbour he decided to split their forces and go in through here. That way they could make their attack on two fronts fooling the enemy into thinking they were a much larger force. He made contact with Razor on the battle radio and quickly outlined his plan. Reception at this point underground wasn't very good but Razor was able to give Jack a progress report before contact was lost.

"No opposition so far Jack."

"We've discovered another way in, you proceed as planned and hope-fully we'll meet up at some point."

"Roger that Jack, see you in hell!"

Jack grinned, hoping that this place would not prove to be home to the devil. Paul was waiting at the entrance with the rest of the men when he received his orders over the radio.

"Send them in one at a time at twenty second intervals," Jack said before going deeper underground.

Three doors stood sentinel flush with the wall and as Jack moved up beside the first he pressed his ear to the wooden panel. He could hear nothing so moving his hand down he tried the handle, it was locked. Turning to the other doors he discovered they were the same. These must be store rooms or offices he guessed before losing interest and moving on. He continued on for another sixty seconds before arriving at another door. This time he could hear noises and pressing his ear up against the panel he soon discovered that the sounds were unmistak-ably human.

He waited for the following man to arrive before gently pulling a grenade from a clip on his belt. Holding it tightly in his hand he pulled the pin feeling the pressure of the detonator release arm against his palm, then placing his other hand against the door he turned his head and gave a nod, ordering his companion to throw it open. For a split second he had a snapshot view of the room, four people sat at work stations of some kind, they were each wearing head phones and he was reminded of an old fashioned telephone exchange. Two men and two women turned their heads to stare at him then one of the women took in a sharp intake of breath her eyes wide with shock as the grenade rolled across the smooth concrete floor. Jack was left with the vision of her levering herself up out of her chair. At that moment one of the men pulled out a pistol and shouting a warning Jack slammed the door shut, throwing himself sideways as two shots splintered the door. Two seconds later the door was blown out and the passageway was filled with dust and smoke.

With hardly a glance Jack was confident that the equipment inside the room had been destroyed, he knew how effective a grenade in close quarters could be. He had no issues with killing women either, these people had been sent to their deaths because they were a threat to the success of his mission, besides, they were wearing military uniforms, the same that he had seen on the hillside in Portugal moments before his Sikorsky helicopter was shot out of the sky. They were terrorists, an organised army who were planning an attack on his country, intent on killing maybe thousands of innocent people and he was not about to let that happen. They had already cost him a ship and taken the life of a scientist who had been working on the Sea Quest. He thought about Roz Stacey, she had been left for dead in the middle of the stone circle and as yet he had no idea what had become of Dr Orlagh Gairne.

Razor and his men were exploring the underground harbour. It was deserted, there were no ships tied up alongside the wall and no one was there to work the cranes and machinery that lay abandoned around the vast unloading area. Systematically the men began checking the offices and other rooms situated along the walls, these were well away from the water's edge. Razor was faced with several options, tunnels ran off in all directions and he had to find the way into the heart of the underground complex, he didn't have time to go exploring.

One of the tunnels was larger than the others and a line of forklifts were parked at the entrance this had to be the main highway, the route that would be taken when shifting goods from the ships to storage areas. Suddenly a group of terrorists appeared and before Razor was able to pull his men together they were spotted. The men were all carrying weapons but they were not expecting to find visitors so in the time it took them to organise themselves Razor reacted and his men took cover.

One of the terrorists called out a warning and Razor recognised the language, a string of orders were issued in German, but he was able to understand their meaning.

Weapons began stuttering, spitting out their deadly fire, in the confined space the noise sounded like thunder. One of Razor's men was hit just seconds before an explosion put a stop to the incoming rounds.

Mac tossed a grenade amongst the terrorists and in the confines of the tunnel they didn't have chance to spread out before the blast caught them. The effect was devastating and before the wounded could respond Razor's men were amongst them and the skirmish was over.

The entrance to the tunnel was a mess huge lumps of concrete had been torn away by ricocheting rounds and from the blast of the grenade, nothing stirred apart from dust particles floating in the air. All the lights in this section had been damaged and before Razor allowed his men to move out he scrutinised the way ahead using night vision glasses. Mac stepped around the bodies observing their uniforms and he frowned, these were Storm Troopers, the type he associated with World War Two German troops.

"They look like extras from a film set," one of the men echoed his thoughts.

"We had better get a move on, the noise must have raised the alarm, keep your eyes peeled."

They had hardly gone far before they were faced with another decision, the passageway split, going left and right.

"Heads or tails?" Mac grinned.

One of the tunnels was larger than the other and clearly had seen more use, the ground underfoot worn smooth by fork lift truck movement. Mac scouted the way ahead and whilst he waited, Razor checked out the man who had been wounded. He had taken a hit in the shoulder, a clean wound the round had passed straight through the soft tissue missing the bone. He patched him up using field dressings from a first aid kit then he heard Mac giving the all clear.

Orlagh is a name which can be spelt in many different ways, (Orla, Orlaith and Orfhlaith), however the pronunciation remains the same. Its origin dates back to pre-Christian Celtic Ireland but is not restricted to Ireland alone. Throughout Europe, notably Denmark, it is a popular masculine name. In the Irish language, *Or* means 'gold' and *flaith* 'prince' or 'sovereign' so Orla is considered as meaning 'golden prince or princess'.

Moonlight touching her pallid skin turned it an unnatural shade of blue, but it was her luxurious hair that remained true to her name. The Torc around her neck was intense with light, energy radiating from its twisted surfaces danced around her head like fairies.

The druids lifted her up and carried her around the auditorium, her hair tumbling over her face like finely gilded silk. The crowd cheered, their voices rising up into the air, dancing and swirling amongst the pillars like smoke from a fire, and Orlagh was resplendent in death.

Needing no light to guide their way they filed out through the opening in the wall their shadows spilling over the undulations in the landscape. The crowd trailing behind were quiet now, their cheering done, their procession a funeral cortege. They took her to a place where she would rest amongst the Gods, the temple of Standing Stones, here the spirits of their ancestors waited. It was a fitting place to be after such a glorious sacrifice. Although the druids knew that something had gone dreadfully wrong during the ceremony they continued to play their part in the hope of restoring order to the spirit world.

Jack and his men went deeper into the underground complex but still they encountered no further resistance. It was as if this whole section had been deliberately abandoned. Jack, scouting the way ahead looked for signs of surveillance equipment, anything which might alert the terrorists to their location, he was uneasy as he glanced sideways at Paul.

"Why is this place so damn quiet?"

Paul could feel his apprehension.

"What do we have here?" Raising his arm Jack halted the men.

Ahead was a pair of double doors set flush into the wall and cautiously he went forward. The doors were decorated with safety and warning posters, although written in German, these were familiar

European standard signs, but one stood out from the others, a warning of radiation.

"Have the men positioned along here," ordered Jack.

Once the defences were in place he moved closer, there was no obvious danger, no wires or laser lights which could trigger an alarm or trap and when he was satisfied Jack placed his left hand flat against one of the doors. Leaning in gently he discovered that they were not locked, Paul was beside him so putting his shoulder to the doors he pushed and they swung open. Rolling around the doorframe they covered each other, one going left the other going right, dropping to their knees they brought their weapons up and surveyed the room, it was clear so, relaxing, they got to their feet.

They had found some kind of a laboratory, a room brightly lit but eerily silent. Equipment was strewn over every work surface indicating that this had recently been a very busy place. Jack glanced up and studied the ceiling. Arc lamps and air grilles were set at intervals amongst the tiles, the atmosphere controlled, the air a few degrees warmer here than in the tunnels.

Paul looked around, although cluttered the place was scrupulously clean, the air was sterile with antiseptic reminding him of a hospital ward. No expense had been spared, the equipment was impressive, someone had gone to a great deal of trouble setting it up and he wanted to know why.

Something at the back of the room caught Jack's attention, a heavy steel box pitted with oxidation had been pushed against a wall, it was completely out of place in its pristine surroundings. He swung quickly across the room.

The top of the box had been hacked off and there was heavy lifting equipment standing to one side which had been used to extract the contents. The last time he had seen this box was in the hold of the Hudson Bay.

"This is what contained the atomic warhead," he said turning towards Paul. "It's the evidence we need, confirmation that the atomic material has been modified here inside this lab."

Paul felt his skin crawl and the colour drained from his face as he realised that the huge missile they had found in the silo was carrying a nuclear warhead.

"Don't worry pal," Jack sympathised. "We've taken care of one weapon, now all we need to do is locate the launch control room and neutralise the other one."

Paul nodded, Jack could be annoyingly confident at times.

"Let's go." Jack whispered.

Jerry Knowles had been right, the missiles were known as Gog and Magog named after the powerful warring giants of ancient times. They were capable of delivering death and destruction on a massive scale and were now resurrected but this time in a different guise. Jerry had insisted all along that these giants would be hidden in a remote place and from the moment they discovered the islands Jack knew they had found the Kingdom of Elmet. It was all there, the answers to his questions, embedded in the texts on the Sonnenrad website, but the words had been jumbled and impossible to translate. These thoughts flooded through Jack's mind as they moved through the tunnel. All the pieces were coming together, the giant silos where the missiles were stored were also known as the Temples of Gog and Magog, but he still didn't understand the pagan element. The elaborate Iron Age village and the circle of Standing Stones, these remained a mystery which he hoped Jerry would explain later. He was still attempting to link all the pieces together when suddenly an explosion shook the tunnel.

"What the hell was that?" Paul was beside him.

A hammer blow drove the air from Jack's body and he was knocked off his feet, his world became a swirling turmoil of pain and confusion as he lay helpless on the ground. His ear drums beat a rhythm against his skull and he was taken to the brink of unconsciousness. The sound of rapid gunfire brought him back and he realised that he'd been hit, so gasping for breath he attempted to inflate his lungs.

"Take it easy pal," the sound of Paul's voice was close beside him. "Take more than a bullet to knock the devil out of you."

Gritting his teeth, Paul fired his weapon, sending short bursts along the tunnel.

The sound of live rounds slapping the air so close above his head was disconcerting and the walls around him began to crumble as clouds of white powder shot into the air. Small chips of stone stung his face and filled his throat, it was a miracle he was not hit as he slithered gradually back the way they had come.

Jack was delirious with pain, the ceramic plate body armour positioned over his heart had taken the full force of the impact, his sternum was probably fractured and a few of his ribs were loose but at least he was still alive. He began to recover his breath and found that he was still clutching his assault rifle. Pain shot through him as he moved, he would have welcomed a shot of morphine but the mission was not over yet, he would need a clear head if he was to continue leading his men. Wiping his hand over his face he swallowed heavily then lifting his weapon, returned fire before giving the order to pull back. Common sense and self preservation told him to withdraw they had to discover what they were up against before they could go forward. Peering through the battle haze he could make out a small force of Storm Troopers, one of the men lay sprawled face down on the floor, his highly polished jack boots reflecting the harsh overhead light.

Jack hardly had time to think about the man's uniform which appeared to come from a time past. Muzzle flashes from modern weapons continued to send the promise of death his way, it was time to move. Glancing over his shoulder he knew he had to clear the tunnel but there was nowhere for them to run. In the distance he could see the laboratory doors but they were too far away, they would never make it before the Storm Troopers cut them down. He was sure he'd seen a tiny side tunnel somewhere along the wall but couldn't remember its exact location. They were running out of time.

His vision blurred as a wave of nausea swept over him and for a moment he couldn't think straight. Something was happening, the rate of incoming fire was easing steadily, either the Storm Troopers were taking heavy casualties or they were simply moving away. If that was the case then he wanted to know where they were going, he couldn't allow them to break away and circle around behind them, his force was not sufficient to fight the enemy on two fronts. Suddenly the gunfire stopped completely, leaving him deafened from the noise of battle. His heart was pounding uncomfortably against his injured ribs and now the initial excitement was over he had time to take stock of his injuries. Sharp pains were shooting through his chest robbing him of breath, he had to pant, draw in short breaths until the burning sensation subsided.

Paul was behind him checking the men, one was lost, face down he didn't react when nudged.

"Jack," Paul touched his shoulder, "we have to move."

Paul was pale faced, streaked with concrete dust and sweat he looked mean but Jack could see through his mask, there were unmistakable shadows of doubt lurking in the dark recesses of his eyes. Jack nodded but as yet he didn't understand why Paul was so concerned, they had been in situations like this before but this one was about to get worse. The underlying noise that he took to be ringing in his ears suddenly turned into the roar of a powerful diesel engine. Tracked wheels clattered and grinding gears growled like an angry beast, then a tank emerged from the tunnel ahead.

"Tell me I'm seeing things!" Paul pleaded as a huge World War Two Mark II Tiger tank squeezed between the walls. Rocking on its tracks it stopped then its turret began to move. It resembled some kind of alien craft seeking out its prey.

"What the hell?" one of the men cried.

"Now I've seen everything," Jack muttered in disbelief.

Rooted to the spot they were in full admiration for the beautifully restored relic but as that emotion quickly evaporated Jack could understand the fear that his grandfather must have felt when facing one of these monsters on the battlefields of France.

Painfully he dragged himself upright, his fight or flight reflexes urging him along the tunnel, closely followed by his men. A hail of lead tore the area apart where seconds before they had been standing, but as the machine gun adjusted its aim Jack spotted the entrance to the small service tunnel. Five men went for a space which would only accommodate one, Jack, Paul and Kylie made it through but the others were ripped apart by hot lead which filled the air around them.

Gasping for breath they made their way frantically along the narrow service tunnel then suddenly an explosion destroyed the entrance. They were thrown forward by the force as huge lumps of concrete tumbled from the walls around them then hot gasses filled the space searing their lungs. After a few seconds they picked themselves up, dazed and bruised they stumbled blindly over the debris. The tunnel ran straight and although it was dark that wouldn't stop bullets from filling the confined space, they would be torn apart once the tank reached the entrance.

Jack realised that he had led them into a trap, their situation was hopeless but there was nothing more he could do so they continued to run. He had lost his bag of explosives, the only weapons they had between them was one assault rifle and a handful of grenades, hardly enough to stop a tank.

The druids arrived at the sacred circle of stones, it presented them with a magnificent sight nestling majestically in a depression in the landscape. They turned towards the moon with their arms raised up and began to chant sacred words. They called to the gods, an incantation of strange poetry that echoed against the stones and the crowd gathered in around them to make their responses.

263

Orlagh, pale and lifeless was held up high so the gods could see, and as they made their way in single file they laid her body out on an alter stone then stepping back bowed their heads in reverence to the goddess. No one noticed Roz who was covered with a silver space blanket, the light from the glare of the moon was lost against the backdrop of stones.

Orlagh was a goddess re-born she had walked amongst them but now had returned to the Spirit world. This was the most powerful sacrifice of all, the red haired woman worshipped during the phase of the full moon. Nothing could be more potent than the Goddess in her Mother aspect and the Spirits would be more than satisfied.

Now things were in place, the final part of the plan was coming together and soon the giants Gog and Magog would rise up out of the ground, take to the air and deliver their terrible blow. The crowd cheered as the druids sang their song of glory, they were relieved that the gods had not become restless. The final part of their ritual was over and now nothing could go wrong.

"Go, go, go," Jack shouted urging them further along the tunnel. A clock was ticking inside his head, the rhythm of a metronome counting down the seconds to the final moment when they would be cut to pieces. When the time came it would be painless, the tunnel would fill with lead and the Reaper would gather up their souls.

Jack was relieved that Paul was there, he could think of no other companion with whom he would rather spend eternity and Kylie was a bonus, their time in hell would be humorous enough, Kylie and his jokes were legendary.

Suddenly another huge explosion rocked the tunnel and they were tossed like rag dolls against the curving walls, rolling over each other they spiralled headlong into the confined space. The small bones in their ears protested as the percussion wave swept over them, the force of it deflating their lungs leaving them gasping for breath.

"What the hell?" Paul wheezed.

He had been thrown further along the tunnel and was now sitting up, a cloud of thick black smoke swirling around his head. Jack pulled himself upright, the shock still ringing in his ears and like a drunkard he stumbled towards Kylie who was lying face down on the floor.

"You okay?" he asked hauling him to his feet.

Kylie opened his eyes and grinned. "Are we in Valhalla?" he looked around him.

"Not sure." Jack choked and glanced towards Paul.

"I can't hear the tank anymore," Paul said as he squeezed up beside them. "What happened?"

"Let's go take a look."

Retracing their steps they made their way cautiously back through the smoke filled tunnel. Thick black fumes were drawn in by the draft making them choke, it stung their eyes, the burning fuel and rubber catching at the back of their throats.

"Something must have gone wrong with the tank." Kylie groaned.

"We can't just go out there," Jack cautioned, "we must have a plan."

Crouching close to the entrance they ducked under the fumes. Paul was still clutching his assault rifle and checking it for damage, he grinned with satisfaction it should still work. Jack pulled the remaining grenades from his belt and handed two to Kylie.

"When we go out there, you go to the right, I'll go left. Paul you hit the ground and cover us as best you can." It wasn't one of his better plans but it was all they had. Each man knew what was expected of him and together they made a formidable team.

Razor and his men could hear the clatter of gunfire and realised that Jack must be close. They were moving through one of the wider tunnels, a main highway that was used to convey equipment around the complex then up ahead Razor spotted a huge pair of steel doors that were sliding open. Halting his men he waited for the doors to open fully, something was about to happen and he had to find out what it was before linking up with Jack. At first nothing appeared, there was only silence, then suddenly they heard the sound of an engine starting, the groans of a monster beginning to stir.

It must be a huge piece of equipment, Razor thought as the growl turned into a deep roar, his imagination going into overdrive, he thought about what might be heading their way. Barking out an order he had his men spread out along the tunnel, then crouching against the wall, he went forward alone to face the monster. The revving engine was now accompanied by a rattle and the ground beneath his feet began to shake, by the time he arrived at the gaping doorway he had a pretty good idea of what to expect.

Peering into the huge open space Razor could see nothing, it was as dark as a coalface and the air was heavy with oil and diesel fumes. Although the void was empty, he got the impression that this place had recently been full of equipment. He had seen this kind of thing before, huge service depots, storage facilities for heavy equipment and ammunition prior to being deployed.

Razor ducked back around the doorframe as a huge tank appeared. It came lumbering out of the darkness like a beast from the underworld and as it drew level with the steel doors it shuddered to a stop. Hot gasses showered over him as he pressed himself flat against the wall, the air reverberating as the monster growled. Razor could hardly believe that it was real. The tank was not one of the latest models it was a type he had not seen before, although this one seemed to have been resurrected from a museum, he had no doubts of its capabilities. Its presence alone was intimidating enough.

He glanced back along the tunnel, his men were out of sight but he knew they were watching. He had no idea which way the tank would go, he assumed it would head towards the sound of gunfire but he couldn't be sure and as he waited for it to make up its mind he offered up a tiny prayer. Suddenly the engine roared and with a cranking of gears the huge machine rolled forward, lurching to the right it lumbered away. Razor remained pressed against the wall in the hope that he would not be seen, the tank was heading in Jack's direction he was in for some serious trouble.

Shouting into his battle radio, Razor attempted to make contact, but in the confines of the tunnel all he got over the airwaves was static. The tank commander was positioned high up in the turret, head and shoulders above the hatch, he was a cliché personified. Dressed in the black overalls typical of tank crews his peaked cap moulded to his head and around his neck a pair of binoculars.

The tank was bristling with weapons, Razor knew he had to do something, he must find a way to stop it. His first thought was to jump up onto the armour plating and drop grenades down the hatch just like he had seen in war movies when a child, but reality wasn't quite that simple. This was a real World War Two tank, almost seventy metric tonnes of armour plating and weapons it was a formidable killing machine. He had to think of something and fast, the tank was accelerating away along the tunnel.

Chasing after it Razor threw himself down and reached out for the towing hitch, there was no time to shoulder his assault rifle so he let it go. He still had his pack of explosives in a bag on his back and slowly hand over hand his legs trailing behind him, he managed to wriggle beneath the hull between the whirring tracks. The engine was situated at the rear along with heavy suspension units, the noise and heat was almost overpowering but once he squeezed under the armour plating he discovered that the smooth underside of the hull offered very little in the way of hand holds.   Luckily the ground was smooth and level so there was no danger of him being thrown around as he hung on. Desperately he searched for inspiration, as yet he had no plan and working on impulse was never a good idea especially when clinging onto the underside of a Tiger tank. Razor's knowledge of this kind of vehicle was limited but he guessed that the armour plating on the hull would not be as substantial as the upper part of the tank. Peering forward to where the underside angled down he spotted a ledge running between the wheels and tracks. Keeping away from the moving parts he did his best to avoid the foul smelling grease and slowly he managed to haul himself hand over hand until he reached the ledge. Here the armour plating looked weaker then he discovered an access panel recessed into the underside, it was held in place by a ring of heavy duty bolts. Razor had no idea what was behind it but he began to unload his bag of explosives. Arranging the packages on the shelf, he laid them out so that they would cause maximum damage, hopefully hit something vital and put a stop to this nightmare.

Suddenly the forward facing machine guns began to clatter; Jack and his team must be within range. The tank slowed to a crawl and lurched clumsily as it changed direction flinging Razor sideways. It took all his strength to hang on, but he managed to recover his hold and the sound of the turret moving made him work faster. He realised that as soon as the tank commander gave the order to fire the huge gun that would be the end of Jack and his team.

With trembling fingers he pushed a detonator between the packs of explosives that were already wedged into place then he attached wires before rigging the whole system to a digital timer. Fixing this into place, he set the timer for thirty seconds then he activated it. Small green numbers began counting down as he shoved it amongst the explosives, then dropping from the ledge he laid flat on the ground. The tank picked up speed and once clear Razor rolled to his feet. Running as fast as he could back along the tunnel, he had to put as much distance as possible between himself and the tank before the deadly bomb went off. He could have used a remote detonator but that would have been too risky, he might have dropped it or have been killed before it could be activated, at least this way the device would detonate automatically. Shouting a warning to his men the ground beneath his feet heaved and Razor was thrown forward by the force of the powerful explosion.

Jack rolled out of the tunnel, adrenalin fuelling his system, he was hardly aware of the pain cleaving at the space between his shoulder blades. Breathless, he turned to face the beast which now lay broken, smoke billowing from the hatch. He was shocked, the huge gun situated on the turret was hanging down at an odd angle and the main hatch and other pieces of metal were strewn further along the tunnel. The remains of the commander were on the ground beside his ruined tank. Jack hobbled forward cautiously, even though he knew it was dead, the tank was still a frightening and intimidating sight.

"Jack," someone called out his name and it took him a few seconds to realise where the sound was coming from.

"Jack, are you okay?"

"Razor?" he replied talking into his battle radio.

Razor appeared from behind the tank. "Man, am I glad to see you!" he said as he clambered over one of the ruined tracks. Five men followed him across the wreckage and like excited school boys they gathered around Jack.

"We are the only ones left," Jack said turning to face Paul and Kylie. "We still have to find the control room, any ideas?"

"It must be that way, it's not back there," Razor nodded in the direction from which they had come. He told Jack about the assembly depot. "Looks like they had a huge amount of equipment stored there including tanks."

"They must have been deployed."

"Yeah, it's my guess they have an army ready to invade once the missiles have gone in."

"The ships carrying all this stuff must be well on their way by now, probably in position, just waiting for the order."

"No wonder this place is deserted, there must have been hundreds of troops stationed here."

"Let's get going, we have to finish this then find Dr Gairne."

Jack didn't expect to find Orlagh in the complex, he told Razor about Roz and how they had found her close to death.

Captain Schiffer scowled at the communications officer.

"What do you mean you have lost contact with the Tiger?"

"Radio contact has been lost Sir."

Schiffer moved quickly across the floor and stopped beside the communications console. There were no C.C.T.V. cameras in that section of the tunnel so he couldn't see what was happening. He glanced up at the digital clock that was counting down the seconds to missile launch. In just under twelve minutes Gog and Magog would be sent on their way. Clasping his hands behind his back he moved back towards the launch control module. He was concerned, something was not right, he had learned over the years never to ignore his instincts. He thought about the men who had followed them out of the Douro valley, he also remembered the helicopter his men had shot down, the same type of aircraft he'd seen snooping over the island earlier.

"Begin operation override, I want to launch the missiles immediately."

The controller glanced up at him, her eyes wide with alarm. She was stunned by his request.

"Do it now," he shouted as he stepped up to the firing buttons.

Nervously her fingers flew over the control panel and in seconds had over ridden the system, now Schiffer had complete control.

269

"Double the guards on the door," he snapped.

Glancing to the back of the room he checked his escape route. A lift door stood open ready to take him up to an underwater chamber which was situated hundreds of feet above them. A type XXIII submarine was waiting for him there. The sound of gunfire alerted him and he pulled his pistol from its holster. Holding it awkwardly in his hand he placed his fingers on the firing buttons, then suddenly the doors burst open.

"Nobody move." Mac shouted as he rushed in.

Schiffer pushed both buttons before bringing his pistol up and firing two rounds in Mac's direction. Jack and his men hit the ground taking cover behind various control cabinets; this gave Schiffer the time he needed to escape. Jack didn't want a shoot out with so much delicate equipment in the way, damaging the electronics might just set off the missile launch system.

"We're too late," Mac said.

Screens above their heads were already displaying lines of trajectory and binary numbers. Telemetry was being fed back to the computers by the departing missiles which were at that moment clearing the top of their towers.

Mac was on his feet. "Everyone remain calm, you're in no danger."

There were five controllers in the room including the communications officer.

Mac reached the launch control panel and began pressing buttons but it was useless, the countdown clock registered a row of zeros.

"They are on their way," he said glancing back towards Jack.

Mac's fingers began dancing over buttons on the keyboard and the view on the overhead screens changed as he began tracking the missiles. Jack, moving towards the communications console, lost valuable seconds as he searched for the V.H.F. setting, but once he located it he began to speak clearly into the microphone.

Gog and Magog rose up majestically from their temples of slumber, both riding on chariots of fire. The villagers turned in awe to face the spectacle and they cheered as the giants climbed into the sky. Soon there would be a new world order in which they would play a leading role.

The electrical system fitted to the explosive charge that Jack had attached to one of the missiles began to function the detonator activated by motion went to standby. It was controlled by a tiny computer linked to an altimeter, this had registered the launch and now a red light was flashing on its micro-screen. This was the first in a sequence that would ultimately lead to its destruction. As the missile rose higher into the sky the air pressure changed, an amber light began to wink taking the place of the red one and a thousand feet higher a green light flashed then a fraction of a second later the charge exploded ripping the missile apart. The nuclear warhead tumbled in the air as the missile disintegrated around it, it continued to rise reaching its zenith before plunging back towards the sea.

The pilot of the RAF Tornado calmly rotated the nose of his aircraft and under full power climbed up into the sky, his routine flight was about to become something more exciting. Suddenly a huge explosion lit up the sky, tearing at the heavens and eclipsing the stars, it was then that an urgent message was sent to the jet fighter.

"Nuclear missile strike, targets unknown, you are clear to engage and destroy."

Without questioning the order the pilot vectored in onto the second missile which was climbing away at speed on an angle to his current course.

"One of the target's down," he reported succinctly.

Magog continued to climb and reaching towards the stars it trailed a banner of hot gasses. Inside the cockpit the Tornado crew worked feverishly, selecting weapon systems and locking onto the rapidly departing target. They had no chance of outrunning the missile but the pilot wanted to be as close as possible, stabilise his aircraft before releasing his weapons.

The target was on his screen and he made a course correction as the onboard computer system analysed incoming information. It began to calculate a deflection firing sequence but precious seconds were lost as the speeding missile continued to pull away. The Tornado was approaching maximum speed and as the pilot tracked slightly to his left he allowed the nose to drift down a few degrees, this increased his air speed slightly then a green light began to flash on his head up display. He fired a Sidewinder heat seeking air-to-air missile and used the brevity code to confirm the launch.

"Fox Two," his calm transmission was heard at RAF Gibraltar.

Jack had no idea when he made his emergency call that the fighter was still on station, for all he knew it could have left Gibraltar hours ago. He was confident that one of the missiles would be brought down by his carefully laid explosive charge and now he was staring at the overhead screen that was tracking the path of the second missile. Razor moved up beside him and together they watched the information coming in when suddenly the screen went blank. A few moments later lines began to dance over the screen as the tracking device attempted to restore communication with Magog, but it was no use, Magog no longer existed.

"I guess that's it then," Razor said, glancing sideways at Jack.

A few seconds later they heard the transmission from the Tornado pilot.

"Target destroyed."

"How can he remain so cool?" Paul grinned. "Bloody speed jockeys."

The atmosphere inside the control room changed, Jack and his men were overjoyed, the first part of the mission was over and now all that remained was to locate Dr Gairne.

The people manning the control room were totally deflated and offered no resistance. The authorities were on their way, British and American warships steaming at full speed towards the islands were expected to arrive within the next few hours. They would secure the islands, arrange for the occupants to be taken into custody and begin a thorough investigation. Jack used the V.H.F. radio to contact the Sikorsky, it was now safe to bring it in.

They made their way towards the Stone Circle but Jack diverted his men to the large buildings that were situated on the outskirts of the village, he felt sure that was where he would find Orlagh.

The druids inside the sacred circle of stones watched open mouthed as an explosion sent the warhead tumbling through the air. They groaned in disbelief as it plunged harmlessly into the sea and it was then they realised that the gods were not pleased, their grand plan was going horribly wrong. They had no idea that Jack and his men had already infiltrated the heart of the underground complex or that the authorities were on their way. Staring at each other in dismay it was clear the sacrifice of the woman had been wrong.

The moon continued on its way slowly towards the horizon, a perfect ball of silver against the night sky. The silver thread of light reflecting against the surface of the sea was like a magic carpet rolled out towards the edge of the world. One of the druids approached the alter stone where Orlagh was laid, his hand brushing against her hair as he reached for the Belgae Torc. He hated her she was perfect her beauty intensified by thin beams of ethereal light that played over her face. He wanted to destroy her, take out his knife, strip away her finely structured looks and plunge his blade deep into her heart, but to desecrate the goddess in such a way was blasphemous, he would be damned for all eternity if he were to defile her in such a way.

Grasping the Torc he slipped it over her head then hid it beneath his robe. His actions would anger the gods even more but he knew it was over, he had to save the Torc and its magical powers, then summoning the power of concealment he disappeared. A submarine was waiting in a secret chamber beneath the harbour so he made good his escape seconds before Jack and his men arrived.

The druids remained silently stunned as they were herded away they were taken to the village and kept under guard along with the rest of the island's population. It was then that Jack and Paul entered the circle of stones. Roz' condition remained the same although her skin was slightly warmer to his touch. Paul checked her over and was satisfied that the saline drip had done its job she was a little more hydrated than before.

"Paul, on me now," the urgency in Jack's voice was palpable.

Snatching up his weapon he ran to where Jack was standing beside another tall stone.

"Dr Gairne," he said in disbelief. Touching the side of her neck he felt for a pulse. "She's alive," he checked for signs of trauma. "She has a strong pulse and is breathing steadily." They did what they could for both women whilst waiting for the helicopter to arrive.

On a level piece of ground beside the monument Razor marked out a safe landing zone. He placed fluorescent tubes in a circle which would act as a beacon to the helicopter pilot. From the air the circle of bright yellow light stood out clearly against the landscape, the pilot was impressed by its near perfection and wondered how they had managed to be so precise working with no surveying tools. He didn't have time to think about the problem, he was fast approaching the landing zone.

Jack used his battle radio to make contact with the pilot as soon as the helicopter was in range giving him details of the female casualties which were then relayed immediately to the hospital on Gibraltar. The moment the Sikorsky landed Orlagh and Roz were evacuated along with Jack's remaining attack force, they left the occupants of the island to the incoming authorities.

Deep under the harbour in a secret chamber a heavily modified World War Two German U-boat was preparing to leave. Captain Schiffer was in command and sealed the hatch as soon as the druid with the Belgae Torc arrived.

"Well done," he nodded, "all is not lost."

The submarine slipped silently along the underwater tunnel which was connected to the huge underground harbour then it made its way out into open water. The systems on board warned them of approaching forces so turning away they left undetected.

EPILOGUE

The terrible ordeal had affected them both in very different ways. Orlagh had a supportive network of friends which she could rely on but it was Roz who suffered the most. Although she had surrounded herself with a tough exterior nothing could prepare her for the horrors that she had experienced and it was proving extremely difficult for her to settle back into her normal life. Working in a male dominated environment didn't help, they couldn't understand the complexity of her moods, her friends and colleagues did their best to support her but nothing they did could ease her pain.

As time went on Roz became progressively more depressed until finally she withdrew from life completely. It was then that she realised the only person who could help was Orlagh, so Roz came to Ireland and from the moment she arrived her life took an immediate upturn. Her time with Orlagh saved her and gradually she became whole again, it was a beautiful experience which filled her with self-realisation and understanding. Orlagh helped Roz through her every crisis, she remained gentle and supportive throughout and for the first time in her life Roz had found a true friend. Caring for Roz salved Orlagh's conscience. She couldn't stop blaming herself for Roz' traumatic experiences, if she hadn't lost her way when the ship was hit by the torpedo, she would have made it out to the helicopter and Roz wouldn't have attempted a rescue.

This was also a time for Orlagh to confront her own demons and together they became stronger. Luckily neither of them suffered physical scars, the tattoos covering Roz' body were made from vegetable dye and henna and over time disappeared.

Orlagh was winding up her talk on Early Iron Age Settlements in Ireland and Jerry Knowles was sitting in his usual place in the front row. He never missed her presentations he had a genuine interest in this period of history, besides he just loved to hear her talk.

One day Orlagh had her hair cut short, her magnificent red hair gone and she immediately regretted her decision, it had been a huge mistake undertaken on a whim when out shopping with Roz. Jerry could hardly believe that she had done such a thing but he remained gently supportive especially when her tears began to flow. This had been one of her lowest points, but now her hair was beginning to recover its body and length and was as luxurious as it had been before.

Jerry was overjoyed at how their relationship was developing their love for each other had deepened. Orlagh revised her paper on Animal Allies and he was amused by her description of Madb, the Wolf and the Stag. He remained faithful to his own beliefs but did nothing to influence hers he would never share his doubts with her. He encouraged her to be true to herself and explore her emotions, she was a convert convinced that her Animal Allies had saved her life. They were never far away, she saw them from time to time, always in her peripheral vision, but whenever she turned to face them they were gone.

At first, Jack kept in touch with Orlagh, mostly by e-mail and the occasional telephone call, they would talk deep into the night but as time went on his communications became less frequent. He had suffered the most financially, complicated insurance and compensation deals kept his financial department fully employed but it was the loss of lives that bothered him the most. He had lost friends before in conflicts all over the world but this time it was different, the situation was not the same. Before they had been servicemen serving in theatres of war, but this time the men had been employed by him to do a job. Good men had died, but the mission was a success and without their sacrifice many thousands of innocent people would have died, the constitution of their country changed forever.

Although Jack's efforts had failed to locate the Belgae Torc, a vast quantity of Nazi gold had been recovered this served as compensation, covering the cost of salvaging the Sea Quest by her sister ship the Nautical Explorer.

Two ships from the invasion fleet had been intercepted by Royal Navy warships and over one thousand Storm Troopers captured, they became prisoners of a war that never was. The rest of the fleet, including at least one submarine, had simply vanished and it was never discovered how large the invading force was. Rough estimates were determined based on evidence found on the islands and from conversations with the prisoners. For weeks following the raid every major port in the world were on high alert, military ships scoured the seas with aircraft in support, even using secret spy satellites the world authorities failed to find any trace of the terrorists force.

Her lecture over, Orlagh and Jerry left the National Museum of Ireland and, arm in arm, made their way across St Stephen's Green.

"At least we know that the Belgae Torc still exists." Jerry said.

"I still can't believe that I actually wore it and survived to tell the tale."

"A tale of which you remember very little," he reminded her with a grin.

276

"Okay," she smiled. "So I admit, I was a little drugged at the time, but the energy from that Torc was just awesome."

Secretly he stifled a yawn she had told him the story many times before, even describing Madb, the character who had supposedly made the thing. As she so rightly said, she had been drugged at the time. Jerry grinned.

"What?" she turned towards him her face smudged by a huge smile.

"Nothing," he replied and slipping his hand into hers they crossed the road and together made their way towards O'Tooles, their favourite bar.

Biography

Kevin Marsh has lived in Whitstable with his wife Maria for thirty years; they have two adult children who are now pursuing their own careers. Kevin has worked in Manufacturing Engineering since leaving school and for the last twelve years has taught the subject in FE colleges. His hobbies include painting using acrylics, he regularly exhibits his work. His interests include history, reading historical novels and he has recently discovered the wonders of e-books.

Acknowledgements

I would like to thank Mark Webb at Paragon Publishing for all his help and guidance in getting my novel into print. Also with the initial proof reading, Anna Christodoulou and Mark Garbutt, who did a sterling job ironing out the wrinkles, any remaining are purely down to me.

Thank you to Maria, my wife, who has become a 'writing widow', as most of my time is spent typing away on my laptop in a spare bedroom, which is now my study.

Lightning Source UK Ltd.
Milton Keynes UK
UKOW041351121012

200492UK00002B/30/P